How to Court a Covert Lady

A LADIES COVERT ACADEMY NOVEL
BOOK ONE

BY JENNY HARTWELL

ARE YOU SIGNED UP FOR DRAGONBLADE'S BLOG?

You'll get the latest news and information on exclusive giveaways, exclusive excerpts, coming releases, sales, free books, cover reveals and more.

Check out our complete list of authors, too!

No spam, no junk. That's a promise!

Sign Up Here

www.dragonbladepublishing.com

Dearest Reader;

Thank you for your support of a small press. At Dragonblade Publishing, we strive to bring you the highest quality Historical Romance from some of the best authors in the business. Without your support, there is no 'us', so we sincerely hope you adore these stories and find some new favorite authors along the way.

Happy Reading!

CEO, Dragonblade Publishing

Dedication

To Molly & Paul who were with me on day 1 of this series

Chapter One

London, 1818

As Miss Philippa Chester surveyed the wooly carnage scattered across her writing desk, she consoled herself with the knowledge that although she was wretched with knitting needles, at least she was skilled with a more useful tool—a blade.

With a sigh, Pippa pulled the bits of completed knitting away from the tangled balls of yarn, noncompliant needles, and scraps of abandoned wool, and plopped them into a wicker basket. Her finished knitting perfectly concealed the dagger lying at the bottom.

The ormolu clock on her bedroom mantle chimed.

"Drat." Pippa peeked at her reflection in the mirror—dark hair mostly tidy, green muslin dress only slightly wrinkled— before dashing out of her bedroom.

Her footsteps echoed through the marble foyer. Despite the time, she needed to make an appearance with her mother before heading to her appointment. Pippa burst into the sitting room where the afternoon sun filtered through gauzy curtains to illuminate her mother and her mother's friend seated before a hearty afternoon tea.

"Good afternoon, Mother." Pippa placed a kiss upon the upturned cheek of Josephine Chester, Lady Everleigh. "And

Eugenia, how nice to see you as well."

"Are you joining us for tea?" her mother asked with a warm smile.

Pippa surveyed the pastries laid out on a silver tray before choosing a plum tart. "Unfortunately, I can't today. I'm off to the Ladies Charitable Association." She took a bite, and the sweet tartness was heaven in her mouth.

"Oh, I was hoping you could catch up on the news with us." Eugenia, Lady Everleigh's bosom friend and frequent visitor, set her newspaper aside.

"You two will have more fun reviewing the latest *on dits* without me, I'm sure." Pippa's mother and Eugenia loved nothing more than an afternoon of pastries and gossip. "And I really am needed at the LCA."

"You young ladies today, always on the go." A smile appeared on Eugenia's round, rosy face. "I must say, I admire you, Pippa, the way you and those other ladies spend so much time helping the poor, the orphans, the sick, those poor war widows—"

"You are too kind," Pippa interjected, uncomfortable at this litany of praise.

"Yes, she is very committed to the LCA," Pippa's mother said. "But it does mean she's rarely available to accompany me to social events." Lady Everleigh gave Pippa a pointed stare.

Pippa shuffled her feet. "I'm sorry, Mother. Perhaps…perhaps some evening soon we could attend a musicale."

Her mother stared.

"Or a dinner party?"

Lady Everleigh swirled her teacup in silence.

Pippa sighed. "Or perhaps a ball?"

Her mother beamed. "What a wonderful idea. Yes, a ball will be just the thing."

Pippa took a bite of tart, hiding her frown.

"Pippa dear," Eugenia said, leaning forward, "before you go, have you happened to hear the latest scandal involving a certain Lord S?" She tapped the newspaper. "I'm assuming it's that notorious Lord Somerset. Why, it says that he was found in a most compromising position—"

"Eugenia," Pippa's mother warned.

"Oh, pish, the girl is twenty," Eugenia protested. "If she's been reading the latest political essay by that firebrand *Democratiam Liberum* fellow, then surely she can discuss a bit of ballroom debauch—"

"Eugenia!" Lady Everleigh's eyebrows were almost at her hairline.

Pippa stifled a snicker.

Apparently looking for a change of topic, her mother leaned forward to peer into Pippa's basket. "Have you been up in your room *knitting* all day?"

Pippa moved herself and her basket to the other side of the tea tray, out of reach of curious fingers. "The Ladies Charitable Association is collecting booties for a foundling house, and I just finished these." She held up one of the booties from her basket.

There was a silence.

Her mother cleared her throat. "Well, those look...quite warm."

"Oh yes." Eugenia jumped in. "Just so cozy...and full of texture."

Pippa bit back on her molars and made a show of examining the lumpy, misshapen booty until the threat of laughter had passed. Truly, it looked as if a band of livid squirrels had attempted to craft a den by twirling the yarn with their bushy tails. She almost felt sorry for whatever poor foundling children received these.

The grandfather clock in the foyer chimed the quarter of the hour.

"Oh, I must be off." If Pippa was late, her instructor would be displeased. She waved farewell with her plum tart as she rushed to the door.

"Don't forget to take your maid," her mother called.

Milly was waiting in the foyer and helped Pippa into her cloak as she took her last bite of tart. While she adjusted the neck closure, Pippa could hear her mother and Eugenia talking through the crack in the unclosed sitting room door.

"What a fine young lady she's turned into," Eugenia said. "And to think, Josephine, you were worried she'd never leave the house."

Pippa flinched.

In the other room, her mother cleared her throat. "Yes, well, I'm glad that's all behind us now. It is quite astonishing, the way she's changed since joining that group."

Milly handed Pippa her gloves, a questioning look in her eyes. Pippa shrugged and her maid rolled her eyes in response. Truly, Milly was most discreet, but it seemed when a servant suspected her charge of getting into mischief, the servant felt a certain familiarity was allowed.

Very well. It *was* allowed. Without Milly's compliance—and subsequent familiarity—Pippa couldn't belong to the LCA.

And without the LCA, she had nothing. She *was* nothing.

"Her membership in the Ladies Charitable Association," her mother was saying from the sitting room, "has quite transformed Pippa, to be honest. She has spirit and confidence now. It's quite astonishing when I think about where she was a year ago. Where she'd been since my Henry passed."

Pippa bowed her head, focusing solely on her gloves while her mother and Eugenia nattered on about Pippa's father's death, how it had upended Pippa's life, and how her little brother, the current Viscount of Everleigh, fared during his time away at Eton.

Pippa's throat thickened with memories of her father. She didn't wish to hear anymore. Her gloves finally adjusted, she inhaled a cleansing breath. Today was a fresh day.

She scooped up her basket of knitting—plus one very sharp weapon—and headed to the door. As she peered outside at the sunny Mayfair street, Pippa's heart beat loudly. Danger could lurk anywhere. In broad daylight. In a fine neighborhood. Even on a well-traveled road.

Touching her basket for courage, she stepped outside. The brisk early fall air cooled her cheeks. Pippa took off down the sidewalk ceaselessly scanning her surroundings, Milly following.

Some things hadn't changed, despite her mother's reference to her new-found "spirit".

Her mother attributed Pippa's rather dramatic transformation in the last year to the LCA, which was correct.

However, imagine Lady Everleigh's surprise if she were ever to discover that the Ladies Charitable Association did not actually exist.

⤜⟫⟫⟫✕⟪⟪⟪⤛

JACK DASHWOOD, EARL of Hartwick, scowled at the towering home in St. James Square, the stately gray stone, gleaming lacquered door, and elegant window dressings cleverly disguising the dwelling's true nature.

This was a house of sin selling innocent women into wretched circumstances.

Or it was the front for a den of thieves stashing purloined merchandise in the basement.

Or…or perhaps it was…

Jack's mind, already overtaxed from a sleepless night and hours of worry, sputtered to a halt. Shoulders slumping, he leaned against a tree at the center of the square.

Or perhaps the house was simply the headquarters for the Ladies Charitable Association.

He'd banged on the door earlier, but the surprisingly burly butler had growled that visitors weren't being received today.

He needed to get into that house. He *had* to get in, or else Lydia—

Jack shook his head. He pushed his hair off his forehead. Perhaps if he restored order to his appearance, he'd regain familiar control over his emotions and this situation.

Feeling desperate, he sized up the building's exterior, searching for toeholds to climb to the balcony. But the sound of approaching footsteps interrupted his plotting. Jack looked over and froze.

A tall, slender woman walked briskly down the sidewalk, followed by a lady's maid who appeared to be in mid-scold.

"...cannot believe ye expect me to lie to your mam yet again, miss," the maid said, wagging her finger, "leavin' ye here for hours at a time!"

The tall woman only shook her head at the maid, and Jack's gaze lingered on her pink lips, curled up at the corners in what looked like an exasperated smile.

Her hair was dark and glossy, pulled back in a loose chignon. Her stylish green gown marked her as someone of means—perhaps an aristocrat or the daughter of a wealthy merchant—but he couldn't recall seeing her at any social events.

And surely, he would remember her, the beautiful lady with a striking, confident presence.

After bidding her frowning maid farewell, she turned toward the very building he so desperately wanted to enter.

Jack's tired, sluggish mind somersaulted to life with a plan. He lurched forward, calculating his rate of approach. Pulling out his pocket watch, he hurried a few more steps, and...

"Oh!" The woman gasped as he collided with her.

He reached out to steady her, his hand curling around her upper arm. The slender limb was firm, with more muscle than he'd expected.

"I-I am terribly sorry." Jack threw in a little stammer for good measure. "I was rushing and checking the time"—he gestured to his watch—"and failed to look where I was walking."

"Er, it's quite all right." She stepped back, reaching one hand into the basket hanging from her arm.

"You are unharmed, I hope?" Jack prayed his smile didn't hint of his desperation.

Her gaze felt stern somehow. "It takes a bit more than a

bump to do me harm."

The lady's voice was low and musical. He imagined sitting in front of a crackling fire beside her as she read aloud or relayed an amusing anecdote from the day. He could envision her soothing voice washing over him, bringing light to the dark places in his mind.

Her lips thinned, and Jack realized he'd been staring for longer than was proper.

He cleared his throat. "Headed to the LCA?" He gestured to the building.

"Yes." She shifted her weight from foot to foot, as men often did when training at Gentleman Jack's boxing club.

"As am I." He smiled. "Allow me to escort you." He held out his arm and waited.

Jack held his breath. But only because he was nervous about his hastily crafted plan. Certainly not because he anticipated her touch.

That would be ludicrous. He'd only just met her.

And Lydia…

Jack straightened his spine and met her deep blue eyes, tinged with suspicion. Their gazes tangled for a moment before she looked him up and down, likely noting both his marginally-tamed disheveled hair and unshaved face and—hopefully—the fine cut of his clothing and gleaming Hoby boots, which would mark him as a man of quality.

Her hand slowly lifted from her basket and settled stiffly on his arm.

As they climbed the steps to the LCA in tandem, Jack drew in a deep breath to clear his thoughts. He needed his wits about him. The potential consequence if he failed was too terrible to contemplate.

PIPPA SMILED AT Jarvis, the hulking servant at the door. The muscles straining against his suit and his cauliflower ears suggested a career as a dockworker rather than a butler to a marchioness. However, as Pippa and her fellow LCA members knew, appearances could be deceiving.

"Good day, Miss Chester," he greeted, a gold tooth winking as he gestured her in.

Pippa watched the butler's version of a smile vanish once his gaze landed on the man at her heels.

"Is this chap with you, miss?" Jarvis turned to face the visitor, squaring his shoulders.

Pippa stepped into the foyer. "Oh, well actually—"

"Miss Chester and I have only recently become acquainted," the mystery man interrupted, as he stepped inside and closed the door behind him. "But I'm sure she can vouch for me to Lady Rowling. I must speak to the lady on an urgent matter."

Pippa stiffened.

"As I already informed you, Lady Rowling isn't home to visitors today," Jarvis growled.

Lady Rowling was the proprietress of the LCA and rarely admitted visitors outside the organization to her residence.

The man's smile didn't reach his eyes. "Ah, but since Miss Chester has invited me—"

Pippa snorted at the man's audacity, but he continued as if she hadn't uttered a peep.

"—I'm quite certain Lady Rowling will see me, since I'm a friend of a friend and such."

Jarvis eyed him in stony silence. Pippa took a moment to give a closer examination to this bold interloper.

Although dressed in the well-tailored clothes of a gentleman, he was wilted and dusty as if he'd been out all night. He was tall, and Pippa suspected his coat didn't rely on padding to achieve his broad shoulders. His dark-blond hair, thick and wavy, was mussed. A hint of stubble darkened his square jaw, and a dimple marked the center of his chin. The warm-brown color of his eyes was countered by their look of flinty determination.

Pippa felt a little flutter low in her belly.

Who are you?

"Lord Hartwick at your service." He swept into a formal bow, and Pippa realized she must have voiced her question aloud.

"Pleased to make your acquaintance, Lord Hartwick." She performed her own little curtsy. *Merciful heavens.* The man had practically forced his way inside, and yet a lifetime of manners and social niceties still dictated their behavior.

"Miss Chester." Lord Hartwick took a step closer. "I beg your forgiveness for my actions, but I'm desperate—*quite* desperate—to see Lady Rowling. If you could arrange for me to speak to her..." He swallowed, his corded neck moving beneath his rumpled cravat. "Please."

The last word was nearly whispered.

Pippa was transfixed by his eyes, so full of entreaty. She didn't know this man or his agenda, but he seemed in desperate straits, and it seemed she had the power to assist him.

"Jarvis," she said, her eyes still locked on Lord Hartwick. "Please ask Lady Rowling to meet me in the sitting room."

"Miss Chester," Jarvis began.

She raised an eyebrow. The butler sighed and nodded in resignation.

"Please, come with me, my lord." Pippa led the way into the front parlor, her basket still tucked under her arm. Although he'd given her a start out on the street, he no longer seemed a threat. However, it was always good to be prepared.

Lord Hartwick declined her invitation to sit. Instead, he paced across the length of the parlor, the thick Aubusson carpet absorbing his footsteps. His trousers pulled tightly across hard thighs as he walked by. Pippa stared from her perch on a velvet settee, entranced at the play of his muscles as they bunched and relaxed with each step. She was so rarely around men; it must have been only the oddity of his masculine muscles that drew her attention.

"You've been involved with the Ladies Charitable Association for some time?"

Pippa's gaze darted up to his face, her cheeks heating. She prayed he hadn't caught her ogling him. "My cousin introduced me to the Association a year ago, and I was most grateful to be taken on as a member."

He nodded.

A rustle of silk announced the arrival of Lady Rowling, proprietress of the LCA.

"Good morning, Miss Chester." A minute smile graced Lady Rowling's face—an almost effusive greeting from the exceptionally contained woman—but it fell away when she turned her attention to the earl. "My lord, to what do I owe the pleasure?"

Pippa slipped toward the door, but Lady Rowling cleared her throat delicately and twitched her chin toward the settee. With a silent sigh, Pippa retraced her steps and sat down once more.

Lady Rowling sank into an ornate chair. Its gilded, ornate carvings were at odds with her ice-blue eyes, austere cheekbones, and severely cut, black gown. Although over two years had passed since her husband's death in India, she continued to dress for mourning.

Lord Hartwick sank down onto the settee next to Pippa. "Lady Rowling, I'm here on a most discreet matter."

A huff of laughter escaped Pippa's mouth. The LCA had discretion down to an art form.

Lady Rowling sent her a silent rebuke with one sharply raised eyebrow before replying, "I shall keep your confidence if I'm able, Lord Hartwick."

"My sister—" Lord Hartwick cleared his throat, his hands clenching on his lap. "My sister is Lydia Dashwood."

Pippa started.

"We are quite fond of Miss Dashwood and her contributions to the LCA." Lady Rowling's face remained coolly impassive.

"She left our residence yesterday afternoon to come here for her usual charity work." He paused, drawing a deep breath. "She never returned home last night."

Pippa held herself perfectly still.

Lydia Dashwood was missing?

Her chest grew tight. She pictured the petite young lady, with her knowing blue eyes and dark blond hair similar to her brother's. Pippa didn't know her well, but she'd seemed kind.

Lady Rowling blanched before quickly resuming her usual impassivity. "I'm quite sorry to hear the news."

"Lydia's maid says my sister sent her away on an errand once they reached here yesterday." Lord Hartwick leaned forward. "After that, I cannot account for her whereabouts. She's just…gone." The man's voice cracked on the last word. He fidgeted with his cravat as if needing to collect his composure.

Pippa squeezed her hands together. How terrifying! His desperation made sense now.

Her heart racing, she turned to the LCA's proprietress. "We can ask Jarvis. He knows all the ladies' comings and goings."

Pippa hurried across the room and tugged the bell pull before returning to the settee. When Jarvis entered with a bow, she opened her mouth to make her inquiry.

However, Lord Hartwick beat her to it, rising to his feet. "What do you know of Miss Dashwood's time here yesterday?"

Jarvis looked to his mistress who nodded her permission.

"Miss Dashwood arrived a bit after noon yesterday, milord," Jarvis said in his gravelly voice, "and left a few hours later."

Lord Hartwick frowned. "Was she with anyone?"

"I believe she arrived with her maid but left alone, milord."

"Did anything about her seem unusual to you?"

Jarvis shook his head.

"Damn," Lord Hartwick said through clenched teeth, sinking back onto the settee.

Lady Rowling excused the butler and folded her hands in her lap. "I hope you're satisfied, Lord Hartwick?"

His head jerked up. "You hope I'm satisfied? My sister disappeared after leaving your establishment, and after a few simple questions, you think I'll be *satisfied*?" He sprang to his feet on the last word, his voice booming.

Pippa shrank back against the settee.

"Did she speak with anyone here yesterday?" Lord Hartwick demanded, looming over Lady Rowling. "Did she receive correspondence? Was she sent out on any errands? She's only nineteen, and she's out there, all alone!"

At Lady Rowling's silence, he threw his hands up in the air and shouted, "For the love of God, woman, do you know anything?"

"Your distress is understandable," Lady Rowling said, apparently choosing to ignore his anger. "However, I fear I have no knowledge of your sister's activities yesterday. Although I'm proprietress of this association, I don't keep records of correspondence or comings and goings."

Lord Hartwick ground his teeth. He drew a deep breath and seemed to stuff the angry beast of his fury back into its cage. When he sat down on the settee once more, his face was a mask of calm. How astounding, Pippa thought, to feel so much and show so little.

He faced Pippa. "Perhaps you saw her here yesterday?"

She swallowed. "I'm so sorry, but I haven't seen her since the day before last."

He closed his eyes briefly, and Pippa fought the sudden urge to reach out and give his arm a comforting squeeze.

"She did seem in a bit of a rush that day though." Pippa cast her mind back. "Her fingers were even more ink-stained than usual, but otherwise, nothing seemed out of the ordinary."

Lord Hartwick nodded. He stared into space, a frown tugging at his lips. "Lady Rowling, if you could discreetly speak to the servants and other members, I'd be most appreciative. I prefer to keep this quiet, but my primary concern is for Lydia's well-being."

The lady inclined her head in acknowledgement and rose to her feet, signaling that the meeting was at an end.

He straightened his shoulders like a weary soldier bracing himself for the next advance. He rose, handed Lady Rowling his card, and bid them both a good day. When he reached the doorway, he paused, glancing over his shoulder at Pippa. Their gazes tangled. In his eyes, Pippa saw straight through to the very center of him: fear for his sister, wild anger, weariness, and even…even something that looked like yearning.

Her skin tingled.

Then he was gone. The room somehow felt emptier without his self-contained energy.

Pippa turned her attention back to Lady Rowling. The woman was running her hand over her face as if to wipe away her anxiety. She stilled, perhaps sensing Pippa's regard. The strange moment of vulnerability was broken when a maid appeared with tea service. Lady Rowling poured and handed Pippa a steaming cup.

"This could cause quite a bit of trouble for us." The LCA's proprietress frowned into her tea. "We cannot handle any additional scrutiny right now."

Pippa leaned forward, shocked by the woman's cavalier attitude. "Trouble for *us*?"

"Among other concerns, there have been whispers amongst the ton questioning the true purpose of the LCA."

Pippa gasped.

Lady Rowling nodded. "I'm sure I don't have to spell out the danger of people growing curious and poking around here." She studied Pippa over the rim of her teacup. "This organization is important to you, yes?"

Pippa clenched her fingers on her delicate cup handle. "You know what it means to me."

"Lord Hartwick must be put off. We cannot become embroiled in any scandal involving his sister's disappearance. It's simply too risky, on top of our other worries."

Pippa tightened her lips together.

Words crowded, hot and spikey, against Pippa's closed

mouth, a startling contrast to the other woman's chilly demeanor.

"You think me uncaring." Lady Rowling leaned back in her seat.

"I don't know all that goes on behind the scenes for the LCA to exist, but Lydia is one of us. If she's in any danger, if she's come to harm—" Pippa broke off, fear for the young woman robbing her of words.

Men with hidden faces. Pistols drawn. Blood on the ground. Screaming—

She blinked away the dangerous images and instead prayed Lydia Dashwood remained safe from such things.

Drawing a deep breath, she worked to steady her voice. "If we can assist in any way, then we must help."

Lady Rowling's expression turned distressed for the quickest moment before she set her teacup down. "I'll certainly look into Lydia's activities here yesterday. Beyond that, however, I don't see what aid we can safely provide. Given the current situation with De—" Lady Rowling broke off.

Pippa frowned. Could she be referring to Dev, the friendly servant in Lady Rowling's retinue who'd traveled with her from India?

Lady Rowling leveled a piercing gaze at Pippa. "Please trust me, Miss Chester, when I tell you the LCA is in a precarious situation. Any scrutiny of our organization right now could prove disastrous." With a regal tilt of her head, Lady Rowling rose and swept from the room.

Pippa exhaled, leaning back on the settee.

Merciful heavens.

Lydia Dashwood was missing. The LCA—Pippa's one true refuge—was in some kind of trouble. And her encounter with Lord Hartwick had left her feeling strangely jittery and off kilter.

There was only one thing to do.

It was time to stab someone.

Chapter Two

ONCE MORE, JACK found himself circling St. James Square, his eyes scouring the building he'd just exited. Unlikely as it was, he couldn't stop himself from searching the grounds for a clue, even the smallest of hints, as to his sister's fate.

He clenched his fists, wishing he could bellow in frustration. However, he didn't wish for Lady Rowling to unleash her hulking butler on him, so he settled for muttering a steady stream of profanity.

Why had the confounded woman been so unhelpful?

He'd harbored a vision of entering the building only to find his sister had been detained by some minor issue—a sprained ankle, or perhaps some knitting-for-orphans related emergency— and had merely forgotten to send word. He would shake his head in exasperation. Lydia would roll her eyes and tease him for his overprotective tendencies.

And then he would bring her home. Home, where he knew she was safe.

Clearly, allowing Lydia to go anywhere without his presence had been a terrible mistake, one he wouldn't repeat. Things only stayed ordered and safe when he was in control.

He sat on a bench in the little grassy area in the square, weariness temporarily winning the battle. He stared at a slim sapling; its slender branches tilted up to the clear autumn sky.

Miss Chester was tall and slim like this tree. He closed his eyes, allowing the memory of their collision on the sidewalk to distract him from his grinding, incessant worry. Respite, just for a moment.

Her lithe form pressed against him. The flash of surprise, of perhaps something more, flaring in the depths of her blue eyes. The solidness of her, the strength he'd felt when he clasped her arms.

Something stirred deep inside him.

A carriage rolled by, its rumble on the cobblestones pulling Jack out of his reverie.

He forced himself to his feet. His minute of daydreaming was over. He had to find his sister. The carriage turned the corner, perhaps headed for the mews behind the grand houses.

Behind the grand houses...

Jack's eyes narrowed.

Behind those houses were stables with sharp-eyed stable boys. There were doors to kitchens where servants and messengers loitered, gossip flowing freely among those unobserved by their masters.

Renewed, Jack followed the path of the carriage around the block and through the alley. He counted off the houses until he found Lady Rowling's. Her backyard was surrounded by a high fence and thick shrubbery on one side and the stable on the other, making it impossible to peer into the garden. Jack trailed his hands along the fence until his fingers detected a gap. Reaching through the narrow opening, he fumbled about until he found a latch. With a small smile of triumph, he eased the hidden fence door open and crept through.

The verdant garden was cast in dappled shade as the early evening sun filtered through the rustling leaves. Bushes adorned with fading flowers hanging onto the memory of summer created the perfect cover for a man wishing to remain incognito.

Tucking behind a cluster of thick bushes, Jack waited.

The soft murmur of a young stable boy speaking—likely to a

horse, based on the sing-song lilt—drifted out the window and into the yard. A kitchen maid clipped herbs from the garden. Otherwise, the back of the house was quiet.

A gray stallion emerged from the mews, the stable boy on the opposite side dwarfed by the massive horse.

Adjustments were made to the saddle and tack, and the horse's feet were inspected. The stable boy walked around the stallion…

…and clearly was not a stable *boy*.

What in the world was going on?

The young woman ran practiced hands over the horse's withers, cooing to the horse as she completed the work usually reserved for the lowest stable servants. She was clad in men's riding gear, and with a quick twist, she tucked her long, red braid up under a hat before springing up onto the saddle and flicking the reins. She set off down the alley.

The woman rode with confidence. Her demeanor and speech indicated she was a well-bred lady, so why was she working in the stables?

Shaking his head, Jack turned his attention back to the house. The kitchen servant was no longer outside. No noise emerged from the stable, and the yard was empty. He crept out of the bushes and slunk about the garden, eyes darting over the ground in search of signs of a struggle, a scrap of Lydia's blue gown, or anything hinting at her fate. After searching the entire yard with frequent glances at the house to be sure he wasn't seen, he stopped behind a tree. *Defeat.*

Perhaps a dropped handkerchief embroidered with Lydia's initials next to a scrap of paper bearing an address was too much to hope for.

The sound of a window sliding open cut through the relative silence in the garden. Jack ducked behind a low shrub.

He peeked around the side. Miss Chester leaned out of a window two floors up. Her cheeks were flushed, and tendrils of hair clung to her temples. Was that how she'd look after passionate kisses, rosy and mussed? Jack's mouth dried.

He exhaled, forcing his mind onto a more logical train of thought. What had Miss Chester been doing up there? Surely knitting booties for the poor wasn't such strenuous work.

"I almost had you with that last feint," she said over her shoulder.

The murmured reply of her companion was too quiet for Jack to make out.

"Yes, but your riposte always bests me. I should have practiced more this week." She wiped her sleeve across her brow.

Jack squinted. She was wearing… a man's lawn shirt?

Miss Chester retreated into the room and closed the window.

Jack sunk to the ground.

Feint.

Riposte.

Those were fencing terms.

Why was Miss Chester discussing fencing? Actually, it appeared she was *practicing* fencing, not merely discussing technique.

A woman who tended to horses and rode about dressed like a man.

A woman who fenced.

What the hell was going on here?

Jack narrowed his eyes. Strange things were afoot at the Ladies Charitable Association and uncovering this mystery might be the key to finding his sister.

PIPPA BOWED TO *Señor* Martín. Her fencing instructor's lean face softened with a smile.

"You do quite well today, *Señorita*." *Señor* Martín hung his *épée* from one of the many hooks lining the wall.

"Thank you, *Señor*," Pippa replied between gulping breaths. The Spaniard hired by Lady Rowling had worked her doubly hard—a welcome distraction after learning nothing helpful about Lydia Dashwood from the other LCA ladies she'd questioned—since she'd missed her usual practice time yesterday.

Occasionally, the ladies of the LCA did actual charity work, and yesterday Pippa and several others had traveled to a workhouse to distribute warm clothes.

The fencer lifted his jacket from another hook to reveal a very feminine parasol hanging behind.

"*Señor* Martín, I'm not sure pink is your color," Pippa teased, determined to set aside her worry for now.

"No, but perhaps it is yours?" He carried the parasol across the room and held it up to Pippa with both his hands as if making an offering.

Pippa stared. "Is this…?"

The man nodded, his eyes sparkling with delight. "It arrived last night. I told the man, if he can make a walking stick with a hidden sword, why not a parasol?"

Pippa reached out a hand, tracing the ornate handle and sturdy pole nestled among the pink frills. Her finger paused at a small button.

"Yes, press there and twist, and the sword releases." *Señor* Martín demonstrated, the thin blade gleaming in the late morning sunshine.

Pippa swallowed. Although she was adequately skilled with a dagger, she never felt as safe as she did with a sword in her hand. Her fencing instructor nodded as if reading her thoughts.

"This is… I can't believe…" She instinctively took the man's hand, squeezing. "Thank you. So very much."

He squeezed in return before sliding the blade back inside the pole with a click. "I shall leave your new toy here, but now you should step into the garden and cool off. Perhaps attack a few leaves—but slowly, very slowly—so your tiny little arms will not turn to rocks."

Pippa gave the wiry man a mock scowl. "Don't speak ill of my muscles. They might take exception and challenge you to a duel."

Señor Martín's face brightened. "Ah, a duel." He placed a graceful hand over his heart. "I remember my first as if it were but yesterday."

Pippa grinned. "I'll let you know if any tree branches feel their honor must be avenged."

After running her hand over the hilt of her new parasol—*her very own parasol sword!*—she headed down the hallway. The familiar sounds of the LCA were audible despite closed doors. A hammer striking a chisel told her Cecily was still in the early phase of her latest marble sculpture. Impatient muttering from behind another door suggested Ophelia hadn't yet cracked that advanced calculus equation. At the end of the hall, Mary was reciting one version of a line and then another as she worked on the draft of her latest play.

The Ladies Covert Academy, the real organization hiding behind the façade of an innocent charity group, was busy as ever, humming with the energy of dozens of women finally free to immerse themselves in pursuits that polite society deemed inappropriate for well-bred ladies. And it was all thanks to the generosity of Lady Rowling. She'd returned from India with more money than Croesus, thanks to her late husband's shrewd investing with the East India Company.

The LCA members shared speculations about their proprietress. The ongoing theory was that Lady Rowling's desire to provide young women with freedom and opportunities stemmed from her parents forcing her to marry a marquess in his sixties. She'd been but seventeen.

Whatever the truth of the group's origins, Pippa thanked her lucky stars—and the cousin who'd sponsored her membership—for the Ladies Covert Academy's existence every day. Without it, she'd still be hiding away in her bedchamber, terrified of an uncertain world that could steal the very life from a man in the time it took to pull a trigger.

Pippa trotted down two sets of stairs into the kitchen for a cool glass of water. She nodded her thanks to the woman peeling vegetables at the counter and her son. The little ragamuffin had a mop of wild, red hair and mischief in his eyes.

"Need me to deliver any letters, miss?" The boy's eyes were alight with the prospect of earning an extra coin.

"Not today." Pippa softened her words with a smile. She slipped him a coin anyway when his mother's back was turned. He tucked it away and gave her a cheeky wink as he took her empty glass.

Pippa bit back a laugh, not wanting to encourage the little scamp, and headed to the back of the kitchen.

She peered through the back door. Hands growing clammy, she searched for any danger. She winced against the self-loathing that pricked her each time her fear overruled her will. Drawing a fortifying breath, she strode out into the yard.

Pippa wandered to the center of the garden. The sky above grew purple as the sun bid this slice of earth farewell until the morrow. Tall trees and shrubs cast much of the garden in shadow. The muffled noises of carriages and pedestrians floated over the fence on cooling air.

Pippa swung her arms in circles. Smiling, she recalled *Señor* Martín's warning that her muscles would tighten into rocks if she didn't follow his prescribed cool-down to the letter. She pulled the protective tip off the end of her sword and stashed it in her pocket. She needed a sharp end for this exercise.

She exhaled slowly, then made a controlled lunge at a dangling tree branch, piercing a leaf with her *épée*. She pulled her arm back and inspected the leaf. Dead center. Her lips curled up at the corners in satisfaction.

Pippa walked in a circle before stabbing another leaf with slow, deliberate movements. Between lunges, she stretched. After a few minutes, her skin was no longer flushed from her exertions inside.

She sighed and tipped back her head. Above her, the thin crescent of the moon was just visible against the darkening twilight. It was a lovely evening. Pippa thought of Lydia Dashwood somewhere out there and her brother, sick with worry, and frowned.

A rustling sound broke through her contemplation. Pippa spun around, sword raised.

"Who's there?" She squinted to see through the shadows.

Silence.

Pippa scanned the garden, her heart thundering in her chest. Was it a burglar, an outlaw? Someone with a pistol in hand, out roaming the mews of Mayfair in the hopes of finding a distracted victim to murder?

Was it a highwayman?

Pippa shivered.

There was nothing there. There was never anything there, and there would likely never be anything there.

Pippa understood this in a logical way, and yet, she couldn't stop herself from standing at alert, straining to hear any suspicious noises. She caught a movement out of the corner of her eye and jumped. A squirrel bounded past before leaping onto a tree trunk.

Pippa's shoulders relaxed. She lowered her sword. Shaking her head at her jumpiness, she walked toward the house. The windows glowed at her in cheery welcome. After she changed back into her dress, she'd collect her new parasol and—

A noise like a twig snapping sounded from behind the bushes to her left. She whirled toward the sound, her skin tightening. Up shot her *épée*.

A shadowy figure loomed up behind the bushes. Pippa's heart stuttered. Her training took over. She lunged forward, her *épée* aimed at the villain's middle.

"Miss Chester!"

At the familiar voice, Pippa pulled back. Her *épée* point was a handbreadth from his stomach. Her stomach flipped over in horror. She'd been a scant inch from killing a man.

Her fingers were as cold as the metal she gripped.

When her voice emerged, it was a choked, desiccated thing. "Lord Hartwick?"

JACK STARED AT the thin blade, the shiny metal winking in the light shining out from the house windows.

He swallowed.

"Miss Chester," he said, forcing a lightness he didn't feel into his voice. "Would you be so kind as to point your sword elsewhere?"

In the faint light glowing from the house, he watched Miss Chester's thoughts pass across her tense face. On one hand, he was an intruder, lurking in the shadows where he didn't belong. Spying on a young woman who'd assumed her privacy was unviolated. But on the other hand, he was an acquaintance now, the brother of her fellow LCA member, and had reason to be searching the grounds with Lydia missing.

What would she decide—was he a criminal or desperate brother? Was it to be disembowelment or mercy?

Her hand twitched.

She lowered her weapon.

Jack's breath whooshed out of him. "Thank you," he said, keeping his voice as mild as if she'd passed him the saltshaker at the dinner table.

She nodded and took a few steps back. He allowed his gaze to roam, his relief at cheating death pumping him full of life, vigor, and a new appreciation for a woman in tight breeches.

He'd seen flashes of her through the thick bushes, however, this unobstructed view of Miss Pippa Chester was hard to ignore. Her snug breeches outlined long, firm legs. A thin, lawn shirt clung to her breasts and trim waist. And thick, glossy hair tumbled down from its pins in distracting dishevelment, as if her locks had been mussed by the hands of a lover. Jack's attention moved to her lips, and a strange hunger gnawed at his belly.

Her eyes grew wide as she witnessed his perusal. The air between them crackled.

Jack tore his gaze away, his face heating as he realized he was openly ogling a gently-bred young lady.

Exhaustion, worry, and the sight of those breeches had apparently addled both his mind and his morals.

"My apologies, Miss Chester." He hoped she wouldn't ask him to expound on his wrongdoings. He didn't think *for mentally undressing the lady in tight breeches* would be well-received.

"What are you doing here?" she demanded. Although she kept her *épée* pointed toward the ground, Miss Chester's confident grip on the handle suggested a fencer at the ready.

"Oh, just out for an evening stroll," Jack tried, voice breezy.

Her eyes narrowed.

"Actually, I'm planning to renovate my backyard." He inspected his fingernails. "I thought while I was in the neighborhood, I'd visit Lady Rowling's garden for inspiration."

He glanced up to find Miss Chester glaring.

Jack sighed. She knew about his sister's disappearance already, so there was no point in lying.

"I came back looking for clues to Lydia's whereabouts. Maybe listen to the servants' gossip, hunt the grounds for signs of a struggle, that sort of thing."

Her *épée* twitched in her hand. "You nearly scared my soul out of my skin." Her mouth tightened. "I thought you were a criminal. I thought—" She broke off and turned her head to the side.

Even in the dim light, he could see her face was tight and pale. He stepped forward, hand up to comfort her, but her *épée* twitched once more.

Jack froze.

"I didn't mean to cause you fright," he said, voice low. "I can see now that I should have announced myself at once. I feared Lady Rowling was setting her mammoth butler on me, so I hid myself." He paused, willing her to look at him.

She kept her face turned, her lips pressed into a grim line.

He broke the silence that had fallen between them. "I'm so sorry."

Miss Chester's chest lifted in a deep breath. She turned back to face him and nodded. "And were you successful?"

Jack frowned as he tried to make sense of her question.

"With your hunt for clues," she clarified.

Jack's muscles tightened. Any brief reprieve he'd gained from his crushing worry while in the lovely Miss Chester's presence evaporated quicker than a penniless second son when it came time to pay the tavern bill.

He shook his head. "I didn't find anything."

Jack pictured Lydia's serene face, her intelligent blue eyes, and clever retorts. He didn't tell his sister often, but he prayed she knew how much he loved her. She was his only family left. It was his duty to not only protect her, but also her reputation. Unfortunately, if word got out that she was missing and unchaperoned, her life in their judgmental world would be ruined forever. His stomach hollowed at the visceral fear shooting through him. Dear God, let her be found so he might tell her he loved her once more.

He must have looked a misery because Miss Chester's expression softened. "I'm so terribly sorry she's missing. I asked around of the ladies who were here today, and no one knew anything about Lydia's whereabouts. Are you quite certain she didn't visit a friend? Perhaps visit a relative out of town?"

Jack ran his hand over his face. "She's the most conscientious person I know. She'd never leave without telling me." He exhaled. "Not of her own free will."

Miss Chester took a step closer. "I wish there was more Lady Rowling and the LCA could do to help your search."

"It didn't seem your proprietress was very keen on assisting," he said, voice dry.

Her lips turned down in sympathy. "I know she seems a

bit...cold." Miss Chester took a step closer. "She has a chilly exterior, but she carries burdens and worries that most of the world cannot see."

Jack frowned. *Burdens the world cannot see?* It seemed Miss Chester knew at least a portion of the mystery surrounding her benefactress. Might she know of any mysteries surrounding the LCA itself, and therefore the cause of his sister's disappearance? She'd already proven herself to be more observant than most, noting the small detail of Lydia's ink-stained fingers.

Jack turned several possibilities over in his mind. He settled on a course of action, and the churning worry in his abdomen quieted.

"Miss Chester, I do believe there is further action your group could undertake to assist." He steeled himself. This wouldn't be easy.

She leaned forward. "I'd be more than happy to pass along any request to Lady Rowling and the other members."

He forced a cold, merciless smile to his face. "Oh, that shan't be an issue."

Her lovely pink lips pulled down in confusion.

"Lady Rowling has proven herself to be less than forthcoming, and I haven't made the acquaintance of the other members." He rocked back and forth on his heels, hiding his hands behind his back. He didn't want their nervous clasping to give him away. "No, there is only one member who has proven helpful thus far. And I shall require her full cooperation in all things."

Her fingers loosened around the sword hilt.

"You, Miss Chester, shall be my eyes and ears into the LCA. You will help me find my sister. And if you don't..."—he leaned forward, feeling nauseous as he added a menacing dip to his voice. *This was for Lydia. Only for her would he behave in this abominable way*— "I shall have no choice but to reveal your secrets."

The sword fell out of Miss Chester's hand and landed on the ground with a thud.

Chapter Three

J ACK SHOULD HAVE known better than to trust a woman with a sword.

He glanced at his pocket watch for the umpteenth time before surveying the crowds of music lovers milling about with their lemonade and ratafia. When he'd suggested they reconvene later in the evening at Lady Frampton's musicale, Miss Chester had readily agreed.

So where was the woman? They had plans to make, sisters to find. How long did it take to throw back a bit of supper, change out of her male garb, wash away the dew from her exertions, and slide into a frock?

His mind stalled at the image of her pulling the thin lawn shirt over her head, running a damp cloth over her creamy skin—

With a whispered curse, he pulled away from the wall he'd been leaning against.

Lydia. Only his sister mattered. He couldn't afford to cloud his mind with fascination over the mysterious Miss Chester. He must focus on the task at hand.

Jack recalled the shock of yesterday evening's discovery. He'd left his study after several hours tending to estate business. It was tedious, draining work. But it was his responsibility. He wouldn't allow the estate to be neglected again.

He'd gone to the parlor to meet Lydia before supper as was

their tradition.

Only, she hadn't been there.

After questioning the servants, he'd discovered she'd been gone all day. Her maid had tearfully recounted Lydia sending her to purchase a pair of gloves on Bond Street once they'd reached the LCA. Lydia had reassured her maid she'd meet her back home in a few hours. When she'd failed to return, the maid had assumed she was stuck with some charity project at the LCA. It wasn't uncommon for her to spend the entire day there, the maid had recounted as she'd twisted a damp handkerchief in her hands.

The panic of discovering she was missing had threatened to cover Jack like a blanket of snow upon the ground, still, icy, and chilling to the marrow. Lydia was his little sister. It was his duty to protect her from harm both real and gossip induced. Unfortunately, aristocratic women of the ton lived and died by the untarnished state of their reputation. He was supposed to keep her safe, and he'd failed.

Jack shook off his woolgathering. He paced along the wide hallway where a few latecomers to the musicale still trickled in.

At least he felt somewhat human again. Despite his impatience and worry, he was glad he'd stopped at home to wash up, change into fresh clothes, and wolf down some food. It was rather astounding how a sleepless night, grubby garments, an empty stomach, and heart-sickening worry could tilt a person so far off-kilter.

Why, he'd gone so far as to break into an aristocrat's back garden and unwittingly spy upon a lone, vulnerable woman— well, perhaps not so vulnerable, considering Miss Chester's sword. And then he'd compounded his sin by threatening to expose her and her group.

He shook his head. He wasn't proud of what he'd done, but it had seemed like the only way to save his sister.

"Hartwick, old man."

Jack looked up. A familiar gentleman approached, a young woman on one arm.

"Hello, Benedict." He smiled to Lord Lovell, his close friend since their days at Eton. "Emilia."

Benedict's sister curtsied and, with a wink, told them she'd leave them to their man-gossip and secure seats near the front before the music began.

"You missed our morning ride," Benedict chided after his sister had left. His open smile took the sting out of his words.

Jack noticed several young women seated at the back of the music room, eyeing his friend over their shoulders. Whether it was Benedict's perfectly-tousled blond hair, blue eyes with a mischievous twinkle, or his vast fortune that piqued their interest, Jack couldn't say, but wherever Benedict went, a bevy of ladies batting their eyelashes followed in his wake. Better Benedict than Jack. He hadn't the time for romance, not with his current duty to repairing his holdings.

He swallowed, preparing himself to lie to a trusted friend. "Er, sorry I wasn't at the park this morning. I've been cooped up at home keeping an eye on Lydia. She's come down with a nasty cold."

Benedict frowned. "I'm sorry to hear that. Perhaps a visit would cheer her up?" He raised his eyebrows hopefully.

Jack shook his head. "Wouldn't want you to catch it. Quite contagious, the doctor said."

His friend made a show of stepping back. "Please refrain from breathing on me, old man. Can't afford a cold, else the ladies will find someone else to moon over." He winked. "Give Lydia my regards." He was quiet for a moment, and then added, his expression intent, "And if you need any help, I hope you know you can count on me."

Gulping, Jack tried to dislodge the sudden lump in his throat. Damn, but exhaustion and worry made him maudlin. "I appreciate that. Hope to see you at the club soon."

Benedict bid him farewell and left to find his sister.

Jack slumped back against the wall as the musicians began their warm up, plucking and tuning their instruments.

He'd lied to his friend. He'd done it to protect Lydia's reputation so that one day she could marry the man of her choosing without the stench of scandal severely limiting her choices, but it had felt wrong to lie just the same. He scrubbed his hand across his face.

Get it together, man.

He'd need his wits about him for when Miss Chester arrived. He was confident she would provide the key to unlocking the mysterious disappearance of his sister.

⟫⟫⟫❳❲⟪⟪⟪

PIPPA MARCHED UP the steps to Lady Frampton's grand Mayfair home, a kernel of hot rage burning in her chest like a coal. *Better rage than fear at least.*

She recalled her run in with Lord Hartwick in the shadowy garden earlier. The man had disarmed her with his sharp words alone.

"You will help me." His voice had been hard as metal. "You have no choice. I need you." He paused, his brown eyes darkening. "And you need me to keep my mouth shut about what I know."

"What do you know?" She'd grasped at straws, but perhaps he was bluffing.

He'd glanced over his shoulder at Lady Rowling's stables before answering. "I know the LCA is more than what it seems."

She'd held her breath, waiting.

"Gently-bred young women doing charity work...and also serving as grooms in the stables?" He'd given her *épée*, lying at her feet, a pointed look. "And studying fencing?"

His words had landed on her like blows from a heavy saber.

"And who knows what else goes on inside this house? I'm sure the ton would be in raptures to hear my tales."

So, it was to be blackmail. The flash of regret she'd glimpsed on his face was surely a trick of the moonlight.

Pippa's breath had come in quick, little pants, and she'd fought to keep her voice even. "Lord Hartwick, I wish I could help you. I truly do."

She'd pictured Lydia's kind smile and the woman's intelligent eyes. If she were braver, if she wasn't crippled in a truly fundamental way by her fear, she'd say yes.

But she wasn't brave.

Something inside her had been broken by what had happened. And she could not say yes.

Lord Hartwick had taken a step forward until he was so close that his scent—clean, masculine soap and rich spice—had filled her nose. She'd shivered.

"Perhaps you don't care for Lydia's well-being, but at least have a care for yourself. For your mysterious charity group. Because I don't make idle threats," he'd growled, leaning closer still. "I will destroy you. I will destroy all of this." He'd waved his hand expansively, taking in the house, the stables, and her sword on the ground. Unless she helped him, he'd destroy the LCA.

Pippa forced his infuriating threats from earlier out of her mind. She charged up the steps of the home sponsoring the musicale—*a musicale! the man was already turning her life upside down*—leaving her mother back on the sidewalk where she greeted a cluster of friends who apparently didn't mind being tardy.

Pippa gripped her new parasol by its ornate, metal handle, using it like a walking stick. Her finger toyed with the little button. Her mother had been confused by Pippa's desire to bring her new parasol—bought at Bond Street just this morning, she'd fibbed—along to an evening outing. Thankfully, she'd been delighted by Pippa's desire to attend at all, so the parasol had been forgotten.

She stormed past the butler manning the front door. How *dare* Lord Hartwick blackmail her? Her outrage over his highhanded threats was at risk of boiling over. Yes, his sister was missing, and yes, Pippa wanted to help, but she couldn't. She just couldn't. Forcing her to assist by threatening to dig into the LCA's secrets was unconscionable. It was the actions of a wretch. A brigand. A pestilence upon the very foundation of society.

As she passed, Pippa noticed a young couple standing together in the foyer. The man's face was red. His stammered comment about the weather was only just audible over the sounds of the musicians tuning their instruments in the other room. The lady smiled shyly at her admirer, peeking up at him from under her eyelashes before suggesting they explore the weather together during a walk through the park tomorrow. The look of pure wonder on the lad's face cooled the angry fire in Pippa's heart. Who could maintain a proper fit of rage in the face of sweet, awkward, young love?

She sighed as her emotions settled. Where was Lord Hartwick? She didn't see the jackal, but there were a few other latecomers milling about in the foyer. Pippa's face heated as a woman stared at her in open interest. She came to social outings so rarely, people treated her as a bizarre curiosity. She hurried along a wide hallway where the first notes of music echoed. Heart racing at the prospect of so many strangers, she stepped into the music room.

Rows of chairs were filled with finely-dressed men and women. Along the perimeter of the room stood even more guests, glasses of refreshment, programs, or fans in their hands.

So many people.

Pippa gripped her parasol handle tightly. Where was her mother? Didn't she know Pippa hated these social events? Her face warming, Pippa struggled to draw breath. She needed to get out. She needed—

"About time," growled a familiar voice.

Pippa breathed shallowly.

Lord Hartwick examined her face and frowned. "It's rather warm in here," he murmured close to her ear. "Let's step out onto the balcony for some air. We'll have more privacy."

"My mother…"

"She'll be able to see you through the glass doors," he assured her as he took her arm and guided her past the table of refreshments at the back of the room and out onto the balcony. He closed the doors behind them.

Pippa leaned against the balustrade, closing her eyes. The cool night air steadied her heartbeat.

"Are you the fainting sort?"

Pippa opened her eyes to find Lord Hartwick watching her, his face inscrutable in the dim lighting.

"Certainly not." Pippa glared, offended. "It was merely too warm for me, that's all."

"If you say so."

Pippa squared her shoulders and looked the man over. The light shining in through the windows at their back reflected the gold in his hair. His snowy-white cravat was neatly pressed, quite a change from his rumpled appearance at the LCA. After submitting to her perusal, he returned the favor. Pippa's heart skipped a beat at the touch of his gaze.

"You're late." His voice was clipped.

"You're an ass," she retorted. Pippa clapped a hand over her mouth. *Where had that come from?*

His eyebrows shot up in surprise.

"Forgive me." She lifted her chin. "I've never been blackmailed before and am uncertain of the protocol."

"Protocol," he repeated, his face impassive.

"Yes. Between the blackmailer and the blackmailed," she replied. "Am I to play the role of polite and proper society miss and curtsy to you? Or is it appropriate for me to show my anger and disdain—quite natural reactions to being blackmailed, I assure you—and speak my mind?"

He stared at her, his mouth a grim line. Pippa gripped the handle of her parasol tightly, but then she noticed the corner of his lips twitch.

"Well," he said, head tilted as if in thought. "I suppose if we are alone, it would be acceptable for you to call me an ass. If you so desire."

His mouth seemed to linger on the word desire, and Pippa tore her eyes away from him, a strange heat unspooling low in her belly.

"Very well," she said. "I shall aim for civility. However, if my anger gets the better of my tongue, don't expect me to wear a hair shirt as penance."

He nodded, and they stared at one another for a moment. It felt as if they were both taking the measure of the other. Did he find her to be as complex and confusing as she did him?

Lord Hartwick turned to face the inky darkness beyond the balcony. His hands rested on the balustrade.

"I know I left you little choice earlier," he said. "Perhaps you won't believe me, but I'm grateful for your assistance. My sister—" He broke off.

Pippa glanced at him. His face remained an impassive mask, but his hands gripped the railing.

"Well," he continued, "we'd best form a plan. I know you began already, but you'll have to question *every* member of the Ladies Charitable Association. Delicately, of course. We don't want word of her disappearance to make its way into the gossip columns. The gossip mongers would love nothing more than to drag the name of an earl's sister through the mud, and then her future will be permanently tarnished. Hopefully, one of the LCA members will have information that will lead us to her."

Strains of music floated on the air around them. The notes were muffled and strangely discordant as if their journey outside of the music room had altered them.

"Her room yielded no clues?" Pippa asked, practicing her grip on the handle of her parasol.

"Her room?" Lord Hartwick frowned.

"I assume you searched her chamber for clues. If her valise is gone, then you know she intended to leave…that sort of thing."

He jerked to face her. Pippa narrowed her eyes.

"I never…" He quickly schooled his face, but not before Pippa saw his stricken expression. She took a step toward him, her hand clenched so tightly around the parasol handle that she feared she'd rip the seams of her glove. "Are you telling me," Pippa ground out, "that before you roamed the streets for the entire night, before you scared me half to death in the garden, before you threatened me with blackmail, you failed to see if your sister had *packed a bag*?" Pippa was shouting by the end.

They faced one another, glaring. His hands clenched into fists at his side. Before her very eyes, he smoothed the expression from his face until only bland politeness remained. It was as if he controlled every facet of his emotion through sheer force of will.

Pippa glanced through the glass doors to check if anyone had heard her. Thankfully, the guests were all facing away from them, suggesting the music had drowned out her raised voice. She spied her mother standing against the far wall with her friends. Her face rapt, she seemed engrossed in the music. Apparently, her mother wasn't at all concerned that her usually social-function-adverse daughter had wandered off with a strange man onto a shadowy balcony.

"Come," Lord Hartwick said, pulling her attention back to the balcony.

Pippa faced him. "What?"

His hand was stretched out to her. "Come to my house. We'll search Lydia's room as you suggested."

She blinked at him. "You want me to come to your house?"

He nodded.

"Unchaperoned?"

He raised an eyebrow.

"Right now?"

"We can't waste any time. Don't you see? If there's a clue, some sort of lead, and we wait, who knows what might happen to her. She's my *sister*. Do you understand? My sister!" His voice, so clipped and controlled, had unraveled by the end. He spoke the last words in a ragged whisper.

Pippa stared.

His guard was down. She saw the naked fear on his face. To refuse him aid seemed the height of cruelty. But his casual neglect to her own reputation and safety when he was so concerned about his sister's was frustrating.

She fingered the small button at the base of her parasol as she weighed her options. The reminder that a simple push and twist would release the sword hidden in its handle renewed her confidence.

Pippa exhaled. "I'll come to your home later tonight."

He opened his mouth, perhaps to argue, so she whipped the parasol up and pointed the end at his stomach.

He dropped his outstretched hand.

"But if you think I'll traipse off into the night and permit any harm to befall myself or my reputation, think again. I'm the woman who was prepared to gut you, remember?" She twitched the parasol tip against his abdomen.

Jack narrowed his eyes. Pippa returned his stare with a steely glare of her own. Their gazes locked and tangled. An epic battle of wills was being waged right here on Lady Frampton's balcony. Entire armies and fortresses could be razed by the fierceness of their stares.

Pippa did not move. She did not blink.

Lord Hartwick exhaled and closed his eyes.

"Fine," he said, voice low.

"I'll tell my mother I have a megrim and head home. Once the house is quiet, I'll come to your place." She forced back a shudder at the thought of travelling the dark streets of London alone. Pippa tapped the button on her parasol for comfort before continuing. "And tomorrow morning, I'll ask the other ladies at the LCA about Lydia. Discreetly, as you said."

He nodded, then gave her his direction. He bid her farewell and left the balcony.

Pippa waited a minute before leaving herself.

"My dear," her mother whispered when Pippa slid in beside her amongst the other musicale guests. "You should have told me to bring my smelling salts."

Pippa leaned close. "What do you mean?"

Her mother's eyes twinkled as she glanced away from the musicians. "My daughter, avoider of all social outings, not only asks to attend a musicale but also finds a dark, cozy corner to flirt with the handsomest man in the room? Why, I'm quite likely to swoon."

"Handsomest man in the room?" Pippa huffed.

Her mother's raised eyebrow spoke of her skepticism.

Pippa scowled. "If you must know, his breath is foul and he's prone to the gout."

While her mother laughed, Pippa made a silent vow. No matter how handsome Lord Hartwick might be—and she most certainly was *not* agreeing with her mother that he was—she would keep her distance. Her involvement was to help a young woman in trouble and protect the LCA and absolutely nothing more.

Chapter Four

PIPPA RECLINED AGAINST her pillows and tried to look pitiful. "I'm so sorry we left the musicale early."

"Oh pish, I'm just sorry you came down with a megrim." Lady Everleigh's silk gown swished as she circled Pippa's chamber, tidying up items that were already tidy. She finally alighted on the edge of Pippa's bed.

"It's just a small headache." Pippa crossed her fingers under the blanket.

Her mother eyed her, lips pursed. "You've been working such long hours with your charity group, it's no wonder you're feeling poorly. I think I'd best sit with you awhile."

Pippa bit her lip. How to get rid of her mother?

Lady Everleigh patted Pippa's hand before turning it over and running a finger across her callouses. She tutted. "I should speak to Lady Rowling, working you until your hands resemble a scullery maid's."

Pippa pulled her hand closed, her mind racing for an acceptable excuse. "Since my stitch is abysmal, they put me on cutting duty for clothes for the work house. I end up using the shears for hours." Yet another lie to her mother. Their necessity did not make her many falsehoods taste any less bitter.

Her mother frowned. "Well, see that you apply some salve."

Pippa nodded before redirecting the conversation. "Mother,

it's only a small headache. What if I drink one of your famous tisanes and then we all get a good night's rest?"

Her mother crinkled up her nose in indecision.

Pippa held her breath.

"Fine, although I leave with a guilty heart." Lady Everleigh rose and shook the wrinkles out of her gown. "I'll send Milly in with the tisane."

After a kiss on the forehead, she departed for her own chambers.

Soon, Milly arrived with the dreaded potion. Pippa dutifully gulped down the noxious drink and reassured Milly she'd soon be asleep.

While she waited for the house to quiet, Pippa decided to do a bit of training. Reaching under her bed, Pippa retrieved a bundle wedged between the frame's wooden support beams. She unwound trousers and a waistcoat and pulled out her newest knife. Although she preferred her *épée*, she couldn't exactly wear it about town. Before she received her parasol, she'd always slipped a dagger into her reticule or pocket, so she was always armed.

She began to practice, flipping the knife into the air and catching it by the handle.

Although *Señor* Martín was an expert at fencing, he knew plenty about knives as well. After a handful of lessons on grip and throwing, he'd left her to her own devices. Clandestine practice sessions like tonight's helped increase her accuracy and confidence.

Pippa winced when she missed a catch, and the blade nicked her hand. Examining the tiny cut, she noticed several small, nearly invisible scars on her hand, symbols of her progress. Thank goodness her mother believed her to be quite inept with a sewing needle and those shears Pippa had claimed to spend so many hours using.

Actually, she *was* quite inept with a sewing needle and shears, but she'd rather be lethal with a dagger than praised for her cross stitch.

When the house was finally quiet, Pippa flung off her night rail and shimmied into her male garb. Hair pinned up, hat shoved on, dagger tucked into her waistband, and with a dark cloak on top, she was ready to sneak out into the night.

She tiptoed down the servants' staircase and made her way through the kitchen. Pippa paused at the back door, surveying the yard. Usually fresh and cheery, the garden was now cloaked in ominous shadows with trees looming up like specters.

There was no one out there. No highwaymen, hiding in the shadows, waiting to rob and kill. Not like the other time. She was safe.

Pippa felt for the dagger at her waist, drew a deep breath, and stepped into the darkness.

She walked a few blocks until she found a hackney stand. Pitching her voice low, she gave the driver Hartwick's address. When they arrived, she fished the fare out of her pocket for the man and strode to the front door, head high and shoulders back. Hopefully anyone passing by would only see a gentleman, some friend of Lord Hartwick, coming by for a game of billiards or whatever it was men did late at night for entertainment.

One possible form of late-night entertainment crossed Pippa's mind. When Lord Hartwick opened the door, her cheeks felt hot with a blush.

He stared for a moment before widening the door and gesturing her in.

"Where's your butler?" she whispered.

"Gave him and the other servants the night off and a bag full of coins to play cards." He locked the door. "Morale, I told them, although it was also a none-too-subtle bribe to keep word quiet on Lydia's absence. Never seen the old fellow move so fast in my life."

Pippa heard the faint sound of laughter from the back of the house.

"They've turned my kitchen into a gambling den." Lord Hartwick shook his head. "It did the trick, but it's possible I've corrupted my servants. They might fall into sinful lives of vice and moral degradation, all because of me."

Pippa imagined a once-dignified old butler opening the door to this grand house with a cigar hanging limply from his mouth, eyes bloodshot, and his words slurring while an ace dangled out his sleeve. She smiled.

"Yes, quite a picture, isn't it?" His eyes crinkled at the corners. He stepped closer.

Pippa stared, his nearness causing her skin to tingle. She breathed deeply, his clean, masculine scent filling her nose. Her foot lifted to step closer.

Closer?

No.

She set her foot back in place. The moment felt fraught, this strange energy between them muddying every thought, word, and movement. "Which way to your sister's room?"

He shook his head as if he too needed to clear himself of whatever this was. But surely that wasn't the case. "Upstairs," he finally replied.

She followed him up the wide staircase. His house was like so many of her acquaintances: stately with thick carpets, luxurious furnishings, and the watchful eyes of disapproving ancestors staring down from the portraits on the wall. The wooden handrail gleamed, a faint scent of lemon and beeswax in the air.

"I saw a few LCA ladies at the musicale after you left and asked them about your sister." She glanced to him at her side.

His head jerked up. "And?"

Pippa paused at the top of the staircase and faced him. "They didn't know anything."

He glanced away and breathed deeply, seeming to need a moment to digest this news. Although he was a complete bounder for blackmailing her, she did feel an ache of compassion. To not know if your loved one was safe or even alive must have been the worst sort of agony.

"I'm sorry," she whispered, her hand twitching as she stopped herself from laying her fingers on him in comfort.

He nodded and continued walking.

"This is Lydia's room." He gestured to a door halfway down the dim hallway.

Pippa pushed open the door, blinking against the blaze of candles.

"I waited for your arrival before starting, but I figured we'd need ample light in our hunt for clues."

She unbuttoned her heavy cloak and draped it over a chair.

Turning, she found Hartwick staring at her men's attire. She'd been similarly garbed earlier in Lady Rowling's backyard, but he must not have been able to see much with the dim lighting. Now his eyes lingered on her bottom half. Pippa's skin prickled with awareness. Perhaps these snug trousers hadn't been the wisest choice.

"So," she said, drawing his gaze back to her face, "this is your sister's room?" Pippa inwardly cursed her clumsy question.

"Ah, yes. I asked the maid if she'd noticed anything out of the ordinary or cleaned up any unusual items, but she said everything had seemed normal when she tidied up yesterday. I don't usually come in here, so I'm not much help in that regard."

Pippa nodded, then gave her full attention to her surroundings.

Lydia Dashwood's chambers were elegant, furnished in soothing blue and cream. Aside from a haphazard stack of books on the side table near her bed, everything was neat and tidy. A large armoire likely held her gowns. The four-poster bed was piled high with fluffy pillows. A writing desk stood against the wall near the window, a spot likely chosen for natural light.

"Where shall we start?" Lord Hartwick asked, and Pippa realized he'd been silently watching her as she'd conducted her survey.

Pippa circled the room, pausing before the armoire. "Let's see if she planned to leave."

Aside from one empty hanger, the armoire was full of dresses.

"She didn't intend to go anywhere," Pippa murmured, idly opening drawers and finding precisely folded stacks of night rails, chemises, and stockings that filled the space.

"Of course, she didn't *intend* this." Lord Hartwick peered over her shoulder at the drawer of stockings. "My sister is at times preoccupied, but she wouldn't have forgotten to tell me about a trip."

Pippa turned around. "Perhaps there's more to your sister than you know."

He stared down into her eyes, and Pippa realized how closely they were standing. She took a step back and bumped into the armoire.

"What are you implying?" he asked, his voice low.

Pippa swallowed, training her gaze on the cleft in his chin. "Just that she might have had interests or friends you didn't know about. A young lady might choose to keep her plans from her family if she wishes to briefly leave town." *Or join a secret academy for women.*

The Ladies Covert Academy did perform actual charity work, but it was the work that went on in the background that made a difference in the lives of its members. Men like Lord Hartwick couldn't understand, would *never* understand, that there were secret depths to a woman's life, dreams, and ambition for herself and what she might do for the world.

He shook his head in sharp denial. "She wouldn't keep plans to leave town from me. She wouldn't." His brown eyes sparked with anger.

Pippa merely shrugged at his certainty that he knew his sister's secrets before stepping to the side. She rifled through Lydia's vanity and peered under the bed, being sure to inspect her own favorite hiding spot in the support slats. Nothing appeared out of the ordinary.

Then she sat in the high-backed chair at the writing desk. The surface was empty, but desks like this had many small drawers and compartments. Pippa began a methodical search.

Hartwick began rummaging through drawers as well. "What are we looking for?"

Pippa pulled out a stack of correspondence from one of the cubbies. "I'm not sure, but I'm hoping we'll know it when we see it."

She shuffled through the letters. "Do you know these women?" She read him the names on the correspondence.

"Friends from finishing school, I believe."

Together, they scanned each letter, but they contained the usual family news, gossip about acquaintances, and discussions of social engagements.

Hartwick sighed and dropped the last letter into the pile. "We've searched the entire room, and we're no better off than I was when I first realized she was missing."

Pippa leaned back in the chair, feeling her shoulders slump. She'd been so certain they'd find something here, something to at least suggest a place to start in their search.

She swiveled in her seat and glanced around the room one more time. Pippa marveled a bit at the tidiness of everything. When she'd encountered Lydia at the LCA, the woman had always seemed a bit scattered, misplacing her reticule and leaving scribbled bits of paper in the dining room.

Pippa's eyes scanned the bed, the night stand, the uneven stack of books, the vanity—

Her eyes shot back to the stack of books. She stood.

"What is it?" the earl asked.

She could hear the worry in his voice—worry over them having no lead in his sister's whereabouts. But something in her gut told her that was about to change.

"The books." She walked around the bed and lifted the top book off the stack.

Lord Hartwick followed. She was conscious of the heat of him at her back, the steady in and out of his breathing. Her skin tingled with awareness.

Focus.

She needed her wits about her. Not only was Lydia's safety at stake, but so was the LCA's very existence.

She thumbed through the top book and tilted it upside down. Holding a side of the cover in each hand, she gently shook. Nothing.

She did the same for the rest of the stack. She and Hartwick stared at the last book in the pile. Pippa shot him a glance. Did he feel this terrible pressure too?

He nodded in encouragement, and she picked up the novel, its tattered edges evidence of a book often read.

"Please," she whispered.

She thumbed through the pages. The book fell open to the center. There, tightly wedged between the pages, was a piece of paper.

Pippa offered the book to Lord Hartwick. His hand hesitated over the paper for a second, then he plucked it up and unfolded it. The creases were worn as if it had been opened and refolded many times.

"It's a letter." He began to read. "'My darling Lydia, it has been two days since I last caught a glimpse of your beloved face.'"

He lowered the page and stared up at the ceiling. "Damn."

Pippa's heart contracted, and she lay a hand on his arm.

He stilled. His arm was firm and warm beneath her hand. Pippa wondered what his skin felt like beneath his sleeve.

Their gazes locked. Pippa's heartbeat filled her ears. Jerking her hand away, she rubbed it against her pant leg.

"What does the rest of the letter say?" she asked, her voice unaccountably husky.

"'My heart cries out to be near you like a hot house flower cut at the stem cries out for the rest of the plant.' What rot," he muttered, with a grimace. "'Please put me out of my heartsick agony and name the time and place where next we shall meet. Your beloved, Aubrey.'"

Hartwick plopped down onto the bed, the letter held loosely in his hand. "How did I not know?"

Pippa plucked up the letter.

"Lydia had a beau, and she kept it from me." He sunk his elbows onto his knees and leaned forward, his hands cradling his head. "I'd have sworn on a stack of bibles she didn't keep any secrets from me."

Pippa examined the letter carefully, rereading the besotted swain's tortured use of the English language.

"She and I are quite close. Or at least," he continued morosely, "I thought we were."

Pippa rubbed the corner of the paper between her fingers. It had a peculiar texture to it, different from usual correspondence like the kind found in Lydia's desk.

"Has she run off with him?" Lord Hartwick ran his hands through his already-disheveled hair. "What if she's ruined?"

Pippa narrowed her eyes. He must have felt the rebuke because a chagrined expression crept across his face.

"Not that *I* would judge her harshly, but society…" He waved his hand about, presumably to indicate the vast, unnamed masses of English citizens who'd summarily conclude his sister was ruined, damaged goods, and a blight on his family's name. In fact, that was why he was keeping her disappearance quiet to begin with. The ton was shockingly quick to renounce a woman as damaged goods—*ruined*—for the slightest hint of impropriety, harming her chances at making a good match and being accepted in polite society.

"You can ruin your gloves," Pippa replied, running a finger over the center of the sheet. "But a *person* cannot be ruined, my lord."

He stilled then let out a long, slow exhale.

Pippa held the letter in front of the candelabra and leaned down to examine it. Her pulse quickened at the information contained on the subtle watermark in the center of the paper.

"You are right, of course." He stared at the wall in front of him. "It's quite a double standard allowing men to sow their oats but castigating a woman for even kissing a man. I just worry, after all I've done to restore our family name after our parents…"

His parents? Pippa's hand drifted down, the letter momentarily forgotten at his words.

"And I know it's not fair. I do. But…" His hands curled into fists on his legs. "But she's my sister and… and I love her." He paused, then spoke again, the words soft. "I love her, and I don't wish for the world to look upon her with disfavor. I wouldn't wish that on anyone."

Pippa felt a strange fluttering in her chest. This man clearly adored his sister, and despite the unlikeliness of it, he was a man of privilege and station who seemed to understand the terrible burden placed upon young women by society's hypocrisy.

To have the devotion of such a man would be a heady thing indeed.

Pippa swallowed.

She placed a hand on Hartwick's shoulder. "I don't think her disfavor with the world is a certainty, at least not yet."

His expression was so hopeless that Pippa had the outrageous inclination to kiss his sadness away.

"The man's first name isn't much to go on," he said, voice gravelly.

"I realize that. But we have more than his name."

Hartwick's eyebrows shot up in surprise.

"I just found his address."

Chapter Five

JACK GLANCED AT his pocket watch as well-heeled shoppers surged past him. Although it was barely midmorning, the shops of Bond Street were bustling. Behind a cluster of giggling misses, he saw a pink parasol above a head of dark, glossy hair.

Pippa.

His pulse sped up.

He'd asked his valet to do a bit of inquiring last night after she'd left, and he now knew quite a bit more about the mysterious Miss Philippa Chester, thanks to his man's secret sources.

She was rarely out in society, however, reports hinted she'd been attending social functions more often this past year. Although considered a beauty, her apparent shunning of society until recently had crossed her off the lists of eligible misses. And of course, she was an LCA member, spending her time doing good deeds under the guidance of their benefactress, Lady Rowling.

His valet had been brimming with gossip on Lady Rowling as well. The marchioness was a bit of a scandal despite her bent for do-gooding.

Apparently, she'd returned from India a couple of years ago after her husband had passed away, leaving her a vast—and unentailed—fortune. Some of the gossip claimed she'd taken an Indian man as her lover. Others said a young Indian woman serving as her secretary was actually her illegitimate daughter. No one seemed to know the truth about Lady Rowling, who although active in society, was chilly to anyone unwise enough to make overly familiar inquiries.

Given his one interaction with the woman, Jack knew that last bit to be true.

"Lord Hartwick," Pippa greeted, finally making her way through the crowds.

Despite her cheerful yellow gown and full lips curved up in a smile, there was a certain pinched tension about her.

"Good morning," Jack said.

Her lady's maid popped out from behind her. "Miss," she said, wringing her hands. "Iffen yer mam finds out I let ye run off on yer own, she's liable to ship me off to Australia!"

"I hear Australia is quite pleasant this time of year." Pippa's eyes sparkled with mischief.

Jack turned to the maid and gave a low bow. "A pleasure to see you again, Miss…?"

The woman blushed as red as a turnip. "Just Milly will do, milord."

"Well, Milly," he replied, offering her his most charming smile. "I do understand the difficult position we're putting you in, but I assure you Miss Chester's safety is my top priority."

The maid's eyelashes fluttered before she seemed to recall herself. "I'm just thinkin' of me post, milord."

Jack nodded. "Your post *is* of great importance, but I wonder…" He trailed off, one hand jingling in his pocket while the other rubbed his chin. "If someone else—say, *me* for instance—served as a substitute for your post…?"

The maid eyed his pocket.

"Have you ever been to Gunter's for ices?" Jack continued. "No? Well, everyone should experience it at least once. Here." He fished out a handful of coins. "My treat."

The maid's hand darted forward, and the coins were out of sight within the blink of an eye. She bobbed a hasty goodbye before vanishing into the crowd.

Pippa shook her head in amusement. "Well, that was neatly done. However, I fear you have set a bad precedent, my lord. My pin money shall never recover."

Jack offered her his arm, and they strolled down Bond Street. "Do you often give her the slip?"

There was so much he wanted to know about Pippa, including the fencing, but he was uncertain how she'd receive his questions.

She shrugged before changing the subject. "The office is four blocks over. I checked on a map this morning."

"Actually," Jack said, shoulders tensing, "we're heading to Bow Street." He turned them down a side street toward his phaeton.

Pippa stopped in her tracks. "You're hiring a runner?"

Jack rubbed the back of his neck. "I initially thought to keep her disappearance a secret to preserve her reputation, but as you said last night…gloves can be ruined but not people."

Pippa nodded slowly.

"I still want to keep things discreet but hiring a Bow Street runner increases our odds of finding her. And surely the runners can investigate this much better than you or I. I'd still like you to accompany me. As a member of the LCA, you could provide valuable insight about her activities."

"You're doing the right thing." Pippa straightened her shoulders. "I'm more than willing to accompany you if my presence will help the runners find Lydia."

Jack's shoulders relaxed. He'd been expecting more of a battle.

Walking the rest of the way in silence, they arrived at Bow Street shortly. Jack held the door to the office open for Pippa. They stood in the entryway, a jumble of men hurrying about the cluttered front room or hunched over desks. One lad seemed to take note of them before disappearing down a dim hallway.

Pippa mumbled under her breath.

Jack turned to her. "What?"

"Not a single woman seems to work here." She watched the busy office through narrowed eyes. "How could they possibly gather intelligence on an organization such as the LCA without a female runner?"

Jack started. "You know, I think you're right."

Pippa raised a dark eyebrow at him. "Well, I shall be sure to mark this date in my diary."

Jack bit back a smile.

Despite their rocky beginnings, Miss Chester was proving to be an entertaining companion. If it weren't for the circumstances—

He shook his head. He needed to focus on finding his sister.

Jack turned at the sound of a throat clearing. A man of average height, build, and altogether average features smiled blandly at them. Jack imagined he'd be unable to recall a single detail about him a minute after leaving his presence.

"Good day, sir, madam." The man nodded to them both. "May I be of service?"

Jack handed the man his card. "I wish to speak to a runner on a delicate matter."

The man inclined his head. "Certainly, Lord Hartwick. I am Mr. Gormley, one of the runners here. I'd be honored to assist you."

Gormley led them through the warren of cramped desks, overstuffed file drawers, and rushing detectives to his office in the back. Clearly the runners didn't want for work.

Pippa sat in one of the chairs across from Gormley's desk, placing her pink parasol beside her with care. Jack frowned. It was neither particularly sunny outside, nor did the weather threaten rain. Perhaps she employed the frilly thing as a fashion accessory?

"How can I assist you, my lord?"

Jack eyed Gormley. Was he really about to divulge the scandalous fact of his sister's disappearance to this nondescript man? Perhaps his very blandness made him good at his job. No one would recall his face or notice him following them.

"My sister is missing." Jack's words hung in the air like a dank London fog. Maybe this was a mistake. He moved to rise from his seat, but he was stopped by a gentle touch.

He glanced down to find Pippa's hand resting on his arm. He met her eyes and felt a jolt to the center of his bones. *Stay,* her gaze seemed to tell him. *Get the help we need.*

The tense muscles in his shoulders relaxed. He wasn't alone in this. The tightness behind his eyes since Lydia's disappearance eased a fraction.

He nodded and her eyelids flickered in reply.

"Your sister is missing," Gormley repeated, his voice without inflection.

"Yes, since the day before yesterday."

Gormley opened a small notebook and began to write with a pencil. "When did you last see her?" he asked, followed by a series of rapid-fire questions ranging from Lydia's typical routine to the color of her hair.

Jack answered the best he could, but Pippa assisted with many of the questions regarding Lydia's involvement with the LCA. She seemed to hesitate before a few of her answers. Perhaps she was nervous to be interviewed by one of the lauded runners. Jack showed the love letter. Pointing out the watermark, Pippa explained finding the law office's address.

Gormley frowned, silently scanning his notes, before leaning back in his chair. He steepled his fingers together.

"I must be frank." His eyes were expressionless. "It's rare that we recover young women after they're taken."

Jack jolted forward in his seat. "Taken?" He gripped the arms of the chair. Good lord, had his sister been kidnapped by her swain? Abused by hardened criminals? Thrown into the Thames? All the terrible scenarios he'd fought to keep at bay since discovering her disappearance howled inside his head.

"There is no evidence she was taken." Pippa's crisp voice sliced through his panic.

Mr. Gormley frowned. "Young lady, given the circum—"

Pippa leaned forward. "Yes, let's look at the circumstances, shall we? There is no evidence of foul play. Perhaps she was called upon to attend to an ill relative and hadn't time to leave a note. Or she was invited to a house party and decided not to tell her brother for fear he'd prevent her from attending. And"—Pippa jabbed her finger toward Gormley—"given the treacly love letter, we cannot rule out Miss Dashwood sneaking off for an assignation."

Pippa's face was lit with a ferocious intensity, her eyes glittering. She was on fire, and nothing, not even the blandest Bow Street runner in the world, could derail her arguments.

Although apparently, it wouldn't stop the man from trying.

"I say," Gormley blustered, "what qualifications do you—I mean, why would you even question…well, of all the…"

Pippa rose to her feet, parasol in hand. "Lord Hartwick expects frequent updates on your investigation. Please notify him immediately if you should learn anything about Miss Dashwood." The look she shot Gormley implied she wasn't holding her breath.

Pippa snatched up the letter and pulled Jack along in her wake as she wove to the exit. A strange buzzing sound filled his ears.

They popped out onto the street.

"Lord Hartwick." Pippa shook his arm. "Lord Hartwick?"

He stared at her, unable to form a coherent thought.

It's rare that we recover young women after they're taken.

Oh, God. Lydia. A clawing, choking sensation gripped his neck.

"Hartwick," Pippa shouted, grabbing him by both shoulders.

His eyes snapped to meet hers. Pippa's eyes blazed with determination.

"Gormley's wrong."

He stared at her, trying to bring her words into focus amidst the roaring noise swirling around inside his head.

"He's done zero investigating into Lydia's case. He has no

evidence of foul play. Do you understand?"

Jack stared.

"We have the address from the letter to check on," Pippa continued. "While Gormley's doing whatever runners do, we'll conduct our own investigation." Her eyes softened, seeming to take in his fear. "We can find her, Hartwick."

Jack nodded.

Pippa's stare bore into him, weighing, assessing. "All right then. The first order of business is the address on the letter."

⟫⟩⟩⟩✕⟨⟨⟨⟪

THEY SAT SIDE by side in his phaeton. Jack focused on navigating the crowded streets, his composure firmly in place once more.

"Last night, how did you know to check Lydia's books?"

She'd rushed home last night, so Pippa had never explained how she'd discerned the location of the mysterious Aubrey. Pippa shifted beside him on the bench, and the graze of her leg against his caused his thigh to tingle.

"It was quite obvious once I noticed." She adjusted her hold on her parasol. "The stack of books was the only thing out of order. Everything else was painstakingly tidy. I'm guessing your sister orders the maid to leave her books alone. Lydia knew they were a safe place to stash something important since the servants wouldn't touch them."

He nodded, impressed. "And how did you know to look for a watermark?"

"It was the paper used for the letter. The texture felt different, similar to paper I've seen my brother's stewards use for legal documents."

Jack nodded.

"So, I held it up to the candles and found the watermark."

Jack pulled on the reins, maneuvering around a slow-moving cart. He knew Pippa was observant—she'd been the one to find the letter and address after all—but this went well beyond his expectations. "I think the Bow Street runners would do well to add you to their payroll."

The corners of her mouth twitched. "I must confess, although I'm still quite put out by you blackmailing me—"

"I did no such thing."

She cocked an eyebrow, and he tilted his head in capitulation.

"As I was saying, although I was miffed by the blackmail, I admit this hunt for clues has been invigorating. I only wish it didn't come at the expense of your sister."

Jack swallowed. It was imperative he kept Lydia front and center in his mind. If he continued to be distracted by Miss Chester, he'd lose focus on what really mattered.

Jack pulled the phaeton to the side of the road. His tiger hopped down, taking hold of the horses. "Walk them, but stay close," he informed the young man before assisting Pippa down.

"There it is." She gestured to an old stone building with *Smythe, Brown, and Clarke* written in precise gold lettering on the shingle.

Jack held the door open. Pippa went in and climbed the staircase, her pink parasol a cheery splash of color guiding him forward. The waiting room was filled with mahogany furniture and shelves of leather-bound books. A hallway led to several closed doors, presumably the attorneys' offices.

"May I help you?" A young man at a desk blinked owlishly behind a pair of thick spectacles.

"We are here to speak to Mr. Aubrey," Jack said.

"*Mr.* Aubrey?" The clerk's eyebrows pulled together.

Jack realized their mistake. "Mr. Aubrey, um…" He snapped his fingers as if trying to remember something and turned to Pippa. "What's Aubrey's last name, dear?"

She blinked, then leapt into the fray. "Oh my, we are so forgetful," she twittered, her hand darting about before landing on her chest. "Oh, how embarrassing!"

"Aubrey Andrews, my lady," the young clerk supplied, leaning forward. "Even the partners mix it up sometimes. Aubrey Andrews, Andrew Aubrey. His name is most forgetful, even if the man himself isn't, with that streak of white through his dark hair." He shook his head in sympathy. "So, you mustn't feel embarrassed."

"Oh, you are too kind." Pippa clasped her hands together. "We shall certainly tell Mr. Aubrey Andrews of your gracious nature."

The clerk beamed.

Jack tried to get them back on track. "May we speak to him please?"

"Oh." The clerk's face fell. "He's not in, but I could see if one of the other attorneys is available." He swiveled in his chair toward the hall.

"I fear it must be him," Jack replied. "When do you expect him back?"

"I'm sorry, but I don't know."

Jack clenched his jaw. *Damn.* How were they ever to find Lydia?

He turned at the sound of sniffling.

"My lady?" Horror was evident in the clerk's voice at the sight of Pippa dabbing at her eyes with a handkerchief.

"Oh, don't mind me," she said, her voice high and quavering. "It's just that Mr. Aubrey Andrews had agreed to help us with a very *sensitive* matter"—she paused to wipe at her eyes once more—"and I fear I'm quite overcome…"

She turned away, her shoulders trembling.

"Oh." The clerk wrung his hands. "Oh, please."

"If only we knew when he'd return," she said over her shoulder, her voice choked. "It might offer us some small measure of solace during this…this trying time."

"I do wish I could help you," the man pleaded.

Muted sobs escaped the handkerchief she held to her face.

Jack almost reached into his pocket to offer his own handkerchief before he recalled she was playing a part. Miss Chester could find great success treading the boards.

"He said he was heading north on urgent business," the clerk blurted out, his face twisted in misery. "He didn't give us a return date. I'm most terribly sorry." He rifled around his desk. "Perhaps you wish to leave him a note?"

Jack put his arm around Pippa, her shoulders still jerking with her alleged sobs.

"We must go, but I thank you for your kindness." Jack hustled her out of the office, and they burst out onto the sidewalk.

"Oh," Pippa gasped, staggering a bit. "That was—"

"That was incredible." Jack shut the door and leaned against it. "*You* were incredible."

"I still feel a bit overwhelmed." Pippa stepped backward on the sidewalk, her parasol dangling at her side.

She rubbed at her wet cheeks with the handkerchief and took another step back until her feet were at the sidewalk's edge.

"Those fake emotions are quite draining." She swayed on her feet, seeming wrung out from her performance. Pippa stumbled and stepped back to catch herself, one foot in the street.

"Oi!" shouted a man.

Jack turned. A carriage pounded down the street, the driver flailing madly with his whip. The horses' powerful legs churned, and their eyes rolled as the carriage careened closer.

Jack's heart leapt in his chest. "Pippa!"

He shot forward. Grabbing her arms, he jerked her back onto the sidewalk.

The carriage thundered by, plowing over the spot where Pippa had stood only a second before.

"Shit." Jack stared in horror at the street.

She was almost run over.

She was almost *killed*.

His arms tightened, and Pippa squeaked. Only then did he realize she was enfolded in his arms, their bodies pressed together with her parasol crushed between them.

He was leaning against the building, the firm brick at his back and Pippa's soft warmth at his front. His blood rushed through his veins. Loosening his hold, Jack allowed her to ease back an inch.

Pippa's eyes were wide pools. "You saved me," she breathed. "I stumbled, and that carriage almost—"

She shook her head as if to physically force away the imagined possibility.

Jack swallowed. "I've got you now," he whispered. His body tingled where she was pressed against him. His arms protested the idea of releasing her.

"Thank you," she whispered in reply. Pippa drew in a deep shuddering breath. "I guess all that fake crying left me dizzy. I didn't even know I *could* fake cry."

"You are a master at fake crying," he said solemnly, wiping away a real tear from her cheek.

She stilled under his finger. Their eyes locked. He saw a flare of heat in her blue depths. He looked down at her plush, pink lips. Her tongue darted out to wet them. Jack groaned. He leaned closer, closer—

—and a cluster of laughing pedestrians walked by, breaking the spell.

He dropped his arms, and she stepped back.

Pippa swallowed. She swiped at her face before tucking her handkerchief into her reticule.

"I wish Mr. Aubrey Andrews had been there for questioning." Pippa kept her eyes on her bag as she fussed with the ties.

Jack stilled. "Urgent business north…"

"Hm?"

"Oh, dear God." There was one simple reason why a couple would rush north. Jack's stomach flipped over, and he ran a hand over his face. "I think he's taking her to Gretna Green."

Pippa frowned.

The walk from the law office to his phaeton passed in a blur.

And Jack couldn't stop his brain from poking at the thought that Andrew Aubrey or Aubrey Andrews, or whatever the scamp's name was, had absconded to Scotland with his sister for a hasty marriage.

Her sudden disappearance. The hidden love letter. *Urgent* business up north.

It was the likeliest explanation. And there was no helping it, but they'd have to travel north to pick up their trail.

"How quickly can you have a bag packed?" he asked Pippa as he took the reins from his tiger.

Pippa blinked a few times. "Bag?"

"If we leave before noon, we'll be able to make inquiries at the first handful of inns along the Great North Road."

He held out his hand to assist her onto the seat. The light pressure of her fingers against his comforted him. He'd been right to insist she help him. With Pippa's keen sense of observation, they'd surely pick up his sister's trail in no time.

"We should swing by Gunter's and collect my maid," Pippa said once they were underway. "And…I cannot go."

Jack maneuvered around a mail coach. "You cannot go to Gunter's?"

Pippa angled toward him, their knees pressing together on the narrow seat. "I cannot go north with you."

Jack squeezed the reins. "That's not acceptable."

"However could I explain it to my mother? 'Quite sorry, but I must dash off to Scotland for a handful of days. Toodaloo!'?"

"I need you there," he replied. "I can't see things the way you can, and I cannot afford to miss any clues. I'll send word to Gormley at Bow Street as well, but he doesn't know her as we do." One of his horses tossed its head in protest, and he realized he'd pulled on the reins in his frustration.

"Lord Hartwick, I cannot simply vanish. My mother would then be in a panic over *my* disappearance the same way you are over Lydia's."

Jack ground his teeth. She was right, but damn it, he needed her. He had to put Lydia first.

"I hate to do this," Jack said, shame bitter in his mouth, "but if you don't come with me, I'll be forced to expose the LCA."

Pippa gasped. "You're despicable."

They drove in silence to collect Pippa's maid, then headed toward the LCA. As Jack navigated, his righteous anger melted away like one of the ices at Gunter's on a hot day.

He *was* despicable, trying to force her to accompany him up the Great North Road. Despite his acute fear for his sister, he couldn't toss aside his values like yesterday's newspaper.

"I'm sorry." He kept his voice low so the maid wouldn't overhear. "It was wrong of me to coerce you."

Pippa still wouldn't look at him, but some of her rigid tension eased.

"I'll head north on my own, and perhaps you can continue to investigate here in town?"

At last, she met his gaze. Jack was shocked to see tears glimmering in her eyes.

"I'm sorry as well." She paused to bite her lip. "I wish I could go with you, but I—I just can't." She looked down at her lap and fiddled with her reticule.

"I understand," Jack said, but in truth, he did not. He knew why she couldn't come, but what caused her tears?

Jack slowed the horses in St. James Square. He began to step down from the phaeton, but Pippa had already climbed down on her side and hurried onto the sidewalk with Milly.

"Good day, Lord Hartwick." She turned to the stairs leading up to the residence but hesitated. Over her shoulder, she said, "And good luck."

Chapter Six

AFTER WATCHING HARTWICK drive away through the front parlor window, Pippa plopped onto a chair and sighed.

Men.

First, they try to blackmail you, and then they apologize for being a lout with such obvious sincerity that you want to consent to their plan.

Only…she couldn't.

The Great North Road was to be avoided at all costs.

"Miss Chester?"

Pippa glanced to the parlor door.

"Good morning, Meera." She smiled at Lady Rowling's secretary, one of the many servants who'd traveled with the marchioness from India. Meera wore a marigold-yellow skirt and top with a swoop of fabric rising across her bare midriff to her shoulder where it draped behind her like a delicate waterfall. Her gowns, which Pippa had learned were called saris, had initially seemed scandalous to Pippa. However, she'd grown accustomed to the colorful clothing with its delicate fabric and ornate embroidery. Once she'd realized that Meera dressing as she liked was akin to a woman learning to fence because she wanted to, she'd been glad the woman continued to wear the beautiful clothing of her homeland.

"*Señor* Martín conveys his apologies," Meera said, "but he

must cancel your lesson today."

"I hope he is not unwell?"

"I've been told it's a minor cold." Meera nodded in farewell.

Pippa rubbed her hands together, feeling the callouses from her hours of training. One day off from their three sessions a week wouldn't impede her progress, but more importantly, she hoped *Señor* Martín made a speedy recovery.

The day stretched before her with its unclaimed hours. She'd better find something to do, or she'd wind up knitting more of those horrid booties. She came upon Jarvis in the foyer cleaning a pistol. Pippa cleared her throat.

The burly butler calmly tucked the weapon into his back waistband. "Anything I can do for you, Miss Chester?"

"Do you know if Jane's about today?"

"Saw her come in an hour ago. Up in her office, I think."

Pippa smiled in thanks before climbing the stairs. She knocked on a door at the end of the hall.

"Come in," came a muffled reply.

Pippa found her cousin, Jane Brickley, bent over a plant whose squat, fuzzy greenery did little to inspire odes to Nature's glory.

"How did your experiment go?" Pippa examined a soil-strewn worktable lining the walls.

"No cross-pollination yet," Jane replied, her voice gloomy. She stretched and squinted against the sunshine streaming in through the many windows. When an LCA member studied botany, she got a corner room.

"Well, at least that thing won't bring any ugly baby plants into this world," Pippa teased.

Jane planted her dirty hands on her apron-covered hips. "Any seedling would be proud to call this plant its sire. I just need to work harder to prepare its stamen for mating."

Pippa snickered.

Jane blinked her long eyelashes over her wide, hazel eyes, her expression one of complete innocence. However, Pippa knew her cousin too well to fall for the *I'm too naive to know what I just said* routine. They were both chaste but spending their days with the very curious, very intelligent women of the LCA meant they both knew about reproduction, whether it be birds, bees, or humans.

Jane hoisted up a watering can. "You haven't been popping by as much as usual."

Pippa's pulse jolted, and she leaned over to inspect a row of seedlings as if they were the famed Elgin Marbles.

"Where have you been?" Jane bumped her gently with her hip as she scooted her over to water the seedlings.

Pippa pretended to yawn while she contemplated and rejected several fabrications.

Plunking the watering can down, Jane narrowed her eyes. "Is it something improper?"

Pippa seized a rag and blotted at the drops of water on the table.

"Well, now I know you're into some sort of mischief." Jane shook her head. "Come on, you'd best confess. You know you can't keep secrets from me. And besides," she said, eyes gleaming as she delivered the *coup de grace*, "you owe me."

Pippa harrumphed. "It's not fair to always bring that up. How many years will I be in your debt for my LCA membership?"

"Oh, I don't know," Jane said breezily, retrieving her watering can. "I was thinking probably until the end of time, but I'm willing to negotiate a year or two if it's important to you."

Pippa rolled her eyes.

Jane stared at her expectantly.

Pippa stared back.

Jane didn't blink.

Pippa's eyes began to water.

"Oh, fine!" Pippa puffed out a breath of air in exasperation. "I've been assisting Lord Hartwick with searching for his missing sister, Lydia."

Jane's eyes grew quite round. "Oh. My."

Pippa nodded. "Yes, that about sums it up."

Hugging the watering can to her chest, Jane began a barrage of questions. "Missing since when? I heard you'd asked if any members had seen her, but is she actually *missing*? Does anyone know where she might have gone? She mostly stayed to herself, but she seemed sweet. Oh! What's *he* like? Is he beastly to you? I heard someone say he practically stormed the door here yesterday. Now I know why. He must be quite fierce! Why ever would you hel—"

"Jane," Pippa interrupted, her hands up to ward off her cousin's torrent of words.

Jane wrinkled her nose sheepishly. "Sorry. I'm just so curious." She bit her lip. "And worried, truth be told. Why are you involved?"

Pippa leaned back against the table. Why *was* she involved?

To save the LCA, of course. She couldn't let him nose around and uncover all their secrets. Too many women relied on the organization. *She* relied on the organization. Without it, she'd once again be a scared little mouse, huddled inside and shying away from the world. For years, the trauma of that night on the Great North Road had left her too afraid to venture outside her home. Only her certainty that she could now defend herself from ruffians—thanks to the LCA's fencing lessons—allowed her to live an almost-normal life. And so, she'd do what was needed to protect the secret organization that had saved her from a life of fear.

But Pippa suspected there was another reason she was helping Lord Hartwick. She wanted to find Lydia, certainly, but beyond that even—

"Miss Brickley?" A deep voice at the door interrupted Pippa's musings.

Beside her, Jane froze.

Pippa turned to smile at the servant in the doorway. "Hello, Dev."

Dev bowed. He was another member of Lady Rowling's retinue from India, and like Meera, he wore the clothing of his home. Lady Rowling's servants and secretaries were a mix of English and Indian with an assortment of languages, religions, and manners of dress among them. Dev was likely of European background based on his coloring. Pippa frowned, remembering Lady Rowling's slip of the tongue yesterday when she'd seemed to mention Dev in relation to the LCA's troubles.

"Did you want something?" Jane asked, finally looking toward the doorway.

The man's blue eyes smiled at Pippa's cousin.

"I want many things, Miss Brickley," he replied, his teeth flashing in a handsome grin.

Jane's mouth opened, but no words emerged.

"For instance," he continued in his slight Indian accent, "I want to know where you wish for me to place the barrel of fertilizer you ordered."

"Oh." Jane's throat moved as she swallowed.

"Miss?" Dev's eyes twinkled.

"Ahem. Yes. Well." Jane shifted from foot to foot. "A few buckets in here and the rest in the storage shed. Please," she added, before looking down at the watering can clutched to her chest.

"It will be my pleasure, miss." With a quick nod, he was gone.

Jane examined her watering can as if it possessed the secrets of cross-pollination.

"So…" Pippa said into the silence of the room.

Jane sprang into movement, dousing the seedlings until water overflowed their little pots.

"Dev says he wants *many things*." Pippa waggled her eyebrows. She pushed against the watering can with one finger to redirect the flow to plants not yet drowning.

"Dev is a dedicated servant," Jane said. "He *wants* to do his job."

"Yes, I'm sure that's all he meant," Pippa teased.

Truly, it was most amusing watching her usually unflappable

cousin lose all composure around Lady Rowling's servant—albeit a very handsome, gentlemanly servant. Truth be told, if he wasn't actually working as a servant, she'd scarcely believe it, he had such a noble bearing.

"So." Jane cleared her throat. "Back to you and Lord Hartwick. What are you planning next?"

Pippa sighed. Given her cousin's clear discombobulation from Dev's visit, she'd allow her to change the subject.

Pippa glanced at the door, and even though Dev had pulled it shut, she still lowered her voice. "Hartwick believes she may have headed north with a man."

Jane's mouth formed an *O*.

"It's all quite shocking. Please swear you won't say anything to anyone."

"I won't."

Pippa nodded. "He's quite distraught. He wanted me to head out with him on the Great Northern Road, but of course, that's impossible." Her heart thumped at the mere thought. "There's the danger, of course." Pippa shuddered before pushing her memories away. "My mother already chafes at how much I'm gone each day with my time here. Not to mention, it wouldn't be proper. And I'm sure he'll do just fine on his own…"

"He's quite the detective, then?"

Pippa snorted. "He's hopeless. He completely overlooked searching his sister's bedroom when he first realized she'd gone missing."

"Poor fellow. I hope he doesn't return empty-handed. He must be sick with worry." Jane shook her head as she continued to water her specimens.

"I *wish* I could help him, of course." Pippa turned a potted plant in a slow circle. "If there was any way, I'd go, but…"

She swallowed. It was true. She did want to help him. And she did want to end her fear of the Great North Road. No one should be scared of a *road*. She knew it was ridiculous, even as she felt the tremble of fear within the marrow of her bones.

More importantly, no one should be left to wonder if their loved one was in danger.

She ran a finger through a pile of soil. "If only there was some plausible reason for me to travel north."

"Hm." Jane plunked her watering can onto the floor.

Biting her lip, Pippa surveyed the room. There were Jane's plants, her piles of journals and notes, bags of soil, special specimens that only grew in certain parts of the country…

She grabbed the edge of the table as an idea took shape. If there was an *official* reason to head north, then surely her mother and Lady Rowling would have no reason to object.

"Jane, weren't you just saying the other day that you need to organize a bunch of LCA members to collect specimens for you?"

Jane wrinkled her nose. "What?"

Clutching her hands together, Pippa bounced on her toes. "Yes, and it will take the entire afternoon, won't it? We might have to pack a picnic. All those plants up north you need to study, and I do believe there's an orphanage up that way as well. Two birds and all that."

This would be perfect. The LCA members could go on a botany expedition with a quick side trip to the orphanage to deliver booties and other clothing to maintain the group's do-gooder façade. Despite its cover for their true purposes, all the ladies did believe in charity. And Pippa could slip away to visit the coaching inns with Hartwick along the terrifying Great North Road—the *formerly* terrifying Great North Road, that was—with the LCA ladies close at hand.

She swallowed before offering her cousin a smile.

Jane rolled her eyes, but the corners of her lips twitched upward.

Pippa headed toward the door. "I'll let the other ladies know we leave in an hour."

WHEN JACK PULLED up in front of his residence, a footman dashed out to take the reins and lead the team around to the mews. Jack trudged up the steps. He already felt travel-weary and he'd yet to begin his journey north.

"My lord." His butler took his hat and gloves. "Mr. Lovell has paid a call. He insisted on waiting in the breakfast room." Although the butler's voice remained placid, Jack detected a devilish spark in the old gent's eye.

Well, this *was* the man who'd led the servants in a gambling party only last night. It made sense he'd approve of Benedict Lovell's cheekiness.

Jack smiled, a fraction of his tension easing at the thought of a quick chat with his best mate before he set off on his quest north.

"Hello, old man," Benedict called from the head of the breakfast room table. "I'd offer to get up and shake your hand, but as you can see, I'm a touch occupied at the moment."

"Yes, one hand busy with my newspaper and the other shoveling my food into the bottomless pit of your stomach," Jack said dryly.

"Can I help it if I'm a growing boy?" Benedict grinned before scooping up a large bite of eggs.

Jack filled a plate from the sideboard and joined his friend at the table. "You know, I ate breakfast hours ago. Why is all this food still here?"

Benedict set the newspaper down and lay a hand over his heart. "Your housekeeper is in love with me and ordered the cook to prepare another meal as a sign of her undying devotion."

Jack snorted. "Mrs. Smythe's at least sixty if she's a day."

"Women ripen with age, my friend, like a good wine. I'm surprised you haven't scooped that jezebel Mrs. Smythe up for yourself and set her up in a little love nest."

Jack laughed, the image of his plump, gray-haired housekeeper swaying her hips as she beckoned him closer with a crooked finger chasing away a portion of his doldrums.

"Good to see you laughing, old man," Benedict said. "In

addition to those missed morning rides, you've been too busy to meet me at the club. Quite dull at White's without you there for cards and brandy. Or to tease."

Jack lowered his teacup from his mouth without taking a sip. "Tease?"

"Oh, you know, a bit of gentle mockery between friends." Benedict lowered his voice and scrunched his face into a frown. "*Duty comes first,* and *it's my responsibility* and all that rubbish. You keep me in stitches for days."

Jack leaned back in his chair, frowning at his friend.

"Yes!" Benedict pointed at his face. "Just like that."

Jack rolled his eyes. "There's nothing wrong with being serious. You should try it."

Benedict smirked. "Just look how serious I can be." He shook open the newspaper. "As long as the House of Commons positions are apportioned through corrupt measures, England will never have justice or fair elections," he read before flinging the newspaper down. "I swear, this *Democratiam Liberum* fellow has everyone's tongues wagging, and I've read every article of his in the paper this past month."

Jack raised an eyebrow.

"That's right. I, Benedict Lovell, incorrigible rake and carefree wastrel am reading the newspaper. And I even looked up what it means. *Democratiam Liberum* is Latin for free democracy. Quick, someone bring me a medal."

Jack shook his head, but he couldn't stop his mouth from tipping up in a smile. To an outsider, he and Benedict were an unlikely pair. He was serious and responsible while Benedict was easygoing, quick with a joke, an unapologetic flirt, and did all in his power to avoid anything smacking of actual work. But somehow, their differences rounded each of them out. If Jack was being honest with himself, he needed some levity in his life.

He hadn't always been so solemn and duty-bound. As a boy, he'd loved his days roaming the estate, climbing trees, and having adventures. He'd been wild and free. But his parents—

"Are you unwell?" Benedict leaned forward. "Your face has turned even more granite-like than usual."

Jack exhaled. "Just woolgathering." He tried to keep his tone light.

They ate in silence for a few minutes.

Benedict cleared his throat. "Well, once you disappear into your study for hours of paperwork, mind if I find Lydia to say hello? I haven't had a chance to pull her braids in an age."

Jack glanced up. His friend was studiously pushing a mound of eggs back and forth across his plate. A ruddy wash of color had swept up Benedict's cheekbones.

Jack narrowed his eyes. "She is not for the likes of you."

Benedict's head shot up, his face tight. Their eyes locked, and then Benedict waved his hand through the air. "Of course not," he said, his voice overly loud. "A smart girl like her and a wastrel like me?" His grin was toothy. "Besides, I'm waiting on Mrs. Smythe, remember?"

Benedict laughed and slapped his own knee, but his mirth lacked its usual warmth.

Jack filed the hints that Benedict might be interested in Lydia away in the back of his mind to be dissected later. There were more pressing issues at hand. "Actually, Lydia's out at the moment."

"Oh." Benedict shrugged. "Off with her charity group I suppose?"

Jack nodded, hoping the movement didn't look as false as it felt.

Even though Jack trusted Benedict, he didn't want Lydia to feel uncomfortable when she returned and discovered others were aware of her unexplained absence. He'd already hired the Bow Street runners to investigate. He'd not involve his friend as well. Damn polite society and it's arbitrary rules dictating the priority of a woman's reputation over her safety.

"Well, help yourself to another round of kippers, but I must excuse myself." Jack stood.

"Will it be the thrilling estate accounts or pleasure reading about crop rotations today?" Benedict drawled.

"Er, business to attend to up north. See you at the club."

Leaving his friend to devour another plate of food, Jack went upstairs to change into riding clothes and grab a few necessities.

The butler brought up a letter on a silver tray. Jack frowned at the unfamiliar handwriting before breaking the seal. He scanned the message and read it a second time.

He exhaled, his tense back muscles relaxing.

"Have the stables ready my horse in an hour," he said to the butler. Jack refolded the note with care and tucked it into his breast pocket near his heart.

Chapter Seven

J ACK TUGGED ON the reins, swearing loudly and fluently as he walked along the Great North Road.

Thankfully, he was alone on this stretch of the highway. He'd hate to corrupt the tender ears of a lady astride her steed.

"Today, of all days?" He glanced behind him.

His gelding neighed in reply and continued limping along the road behind him. Hopefully one of the inns would have a stable that could re-shoe his mount.

Jack crested a hill. Down to the right stretched an open meadow with carriages gleaming in the afternoon sun. Ladies dotted the field, their colorful gowns like wildflowers amidst the grass. Some were bent over picking plants while others sat on blankets with open wicker baskets.

He shielded his eyes and saw a tall, slim figure rise from one of the blankets.

Pippa.

She pointed with her head, seeming to indicate she'd meet him farther along the road.

He clicked to his horse and continued on. Near the bottom of the hill, Pippa emerged from a thicket with a horse. Her cheeks were rosy, and a blue riding habit hugged her trim figure.

"Hello," Jack said, his throat suddenly dry.

She smiled. His chest tightened in response to the sweet

curve of her lips.

"I'm glad you found us," she said. "I wasn't sure we'd make it all the way to South Mimms, and I didn't know any landmarks to tell you."

"Your note was thorough. You organized this LCA outing just for our search?"

"Well, I couldn't just take off on the Great North Road with you by myself, could I?" Her lips thinned. "My mother would demand to know my whereabouts, and I—"

Jack held up his hands. "Pippa."

Her eyes widened.

Damn. He hadn't meant to use her given name, but he'd stopped thinking of her as Miss Chester some time ago and it had slipped out.

He inhaled. "Perhaps you should call me Jack."

She cocked her head, studying him. He tried not to fidget under the intensity of her gaze.

"Only if you feel comfortable with it," he amended.

The corner of her lips twitched. "Well, as we're partners in a clandestine mission, I suppose we can dispense with formalities. When we're alone," she added.

"What I was trying to say before, Pippa," he said, savoring the sweet pop of the p's on his lips, "is I'm impressed with your planning. And…I appreciate your assistance. Very much."

Her deep blue eyes were twin lakes, pulling him into their refreshing fathoms.

"Why'd you change your mind?" he asked, his throat tight.

She stepped closer, and his body tingled with awareness.

"I want to save the LCA from scandal." Her eyes flickered away. "And, perhaps…perhaps I decided I *can* be of use to you. The fear of losing a family member…" She trailed off and swallowed. "We must find Lydia. It's as simple as that."

Something flipped over in his chest. *It's as simple as that.*

If only that were true. It seemed there was nothing simple in the way he responded to this mysterious woman.

She met his gaze once more, and the shock of the connection, the current between them, was too much. Now it was his turn to look away.

"Well, I was glad to receive your note. It seems you're quite adept at giving your chaperones the slip."

Her mouth tightened. "Jack."

The melodic sound of his name on her lips was honey, dripping from a spoon. God, he wanted to hear her say it again.

She glared, seeming to realize she'd lost his attention. "Listen, this is important. Perhaps you think because I snuck out last night and occasionally give my maid the slip, I have no care for my reputation or safety. But that's not the case. My safety is *quite* important to me."

Her words vibrated with intensity, and Jack studied her, unsure of the cause.

She looked down the road, ending the discussion.

"There are a few coaching inns the next few miles. We can make inquiries—discreetly, of course—to see if your sister or Andrew Aubrey came through."

"Aubrey Andrews."

"What?"

"The bounder's name. I think it's Aubrey Andrews." He paused and rubbed his chin. "Or *was* it Andrew Aubrey? Blast, now I can't remember."

Pippa smiled. "Either way, I'm sure we'll find them."

Jack tilted his head toward the meadow. "They won't notice you've left?"

Pippa patted her horse's neck. "My cousin will cover for me. Let's ride."

"Actually, my mount threw a shoe a way back."

She seemed to take in the fact that he was walking for the first time.

He eyed her horse, a sturdy-looking gelding. "We'll have to ride double."

Her eyes flew to his face. She swallowed and gave a jerky

nod.

"I imagine the first inn will have a stable that can sort it out."

Jack made quick work of trading the saddles—Pippa's side saddle would never do—before tying the reins of his horse to the back of her gelding and mounting up.

"Here." He reached out his hand.

She squared her shoulders and placed her gloved hand in his. He tugged her up, so she sat sideways across his lap. She shifted, trying to find a comfortable fit. Jack nearly groaned at the exquisite torture of her firm bottom and thigh pressed against him.

"I'll hold you." He wrapped an arm around her waist and pulled her against his chest. She remained stiff and unyielding.

Jack pressed his heels into the mount's sides, and the horse began an easy canter. Pippa crashed into him with each jostling movement. After a few moments, she must have realized resistance was futile. She sighed and relaxed her posture, sinking against him so they could keep their balance and protect her mount from the heavy load of two passengers.

Jack tried to concentrate on navigating, but as the road carried on in a straight line, this required little focus. His senses shifted to her.

The clean, floral scent of her hair.

The warmth of her waist beneath his hand.

The firm press of her bottom and thigh against him.

He tightened his arm, and her head came to rest on his shoulder. Jack glanced down, wondering what expression he'd find on her face.

Her eyes were closed, her face nuzzled against him. She was soft and pliant in his arms. Something in his chest loosened and eased. The sensation of her nestled against him felt so good, so right, that it seemed preordained.

He dipped his head, stroking his mouth and nose along the top of her glossy, dark hair.

Her breath hitched.

My God.

He wanted to inhale her, to bite her, to consume her until they were one.

He lowered his face farther, knowing only a few inches separated their mouths. A kiss. Yes, a kiss.

She tilted her face up. Her lips were parted, pink and soft. Pippa's eyelashes fluttered. In the depths of her blue eyes, he saw a flicker of want. He felt it too. A want so urgent that it drowned out all other concerns—

Jack stiffened. *Damn.*

He pulled back, loosening his hold around her waist.

What in the bloody hell was he thinking? His sister Lydia was missing, and he wanted to become intimately acquainted with this woman on the back of a horse along the Great North Road?

Madness.

She shifted, putting another inch or two between them.

"I believe the first inn should be around this next bend," she said, her voice breathless.

Jack cleared his throat. "Perhaps you can speak to the owner while I see to my horse?"

She nodded.

He risked a glance, and their eyes locked for a heartbeat before hers skittered away.

They pulled up in front of a coaching inn, its wooden sign proclaiming it The Golden Lion. A boy scurried toward them, but before he arrived or Jack could offer her a hand, Pippa slid to the ground, straightened her riding habit, and dashed inside.

❧⟫⟫⟫⟨⟨⟨❧

PIPPA BARRELED INSIDE the squat, sturdy building, nearly knocking over an elderly patron in her haste.

"My apologies," she murmured, backing away from the scowling fellow.

Pippa ran a hand over her gown to smooth out the wrinkles.

If only she could smooth out her nerves as easily.

What on earth had just happened?

She remembered Jack's arms tightening about her as he'd nuzzled her hair, inhaling her scent. Then his eyes gleamed as he'd lowered his head toward hers, his gaze on her mouth, his lips coming closer and closer—

The door banged. She glanced over her shoulder and found the object of her musings standing uncertainly in the entryway.

Oh, for heaven's sake! They couldn't *both* be rendered awkward and uncomfortable by what just happened—or didn't happen, as the case may be. Who would question the innkeeper otherwise?

"Can they fix your horse's shoe?"

Her direct question seemed to shake him out of his uncertainty. "They'll have him ready in a couple of hours."

Pippa nodded.

"They're saddling up another mount for me, so we won't have to ride double."

Pippa swallowed against an emotion—disappointment? relief?—that was probably best left unexamined. Plastering on a smile, she said, "Wonderful. Shall we proceed?" She tilted her head toward a plump man in an apron wiping down a table.

Jack offered his arm and led her to the table.

"Good afternoon, sir, ma'am." The innkeeper nodded to them. "Can I interest you in a meat pie or cool mug of ale?"

"Ale for me," Jack answered. He glanced at Pippa who merely shrugged. "And one for the lady."

Pippa leaned forward while the innkeeper saw to their drinks. "What are you going to say?"

"I think I'll describe Aubrey Andrews and try to keep the focus off Lydia."

Pippa nodded. It was a good plan. Asking too many questions about a gently-born lady traveling under mysterious circumstances was bound to lead to curiosity, rumors, and perhaps even scandal.

The innkeeper returned. He plunked down foaming tankards in front of each of them.

"Brewed it myself." His eyebrows lifted as if awaiting their verdict. "Call it Babcock's Ale, on account of me being John Babcock."

Pippa took a sip under Babcock's watchful gaze, then hummed in appreciation. She'd never tasted ale before, but the beverage was refreshing after a day of travel.

"I was hoping to learn if a friend of mine has come through in the last two days." Jack leaned back as if the question was born only of idle curiosity.

"Lots of visitors come through my doors, on account of the excellent ale." Babcock nodded toward their mugs.

"Best on the whole north road," Jack agreed, smiling at the man.

The innkeeper's chest puffed up with pride. "Aye, the secret's in the hops, you see—"

Jack interrupted him with a jingle of coins in his pocket. "I'd be most appreciative if you'd try to recollect. You see, I have an important message to deliver to my friend, but I'm not sure of his exact route."

Babcock pinched his mouth shut. Apparently, the innkeeper had been quite keen on sharing his hoppy tale. After a beat, however, he eyed Jack's pocket and nodded.

"My friend has dark hair with a shock of white through it," Jack said, recounting the description supplied by the law office clerk. "He may have been traveling with a woman."

The innkeeper scratched his chin.

Pippa held her breath.

"Can't say as I recall seeing anyone of that description," Babcock finally answered. "Wish I could be of assistance to you though."

Jack's hand clenched tightly around the handle of his tankard. "If you see this man come through, I'd be most grateful if you'd send word." Jack slipped a coin and his card onto the table.

The innkeeper scooped them up with a practiced hand and murmured his assent.

Pippa slouched in her chair, speaking once the innkeeper was out of earshot. "Well, I don't know if we should be relieved or disappointed."

Jack ran a hand through his hair and sighed. "I'd prefer to learn she hadn't traveled to Gretna with that bounder, but I wish we at least knew *something*."

Pippa gulped a few mouthfuls of ale. "Well, we've got more inns to visit. Perhaps one of them will have information about Lydia."

Jack left her money to settle their bill while he collected the horses.

They rode toward the next inn, which the stable master had told Jack was about five miles further along the Great North Road.

"There's something I've been quite curious about," Jack said, interrupting their companionable silence.

Pippa's shoulders tensed.

"Well, according to my maid, the secret is using tongs that are hot, but not *too* hot," she quipped, hoping to deflect the question she assumed was coming.

"What?" He stared as if she'd recited Shakespeare while balancing a cat on her head.

"You're curious about how my hair holds a curl for so long, yes?"

"That's not what I was going to ask." Jack's warm-brown eyes twinkled. "However, I'll be sure to pass along the advice to my valet."

Pippa's lips twitched.

"How is it you've come to learn fencing?"

Her smile vanished. She glanced over, worried she'd find disdain on his face. She knew a woman who used a sword didn't match society's perception of femininity. However, his expression was merely one of friendly curiosity.

"Well," she began, uncertain how to answer without reveal-ing the Ladies Covert Academy's secrets. "I *enjoy* fencing."

"But why?"

"Why does any man fence?"

Jack furrowed his brow. "Exercise, I suppose, and a love of sport and competition."

She raised an eyebrow at him. "And that can't be true of women?"

"But women don't engage in sports."

Pippa rolled her eyes. "And here I thought you were more enlightened than the average man." Although she knew—she *knew*!—not to expect understanding from a man raised in a society with so many prejudices against women, a knot of disappointment still formed in her stomach.

She recalled one of *Señor* Martín's expressions. *You shall not defeat your foe with one lunge.*

She shifted on her horse. "Some men love hunting while others find pleasure at the card table or reading history. It's the same for women. One woman might enjoy needlepoint, another watercolor painting, and someone else playing the pianoforte. *I* happen to enjoy fencing. It's really that simple."

Jack shook his head. "But how'd you learn? It's not like you can stroll into Angelo's School of Arms for a lesson."

"I have a private instructor." She raised her chin. Her horse whinnied as if adding his support.

He watched her through narrowed, assessing eyes. "And your mother arranged this?"

Pippa opened her mouth. She inspected her reins, then ad-justed her gloves. "She doesn't know."

"Your mother doesn't know." He shook his head, clucking his tongue. "You're quite a rascal, aren't you Miss Philippa Chester?"

She glanced at him and caught the laughter dancing in his eyes. Her lips twitched in response. "Maybe just a little bit." She held her thumb and forefinger an inch apart, and he laughed.

"Well, you can keep your secrets, I suppose. I'm not completely unenlightened."

"Oh?" she said, drawing out the word.

"Well, I allowed my sister to join the LCA, didn't I?" Jack sat up straight in his saddle as if this were an impressive accomplishment.

"*Allowed* her, did you?" Pippa didn't disguise her sarcasm.

"You know what I mean."

"I think your sister deserves more respect and autonomy than it seems you grant her. She's a woman fully grown after all."

"Yes, a woman who ran off with her lover." His expression darkened.

"We don't know that yet." Pippa clenched her reins. "Perhaps every innkeeper along this road will have the same answer as the last one because she did not, in fact, dash off to Gretna Green with Andrew Aubrey—"

"Aubrey Andrews," he interjected.

"Oh, stuff it." She scowled. "You know perfectly well the dratted name isn't the issue. What matters is that you're too controlling of your sister." She shot him a look, daring him to disagree.

"I protect her."

"You *stifle* her."

Now he scowled.

Before Pippa could further show him the error of his ways, they arrived at the next inn. They ordered ale again, as this seemed to be the initial payment required to earn a conversation with the innkeeper. Pippa was surprised to discover the ale at the first establishment was, in fact, quite superior.

Like before, this innkeeper hadn't seen anyone matching Aubrey Andrew's description. Jack again left a coin and his direction in case the dark-haired man with the white streak made himself known.

They were a mile past the inn when a rider came tearing down the road. Crouched low over his horse, the man's face was shadowed by his hat and the high collar of his coat.

Pippa gripped her reins. Her heart raced. Shifting nervously, her mount skittered sideways on the road.

"Easy," Jack murmured, riding up beside her and laying a hand on the horse's neck.

His other hand reached inside his jacket.

Pippa's heart was in her mouth. Closer the man thundered, the pounding of his horse's hooves only slightly louder than her drumming pulse. The rider flew past them without even a sideways glance and was out of sight within seconds.

Pippa's breath whooshed out of her in relief. She sagged in her saddle, wondering for a moment if her suddenly boneless frame could keep her in the saddle.

Jack's hand emerged empty from his jacket. "Wasn't sure if he was out for a sporting gallop or had something more nefarious on his mind."

He didn't seem to notice that Pippa was a puddle of hollow flesh. He clicked to his mount, and Pippa's gelding followed. It took several minutes for her pulse to slow to normal and she could breathe with ease once more.

"You're armed?" she asked, eyes on the road ahead of them.

"Yes."

"A pistol?"

"I always bring one along when I'm traveling like this. You never know when a highwayman might turn up."

Pippa gulped.

The horses trotted side by side down the road, the dappled afternoon light filtering through the canopy of leaves overhead.

"I wonder," she asked, her gaze pointed between her horse's ears, "if you might teach me."

"Teach you?"

She cleared her throat. "To shoot."

Silence.

She snuck a peek. He was staring at her, his expression inscrutable.

"It seems like a useful skill." She worked to keep her voice even. "And since we're out here in the countryside, it's a perfect opportunity really. You have the pistol with you now, so…" She trailed off, uncertain how much to tell him.

He appeared to study the road ahead of them, the entire long, straight, unimpeded length.

"No."

"No?" She gaped at him. "Just like that?"

"Just like that." He wouldn't meet her gaze.

A bird trilled a cheery tune, its sweet melody at odds with the tension between them.

"Why?" she asked.

He sat stiffly on his mount.

"Jack."

He finally looked at her. "I have the pistol. I'm here to protect you. You don't need to know how to shoot."

"But I want to know how," she said through gritted teeth.

"You're a *woman*," he bit out.

"I *know* that."

They glared at each other, the few feet of space between their mounts suddenly a chasm.

He looked away first.

Pippa swallowed against the lump in her throat, blinking rapidly.

They only broke their silence when they reached the next inn and inquired once more about the elusive Aubrey Andrews and his female companion.

Chapter Eight

T HE SUN HUNG low in the sky, casting long shadows across the road when Jack and Pippa arrived at the orphanage. They'd visited a total of five inns before turning around. None had reported seeing a man fitting Aubrey Andrews's description.

Jack handed the reins of his horse—retrieved on their return journey—to a boy before assisting Pippa. His hands at her waist warmed Pippa's skin through the wool of her habit. He lifted her down, her chest sliding against his before her feet landed on the grass. Her breasts tingled from the firm contact.

"Thank you." She stepped back, embarrassed by her breathless voice.

Glancing up, she caught him pulling his gaze from her chest. His cheeks grew ruddy.

He'd been staring at her breasts! Now *her* cheeks heated.

Pippa swallowed before asking the boy, "The other ladies are inside already?"

"Yes, miss. Just follow the noise. You can't miss 'em."

They turned toward the orphanage. The faint shrieks of excited children sounded from the brick, three-story edifice.

"Are you certain you wish to go in?" she asked Jack. "I need to make an appearance since Lady Rowling's servants will notice if I'm not at this portion of the outing, but I no longer need an escort since I can ride back in one of the carriages. I'm sure one of the grooms can attend to my horse."

Jack nodded. "I'd like to see the sort of work my sister was involved in. She rarely spoke about her projects with the LCA although she spent almost every day there."

Pippa bit her lip against a twinge of guilt.

"Well, let's go visit some orphans then." She lay her hand upon his arm, and they strolled to the front door.

No one answered her knock. Jack shrugged, so she opened the door. Echoes of high-pitched voices and the deeper rumbles of adults sounded from the right. They followed the hallway until they came into a large room filled with long tables and benches. Dozens of children dashed about. Some clutched rag dolls and others waved knit stockings above their heads. Very lumpy, misshapen stockings. Well, at least Pippa's booties would be in good company.

Amid the chaos, a tiny woman attempted to corral the children. Dev stood beside several large trunks, pulling out bundles of clothing and toys. Meera scribbled onto a sheaf of paper with a pencil.

Lady Rowling's secretary waved them over. "Ah, Lord Hartwick, thank you for joining us here today. Miss Chester told me you were considering a donation to the orphanage but wanted to visit first?"

Pippa bit her lip. With everything else going on, she'd completely forgotten about her fib to Lady Rowling and Meera that would explain his potential presence today.

"Yes, I dislike having requests sprung on me," he said, flicking his eyes to Pippa, "so I prefer to research before committing to a donation."

Pippa coughed to hide her smile.

"Lord Hartwick and Miss Chester, this is Mrs. Leary, the orphanage director." Meera gestured to the petite woman who by turns scolded the children for their rowdy behavior and beamed at them with obvious affection.

"I do apologize." Mrs. Leary raised her voice to be heard

above the din. "The children are usually well-behaved, but it's as if Christmas has suddenly appeared."

Meera handed her a package wrapped in brown paper. "Here are your items, Miss Chester. We thought each LCA member could distribute her own contributions."

Unwrapping the small bundle, Pippa pulled out a familiar lumpy booty, the toe area twice as wide as the heel.

"It seems your *épée* skills don't translate to knitting needles." Jack's murmur into her ear made her shiver.

"I'll have you know I'm an expert knitter, and I meant for the bootie to be this shape. You'd be surprised how many children have wide toes."

"And this is for you, my lord." Meera took a package from Dev and handed it to Jack.

He turned the bundle over in his hands. "I don't wish to upset a lady by passing out her work."

"It's your sister's," Meera replied before returning her attention to the list on her paper. "I found it in her room at the LCA."

Pippa inhaled. She turned to Jack, her mouth open to speak, but then she saw his expression. With his lips compressed and jaw clenched, it was clear he was wrestling to control his emotions.

She lay a hand on his arm. "If you'd rather wait outside—"

"No, I—I'd like to see what she made."

Pippa nodded. He tore into the package, pulling out a neat stack of white cotton pinafores.

Pippa traced the edge of one with her finger. "Beautiful." The little sleeveless gown would slip over a child's dress and tie in the back. Each precise stitch was even, the seams aligned, and the yoke decorated with embroidered flowers. "I didn't know your sister was so skilled with a needle."

Jack continued to stare at the garments. "Neither did I."

Pippa touched his arm. "Shall we find some girls in need of pinafores?"

He gave a jerky nod and followed her across the room. Soon, a bevy of little girls surrounded him. Each one clambered for a "fancy dress".

Once he seemed comfortable passing them out to the children, Pippa snuck away for a minute to check in with Jane.

"Did everything go well with the plant collecting?"

"Your idea to invite all the LCA members to help was brilliant. I have so many new specimens…" Jane trailed off, staring at something just over Pippa's shoulder.

Pippa turned to see what had caught her attention. Dev strode by, a large trunk propped on each shoulder. Pippa turned back to find her cousin pink-cheeked.

"Ah, yes, ahem." Jane restacked the perfectly stacked aprons she'd sewed for the children. "As I was saying, I'm well-stocked on plants now. How'd things go with Lord Hartwick?"

"We inquired at several inns, but no one saw Lydia."

Pippa glanced back to see how Jack was faring. He was sliding a pinafore over a cherubic little girl's head. He bent over, trying to tie the ribbons behind the child. Instead, she scooted forward, flung her arms around his leg, and sat down on his boot.

Even with the din in the room, Pippa could hear the child's high-pitched voice commanding Jack to "giddy up."

He stood frozen.

Pippa took a step toward him and the child, but Jane halted her with a light touch.

"Wait," Jane suggested. "Give him a minute to sort it out."

"Giddy up," the child crowed again, tugging on his pant leg as if it were her reins.

Jack took one step with his unencumbered leg. He swung his other leg high, lifting the child through the air with a giant stride. She shrieked, her sweet little face lit up with an adorable grin.

A feeling of lightness bubbled up in Pippa's chest.

Soon, he'd reached the other side of the room, and another child demanded a ride. Within minutes, he had not only a child on his foot but also one on his back and another dangling from an arm as he marched about.

Jack smiled and laughed, his face open and easy. Pippa inched closer, mesmerized by the sight. She started when he began to sing.

"Hickory dickory dock, the mouse ran up the clock..."

Pippa's mouth fell open.

Other children began to dance about him, singing along. The petite orphanage director hurried over. Pippa bit her lip, uncertain how the woman would react to the spontaneous gaiety. However, the director scooped up a child and began to dance about. Jane, Meera, Dev, and several other women from the LCA joined in, clapping and singing along or grabbing children by the hands to twirl.

A little boy approached Pippa and began to jig. Pippa curtseyed low. Lifting the edge of her skirt in one hand, she tried to copy his steps and soon they were both laughing and bouncing about.

An arm hooked around her waist, and Pippa was pulled into a hop step. She grinned up at Jack, the little girl in the pinafore held in between them.

"Quite a party," she shouted above the din.

His arms tightened about her waist, drawing her a few inches closer. He smiled. With his brown eyes twinkling and a lock of dark hair curling over his forehead, his face was relaxed and easy. Something inside Pippa's chest shifted at the sight, and she had to look away, fearful he'd see her feelings.

Her *feelings?*

She shook her head, expelling the notion, and gave herself up to the swirling, twirling fun.

After a few more songs, the dance party concluded. The adults sipped tea and munched on scones brought out by a kitchen servant while they all caught their breath. The children, flushed and giggling, drank mugs of frothy milk and pastries liberally smeared with jam. Every child wore a new article of clothing or held a simple toy.

Meera and Jane sat across the table from Pippa. Jack was at her side. The quiet warmth of his presence was strangely comforting.

"Lady Rowling shall be quite pleased when I make my report," Meera told Jane and Pippa, stirring her tea. She took a sip and shuddered, setting the cup down. "You English have much to learn about the art of tea."

Pippa saw a sparkle in Meera's eyes and smiled in return.

"Perhaps you could give us instructions one day on how to brew a proper cup."

Meera nodded, then scanned her paper. "Miss Chester, I have not marked off the distribution of your items."

Jane snickered, and Pippa shot her cousin a dirty look.

"What's so funny about Miss Chester's contribution to the orphans?" Jack looked rather offended by Jane's laughter.

"Those baby booties are the sorriest bit of knitting I've ever seen," her cousin explained. "I actually feel sorry for the babies."

"Hey!" Pippa plunked her teacup down.

"Perhaps if you could knit with an *épée* instead of knitting needles—" Jane slapped her hand over her mouth, staring at Jack in horror.

"It's all right," Pippa said, voice low. "He already knows."

Jane lowered her hand. "Phew. I thought for a moment there that I'd given away the secret of the Ladies Cov—" Jane broke off in a yelp.

Probably because Pippa had kicked her under the table.

"Well," Pippa said, rising. "We really ought to deliver those booties. Lord Hartwick?"

She grabbed his hand and pulled him to the last trunk in the center of the room, the bundle of booties she'd set down to help Jack with the pinafores the only item laying at the bottom.

After quick directions to the nursery from the orphanage director, they headed to the stairs.

"What was that about?" Jack asked, following behind her.

"What?"

"Your cousin. She was about to say something about the LCA."

Pippa nearly missed a step. "I'm not sure what she was babbling about. I think all that dancing went to her head."

"Hm."

"There was something I was going to say to you earlier, but I've forgotten what it was with all the hubbub," Pippa mused, glad to change the topic. She wrinkled up her nose. There was something she'd realized earlier, something important…

A baby's cry announced they were close to the nursery, interrupting her elusive thought. Pippa eased the door open and found two women in the large, airy room filled with cribs. One rocked a child in the corner by the window. The other changed a nappy.

"Perhaps I'll just wait in the hall," Jack murmured.

"Oh no, you don't." Pippa grabbed hold of his arm. "If I have to be here, then so do you."

The woman in the rocking chair smiled. "May we help you?"

Pippa made introductions and held up her package. "I have baby booties for you."

The woman rose, tucking the baby in one arm. She plucked up a bootie and examined the lumpy heap of oatmeal-colored knitting. "Oh. This is quite…unique. How very thoughtful of you." She cleared her throat, seeming to need an extra moment to come up with some positive words about Pippa's dreadful creation. "With winter coming, we are grateful for warm clothing, even garments that aren't considered—er—the first blush of fashion."

Pippa bit her lip, inwardly cringing.

The woman held the bootie up to the baby, cooing, "Look at this little stocking, darling."

The baby began to wail, the tot's face scrunching up like a prune.

Pippa's cheeks flamed.

Jack emitted a noise sounding suspiciously like a strangled laugh. She jabbed him in the ribs with her elbow.

"Well, we'd best be on our way," Pippa chirped, handing over the package before backing up toward the door. "Thank you for your incredible work with these children. They are clearly in good care."

With murmurs of thanks, the women bid them farewell, and Pippa and Jack made a hasty retreat.

"Don't say a word," Pippa grumbled, marching down the hallway.

"I wouldn't dream of it." Even though Jack was behind her, she could tell he was grinning.

"You wouldn't believe how many hours I spent cooped up in my room trying to make those." She stomped down the stairs.

Jack laughed. "I believe *trying* is the critical part of that statement."

Pippa stopped halfway down the staircase. Jack bumped into her.

"What?" His long, warm body pressed against her back. "Have you decided to join a knitting club?"

Pippa spun around on the step and craned her neck to look up at him. "I just remembered!"

"Remembered what?"

She gripped his arm in excitement. *"Cooped up in my room.* We never checked your sister's room!"

Jack frowned. "What? We already searched Lydia's room and found the letter from that jackanape."

Pippa beamed at him. "I can't believe we didn't think of this before. Meera mentioned it when she gave you the pinafores, but I got so distracted right away that I forgot." Pippa took his hand in hers and squeezed. "We never searched Lydia's room at the LCA."

Chapter Nine

AFTER A WEARY ride back to London, Pippa and Jack arrived at Lady Rowling's house. Before climbing a narrow back staircase, they snagged a bit of bread, cheese, and cold meat along with a candle from a servant who was used to not asking questions.

Pippa led them into a room halfway down the hallway. As she lit more candles, his sister's room at the LCA was illuminated in pieces. A bookshelf. A cozy, upholstered chair near the window. A desk strewn with paper and quills.

Jack turned in a circle, taking it all in. He'd expected to find scraps of cotton and pincushions from all those pinafores. He had *not* expected a small-scale version of his study.

What on earth did Lydia do here?

"I really don't know."

Pippa's voice startled him. He must have spoken aloud.

"Your sister mostly kept to herself, so I don't really know what her work entailed."

"Her work?"

Pippa bit the inside of her lip. "For the Ladies Charitable Association, of course. I knit, she sewed..." Pippa flapped her hand as if to include the myriad charity activities of the LCA.

Only, Jack was beginning to realize that charity wasn't the sole purpose of their organization. "What's going on here?" He took a step closer. "Tell me the truth."

"I told you—"

"Stop lying."

"Listen." She jabbed his chest with her forefinger. "You said if I helped you find Lydia, you wouldn't poke around into the LCA's affairs. And yet, you keep asking questions." Her whisper was as sharp as her finger against his sternum.

He grabbed the digit, wrapping her hand in his. "Perhaps I wouldn't ask questions if the members didn't behave so strangely. I need to know what sort of group my sister belongs to."

He continued to hold Pippa's finger, his chest tightening. He wasn't being entirely truthful. He did want to know about the LCA because of his sister. But he also wanted to know because of Pippa. He wanted to know what she did and if she was staying out of danger.

He wanted to know *her*.

Jack gritted his teeth. The truth was, *he* had brought danger to her doorstep. The possibility of damage to her reputation from visiting those inns hadn't escaped him. He'd put her at risk.

They stood together in silence. Releasing her hand, Jack leaned forward, slowly closing the inches between them. He rested his forehead against hers.

"I'm sorry," he whispered.

"For what?" Her breath brushed against him.

The comfort of leaning into her was sweet beyond measure. It was only now when he had someone to lean on, even just for a moment, that he saw how lonely it was carrying his burdens alone. Feeling Pippa here next to him with her strength and clear sense of self allowed him to set aside his troubles, even if it was just for the span of a few heartbeats.

"I'm sorry for all of this," he finally answered. "For forcing you to help me. For placing you in harm's way."

She laughed, the sound tinged with bitterness. "I've seen danger before, and this isn't it." She pulled away slowly and glanced around the room, breaking the bubble of intimacy between them.

She ran her hand over Lydia's cluttered desk. "Your sister always had ink stains on her fingers." Pippa grabbed a piece of paper and held it to the light. "She was writing something."

Jack picked up a sheaf of papers, scanning the familiar handwriting. "...the illogical distribution of House of Commons seats due to the continuation of rotten boroughs deprives English citizens of equal representation in government," he read aloud. Frowning in confusion, Jack glanced up at Pippa. "What is this?"

She shuffled through a stack of papers, then sank onto the wooden chair at the desk. "Is your sister very...political?"

Jack shook his head. "Lydia is quiet and sweet. She has no interest in politics or whatever this is." He waved the papers in his hand.

"This sounds like the work of *Democratiam Liberum*," she murmured, scanning a paper.

Jack stilled. "The political firebrand in the newspaper?"

Pippa looked up at him. "Is it possible Lydia could be—"

"No," he interrupted. "Lydia would never—I mean what sort of nonsense..." He trailed off. This was madness. It couldn't be true. Surely not...

Everything he thought he knew about his sister—his only real family—was crashing down about him. Pippa was wrong. This was her fault.

"Listen," he said through gritted teeth, "just because *you* like to act like a man doesn't mean my sister does."

Pippa flinched.

He cursed, running his fingers through his hair. He was being terrible. This most certainly *wasn't* her fault. None of it was. He took a deep breath before saying, "I apologize. I didn't mean that to come out the way it did."

Pippa crossed her arms and leaned back in the chair. "I think it came out exactly as you meant it to." She paused. "You are prejudiced against women."

The whooshing of his heartbeat was loud in his ears. "That's not it."

"Then what is it?" Pippa's voice revealed he'd hurt her. Yet again.

"I—I struggle with—I always have to—" Jack paced the narrow confines of the room, his heart pounding so furiously it seemed as if the damn organ wanted to flee from his chest.

Pippa remained silent.

"I have to be in charge," he blurted out, freezing in place.

The room was silent except for the ticking of a clock. Jack felt as if he'd tossed a rock off a cliff and waited, waited, waited to hear the sound of it crashing to the ground far below. He'd never said those words aloud. He'd never even thought them, but now…he realized they were the truest thing he'd ever said.

"Why do you have to be in charge?" she finally asked.

Jack exhaled. The steady sound of her voice after his confession rebalanced him somehow.

He shook his head. "It's complicated."

Pippa was waiting for more, he could tell, but that was all he could say.

Eventually, she sighed. "Well, we'd best finish our search."

The sound of shuffling paper and drawers opening pierced his stupor. They searched the office together for several minutes in silence.

Pippa huffed in frustration and rose to her feet. "I need more light to read all these papers. I'll get more candles."

The room felt empty with her gone. Jack finished searching the last book on Lydia's bookshelf, disappointment dragging at his shoulders. He'd found nothing.

Turning to the papers on the desk, he picked one up at random and began to read.

The county of Middlesex includes London, a city with an estimated one million citizens. Middlesex sends only eight members to the House of Commons. By contrast, the county of Cornwall, infinitesimally smaller than London, sends forty-four members. This undemocratic distribution of votes allows small pockets of the population to yield great power in parliament. As a result, corruption, vice, and backroom dealings flourish in the den of spoils we refer to as the House of Commons...

Jack dropped the paper onto the desk. He rubbed his eyes. As a member of the House of Lords, he was quite familiar with parliament's upper chamber, but he didn't realize the votes in the lower chamber were so unequally distributed, if this claim was true.

And why was his sister writing this down anyway? It was clearly her handwriting. Was she copying articles out of the newspaper for some reason? Maybe she served as secretary for the author of these inflammatory essays? Could the author be that scoundrel, Aubrey Andrews?

His head ached just contemplating all the potential scenarios.

"...am quite disappointed at the reports I've been hearing, Miss Chester."

Jack stilled at the sound of a voice from down the hallway. When Pippa had left to fetch candles, she'd left the door cracked.

"I'm sure I don't know what you mean." Pippa's clear voice was unmistakable, but Jack was uncertain who she addressed.

"Meera mentioned you left the group for several hours today and arrived at the orphanage in the company of Lord Hartwick."

Ah, his old friend Lady Rowling. That icy voice could belong to no other.

"He was heading to the orphanage to discuss a donation, and he saw our group collecting specimens for Jane," Pippa said. "He asked me to ride with him so we could discuss his sister."

"His sister is not your concern."

Jack frowned. What was Lady Rowling trying to hide?

"My lady, I most vehemently disagree. Lydia is a member of our organization, and she's been missing for three days now. I *will* help Lord Hartwick in any way I can."

"You are putting the LCA in jeopardy," came Lady Rowling's reply. "I know you cannot see it, but *I* can. You must desist."

"Lady Rowling," Pippa said, frustration in her voice. "I value the LCA. You know I do. But I cannot turn my back on a friend in need."

"You are young and foolish." Lady Rowling answered at last. She sounded almost weary. "There are forces at work you cannot comprehend. If you knew what we were up against…" She trailed off. "But I see I cannot dissuade you. I pray you don't bring ruin down on us."

Light footsteps and the swish of silk passed by the door. A moment later, Pippa returned, clutching a candelabra to her chest. She pushed the door closed behind her.

"I suppose you heard?" She set the candelabra down.

Jack nodded, uncertain what to say. She had put her position here—a position which obviously meant a great deal to her—on the line. For Lydia.

For him.

"Thank you." The words seemed inadequate, so he stepped forward to take her hand. "Thank you, Pippa. I honestly don't know what I'd do without you."

Her tongue darted out to moisten her lips. Jack nearly groaned at the sight. He gently tugged her close, then bent down, brushing a soft kiss beside her mouth. Her skin was smooth as satin. Blood whooshed through his veins as his lips lingered upon her cheek.

Pippa didn't move. He pulled back, finding her eyes wide in her face. The air pulsed between them with something hot and heavy.

"A thank you kiss," he said, although it cost him dearly to pretend. The desire to kiss her in full, for their lips to explore and tantalize, was almost overwhelming. He forced himself to take a step back.

She nodded and tore her gaze away.

He took another step back before saying, "There was nothing in the books, so I can assist with the papers on her desk."

The task was much easier with the extra candles. He found more treatises on the House of Commons, including what appeared to be a well-researched examination of the so-called "rotten boroughs", or areas of land on the edge of a sea cliff or in inhospitable wilderness areas. Such lands were within the border of a nobleman's estate, however, and since the nobleman controlled his tenants, he could control who won the seat. The position in the House of Commons was often given to a second son or sold to the highest bidder. There was no free voting by citizens. No democracy. No *common* in those House of Commons elections whatsoever.

"I might have something." Pippa handed him a paper. "There's an address written at the top here, along with a date from several months ago."

Jack stared at the address written, like all the other papers, in his sister's hand.

"We should go there." Pippa stood. "We can hire a hackney. Just let me change—"

"No."

"What?" She stared at him.

"We're both exhausted from today's journey. This can wait until tomorrow."

Pippa crossed her arms over her chest. "You're planning to go without me, aren't you?"

Jack pressed his lips into a line.

"Well," Pippa said, plucking the address from his hands. "I'm going to pay this establishment a visit now, and I won't say no to your company." She flounced out of the room.

Jack sighed, picked up a candle, and followed her down the hall.

PIPPA FIDGETED ON the dark sidewalk while Jack paid the driver. She'd taken a few minutes before leaving to slip into her male garb, and at the last minute, had grabbed her parasol.

A woman dressed as a man carrying a pink parasol about

town might elicit unwanted scrutiny, but hopefully, no one would notice in the dark. When Jack had raised an eyebrow in question at her pink accessory, she'd merely informed him that a person should always be prepared for adverse weather.

Besides, quite a bit of confidence was instilled by a disguised sword and enough knives to arm a small regiment. Surely, she needn't still feel on edge when she went outside? And yet…

Skulking about the seedier side of London in the dark wasn't the safest endeavor, despite Jack and his pistol.

His pistol he wouldn't teach her to shoot.

She made a face at him, but as his back was still turned, it was doubtful he'd be flooded with remorse.

Jack returned. "The driver says the address is a block to the left."

Keeping to the shadows, they walked on silent feet. They were a handful of blocks from the docks on the Thames, and the area here was mostly warehouses and a few shops with shutters drawn.

Jack paused to read a worn address on a faded store sign. "It should just be around the corner."

Pippa peeked around the building at the end of the block. Her heart sank. "We've got company," she murmured.

Jack leaned against her, peering over her head. He muttered a curse.

The warm press of him shot white hot sparks of desire along her backside and through her body, momentarily blinding all rational thought. She inched forward to create some distance although a part of her wished to do nothing more than snuggle more tightly against him.

"Who do you think they are?" she finally whispered.

They watched as a handful of men backed a horse-drawn wagon to the building around the corner—the very building they were supposed to investigate.

"I don't know. I suppose we have no choice but to wait them out." Jack's breath was warm in her ear.

Pippa shivered, goosebumps breaking out across her skin.

"I see a stack of barrels a bit closer," he said. "Let's move there for a better view."

One of the horses attached to the wagon reared up, causing the wagon to totter side to side. All the men rushed to help, their attention on the animal.

Jack whispered, "Now."

Pippa crouched low and scurried to the barrels. Jack was right behind her. The stack of barrels was tall enough that they could stand and remain hidden.

The men calmed the horse and continued with their work. Pippa and Jack's new vantage point through the gaps in the barrel stacks gave them a clearer look at the men.

They wore the rough clothes of working-class men, but none appeared unkempt. None of the men brandished a worn map with an X marking the spot or threw back his head and cackled like a villain. None had a woman trussed up and slung over his shoulder.

In short, they looked like average men going about their work.

Pippa sighed. She'd hoped for something more obvious to come from this hunt. If Jack was half as tired as she was, then he was nearly dead on his feet. His suggestion back at the LCA to wait until morning had tempted her, but he'd been unable to meet her eyes when he'd said it. She'd known in a flash he meant to go alone.

What a change from that morning when he'd practically blackmailed her—yet again—to help find his sister by accompanying him north.

What had caused his changed attitude?

Had all the time they'd spent together today made him doubt her ability to assist him? That was unlikely, or else they wouldn't be here crouched behind these old barrels.

Or did the cause stem from something more tender?

Pippa swallowed and forced her mind back to the men.

Only she couldn't.

The narrow space behind the barrels kept them close, and Jack's muscular chest warmed her back. Each breath stirred the wispy, escaped hairs from her hat, tickling her ear in a way that wasn't quite ticklish.

Was he as aware of her as she was of him?

Perhaps a small experiment was in order.

Pippa recalled the previous night when she'd arrived at his home dressed in trousers. Several times she'd caught him staring at her bottom, a hot look in his eyes. It seemed Jack liked *derrieres*.

Pippa leaned her parasol against one of the barrels. She faked a yawn, arching her back and raising her hand to cover her mouth. Her bottom pushed back, snug against his pelvis.

She heard his quick inhalation and smiled. Despite her male garb, she felt quite feminine.

Pretending to look left and right, she subtly shifted her body, rubbing her bottom back and forth.

Jack choked out a curse and dropped heavy hands onto her hips.

"What are you doing?" His whisper was curt.

Pippa peered over her shoulder, blinking innocently. "What do you mean?"

Jack's jaw tightened. Even in the darkness, she could see the hot blaze in his eyes.

"You're playing with fire," he growled.

Pippa's heartbeat thundered in her ears. She licked her lips, and his gaze locked on her mouth. Sparks shot through her just from his look. Rational thought fled. Pippa acted purely on instinct, turning around to face him.

Their bodies touched knee to chest.

She tilted her chin up, whispering, "Kiss me."

She was stunned by her own boldness, but then his mouth was on hers, and her only thought was *more*.

His mouth was warm, his lips gentle as they moved over hers. Pippa's eyes slid shut as all her senses focused on his touch.

He seemed to want something from her. He slid his hands across her hips to her rear and squeezed. Pippa gasped with both shock and pleasure, her mouth opening. Jack's tongue slipped inside. She clenched his jacket in surprise.

His mouth and hers were a strange, magical tangle of heat and movement and slick tongues and lips. Soon, she understood the rhythm, the give and take as their mouths moved together.

She pressed closer against him, her breasts aching at the firm pressure of his chest. His hands squeezed her bottom again. He moaned, the sound vibrating through her to the juncture of her thighs. She felt a strange tingle there and leaned forward, trying to alleviate the ache.

A hard length pressed against her core. Pippa had heard whispers about this when the maids thought no one was around. She gasped at the aching throb caused by the pressure.

"Pippa," he whispered, trailing kisses along her jaw and neck.

Her skin was aflame, each kiss and touch adding fuel to their desire. Her body wanted something she didn't understand. She'd never been kissed before, but now she burned. *More.*

"Oh, please," she gasped, unsure what she asked for.

His lips nibbled across her neck and to her ear. The stubble on his chin scraped along her tender flesh there, the light abrasion heightening each touch. How could a neck be so sensitive?

She mewled in pleasure, running her hands over the hard planes of his chest and shoulders. She wanted to feel more of him, to explore his muscles and sinews and flesh. Her hands burrowed inside his coat, and she rejoiced at touching him without its bulky interference. Despite the layer of his shirt and waistcoat, she could feel his heat and strength. She lay her palm across the center of his chest, the pounding of his heart proving he was just as affected by their passion.

"Jack," she whispered. *More.*

He hummed in reply, his mouth trailing back up her neck to her mouth.

This time, she parted her lips at the first touch of his mouth.

Her tongue flicked against his shyly. He moaned. She wanted to sink into him, cocooned inside this little haven of darkness, and be locked together like this with him forever.

The shrieking yowl of a cat split the night air.

Pippa jerked back, panting. She scanned the area, and the reality of their surroundings resurfaced.

Jack blinked, his breathing harsh. "Damn."

Pippa swallowed, fighting against the lump in her throat.

"I apologize." He ran his hand through his hair, not meeting her gaze with his own. "That was ungentlemanly of me. It won't happen again."

She sucked in a breath at the sting of his words.

He was sorry. It wouldn't happen again.

"Just…just passing the time while we waited," she croaked out. Pippa's chest ached.

Merciful heavens, what did he think of her? He admitted to ungentlemanly behavior, so what did that make her?

Her cheeks burned. Her *entire body* burned. Desire coated in shame coated in rage led to quite an internal fire. How dare he make her feel this way. She turned away, biting her lips to keep the angry torrent inside her from spewing forth. But biting her kiss-swollen lips just reminded her of his touch.

She glared out at the street. The *empty* street. "They're gone," she gasped.

Jack peeked around the barrels and cursed.

"I'm sorry." Pippa's stomach was full of ash.

He swore again, then exhaled. "We both missed them." Jack shook his head. "After all, they were only driving a team of uncooperative horses and a rickety cart filled with mystery cargo across cobblestones." He laughed, the sound totally without mirth.

Pippa peeked at him, and their eyes locked.

His gaze dropped down to her mouth, and the tight line of his lips softened before he cleared his throat and looked away. "Well, we were hoping to investigate the building, so I guess it doesn't matter that we missed their departure. Shall we?"

Pippa nodded, not trusting her voice. After one last check of their surroundings, Jack stepped out of their hiding spot. Pippa grabbed her parasol and followed.

The brick building sprawled across half of the block. Jack tested the large double doors the wagon had been backed against, but they were locked. The windows were too high for them to peek inside. Maybe if they pulled a barrel over, they could clamber up and peek in?

"They're too heavy," he said, following her train of thought. "I'll lift you."

"You'll lift *me?*" Pippa raised an eyebrow.

He raised an eyebrow back at her. "Do you have a better idea?"

Pippa huffed.

He took position under a window, bracing his legs wide and linking his fingers together. "Put your foot here."

He lifted and up she went, steadying herself against the building. She reached the window where she grabbed the edge of the sill to take some of her weight from him.

"What do you see?"

Pippa squinted, then rubbed her forearm against the glass, removing a layer of grime. Inside was machinery, barrels, stacks of paper…

"It's a printing press." Despite her suspicions about Jack's sister, she was still surprised at the evidence before her.

"Down you come," he warned, lowering her to the ground.

She stepped out of his handhold, and he steadied her, his hands on her hips. Pippa pulled back, hoping he didn't notice her shiver at the heat of his touch.

A gust of wind blew through the street, swirling the detritus of the city around their feet. A newspaper wrapped around Jack's leg. He shifted his weight to one foot to shake it off. Before he could jiggle his leg, Pippa grabbed it.

The scent of fresh ink filled her nose. "It's new."

"So?"

"It probably fell off the cart when they were loading. This has tomorrow's date on it, and if I'm right..." She trailed off, the moonlight providing enough illumination for her to scan the headlines of the first few pages.

Pippa's stomach lurched. *There it was.*

Although she usually relished being right, she'd gladly have forgone this victory.

"Look." She held up the paper, edges flapping in the breeze. "It's another *Democratiam Liberum* article."

He folded his arms over his chest.

Pippa stared at him, tapping her foot. "You're really going to pretend you don't know what this proves?"

"It doesn't prove anything." He made a great show of examining his fingernails. In the middle of a dirty street. In the dim shadows of night.

Pippa rolled her eyes. "Let's examine the evidence piece by piece, hm? One, your sister's office at the LCA is filled with political essays in her handwriting." She ticked off a finger. "Two, she had the address for a newspaper's printing press jotted down. Three, the same newspaper is running political essays matching the tone and message of the essays in her office. Four, the essays in the paper are attributed to *Democratiam Liberum*. Ipso facto," she concluded, throwing in some Latin for good measure, "your sister, Lydia Dashwood, *is Democratiam Liberum*. LD, DL...they're the same person."

"That's..." Jack's mouth worked as he seemed to search for the right word. "...*preposterous*." He glared. "She belongs to a charity group, not some radical political organization. I mean, how could this even happen?"

Pippa's pulse sped up.

She wasn't supposed to tell anyone. No one at all. But if it was the only way to get him to believe, the only way for them to look in the right direction for his sister...

There really wasn't any choice.

"The Ladies Charitable Association isn't real." She hoped he didn't notice the tremor in her voice. "We use it as a cover for our real organization."

Other than a narrowing of his eyes, Jack didn't move.

She swallowed. "Your sister belongs to the Ladies Covert Academy." She braced herself for his reaction.

Jack blinked.

"Did you hear me?"

He stared at her, the wind ruffling his hair.

"It's a secret school for young women," she continued. "We can study whatever we want. Learn any skill. Perfect any area of academics, art, or occupation. I study fencing. My cousin is a botanist. We have architects, poets, mathematicians, a sculptor, a horse trainer. Your sister was—is—clearly a political writer."

"That is…" He trailed off. His eyes burned. She hadn't seen such a hard look on his face before.

"I know it sounds outrageous, but it's true. When Lady Rowling's husband died, she inherited everything that wasn't entailed. She returned from India with a massive fortune. She'd been quite stifled over there and wanted to give young women the opportunities she never had. So, she started the whole thing. She pays for the tutors and the supplies. Her house is the school. And it's all kept perfectly quiet under the disguise of charity work. And who'd question it?" Pippa shrugged. "Who'd *ever* think proper young women were enrolled in a secret academy?"

She breathed deeply, standing straight with her shoulders back.

She felt…unburdened. She wasn't supposed to share the secret, but she'd done it and she had no regrets. But what was Jack thinking?

"Lookee what we 'ave 'ere."

Pippa whirled around. Four men, roughly-dressed and sporting various scars, flanked them. Each held a weapon.

One, apparently the leader, grinned to display teeth like crooked tombstones. "Two plump birds waitin' to be plucked, wouldn't ye say mates?"

His three companions agreed, stepping closer.

Pippa's heart beat double-time.

She lifted her parasol and pushed the button.

Chapter Ten

The Ladies Covert Academy.

JACK'S MIND RESEMBLED a violent winter storm. Information howled like the wind, thoughts were jagged lightning, and conclusions dropped from the sky only to vanish from sight like rain absorbed by parched earth.

What the hell was happening?

The sight of Pippa drawing a sword from her frilly, pink parasol broke through the tempest.

Four men had surrounded them on this dim, deserted road. The apparent leader grinned, displaying the most crooked mouthful of teeth Jack had ever seen. He held a knife, the edge of the blade gleaming in the moonlight. Another man with a patch covering one eye rhythmically smacked a club against his hand as if testing its heft. The third ruffian swung a length of heavy chain at his side. His round face was half-hidden by a wild, tangled beard. And the last, a giant hulk of a man, popped the knuckles on the only weapons he required—his heavy, scarred fists.

Jack's skin tightened. Reaching into his pocket, he pulled out his pistol. He only had one shot, and there were four assailants.

The odds weren't in his favor.

"The swell's got a snapper, thinks 'e can fight the lot of us." The leader's snaggled grin showed a marked lack of fear. The man also seemed to realize the odds weren't in Jack and Pippa's favor.

"Stay back," Pippa commanded, her sword outstretched. Sweet Jesus, she'd had a sword hidden in her parasol all along. "I'd hate to run you through, but I'll do it if you come closer."

"Oo, the rum duke thinks 'e can run us through," Snaggle jeered, tossing his knife from one hand to the other. "There's four a us an' only two o' you coves. I bet a ha'pence you don't even know wot to do with that tilter."

"Come and find out," Pippa retorted.

Jack heard a slight waver in her voice.

The thieves moved a step closer, the circle around them tightening like a snare line around a hare's leg. A trickle of sweat ran down Jack's spine.

"Listen here," he barked, sighting his pistol at each of the bounders by turn. "I'll toss you my purse, and no one gets hurt."

"'And it over then, an' you'd best not cry beef." Snaggle reached out his hand and wiggled his fingers impatiently.

Jack fished his coin purse out of his pocket and tossed it. The thieves' leader weighed its heft before stashing it inside his coat.

"Now you, cub," Snaggle ordered Pippa.

"I—I don't have a purse."

Snaggle narrowed his eyes, and the thieves all took another step forward. Jack and Pippa shifted back, and he felt the wall at his back.

Hell and damnation.

"Search 'im," Snaggle ordered, pointing at Pippa with his chin.

"No," she cried.

The ruffian with the beard and chain crept forward.

Jack pulled Pippa behind him. If these ruffians searched her, they'd certainly discover she was a woman, and then…

He clenched his teeth.

That wouldn't happen. He wouldn't allow it.

Jack stared down the sight of his pistol at Beardface. "One

step closer, and I'll put a hole through you," he growled.

Beardface halted, but his beady eyes flicked left and right to his companions. The giant man inched closer on one side and the criminal with the eyepatch and club moved in on the other.

Jack swore.

He pulled the trigger.

Beardface jerked back. Jack reversed his hold on his pistol and pivoted, swinging at Giant. The butt of his gun smashed into the man's face. Giant only grinned and wound up for a punch.

Jack ducked and circled the man. He was enormous, but he was slow.

From the corner of his eye, Jack saw Pippa circling Snaggle. She held her sword at the ready. Snaggle feinted with his dagger, seeming to test her defenses. The man with the eyepatch snuck up behind her, his club lifted over his head.

Jack's heart stopped. "Look out!"

Pippa swiveled, slashing at One Eye's abdomen before he leapt back.

Jack's face exploded. He fell to the ground, cupping his jaw and seeing stars.

Giant stood over him, his hand in a fist. The thief's granite face was split by a grin.

Jack staggered to his feet. "That was unwise," he growled.

He and Giant circled one another again. Jack shook his head, trying to clear the disorientation. When massive thief's next lumbering punch came, Jack lunged sideways. He bashed the man with his pistol butt again before darting out of reach of those hammer fists.

To the side, Pippa had dispatched One Eye. The thief was slumped on the ground, the sleeve of his grubby shirt dark with blood in the moonlight.

Beardface was staggering away down the street, clutching his shoulder where Jack had shot him.

Jack evaded another punch and bashed Giant in the back of his head. The man grunted but kept coming.

Snaggle continued to slash at Pippa, but she kept him at bay with her sword. Although Jack put himself at risk of another surprise hit from Giant, he kept glancing over.

Truth be told, it was hard to look away from her.

Pippa was magnificent.

Her form, her quick footwork, her utter concentration—

Bam.

Jack blinked up at the moon. He was on the ground again. The splitting pain on the other side of his face confirmed Giant had landed another punch. His adversary loomed over him. He drew his foot back, aiming for Jack's ribs.

Jack rolled. Using the side of the building, he hauled himself up. The massive thief came for him, fist pulled back. Jack darted to the side. Giant's fist bashed into the side of the building. The man howled in pain, shaking his hand.

Jack's eyes darted along the ground. His gun had skittered out of his hand when he'd fallen.

There.

He scooped it up. Drawing his arm back, Jack brought the butt of the pistol down on the thief's head with all his might.

Giant swayed. Jack raised the pistol, ready to strike again if the man didn't go down. At last, he began to topple like an ancient tree sawed down in the forest. Before the man hit the ground, Jack pivoted.

Pippa and Snaggle still battled. Snaggle's left arm hung useless at his side, sleeve torn to reveal a bloody gash.

Jack scanned Pippa, holding his breath until he'd confirmed she was uninjured.

So far.

He didn't want to distract her fierce concentration. Perhaps if he threw the pistol at Snaggle, it would distract the man long enough for Pippa to dispatch him? Jack pulled his arm back, but before he could toss his weapon, Pippa feinted to the left and then lunged, stabbing Snaggle in the side.

The man grunted, hunching over. Pippa knocked the knife

out of his hand with her sword.

Jack hurried over, yanking off his cravat. Snaggle cursed while Jack tied his hands behind his back. While he secured the leader of the gang, Pippa stalked toward Beardface who still staggered down the street. She raised her sword in the air and whacked the handle against the back of his head. He crumpled to the ground.

Three of the thieves were unconscious, and the fourth was injured and bound.

Jack ran to Pippa, running his hands over her arms and shoulders. "Were you hit?" He had to be sure.

Pippa shook her head.

Jack closed his eyes for a moment, limp with relief. Pippa pulled back, and he stared at her pale, drawn face.

He wanted to pull her tightly against him. He wanted to run his hands over her entire body to be certain she hadn't been hurt. He wanted to kiss her again. He wanted to shoot and pummel the cutthroats a second time for threatening her safety.

And he wanted to raise her arm in the air in triumph.

She was a wonder.

She'd calmly fought off two hardened criminals entirely on her own. Most women of the ton—and even most men, come to think of it—would have fainted or run for the hills at the first sign of danger. Rather than retreat, Pippa had drawn her weapon and defended herself—and him—with skill and surety.

Instead of celebrating their win over death with a kiss or shout of victory, Jack gathered about him the mantle of efficient, level-headedness he'd long ago adopted. He inspected his pistol. He tucked it into his pocket. He retrieved his purse and her parasol.

Her parasol with a hidden sword. Damn.

"We'll send a constable once we find a hack."

Pippa nodded.

They walked in silence until they found a hackney a few blocks away. He instructed the driver to find a constable along the busy waterfront. Once Jack had told the lawman about the attack and the location of the thieves, he gave the driver Lady Rowling's address. If Pippa was surprised he'd remembered her need to change back into her gown, she didn't show it.

In fact, Pippa hadn't spoken a word.

As the hack rolled toward Mayfair, Jack studied her in the shadowed darkness. "Pippa, are you…" He trailed off, uncertain what to ask.

After a worrisome pause, she spoke. "I've never hurt anyone before." Her voice was thin.

Jack crossed to her seat and took her hand. It was icy-cold, so he gently chaffed her hand between his own. He felt the callouses on her palms, proof of her dedication to fencing.

"I've been training almost every day for a year," she continued. "I've sparred with *Señor* Martín so many times. But I've never actually…"

He heard her swallow.

"You had to," Jack replied. "It was us or them. That's what all the training and sparring is for—to defend yourself against harm."

He took her other hand and began to warm it as well.

"I know you're right," she said. "It's just…I feel…" Pippa sighed.

Jack squeezed her hand, and they rode the rest of the way in companionable silence.

WHEN THE HACKNEY pulled up in front of Pippa's home, the windows were ablaze with light. Pippa peered out the window. "What time is it?"

Jack pulled out his pocket watch. "Half past one."

She groaned and banged her forehead against the window.

"What reason did you give your mother for your absence today?"

Pippa closed her eyes. "I didn't."

"*What?*"

Maybe she'd been mistaken, and it was the neighbor's house all lit up. Yes, surely her mother was abed by now, and all the servants had retired for the night. She cracked one eye open.

No, that was her house all right. She groaned again.

A figure crossed the front parlor window. Pippa's eyes widened. Oh, merciful heavens, her mother was *pacing* in front of the window.

"What should I tell her?"

Jack ran a finger over his lips while he thought.

His soft, kissable lips. Pippa looked away.

"Stick to the truth as much as possible. Tell her about the LCA outing but add that the group was delayed. A broken carriage wheel perhaps."

Pippa risked a peek at him. Despite the long day of visiting Bow Street, investigating the law office, riding miles on the Great North Road, surviving the orphanage melee, searching through every scrap of paper in Lydia's office, and fending off a band of armed thieves in the dirty streets of London, Jack somehow still looked like the perfect English aristocrat.

Minus his cravat which had been repurposed as a restraint.

And his hair was quite mussed, although that only lent him a certain dashing air. Perhaps it was the contrast between his rigid self-discipline and those untamable waves of hair, but every time she saw a lock cascading down the center of his forehead, her fingers itched to plow through his wavy locks.

"I imagine if you don't go in soon, she'll send out a search party." Jack's lips twitched.

Pippa nodded and reached for the door.

"We'll resume our search tomorrow?" he asked.

Pippa stared in astonishment. He was asking instead of coercing? It seemed something had shifted between them today.

"Tomorrow." Pippa nodded and slipped out of the hackney.

As each footstep carried her closer to her doom, Pippa offered a silent thanks to Jack for his foresight to visit the LCA first so she could change back into her dress.

Hello dear. Why are you dressed like a bedraggled baronet? she imagined her mother asking.

Oh, just the usual—traipsing down by the docks and stabbing murderous thieves with my sword.

Sounds lovely. Tea?

A giggle escaped. Pippa clapped her hand over her mouth. Had she lost her mind? She was practically swaying on her feet with exhaustion, so it wasn't entirely impossible.

The door swung open to reveal the stern face of the butler. "Your mother awaits you in the parlor, miss."

Pippa drew a deep breath before entering the parlor.

Her mother rushed over, gathering Pippa in her arms. "Oh, I've been so worried!"

Guilt roiled in Pippa's stomach.

"I—I'm so sorry, Mother. The LCA took a trip to an orphanage and the carriage wheel broke."

Her mother pulled back, eyes narrowed.

Pippa swallowed.

"I sent a note to your aunt and uncle's asking if Jane had come home." Her mother crossed her arms over her chest. "They told me she'd returned from the LCA outing hours ago."

Pippa's mind swirled. What possible explanation could she give?

Her mother gestured to the divan, and Pippa sank into the cushions.

"I imagine you've come from Lady Rowling's?" Her mother folded her hands in her lap.

Pippa nodded. With her wardrobe change at the LCA, at least that much was true.

"I know what's going on, Philippa."

Pippa blanched. How had she found out? If Lady Rowling thought she could thwart her work to find Lydia by turning her mother against her—

"You're using the LCA as a cover."

Pippa gasped. Her mother nodded at her shocked expression. "Oh yes, I've put the pieces together."

Pippa leaned forward, resting her head in her hands. Tears pricked her eyes. Everything was crumbling down around her. She'd finally found something that cast a bright light into the shadow of her fears, and now she'd lose it. She'd once again be the girl frightened by every noise, every person who rushed by every stranger. She'd be afraid to venture out of the house. She'd lose her lessons with *Señor* Martín. She'd no longer be able to tease Jane about her crush on Dev.

She would no longer see Jack.

Pippa's insides were hollow. She breathed deeply, trying to push back her tears.

"Darling," her mother said, laying a comforting hand on her back, "you don't need to rake yourself across the coals. I understand why you did it."

Pippa raised her head. "You do?"

Her mother nodded, brushing a tendril of Pippa's hair back behind her ear. "Of course, my dear. This problem is hardly new, is it?"

Pippa stared at her mother, uncertain of her meaning.

"I suppose if I have to explain why my daughter is unable to attend yet another social function, saying she was detained by her charity work isn't the worst excuse."

"It's not?" Pippa's mind swirled in confusion.

Lady Everleigh smiled at Pippa with such a tender love that it nearly undid her. The urge to lay her head on her mother's shoulder and weep all her secrets was almost overwhelming.

"I know why you chose to stay home for so many years. After what happened to your father, well, I can't say I blame you. But my hopes had been raised by your ventures out into society this past year, especially your eagerness to attend Lady Frampton's musicale yesterday. I have such dreams for you Pippa. A husband. Children of your own." Her mother grasped her hand. "Now you're avoiding society again, but this time you're using the LCA as an excuse to stay away."

Pippa blinked.

Her mother didn't know.

Her mother *putting the pieces together* as she'd claimed was merely her incorrect speculation about why Pippa had been away so much the last couple of days, not because she'd uncovered the truth about the LCA.

Pippa's body went limp with relief. She leaned back against the divan, closing her eyes in gratitude. Her secret was safe.

The LCA was safe.

And she could continue to see Jack. Well, continue to *help* Jack. That was all it was.

Pippa offered her mother a smile. "I'm so sorry I've worried you. I admit that leaving the safety of home to socialize has long been a challenge for me, but I'll make more of an effort."

Her mother squeezed her hand and beamed. "I'm so glad to hear it. Lady Adderly's ball tomorrow will be the perfect opportunity."

"A ball?" If Pippa had the wherewithal to kick herself, she would. Hard.

"Oh yes. Why, it was your idea just the other day, remember? Everyone will be there. I put in an order with the modiste last month for a new gown, just in case. It's hanging in your room." Her mother clapped her hands together. "You shall look a picture. I'm so happy, my dear."

Pippa pasted a smile on her face.

A ball.

What every woman who eschewed society, fenced, and was embroiled in a dangerous, clandestine investigation yearned for.

Chapter Eleven

JACK DIPPED THE corner of his toast into his egg yolk and sighed. Sleeping in late this morning had been restorative. After a long day of travel and a late night of fending off criminals, not to mention an erotic dream about a certain fencing female who kissed like a courtesan, he'd needed the extra hours of shut-eye this morning.

Guilt returned. Those were hours he could've been hunting for Lydia.

Truth be told, he hadn't the foggiest where to look next. He'd dashed off a quick note to Gormley at Bow Street earlier this morning asking if the runner had any updates for him. Hopefully, the man would have at least some news. Good news. It had to be good news.

Jack frowned at his eggs.

"My lord," his butler said from the doorway. "You have a visitor. Shall I tell her you are not receiving this morning?"

Jack dropped his toast to his plate. "Who is it?" he asked, although he already knew the answer.

"It's Miss Chester, my lord." The butler's lips thinned in disapproval.

"Show her in." Jack dabbed at his mouth with a napkin. Best to avoid egg on one's face and all that.

Hearing light footsteps in the hall, his heartbeat sped up.

Surely his reaction stemmed from his eagerness to hunt for more clues.

Pippa glided into the breakfast room, a basket over her arm and her maid trailing behind her. The woman was whispering in Pippa's ear, scowling all the while.

"Ah, my dear Milly." Jack moved around the table to take the maid's hand.

Milly blushed, and Jack peeked at Pippa in time to see her rolling her eyes.

He bussed the back of the maid's hand before letting go. "It's so lovely to see you again. I trust you are well this morning?"

"Quite well, milord." She giggled.

"Milly was just telling me she simply wouldn't dream of leaving me unchaperoned with a man of unknown moral turpitude like you, Lord Hartwick," Pippa drawled.

"Oh, I never said the like, miss!" Milly's face grew even redder if such a thing was possible. "I'm just looking out for me post, I am."

"Such loyalty to your mistress is to be admired." Jack nodded to demonstrate his solidarity with the woman. "I wonder, though, if you are perhaps a bit hungry?"

Milly glanced at the sideboard laden with breakfast food. Her stomach promptly growled.

"Oh, that's been sitting out an hour or more." Jack waved his hand in dismissal. "A young lady of your high standards deserves a nice, hot meal. Why don't I ask my butler to escort you down to the kitchen where Cook will whip up something fresh, just for you?"

Milly bit her lip in indecision.

Jack reached into his pocket. "And know that my feelings will be hurt if you turn down this small token of my appreciation."

The coin disappeared from his hand with astounding speed. Jack walked Milly out to the hallway, handing her off to a footman with instructions to accompany her to the kitchen.

He returned to the breakfast room, finding Pippa loading a

plate from the sideboard. He drank in the sight of her like a man who'd been wandering the desert. Her tall, elegant form. The pretty sapphire shade of her gown which showed off her startling blue eyes. The glossy locks of hair pinned in a simple chignon.

"The eggs aren't *too* cold," she commented.

Jack shook himself out of his reverie. "I can send for a fresh plate if you wish."

Pippa turned, shaking her head. "I'm giving you a hard time since you were more concerned about my maid's meal than my own." She offered a tentative smile, and her eyes sparkled.

Jack smiled in return. His chest warmed as he remembered the feel of her in his arms last night, her soft breasts pressed against his chest and her lips so supple and responsive.

Perhaps a measure of his thoughts showed on his face for Pippa's cheeks pinkened, and she looked away.

"Please," he said, "join me at the table and we can discuss our next steps."

Pippa slid into the chair next to his and tucked into her food with obvious relish. "Mm, this scone is delicious."

Jack tried to keep the strain out of his voice, but the way she closed her eyes and hummed in pleasure after taking a bite made the front of his breeches rather tight. "Ahem. Yes, well, my cook is quite adept at pastries."

He tore his gaze away and surveyed his own plate. His egg yolk had congealed, and the toast was cold. He picked up a scone as well and took a bite. It *was* delicious. Had he ever really appreciated a well-baked pastry before?

"I brought a bunch of newspapers." Pippa tilted her head to a basket on the table. It overflowed with newspapers, most looking as if they'd already been tossed into a kindling pile.

He quirked a brow. "Are we to pay a visit to the fishmonger?"

Pippa shot him an impatient look. "We're going to research all of *Democratiam Liberum*'s recent articles."

Jack tightened his jaw.

Pippa lifted a hand in appeasement. "I know we disagree on

Lydia's role in *Democratiam Liberum*'s writing, but surely you can admit they're somehow connected to her disappearance?"

Jack forced himself to relax his jaw. It would be nice to have his molars left when this whole affair was resolved.

"I admit, it does seem Lydia and this *Democratiam Liberum* figure are perhaps tangentially connected."

Pippa's grip on her fork relaxed, and Jack felt like a cad for his behavior. She'd made all this effort to help, and he'd not shown an ounce of gratitude.

He lay his fingers across the back of her hand. "I *do* appreciate your assistance. I hope you know that." He ran his thumb over her wrist, marveling anew at both the softness of her skin and also the strength evident in her capable hands. Hands that could fight off armed thieves.

He pulled back, busying himself with his coffee cup.

"I...I'm glad to help." She stared down at her plate. The pulse in her neck fluttered rapidly.

Was she that affected by his touch? Well, if the mere sight of her chewing eggs stirred him, at least there was some comfort in knowing she was similarly affected.

He gulped back a mouthful of tepid coffee and grimaced. "Shall we begin with the articles? This large table would allow us to lay them all out."

Pippa nodded.

Jack cleared their dishes to the sideboard. "Being an earl isn't what it used to be, I'm afraid."

Pippa looked up from her basket. "Oh?"

"An earldom used to mean brandy, powdered wigs, and commoners bowing all day long. But we modern earls have to deal with knife fights on dark streets and clearing away dishes." He shook his head in mock sorrow. "One day, my descendants will be reduced to herding sheep."

Pippa's lips twitched, and Jack felt inordinately proud at putting some semblance of a smile on her face.

"Such a hard life you lead, my lord. Once you've finished the laundry and mopping, perhaps you can assist me with sorting these papers?" She handed Jack half the stack.

In addition to a headline about *Democratiam Liberum*, he saw stories in the newspaper at the top of his pile about Nathaniel Hinds, who was pressuring the House of Commons to pass a law beneficial to his coal empire, as well as a piece on the Prince Regent's latest architectural project.

"I asked a servant to gather them from the kitchen this morning," Pippa said, sorting through her own stack, "so they're out of order. I haven't had a chance to read this morning's article yet."

They both shuffled through their piles. Soon the papers were sorted and laying in order from one end of the dining room table to the other.

Pippa surveyed their work, her mouth scrunched up in concentration. It was adorable. Jack wondered what she'd do if he kissed her. He forced his gaze back to the row of papers.

"I think we should jot down notes as we read," she announced. "We can keep track of each article's topic, its date of publication, and anything smacking of a clue."

"Smacking of a clue?"

Pippa rolled her eyes. "Anything pointing to your sister or what may have happened to her."

"You think that would be in the articles?" Jack eyed the papers with skepticism.

Pippa shrugged. "As we're at a dead end and we haven't heard from Gormley at Bow Street yet, I say we look for clues anywhere we can."

Jack nodded. He called out to a passing footman to fetch writing supplies from his study. Within minutes, they were ready to proceed.

"Shall I read aloud or take notes?" Pippa asked.

Jack recalled his impression from the day they met—that he'd be happy to sit and listen to her melodic voice for a long time.

"You read." He took a seat and dipped the quill into the inkwell.

Pippa started with the first paper on the table, and Jack scribbled as she read. The first *Democratiam Liberum* piece dealt with noblemen granting their second sons seats in the House of Commons by pressuring their tenants to vote as they dictated. The next article explained the existence of rotten borough. The author explained these were seats in the House of Commons representing an area of land including a bog, a sea cliff, or some other inhospitable place, allowing whatever aristocrat controlled the area to select the member of parliament instead of a vote by the people. The third piece dealt with corruption within the House of Commons itself. Rumors of bribery, kickbacks, and seats for sale were analyzed and corroborated.

Jack set down the quill and leaned back in his chair when Pippa finished. "This is…" He ran his hands through his hair.

"I know." Pippa refolded the newspaper, smoothing out its wrinkles. "I assumed the House of Commons represented the will of the people of England. But this…" She gestured at the row of newspapers. "This is some havey-cavey business."

Jack continued to write notes as Pippa worked her way across the table. Her soothing voice and the gentle scratching of the quill against paper were in stark contrast to the wretched corruption and undemocratic practices illuminated by *Democratiam Liberum*'s writing.

At last, Pippa picked up the final newspaper, delivered only this morning. "This looks familiar." She waved the paper in his direction.

"I suppose we ought to be grateful those cutthroats didn't bleed all over it?" Jack said wryly. Perhaps if they joked about last night's attack, they could prevent it from hanging over them like a dark cloud.

Pippa's wrinkled her nose at him before flicking open the newspaper. A furrow formed between her eyebrows as she scanned the piece.

"Did you read any of this last night?" she asked, her eyes still on the newspaper.

"No, it was too dark. Why?"

She shook her head. "This doesn't make any sense. It says, 'While under the spell of certain false assertions, this author penned many an article attacking the noble and hallowed institution of the House of Commons. After further study on the subject, it is clear the House of Commons not only represents the finest ideals of English representative democracy but is also a body made up entirely of moral men with only the good of the people in mind.'"

Pippa continued to read. Jack stared at the blank paper in front of him, unable to write a single letter down.

What did this mean?

Lydia had vanished three days ago. Without the articles, they hadn't a single lead to follow.

Jack tossed the quill onto the paper and pushed up out of his chair.

Pippa stopped mid-sentence. "You don't wish to hear the rest?"

He paced the dining room. "I don't know. I don't know what to do. I don't know where to look. I don't know if it was wise putting faith in the Bow Street runners." He ran his hand over his face. "How can we find her? Where has she gone? *Where's my sister?*" His voice rose in volume until he was shouting.

Pippa's eyes widened.

Jack's chest rose and fell like bellows. He wanted to break something. He wanted to punch someone.

He was *failing*.

He was inept, just like his parents. He swallowed hard against the lump in his throat. "Please leave."

"Leave? But—"

He cut her off with a slash of his hand through the air. "Pippa, please."

The hurt in her eyes as she gathered her basket caused his chest to ache with regret, but he couldn't allow her to stay. He couldn't allow her to see him like this, felled by his failure.

She paused in the doorway. He felt her eyes on him, but he wouldn't meet her gaze.

"I'll be at the Adderly ball tonight," she said.

Jack nodded, eyes still averted.

Pippa's footsteps echoed through the hallway as she left him.

PIPPA LUNGED FORWARD, but her opponent knocked her *épée* aside and parried, forcing her back. Her sword blocked his advance, their two blades dancing in a blur of flicks, thrusts, and hits.

Pippa's chest heaved. Her feet carried her forward and back again and again as they fought for dominance. She feinted to the right, then with lightning speed, pressed forward on the left side, pressing the covered tip of her *épée* into *Señor* Martín's abdomen.

He backed up and pointed his sword to the floor.

"Well done, *señorita*." Her instructor smiled, his dark eyes crinkling at the corners. "You fence with a fire inside you today, *si?*"

Pippa wiped her damp brow with her sleeve. "I had…a difficult…morning," she said between deep gulping breaths.

She opened the window. Leaning against the sill, the breeze refreshed her heated face. *Señor* Martín had pressed her harder than usual today, but she'd been up for the challenge. He was right—she did have a fire inside her. It had been lit in Jack's breakfast room just a couple of hours ago.

Pippa ground her teeth together. Her view of the back garden was serene with birds chirping and leaves rustling in the breeze. Too bad its peace wasn't transferable. Inside, Pippa stormed with anger.

Jack had treated her abominably. He'd been rude, insufferable, and demeaning. He was completely illogical when it came to his sister and her articles.

Pippa bit her lip. The turnabout in the article's message today was significant.

Could it mean that Lydia—

Movement outside interrupted Pippa's thoughts.

"Jane," she called down to her cousin in the garden.

Jane shielded her eyes as she peered up at the house. "Oh, hello," she replied once she caught sight of Pippa. "I'm just filling a bucket with fertilizer. Meet me in my room in a bit?"

Pippa agreed, her anger cooling a few degrees.

She closed the window. *Señor* Martín explained the finer details of the passata sotto maneuver when a fencer dropped to the ground, planted a hand, and attacked from under the opponent's weapon. Pippa practiced the maneuver, knowing after her experience with the cutthroats last night that such moves could actually save her life. After thanking *Señor* Martín for the lesson, she journeyed down the hall to Jane's room.

Pippa wrinkled her nose. "What's that horrible smell?"

Jane grinned. "It's my new fertilizer. Isn't it wonderful?"

Pippa threw open the windows before answering. Thankfully, the stench of rotting fish, cow manure, and heaven knew what else dissipated with the help of a cross breeze.

"If by wonderful, you mean wonderfully vile, then yes, you're absolutely right."

Jane shook her head. "You have no appreciation for the hard work that goes into botany."

Pippa leaned against a worktable covered with plants. "I can definitely appreciate that Dev deals with the fertilizer instead of me."

Jane picked a spent flower off a plant and switched topics. "I heard your mother was quite worried about you last night. My apologies that my parents blew your cover."

Pippa shrugged. "It wasn't your fault."

"Was she terribly upset?"

Pippa joined her in plucking the dead flowers off the specimens. "I scared her. I didn't get home until well past midnight."

Jane turned, her mouth hanging open. "You were with Lord

Hartwick all that time?"

Pippa waved her hand. "It was nothing. After the Great North Road, I just snuck him into Lydia's room here to search for clues, we followed a lead to a warehouse near the docks, and then we fought off a band of thieves."

Jane laughed. "Right. And I was engaged in a mighty battle with a mutated flesh-eating plant until dawn."

Pippa tilted her head and shot her cousin a look.

Jane's smile dropped from her face. "Oh, you weren't teasing."

Pippa shook her head. "All true."

"Good gracious!" Jane lay her hand on her chest. "Pippa, how terrifying."

Pippa closed her eyes, remembering the feel of her blade slipping through the layers of the thief's clothing and flesh. She shuddered.

Jane took hold of her hand. "Were you or Lord Hartwick hurt?"

Pippa gave her cousin a gentle squeeze. "We escaped unscathed. But the thieves…" Pippa swallowed. "Well, I had to use my sword to fight them off. And Hartwick shot one of them."

Jane's fingers tightened around her own.

Pippa's stomach dropped. Perhaps she hadn't really processed all that had happened. There'd been the kiss, which proved quite distracting. Later she'd been so tired, and then her mother had descended upon her. And this morning, she'd been consumed by their investigation into the articles and then Jack's churlish behavior.

But truly, fighting for their very lives against the thieves had been a shocking, frightening incident.

Jane's brow furrowed in worry. "Do you want to talk about it more?"

Pippa shrugged.

Jane led her to a set of wooden chairs in the corner. "Tell me everything."

Pippa relayed the evening's events in detail, starting with their return to town from the Great North Road. She did skip the kissing, however. By the time she finished her tale of Jack's behavior this morning, her throat was dry from talking for so long.

Jane stared out the window, frowning. "Something about his actions this morning feels off. What did he say right before he demanded you leave?"

Pippa bit her lip, trying to recall his words. "He was getting agitated, saying he didn't know what to do next and asking where his sister was. Then he told me to get out."

Jane drummed her fingers on the top of her leg. "He didn't know what to do," she murmured.

Pippa could hear his voice echoing in her mind. *I don't know what to do. I don't know where to look. How can we find her? Where has she gone?*

She thought of Jack's usual self-control, need for command, and love of order. Maybe his reaction wasn't to her but stemmed from something else, something deep inside him.

Pippa had struggled with her terror of strangers and leaving her house for years because of her past. Perhaps it was the same for Jack. Perhaps he had a secret, some pain he kept locked away, and he was reacting to it now because he couldn't control things.

Pippa leaned back in her chair.

"I think," she said slowly, "that perhaps his actions weren't about me at all. I think it was about *him*, about something he hasn't revealed yet."

Jane pursed her lips. "That's a sound hypothesis. Now you have to test it."

"Test it?" Did everything turn into a science experiment with her cousin?

"Are you two meeting up today for more investigating?"

Pippa groaned. "I promised my mother I'd attend the Adderly ball tonight. It was the only way to appease her after I was gone for so long yesterday."

Jane eyed Pippa thoughtfully. "This might be the perfect opportunity. In a social setting, it's completely natural to engage in conversation about things other than missing sisters. Send him a note. Tell him to meet you at the ball. Say you must discuss the investigation. And then ask him questions about his past, his family, and his relationship with Lydia. If you can uncover what's in his past, then you'll know why he sent you away from his home."

Pippa stared down at her calloused palms. "It was only when you helped me see myself and see the way forward that I was able to change."

"Exactly," Jane agreed. "And if he can't move forward," she added, her voice grim, "then the likelihood of you two working together to find his sister evaporates quicker than damp soil on a summer day."

Chapter Twelve

J ACK WAS PLAYING spy.

The rooms at Whites provided ample opportunity to sedately stroll, listening in on quiet conversations and peeking at the betting book. After finishing his promenade through the club, Jack sighed in relief. No one was speaking of his sister's absence.

He sank into a chair. A servant promptly arrived with a brandy, newspaper, and promises of a meal.

Jack sipped his brandy, trying to relax the tight band of tension around his chest. He swirled his glass, watching the amber liquor spin in circles, getting nowhere. Just like his life.

Clearly his fear over his sister's disappearance was giving him a case of the blue devils. It had nothing to do with Pippa, whom he'd treated so abominably that morning. And it certainly had nothing to do with the structure and rules he'd created for his life. The structure was as necessary as air. He'd seen what happened when people did as they pleased without care or concern for their obligations, their duty, or the well-being of those in their charge.

He shook his head and distracted himself with the newspaper, flinching when he spied the latest *Democratiam Liberum* article.

"Might as well," he mumbled.

The first part sounded familiar from Pippa's read-aloud that morning: praise for the hallowed institution of the House of Commons, mention of the honorable men who served not only their boroughs but also the great nation of England, and other fawning compliments.

Jack frowned.

This really was a complete reversal for *Democratiam Liberum*. Could the author truly have had an awakening as claimed in the opening? Or was something nefarious underfoot?

Jack continued reading. *And this year alone, the industrious House of Commons passed numerous acts to benefit the nation regarding tariff regulation, regulation of coal shipping, and habeas corpus. In addition to these acts and writs, we can add the Statute of Militia edicts Regulating Services, etc. & Taxation. Truly, the House of Commons is prodigious in its dedication to protecting England and its citizens and preserving its finest institutions.*

Jack reread the paragraph. Not only was its tone strange, but it mentioned something called the Statute of Militia edicts Regulating Services, etc. & Taxation. As a member of the House of Lords, he knew every act passed by parliament, and this wasn't one of them.

Inventing an act of parliament because the author was too lazy to conduct basic research? Clearly, the author was an idiot.

Lydia was no idiot. She couldn't be *Democratiam Liberum*. Jack's shoulders relaxed.

He hadn't realized how much doubt Pippa had cast in his mind. It seemed he'd actually entertained her outlandish theory because now that he had evidence to the contrary, he was filled with relief.

Lydia was intelligent. She valued accuracy and precision. She'd never fabricate an act of parliament from thin air. Jack folded the newspaper and tossed it across the table.

"I say!"

Jack's head shot up. His friend Benedict sat across the table, glowering as he lifted the newspaper off his arm.

"Apologies," Jack said. "Didn't see you there."

"Well, that's a fine thing to say to a friend. As if I were an aging mistress you only kept around out of pity." Benedict grabbed Jack's glass of brandy and belted back a mouthful.

Jack gave him a pointed stare.

Benedict grinned. "Tell me, how's your sister? Thought I might send around a bouquet of flowers from my hothouse."

Jack narrowed his eyes.

"To help cheer up her sickroom," Benedict clarified. "That's all. Damn, old man, you're pricklier than a porcupine these last few days. Are you certain there isn't more going on?"

Jack's breath caught in his throat.

"Aha!" His friend pointed a finger at him in triumph. "I knew there was something else. Tell your Uncle Benedict everything."

"There's nothing—"

Benedict interrupted, lifting his index finger. "It's a woman, isn't it?"

Jack attempted to school his features, but something must have given him away.

"Now who is she? You haven't gone and stolen my lady love, Mrs. Smythe the housekeeper, have you?"

"Yes, that's it," Jack replied dryly, glad his friend's attempts to uncover the truth had been usurped by his sense of humor. "I'm applying for a special license on the morrow."

Benedict laughed.

A servant arrived with his meal, and Jack made a show of checking his pocket watch. "Do me a favor and take over here?" He rose from the table. "I just recalled a prior engagement."

"But—"

"Must dash off. Goodbye." Jack strode out of the club, guilt nipping at his heels. But what could he do? Deception wasn't his strong point, and he couldn't risk his friend uncovering the truth about Lydia... or his situation with Pippa.

Jack began walking toward home.

What *was* the situation with Pippa? He certainly needed her for the investigation. She had an instinctual understanding of his sister and was the most observant person he'd ever met.

He definitely owed her an apology after his terrible behavior that morning.

And the truth of the matter was…he desired her.

Pippa's kisses last night had enflamed him. Even though it was unwise, even though she was a lady—and likely untouched—he wanted her.

His breeches felt tight at the mere thought of her. How she'd pressed her round bottom against him behind those barrels. The taste of her lips when she'd turned in his arms. The quiet moans of pleasure she'd made in the back of her throat…

Jack blinked as the butler opened his front door. The walk home has passed in a blur.

"Your man requested I tell you he's returned from his errand, my lord," the butler said.

Jack nodded and hurried up the wide staircase to his bedroom. His valet was in his dressing room, arranging a pile of freshly starched cravats.

"Thorpe, what did you find?"

"I had a time of it, my lord, seeing as how I'm not chummy with any of the men working down at the newspaper. But," Thorpe paused to waggle his eyebrows, "turns out they have a few women in their employ. So, I turned on my old charm, and out spilled the secrets, easy as pie."

Thorpe leaned back on his heels in satisfaction.

"What did they tell you?"

"Well, it turns out the editor-in-chief's the only one that handles the special articles from *Democratiam Liberum*. Makes a big to do about it being classified. The lass I spoke to said a little street urchin arrives like clockwork, delivering a message to the editor, and then what do you know? An hour later, the editor delivers the *Democratiam Liberum* article to the printers."

Jack frowned. "So, no one knows who *Democratiam Liberum* is or where she lives?"

"Where *he* lives, you mean?"

"Right, that's what I said." Jack's face heated.

Thorpe eyed him before continuing. "It's completely hush-

hush. With all the hullaballoo over *Democratiam Liberum*, the men at the newspaper are placing bets on his identity. There's quite a fat purse for the one who uncovers the truth. But so far, no one's cracked it."

Jack exhaled.

None of this mattered. He'd ruled Lydia out as the mystery writer behind the *Democratiam Liberum* articles. And yet... it niggled at the back of his mind.

A knock at the door interrupted his thoughts. "Come."

A servant entered the room with a note on a silver tray. Jack broke the seal.

I must speak to you. Please come to the Adderly ball tonight. –P

Jack's heart skipped a beat.

He turned to his valet. "Have my evening clothes ready for tonight. I've a ball to attend."

⇶⬻

PIPPA CIRCUMNAVIGATED THE ballroom, her eyes roving the throngs of well-heeled aristocrats. She searched through the couples floating across the dance floor, between clusters of gossiping matrons, and around young ladies smiling over their fans.

Jack wasn't here.

Her cheeks burned, his rejection of her request to meet scalding her pride. She needed to talk to him, to unravel the mystery of his actions.

And more than that, she needed to see him, needed their eyes to connect across the room, needed his lips to twitch from a shared amusement.

Pippa's gaze fell upon the double doors open to the terrace. Perhaps he'd sought reprieve from the warmth of the crowded ballroom.

Pippa wove her way through the throng, accepting a glass of champagne from a passing footman. She sipped, savoring the tickle of bubbles.

Heads tilted together as she passed, engaging in the ancient art of gossip.

"…used to hide in the corners and leave early…"

"…heard her mother forces her to attend or she'll lose her dowry…"

"…quite a pretty girl, if she'd smile more…"

Pippa's hand convulsed around the delicate stem of her champagne glass. She lifted her chin. Meeting the eyes of the gossipers as she passed, most looked away, unable to match the ferocity of her gaze.

Yes, she knew she was the object of speculation. Where'd she been all those years? And if she were to tell them, to stride up to their little clusters of catty whispers and announce she'd witnessed her father's murder and it had scared her, what then? Would they press their hands to hers and offer their condolences? Or would their eyes widen in horror at this new affront to their tender sensibilities—the unimaginable horror of plain, honest talk?

At last, she passed through the gauntlet of gossip to the double doors. They opened to a stone terrace with a staircase on one side leading down to the garden.

Several torches cast flickering light across the various couples seeking privacy outside. Soft murmurs and intimate laughter intertwined with the muted strains of the orchestra.

Her breath caught as her gaze landed on him.

Jack.

His back was to her, his black jacket perfectly tailored to his broad shoulders. The torchlight burnished his hair.

Heavens, she was a ninny, but just seeing him, just knowing he was here eased something tight inside her. The tension came from her fear of being among people, from the gossip, but it was older than that. It felt ancient, it had been with her so long.

But when she was with him—

Jack shifted to the side, revealing his companion. A petite woman in a deep scarlet dress smiled up at him, her eyes slumberous as she ran a finger up his sleeve.

Pippa's chest seized.

He murmured something to the woman, and she threw her head back and laughed, the deep expanse of her bare cleavage jiggling with her movements.

A creature, red and ferocious, clawed at Pippa's tender insides. She had to get away. The anonymous darkness of the garden beckoned, and she dashed across the terrace to the steps.

"Pippa."

At the sound of her name, she broke into a sprint.

She couldn't see him. She couldn't meet the woman with the red dress and knowing eyes. She couldn't fake her way through small talk while daggers sliced her to shreds. She knew she was overreacting, that she hadn't the right to such possessiveness. But last night as they'd kissed, her first taste of such intimacy, something inside her had changed.

Something that couldn't be undone.

And so, she had to get away. Deeper into the garden she ran, the sounds of the ball vanishing behind her.

She rounded a hedge and ran full force into someone.

She staggered back. Arms reached out to steady her.

"My dear girl, are you quite all right?"

Pippa froze.

The scent of spirits wafted off the tall, slender man with blond hair. He smiled, revealing an inordinate amount of teeth.

"Well, this is my lucky evening." He eyed her slowly. "Here I was wishing for a pretty girl to stroll with me through the gardens, and *voila*." He released her arms and gave a flourish with his hand.

"I must return." Pippa inched backward.

"Nonsense. We've yet to acquaint ourselves. I'm Lord Westerly, your humble servant." He bowed gracefully then took her hand in his. "And may I have the pleasure of your name?"

"I'm…I'm needed back at the ball," she stuttered, unease swirling in her stomach. She didn't know why the man set her on edge, but she trusted her instincts.

"Certainly." He flashed his teeth once more. "I'd be honored to escort you."

Pippa's shoulders relaxed an inch. She fell into step beside him as they headed toward the house.

"These events can be so tedious," he said, his voice smooth as gossamer, "but then *you* came along." Westerly's feet slowed. "It's almost as if fate conspired for us to meet."

Pippa kept walking, but he clamped down on her arm, holding her in place. "I'd hate for this opportunity to pass us by," he whispered.

The familiar weight of her reticule dangling from her wrist steadied her nerves. It would be the work of mere seconds to have her dagger in her hand.

"You are so lovely." He leaned forward.

"Stop." She raised her free hand and pushed against his chest.

"But my darling," Westerly murmured, his eyes glittering in the faint light, "why else would you be wandering around in the dark garden alone if not in search of this?"

His hand snaked around and cupped her bottom, pulling her flush against him. His mouth dropped, grinding her lips against her teeth.

Pippa's heart stuttered. She shoved, but he was as immovable as a mountain. The noxious fumes of his earlier drinks engulfed her. She fought the bile rising in her throat.

Pippa bit his lip. As he reared back in shock, she tore into her reticule and pulled out her knife.

"You bastard," she spat, stepping back.

She brandished the knife at him, and his eyes widened as he took in the weapon and the ease with which she held it.

"You don't get to touch women because *you* want to." Her hand was steady despite the rush of blood through her veins.

"You don't decide why a woman might be in the garden at night. It's certainly not for *your* pleasure."

Westerly's gaze darted between the knife and her face, and she could see the moment he decided she was bluffing. He stepped forward, his arms coming up as if to grab her.

She flipped the dagger into the air and caught it with practiced movements, her eyes on him all the while.

"Try it," she whispered, "and you'll wear the scars for the rest of your life."

He blanched, his arms freezing mid-air.

Pippa's teeth ached from clenching her jaw.

She raised her left hand to her mouth and took the tip of her glove between her teeth. She wriggled her hand until she'd pulled free of the white fabric. Taking the glove from her mouth, she stepped forward, careful to keep the knife in his line of sight.

And she slapped him across the cheek with her glove.

"Swords at dawn." Her soft words landed like a felled tree in the silence of the night.

Westerly gaped. "I don't...what do you..."

"I've just challenged you to a duel." Her hot surge of satisfaction surprised her, and she thought of *Señor* Martín and his love of dueling. She could understand it now.

The man adopted an affronted air, adjusting the cuffs of his jacket as if she were responsible for mussing him. "Clearly you're insane." He sniffed. "Women don't duel."

A rustle sounded from the bushes to the side. "But I do."

Pippa stiffened at the familiar voice. A figure emerged from the shadows.

"It's clear you have disrespected this lady." Jack approached their little tableau, her with a glove in one hand and a knife in the other while Westerly had frozen, mid cuff adjustment. "And I demand satisfaction."

"No," Pippa protested, her cheeks burning as outrage and longing waged a mighty battle. "*I* challenged—"

She stopped mid-sentence at his searing glare.

"Westerly, I'll send my second to your residence in an hour's time."

The man gaped once more. "But I—"

"Don't." Jack's voice was arctic. "I've seen her fight, and I'd hate for you to be carved up before I get a chance to shoot you."

Jack held out his hand to her. "Come."

Pippa went to him, having time for only a quick peek over her shoulder before he pulled her around the shrubbery and out of sight of bug-eyed Westerly.

"I can defend myself," she hissed at Jack, nearly trotting to keep pace with his long, angry stride.

He didn't reply.

"I didn't need you to rescue me. I had him at knifepoint."

He stopped abruptly, spinning her around to face him. "Did he hurt you?" The fierce growl of his voice was at odds with his look of tender concern. He ran his hands up her arms and over her back and shoulders as if checking for injuries.

Pippa's skin sang under his gentle touch.

"He kissed me."

Jack's hands froze.

"But I stopped him before he could do more."

His hands relaxed. A long exhalation tickled the fine hairs at Pippa's temples.

Slowly, he pulled her closer, the light pressure on her back so different from the forceful grasp she'd experienced only minutes before. She could pull away with the slightest movement.

If she wanted to.

"Pippa," he whispered, her name like a benediction.

He stared at her mouth, and her heart sang. Instead of kissing her, though, he pulled away with a sigh.

"I'm taking you home." He engulfed her hand in his. He led her along the side of the house and through a gate. Slipping through the shadows between the queue of carriages, they came to a coach emblazoned with his family crest. Jack opened the door for her, and as she clambered in, she could hear his muffled words to a footman.

Jack entered the carriage and sat beside her.

"I've sent your mother a message that you fell ill and are going home." He gave a rap to the roof, and the carriage lumbered into motion.

The last remnants of hot exhilaration from her duel challenge faded away. Pippa shivered.

Jack wrapped his arm around her, pulling her close. "Better?" he murmured against her hair.

She nodded, inhaling his clean, masculine scent. She closed her eyes and nestled against his shoulder.

"Why did you run off into the garden alone?" he asked.

Her eyes flew open.

JACK FELT PIPPA stiffen beside him.

"I felt like some fresh air," she said pulling away.

He felt bereft without her gentle weight against him, but she was already pressed against the far side of the carriage, pulling her glove back on with jerky movements.

"Fresh air," he repeated, uncertain what to make of her coolness.

"It looked like the air around *you* was rather warm, though." She stared out the window.

Jack's brows came down, then he recalled how Lady Wayland had cornered him on the terrace, running her finger along his arm while boldly undressing him with her eyes.

As she was a friend of Benedict, he'd tried to extricate himself as delicately as possible…until he'd seen Pippa dash past. He'd followed her into the garden without a single word of farewell to the woman.

Pippa was jealous.

Warmth spread through his chest.

He traced a finger along the back of her neck and down the

exposed skin of her shoulders until he reached the edge of her silk gown.

"If there was any heat on that terrace, it didn't come from me," he murmured, feathering his fingers across the smooth skin at her nape.

Pippa shivered under his touch and leaned back toward him.

"That woman left me cold." He shifted closer on the bench.

Leaning forward, he pressed his cheek against the silky coolness of her hair. She smelled of flowers. Jack closed his eyes, the sound of their uneven breaths the only noise in the carriage.

"But there *is* someone who lights a fire in me," he whispered.

His fingers journeyed around the sides of her neck and traced her clavicles. Pippa arched her head back. A faint gasp escaped her lips as his fingers moved downward. Back and forth, he traced her skin, the satin texture delicate under his fingertips.

But he knew she wasn't delicate. She was a fighter. She was strength and power and fierceness wrapped in a silky, flower-scented package.

His fingers reached the sweet roundness exposed by her gown's neckline. Pippa's breath came in shuddery little gasps now. He kissed the side of her neck, and she moaned, her head thrown back completely against his shoulder.

"You are delicious," he whispered between feathery kisses along the column of her neck, the tender flesh behind her ear, the delicate ridge of her jaw.

And all the while, his fingers moved lower and lower until he reached the edge of her bodice.

He felt her hold her breath when his fingers paused, tracing the seam of her décolletage.

"May I?" he whispered into her ear.

Now *he* held his breath as he waited for her answer.

Pippa's head jerked in a nod, and heat seared his veins at the pleasure of her consent.

Slowly, slowly, his fingers dipped inside her bodice. He touched the delicate fabric of her chemise, the stiffer barrier of her stays. And then… his fingers reached the puckered tips of her breasts.

He groaned, cupping her more fully. "Oh, Pippa."

She pressed her breasts against his hands. "Jack," she sighed, shifting against her seat.

Smiling in wicked delight, he suspected she ached to be touched elsewhere as well.

He lightly pinched her nipples. She mewled her pleasure. He pinched harder, and she gasped. He ran his cheek against hers. She turned, and their mouths met. Her lips were soft and open in invitation. He kissed her, all the longing and desire inside him pouring forth from his lips to hers. His tongue traced the slick heat of her mouth, and he swallowed her moans of passion.

He never wanted to stop kissing her. He never wanted this carriage ride to end. He never wanted to leave her to shoot a man in a duel.

The thought was a handful of snow down the back of his jacket. Jack stilled, his hands on her breasts, his lips pressed to hers.

A man had touched her without her consent. Jack had issued a challenge. There was much to do—ask Benedict to be his second, pick the place, and check his pistols.

He could die.

Jack eased his hands out of her bodice and shifted away on the bench.

"Jack?" Her voice trembled.

For a moment, he hated himself for what he'd done, for starting something he could never allow them to finish. "I'm sorry." The words sounded trite, but he couldn't think of others to offer.

She jerked back as if he'd slapped her. "You're sorry? *Again?*"

Jack winced. He'd apologized after their kiss behind the barrels last night as well. Damn, it seemed he was consistently making a hash of things with her.

Pippa narrowed her eyes as his silence dragged on. "I see."

He couldn't let her think he regretted touching her. "No, I—"

She held up a hand. "I don't want to hear another word."

They rode in silence. Jack wavered between reliving the bone-deep pleasure from just moments before and tension over thoughts of not only the duel ahead but also the fact that he'd hurt her. Again. And they'd never even had a chance to discuss why she'd asked him to meet her at the ball in the first place.

The carriage slowed to a stop. Pippa maneuvered around him to the door. "Jack, about Westerly. I really think I—"

"No. That bastard is for me to deal with."

She stared at him, confusion, hurt, and anger swirling in her blue eyes. Her face hardened, and she exited the carriage. He watched until she disappeared inside her house.

"Where to, sir?" asked the footman at the open carriage door.

"Home."

There was much to be done.

Chapter Thirteen

PIPPA SHIMMIED ALONG the tree branch, glad she'd worn gloves to protect her hands from the rough bark. The light of the moon limned the leaves in silver shadows. Just a little further, a little squirm, and….

Her fingers gripped the balustrade around the small balcony. With controlled movements, she swung herself off the branch, landing on silent feet. She froze. Listening intently, she exhaled in relief when she heard only the quiet of night.

She'd waited in the yard for an hour after the lights had been extinguished. Patiently. It had been a long, cold hour, but each minute that passed increased the likelihood he was asleep.

And each minute that passed had been time to reconsider her plan. But she needed to do this. To live without fear, she needed to fight her own battles, scandalous though they may be.

Pippa crept to the window. Slowly, carefully, she pushed up on the glass, closing her eyes in gratitude when it lifted. Her male garb allowed her to easily maneuver into the dim bedroom, the embers in the fire providing a faint glow.

The room was spacious. The shadowy outlines of furniture suggested a dresser, desk, and pair of chairs by the fireplace.

And a bed.

A large, masculine bed containing a large, masculine figure supine in sleep. The soft, easy breaths confirmed he slumbered.

Pippa tiptoed across the thick carpet. She stared down at Jack, the contours and planes of his face relaxed as he slept. In a moment of clarity, she realized that he always—except in the peaceful darkness of sleep it seemed—carried a measure of strain on his face. She could easily picture the small pucker of worry between his brows or a tightening at the corners of his mouth.

But now there was only peace.

What burdens did he carry throughout his waking hours that pinched him so?

Pippa frowned, realizing she'd never confronted him about his behavior in the breakfast room. And she'd completely forgotten to dig into his past to learn what shaped him into the man he was today. Would he even ask her about her reason she'd invited him to the ball? They'd both been a bit preoccupied, what with the lady in red, the garden incident, the glove across Westerly's face—

Yes, Westerly. The reason she was here. She took a deep breath, finding her inner center of calm like *Señor* Martín instructed before a fencing bout.

Praying Jack was a deep sleeper, Pippa tucked her gloves into her waistband and uncoiled the length of rope strapped to her side. With fingers light as thistledown, she tied one end around his wrist.

She smiled, remembering her young brother's enthusiasm for tying knots.

"And this one will never, ever come undone," he'd pronounced after demonstrating a complicated loop, twist, and loop.

Thank goodness for little brothers and their obsession with playing pirates.

She tied the other end to the post at the top of Jack's bed, then prowled to the other side to repeat her work. Both arms were now tied, one to each corner of the bed, with enough slack for comfort but not enough so he could reach one hand with the other.

Jack stirred.

A lock of hair fell over his brow, and she could no more stop her hand from smoothing it back than she could stop the sun from rising in two hours' time.

His hair was soft as rabbit's fur beneath her fingers.

She knew she should leave. Staying was the height of folly. Exhaling, she tried to push the wanting away, but it didn't leave her.

And so, allowing the inevitable to pull her to the bed like the very force of gravity, she sat beside him and ran her hands through his thick locks.

His eyes fluttered.

She stilled, her fingers entwined in his hair.

Jack's eyes found her, and a spark lit in their sleepy depths.

"A dream," he murmured, raising his head.

She leaned down to meet him, lips pressing against lips. She twisted so she lay alongside him, stroking his cheeks, his jaw, the strong column of his neck with her fingers. All the while, they kissed.

This kiss was so different from the hurried passion that had exploded in the carriage. This was slow and leisurely—an exploration. His tongue traced the seam of her lips and she parted for him, their mouths meeting in a slow tangle. Lazy, drugging kisses filled her senses, filled every empty place in her heart.

This.

This was what she wanted.

He moaned, his chest and shoulder muscles bunching as he moved his arms.

As he *tried* to move his arms.

"What—" He jerked, and Pippa pulled back, regret constricting her like a punishing corset.

Jack's head swiveled, taking in the ropes. "What have you done?" he growled.

Pippa shivered, pulling away. "I cannot let you duel that man."

His arms flexed as he pulled against his bonds. "Pippa."

"*I* challenged him." She slid off the side of the bed. "*My* honor was impugned by his actions." Her hands clenched at her sides. Already, the soft coolness of his hair through her fingers felt like a distant memory.

"I cannot let you fight him," Jack said, teeth clenched. He continued to pull at the ropes.

"What I do is not up to you." She felt the truth of her words once spoken. She had to do this, to show the fear no longer ruled her. If he fought her battle for her, she'd never know if she had truly conquered her past.

"*I* will duel this man. *I* will win. *I* will regain my honor. And then," she stepped closer, "I will return to release you."

She ran her hand along the rope, pulled taut with his straining. "Please don't pull so tightly. I don't want you to hurt yourself."

His eyes flashed in the darkness. "Pippa, please release me. *Please.*"

The note of fear in his voice—fear for *her*—almost tempted her. But no. Untying him wasn't an option. Better to leave quickly before his concern swayed her actions.

"I assume Hyde Park at dawn?" She pulled her gloves on.

He jerked his head to the side, but his startled expression confirmed this duel was to be conducted at the usual place.

She glanced around the room, spying his clothing from the night before draped over a chair. She eyed his hat and great coat. They would suffice. She pulled his hat low before checking that her hair was tucked up inside. Sliding into his coat, she tugged the high collar to shield her face.

"I'll be sure it's returned to you in mint condition," she promised from behind her mask of shadow.

He glared at her in stony silence.

One last thing to do. She pulled a handkerchief with her embroidered initials out of her pocket, making sure he saw it before tossing it to the floor.

"Do us both a favor and don't call for help. If your servants find you tied up and my handkerchief here, my reputation will be ruined forever."

He swore, quietly and profusely.

"I'll be back soon, and then we can plan our next steps to find Lydia." With one last glance over her shoulder, Pippa climbed out the window.

⠀⠀⠀⠀

"I'LL DOUBLE THIS if you wait," Pippa told the hackney driver, deepening her voice. She dropped coins into his hand.

He grunted his assent before reclining in his seat and pulling his hat down over his eyes.

Pippa climbed the hill, the two *épées* clanging against her legs. Pausing as she neared the top, she adjusted the borrowed hat and coat. She had to cover her face as much as possible if this was to succeed. Only the faintest pearly glow on the horizon indicated the approach of dawn. If she could convince them to start right away, the dark would assist her disguise.

She'd put lifts—scrounged from an old dress-up box in her brother's room—in her boots and worn several layers under her jacket, increasing her height and bulk. But would it be enough?

Please let it be enough.

Pippa drew a deep breath to steady her nerves, then crested the hill.

Two men stood off to one side, barely visible in the darkness. They passed what appeared to be a flask back and forth. Near the carriage, another man paced. He pulled his pocket watch out and glanced around before spying her on the hill. He raised a hand in greeting.

Pippa strode toward him, lengthening her stride. She tilted her hat, so it was even further down her face.

"Hello, old man," the gentleman greeted, squinting at her. "I knew you wouldn't cry off, but you're cutting it a bit close, eh?"

Pippa shrugged.

The man—presumably Jack's second—gestured toward the carriage with his thumb. "The surgeon is sleeping." He leaned forward. "Are you sure you want to do this?"

Pippa nodded.

He shook his head and sighed. "Where are your pistols?"

"Swords," Pippa rasped.

"Bloody hell, have you come down with a cold? Got it from Lydia I'd wager. Well, I'll go sort it out with Westerly."

The second held his hand out, and Pippa stared, uncertain. Did he want to shake her hand for good luck?

"They'll want to inspect the weapons." He jerked his hand in impatience.

Pippa pulled both *épées* from their sheaths. He trotted over to Westerly and his second, who was looking a little wobbly on his feet. Hopefully, the wretched lecher hadn't imbibed as much as his companion. It wouldn't do to duel someone incapacitated by drink.

Pippa shook her head. Men were such imbeciles sometimes.

Jack's second trotted back. "Westerly agreed to swords."

Pippa nodded, relieved. She hadn't even considered that he might demand pistols which she had no experience in.

Pippa took her *épée* back from the second. She swung and lunged a few times to warm up her arm. She gave the gentleman a nod and started toward Westerly.

"Um, the tip?" he called after her.

Pippa froze.

She raised her *épée* and slowly removed the protective tip at the end. The little device ensured no one was injured during training and practice activities. She swallowed. She'd never taken one off before. Her parasol sword didn't have one. Unease slithered along her spine. Pippa glanced at Westerly and his pompous, smirking, toothy face. Oh no, he was not getting away with it.

Pippa tightened her grip on her *épée*. She gave the second a nod. He peered at her through the early morning gloom, his mouth screwed up in consternation.

Oh, merciful heavens, was he beginning to question her identity?

Throwing her shoulders back, Pippa strode to the center of the field, trying to radiate confidence. Westerly approached, a lurid grin across his face.

"I say, Hartwick, based on what I've seen at the fencing club, I'm surprised you picked swords." He brandished the *épée*, completing a series of flashy maneuvers.

Pippa recalled *Señor* Martín's words. *A peacock does not win a fight with a wolf.*

She must be the wolf. She would use her fencing skill and her anger at what this man had done to her to get past his showy twirls and cut him down to size.

She could do this. She *had* to do this. For all women who should be safe at a ball or walking in a dark garden. And for herself.

Pippa raised her sword in front of her face in salute, and he followed suit.

She took her position. Standing sideways, she spread her feet with her right arm holding the *épée* in front while her left arm stretched behind her.

"*En garde*," she rasped.

Westerly lunged and she parried, deflecting his sword. He twirled around and lunged again, his movements large and showy.

Pippa easily parried his attack. She kept her movements precise and controlled. The clanging of metal-on-metal filled her ears, the sound as familiar as her mother's voice.

Footwork was challenging on the dew-covered grass, and the lifts in her boots didn't help the situation. Her foot slipped as she parried an attack. Westerly's *épée* darted past her defense as she wobbled, nicking her upper arm.

Pippa inhaled sharply. She'd never been injured from fencing before. The slice stung, but she pushed it aside. She had to win, otherwise, her identity would be discovered. She'd be unable to help Jack find Lydia. The stakes were too high for a little blood to stop her.

Focus, balance, speed. Señor Martín's words echoed in her mind, and she adjusted her stance to counter the wet grass.

Back and forth they lunged and parried. Her daily practice and sessions with *Señor* Martín held her in good stead. Her thoughts narrowed until all she saw, all she knew, was the clash of *épée* against *épée*, the feint, lunge, and parry of this dance.

"You can surrender now if you wish," Westerly gasped, signaling his attack with obvious footwork. Pippa knocked his lunge aside.

"I make you the same offer." She kept her voice raspy.

Her arm was loose, the muscles used to the rapid flicks and twists. Underneath her layers of clothing, her skin was only beginning to dew from exertion.

Lunge, parry. Lunge, parry. Back and forth they went on the wet grass, the clanging of their blades echoing through the silence of the park.

Westerly was audibly panting now. His red face was clear even in the hazy dimness of dawn.

Pippa had seen enough. She knew he favored showy lunges over precise attacks. His left shoulder was often exposed. Although he had more force due to his larger size, he was sloppy and imprecise.

It was time to make her move.

"Women are not your playthings," she growled, feinting to the right.

He fell for her rouse, and she stabbed at his shoulder, slicing through the seam of his jacket but not touching his skin.

He started, clearly surprised by the hit.

"Don't touch them without their consent." She feinted, and once again he followed her sword, opening up his side. She lunged, slicing apart his jacket.

"Anywhere you go, I'll be watching you." Pippa picked up the pace, attacking with a vengeance now.

Her anger fueled her, the memory of his pawing hands and crushing lips lending speed to her feet and arm.

"I'll be there, in the shadows."

He fell back, struggling to defend against her onslaught.

"And if you ever…"

She sliced the seam on his other shoulder.

"…harm a woman again…"

She severed the buttons from the front of his waistcoat.

"…*I'll kill you.*"

She struck his *épée* from his hands.

Westerly froze, his empty hand outstretched. His clothes flapped about his body in neatly sliced tatters. Not a drop of his blood had been spilled.

Pippa leaned forward, pressing the point of her sword into his groin.

He gulped.

"Do you understand?" Her voice was alien to her, raspy, hard, and filled with icy savagery.

Westerly nodded.

"And you'll send a written apology to the lady."

"Y-yes."

The park began to glow with the approach of sunrise. Pippa had only moments until the light of dawn would pierce her disguise.

She stepped back and saluted the panting, red-faced pig with her *épée*. After collecting the second sword from the ground, she hurried across the hill where the hackney hopefully waited on the other side for her. She rotated her arms in small circles as she walked. The routine of cooling down after a bout was automatic after a year of training with *Señor* Martín. He was fond of predicting her muscles would knot up—turn into rocks, he'd tease—if she failed to stretch.

"I say, Hartwick," the second called.

She waved her hand in acknowledgment but didn't stop.

Once she was over the crest of hill, Pippa broke into a run.

She exhaled in relief when she rounded a cluster of trees and saw the hackney.

"Time to go," she said, rousing the snoring driver. She gave him Hartwick's address and clambered inside.

Pippa leaned back against the seat. Her fury-fueled energy vanished. Fine tremors wracked her body. Closing her eyes, she gulped shaky breaths of air.

Dear lord.

She'd dueled a man. She'd dueled and *won*.

This was different from the quick and dirty fight against the thieves in the alley with her sword stick. This had been a true duel. Premeditated. Intentional.

She'd fought for her honor, for her safety, and for herself.

And now she knew she could fight and win.

Eyes still closed, Pippa recalled another carriage ride so many years ago.

Snuggled between her father and mother as their coach rumbled along toward their country estate. Gunshots piercing the air. The carriage rocking to a halt.

Her father loading a pistol. Kissing her before leaving the carriage.

And then…

Pippa covered her face as if she could block out what her ten-year-old self had seen. Men on horseback, their faces covered. Loud bangs. The slumping figure of a man. Her father. On the ground. Fleeing horsemen. Screaming. Blood. Screaming that went on and on and wouldn't stop. Screaming that came from her mouth and filled her ears and her heart and her soul.

With a soft cry, Pippa jerked forward in the hackney seat, pressing her face to the window. She gulped in shuddering breaths, forcing her eyes to stay open, to see what was outside of *this* carriage.

London. Shopkeepers just setting out their wares. Maids with baskets. Horses.

No dead father on the ground.

And so, she rode, dry-eyed and staring until the hackney rolled to a stop in front of Jack's house.

Chapter Fourteen

J ACK EYED THE anemic morning light creeping through his curtains and swore.

Where was she?

He yanked half-heartedly on one of the ropes. He had to hand it to Pippa—the woman knew how to tie knots. After an hour of fruitless struggling, he'd realized the only way he was leaving his bed was either with the vexing woman crawling back through the window to release him or a servant finding him in his nightclothes beside her damning handkerchief.

When her head had vanished through the window over an hour ago, he'd almost shouted for his servants. But the thought of ruining her reputation forever had given him pause. For endless minutes, he'd wavered back and forth.

If he didn't call for help, she could be killed.

But if she won, then he'd have ruined her for nothing.

But ruination was a small price to pay for not being run through.

But he'd seen her with a sword, and she was actually quite good.

That had decided it. While his own fencing skills were middling at best, he'd witnessed her talent beating back knife-wielding thieves. Her lightning-quick movements and confidence with her blade all spoke of a highly-skilled fencer.

And so, he held his tongue.

But God, if anything happened to her…

He imagined her lying still and chalky on the grass, her heart pierced by that bounder's sword.

No!

No, he wouldn't allow it.

Gritting his teeth, Jack strained against the ropes. He needed to get to her. He needed—

"Jack!"

At the muffled exclamation, he froze, opening one eye. Pippa loomed over him, reaching toward the ropes.

"Your wrists," she murmured, her eyebrows drawn together in concern.

He devoured her with his eyes, looking for blood, a scratch, any sign of injury at all.

When he saw none, the howling cries of fury and helplessness inside him quieted. He felt able to take a full breath for the first time since he'd realized his arms were bound.

"Untie me," he commanded.

Pippa pulled a knife out of her boot and sliced through the ropes.

He waited until she'd set the knife down on the nightstand, then his arms darted out, pulling her on top of him.

Pippa's eyes widened, but she didn't struggle.

"Don't you ever," he growled, "do that again."

And then he kissed her.

He poured every ounce of his feelings into the kiss—his fear, his helplessness, and his startling awareness of how very precious she'd become to him.

Her lips were soft and warm, and he clung to her, her weight on top of him a comfort.

She was here.

She was alive.

"I was so worried," he murmured between kisses. "I was so scared for you." The admissions slipped out unbidden.

"Jack." She pulled back to look at him, resting her hand on his cheek.

His eyes roamed her fierce, lovely face. Her soft touch and calloused hand against his cheek were somehow more intimate than the press of their entire bodies.

"If anything had happened to you…" He swallowed.

"I'm here." Her eyes lowered to his mouth. She licked her lips and then leaned down, pressing soft kisses against his.

He opened his mouth and nipped at her lips. Pippa opened for him, the slick heat of her mouth searing him.

The sweet taste of her only made him hungry for more. Jack trailed hot, open-mouthed kisses down her cheek to her jaw. He cursed the barricade of a cravat impeding his progress along her neck. He lifted her back enough to unwind the fabric. Each inch of newly-exposed skin cried out to be tasted.

"You are so beautiful," he murmured, tracing his lips along the long column of her neck and the little dip at the base of her throat.

"Jack." She ran her fingers through his hair and squirmed on top of him.

The press of her body inflamed him. His mouth was ravenous, returning to plunder the silky interior of her mouth. She moaned, the sound urging him on. Trailing his hand down her back, he cupped her derriere through her breeches. Her bottom was round and firm, the perfect shape for his hand. He squeezed. Pippa ground against him.

Lightning-quick, he rolled so he was on top. She gasped, then pressed her lips to his for more kisses. Their tongues swirled together, and he rocked his aching erection against the sweet cradle between her thighs.

Pippa moaned, swiveling her hips against him.

He pressed against her, showing her the rhythm, the cadence of a man and woman moving together as one.

Her eyes sparked with passion.

Need seared his veins at the pleasure of them grinding together, his cock rubbing her feminine core. He could feel the heat of her desire through their clothes. He thrust, wishing the layers between them would evaporate.

"Pippa," he whispered. "I want to touch you."

Her eyes fluttered open. "Yes."

Primitive joy at her consent raced through him. *Yes.*

He could touch her.

He could give her pleasure.

Time slowed as he rolled to the side and trailed his hand down her stomach. She quivered as his fingers slid to the placket of her breeches. He slipped the first button through the hole, taking his time to savor the act of undressing her. Her chest rose and fell with rapid breaths. He slipped the second button loose, then the third. He watched her all the while. She looked up at him through slitted eyes, her cheeks pink.

He slipped the final button through and slid his hand inside. Instead of drawers, his fingers encountered downy hair. She inhaled with a shudder at his touch.

Lightly, he stroked over her soft curls. He explored slowly, savoring each step, each touch, each new bit of Pippa she shared. His heart raced. Jack was a lantern, beaming brightly with unadulterated joy from being with her like this.

"You are so lovely," he whispered, sliding one finger between her folds.

She gasped, arching her hips toward him.

Softly he touched, allowing that one finger to gently explore her heat. His finger slid along her slick core, and he moaned at the proof of her desire.

"Oh, Jack," she gasped.

Lust pounded a mighty beat through him. Jack fought the urge to plunder, to take, to sink in deep. His cock strained against his breeches, aching for more.

He kissed her, the tangle of their tongues mimicking his fingers as he increased his touch, parting her seam. She was so responsive, her body growing even wetter with his caresses. She clutched his shoulder and opened her legs wider for him.

His fingers explored her secret terrain, finding her sensitive nub. She moaned, and he circled her there.

"Oh, Jack!" Her hips undulated against his touch.

"Pippa," he growled before kissing her again.

He ached to rip off his clothes and sink into her welcoming heat, but instead, he pressed himself to her hip, thrusting against her side while he continued to stroke the center of her pleasure.

He kissed deeply into her mouth as his fingers circled her faster and faster. Beneath him, she writhed and panted. His own breath was loud in his ears. Pleasure spread from his cock through his entire body as he ground against her.

He rubbed and flicked and lightly pinched, and Pippa's body grew tighter and tighter until she exploded in his arms, shuddering and moaning as she tipped into her release.

Her head was arched back, her mouth open wide as she became incandescent with pleasure. The sight of her orgasm and the sound of her wild cries pushed him over the edge.

With a shout, Jack's own pleasure shot through him. He ground against her hip, his release powerful as a volcano.

With a final shudder, he stilled, his fingers gentling as they came down from the pinnacle.

She panted, her eyes closed.

Jack swallowed. He tried to put the different parts of himself back together before she noticed he'd come completely undone by their shared passion.

Exhaling, he pulled his hand from her trousers. He kissed her softly before pulling her tight against him, one hand cradling her head against his chest while the other stroked her side and back.

Although his mind was a maelstrom of swirling thoughts, one fact was quite clear.

Things would never be the same again.

Pulling back, Jack shifted his weight onto one arm. He brushed her upper arm, and Pippa winced.

"What?" He stilled instantly, fear drying his mouth.

"It's nothing."

Jack rolled to the side and examined her arm. The sliced fabric revealed a cut along her upper arm.

"Blood hell," he said through gritted teeth. He reached for the edge of the jacket.

"I don't need—"

"You need to be quiet right now," he growled, "or I swear I'll send my servants for a surgeon—damn the consequences to your reputation—before I take off to hunt down that bastard and strangle the very life out of him."

She wisely shut her mouth.

"Unless you killed him already?" He flicked his eyes up from his work removing the jacket to see her shake her head.

"Pity," he murmured.

Jack eased the sleeve down her arm, pausing once when she hissed in pain. Her white shirt was wet with blood near the cut. He reached for the top button, but she stayed his hand.

"I can't disrobe in front of you," she said. "It wouldn't be proper."

Despite the maelstrom of fear and anger and worry swirling inside him, Jack's lips twitched. "There's little that's been proper between you and me."

Her expression softened. "That's true."

They remained still, her hand covering his where it rested against her shirt opening. Their eyes were locked together.

The world shrunk to the two of them on his bed, the gentle rise and fall of her chest beneath his hand the only movement in the entire world. He could fall into her eyes, blue like the sea at summertime, bottomless and mysterious. The callouses on her fingers gently stroked the back of his hand. Her scent—soap, flowers, and woman—filled his nose.

"Pippa, I—"

They both started at the sound of footsteps in the hallway. He untangled his hand, and the cool air of the morning against his skin instead of her warm touch felt inexplicably wrong.

"See if you can at least pull your arm out," he murmured as he threw on a banyan from the foot of the bed and dashed to the door.

Fabric rustled behind him even as he opened the door a crack. He instructed the maid in the hallway to send warm water and bandages to the room. "Just knock and leave them in the hall."

Then he locked the door.

One entry addressed and one to go.

Jack opened the door to his dressing room, quickly pulling it shut behind him. His valet was inside, brushing one of his jackets.

"I wish to sleep in today," he told Thorpe. "Please see I'm not disturbed for at least another hour." He left, shutting the door and turning the key before the man could reply.

"May I turn around?" he asked, face turned away from Pippa.

The rustling ceased from the bed. "Yes."

Jack turned.

He stared, his mouth going dry.

She'd pulled her arm out of the shirt sleeve, and the early morning light gilded the skin of her chest, shoulder, and arm. She'd kept the bottom half of the shirt buttoned and clasped the open top against her breasts. A gentle pink suffused her chest and traveled up her neck to her cheeks.

A knock at the door sounded. He found the hallway empty save for the requested items and a tray of food.

Once he'd ferried everything to a nearby table, he sat beside her on the bed.

"I'm going to clean the cut," he said, working to keep his voice even. Her exposed injury threatened his tenuous hold on his temper. The desire to hunt down that son of a bitch Westerly and pound him into oblivion beat fiercely against his restraint.

As he cleaned away the blood, he was relieved to see the cut was shallow. Likely, the bastard's *épée* had merely grazed her arm as the tip of his sword sliced her sleeve. Still, the red gash against her soft, delicate skin pained him, and he would take a thousand such cuts to spare her.

After a few calming breaths, he said, "I don't think you need any stitches."

She sniffed. "I told you it was nothing."

He reared back and pinned her with her gaze. "You were struck with a sword by a man who could have killed you," he said through gritted teeth. "Never say it was nothing." His heart pounded, and a hot fierceness lay claim to his very core.

No one could hurt her. No one would hurt her ever again, not while he drew breath.

Pippa stared for a moment, seeming to absorb a portion of his resolve. She nodded.

He finished dressing the wound and offered her his shirt from yesterday, still lying over the back of a chair.

"You wouldn't want to get the blood from your shirt on the clean bandage," he said gruffly, turning away.

The idea of her wrapped up in *his* shirt called to something primitive inside him. Something that wanted to grab her and say "mine". He shook his head. Despite this strange, elemental response he had to her, they were working together to find his sister. That was the extent of their connection when all was said and done.

Pippa cleared her throat. "I'm dressed."

Once again, she was fully garbed in her manly outfit, including his outerwear.

She pointed to his coat. "Mind if I borrow this?"

"Since it has your blood on it now, it only seems fair you keep it," he answered dryly.

She rolled her eyes before strolling to the window.

Something nagged at the back of his mind. "Pippa, why did you ask me to meet you at that ball last night anyway?"

She stilled, facing the open window. After a pause, she said, "I wanted to talk to you. I was mad that you'd sent me away earlier. I was hoping..."—her shoulders moved as if she'd drawn a deep breath—"I was hoping you'd share a bit more about yourself with me, so I could understand you better."

Jack's breath froze in his lungs.

Silence stretched between them. She was waiting, he knew, for him to speak. For him to open up. But no words would come.

Pippa sighed, the sound tinged with disappointment. "Thanks for patching me up." She slid one leg over before hesitating. "Would you really have strangled him if he'd hurt me?"

"I really would have."

She examined his face, seeming to search for something. He met her stare unwaveringly, although inside he felt small for his silence to her question. Pippa nodded as if coming to a conclusion, then pulled her other leg through the window and disappeared from sight.

Chapter Fifteen

L ONG, NIMBLE FINGERS stroked her breasts. Tingles shot down her chest to her very core. She moaned, pressing herself against his hands.

Jack's hands.

His lips brushed against her, and she opened for him, his taste now familiar. His slick tongue tangled with hers.

More. He complied.

"Pippa."

The world went hazy at the edges. *Don't leave.*

Jack's hand grew wispy, his mouth like fog. Where was he going?

"Pippa."

He was shaking her, his hand on her shoulder.

Her eyes fluttered open. It wasn't the languid face of her lover that met her gaze.

"Jane!" she screeched, jerking back.

Her cousin stepped back, her eyes glinting with humor. "Your mother said you'd likely be tired, but I didn't think waking you up would be like resurrecting a corpse."

Pippa blinked.

The sun streamed through the open curtains of her bedroom. She was in her rumpled night rail, and Jane, fresh in a lovely peach-colored day dress, stood at the side of her bed.

It had been a dream.

She ran her hand over her face, trying to cast off the last vestiges of her slumber. Had she spoken aloud? Her cheeks heated as she contemplated what her cousin might have witnessed while waking her.

"Was I…" Pippa cleared her throat. "Was I talking in my sleep?" She risked a peek at her cousin.

Jane shook her head. "You were a log. How late did you stay at the ball last night?"

Pippa recalled climbing through her window as the birds chirped an early morning welcome. She'd barely had the energy to don her night rail and stash her *épée* and male clothing before collapsing into bed.

"I don't even recall," she answered truthfully. "What time is it now?"

"It's past noon. You need to get up." Jane moved to one of the chairs by the window.

Pippa rolled out of bed, wincing when her arm brushed against the mattress. She'd best wear long sleeves today.

She poured water into a basin. "I know you love to see me, but I'm a bit surprised by the personal wake up."

"We are needed at the LCA." Jane paused. "It, ah, sounds urgent."

Pippa spun around, water dripping from her face. "What's going on?"

Jane toyed with the fabric of her skirt. "I'm not sure. I received a message from Lady Rowling this morning. She said all members needed to come. At once."

Jane finally looked up, her brow knit with worry. Pippa's stomach plummeted.

The LCA.

Oh, merciful heavens. Nothing could happen to it. Nothing *would* happen to it. It meant too much to her, to Jane, and to all the members.

Pippa rushed through the rest of her toilette. Jane was so

distracted she didn't even notice the bandage on Pippa's arm when she dressed.

They flew down the stairs.

"Hello, darling," her mother called out as they passed the sitting room. "Do come in and have a bit of tea."

Jane shot Pippa a look.

"Actually, Aunt Josephine, we are in a bit of a rush." Jane inched her way back from the doorway. "Emergency at the Ladies Charitable Association. We have to, erm, roll bandages for the militia. The need is quite urgent."

Pippa's mother frowned. "I didn't see anything in the paper about the militia. How strange." She began to shuffle through the stack of newspapers on the table in front of her. "Come and have a bite at least before you dash off. And Pippa, how's your headache?"

"Hm?" Pippa said before recalling Jack dashing her away from the ball last night with a message of poor health sent to her mother. "Oh, I'm feeling quite better this morning. But yes, terrible headache last night. I was so glad to get a ride home, with...ah..."

"Yes," her mother said, distracted as she continued to rifle through the newspapers. "A footman told me you'd taken our coach home, but don't worry, it had returned for me by the time I left."

Pippa slumped against the doorway in relief. All this deception and evasion was rapidly approaching a state of unsustainability. How could she keep all her stories straight? Lies to her mother, lies to Lady Rowling, and even lies to herself if she was being honest. But she wasn't being honest. How confusing.

"Well, I'm relieved to hear you're feeling better," her mother continued, flipping pages. "That's your second headache this week."

Jane glanced over, her eyes glinting with curiosity.

"I don't see anything about the militia in here, but there is another article by that *Democratiam Liberum* fellow." Her mother held up the newspaper. "It's all anyone could talk about at the ball last night. Such strange goings-on, with the House of Commons elections just next month. And now there are rumors about a certain Mr. Nathaniel Hinds—a coal investor—who some say will push to get laws favorable to his financial interests before the Commons. Although I'm certain such a thing would be impossible. It's a wonder men can decide which way to vote, what with all these people clambering for their attention and contradictory messages. Why Eugenia was just saying to me—"

"Mother, Jane and I must be off," Pippa interrupted.

Her mother sighed in exasperation. "Well, at least take a pastry along for the carriage ride."

Pippa darted over to grab a pastry, dropped a kiss on her mother's cheek, and then she and Jane were out the door and in Jane's carriage.

"So, another headache?" Jane raised an eyebrow as they rumbled down the street.

Pippa made a great show of examining her scone for currants. "Ah, well…"

Jane poked her in the ribs. "You were out again with *him* last night!"

Pippa rested her head back against the seat. "Last night was more of…a personal situation."

Pippa felt her cousin watching her. She sighed. Truly, she didn't have the energy to conjure another lie.

While the carriage rumbled to the LCA, Pippa filled her cousin in on the events of the previous night and early morning, omitting the private interludes that brought a blush to Pippa's face just from the memories.

He'd touched her.

There.

"A duel—good heavens!" Jane's eyes were round as guineas by the time she concluded her tale. "I'm…" She trailed off, staring at Pippa unblinking. "You've gone rather pink. Has rehashing all of this upset you?"

Pippa snorted. If her cousin only knew the thoughts racing through her head.

She stared out the window. "I'm not upset," Pippa finally answered. "In fact, I'm rather proud of myself. I fought off a vile lecher, I challenged him to a duel to defend my honor, I successfully impersonated Ja—Lord Hartwick, and I won."

Pippa turned to her cousin, full of wonder as what had happened really sunk in. "I *won*."

Jane took her hand and gave it a squeeze. "I'm proud of you too."

Pippa's chest felt tight. She squeezed Jane's hand in return. "All of this, I owe to you. If you hadn't sponsored me to join the LCA, I'd still be hiding at home."

The carriage stopped, and Pippa followed her cousin up the steps to the LCA. Jarvis opened the door a crack, his face granite. The butler poked his head out, looking left and right before opening the door fully and rushing them inside.

Several servants scurried by, arms full of piles of paper, brooms, or broken crockery. What in the world was going on?

Jane nudged her with her elbow and nodded to the end of the hall. Lady Rowling was frowning at Dev. The handsome servant spoke to the marchioness in a voice too quiet for Pippa to make out, but his agitated hand gestures indicated all was not well. Dev glanced up, his eyes lingering on Jane before he stormed away.

Pippa's stomach knotted.

She followed her cousin into Lady Rowling's sitting room. More members trickled in, each one looking bewildered and worried. Soon every member of the Ladies Covert Academy— except Lydia—was present.

Heads were together as ladies who studied mathematics, carved sculptures, and wrote plays whispered nervously. They all waited to hear the fate of their school, their community, and the one thing that gave them each meaning, satisfaction, and a feeling of completion.

Pippa clenched her hands on her lap.

At last, Lady Rowling swept into the fireplace mantle at the front of the room. Behind her trailed Meera, her face cast in stone.

Lady Rowling cleared her throat, but she already had every eye upon her. Her face was so pale it practically blended into her platinum blond hair.

"Thank you for arriving so promptly." She clasped her hands in front of her. "I have news of…" She paused, her throat working as she swallowed. "…news of a distressing nature."

The room was so silent Pippa imagined she could hear the blood racing through the veins of every woman present.

Lady Rowling continued. "Effectively immediately, the Ladies Covert Academy is closed."

Protests erupted throughout the room.

Pippa's head swam, and tiny spots floated across her vision.

This couldn't be happening.

Lady Rowling held up her hand for silence. Her face was a mask betraying no emotion, but her hand shook. "There has been a robbery. Many of you will find your rooms are in shambles."

Pippa glanced at Jane. She imagined her own expression was similar to her cousin's—a mix of disbelief, anguish, and anger.

Ladies began to call out questions, many rising to their feet.

Lady Rowling stepped forward and the women quieted once more. "It's no longer safe for you here. We don't know who did this or why, but there's a very real possibility of exposure of the LCA's true purpose—or worse." She swallowed. "Thankfully no one was harmed as the household was asleep and the intruders were very quiet. But we can't put any of you at risk by continuing our operation. I'm truly sorry."

She swept out of the room, and a cacophony of questions and exclamations erupted among the LCA members.

Pippa blinked, fighting back the heat gathering in her eyes.

The LCA was no more.

Meera circulated the room, murmuring instructions to the women to collect their belongings from their rooms.

Jane rose from her seat. "Let's go upstairs."

Pippa followed, her hand trailing on the familiar staircase railing. She wanted to wrap her fingers around the wood, dig her nails in, and cling to the posts. She wanted to cry and howl and kick her feet. She wanted to hide. She wanted to fight.

They opened Jane's door.

Her cousin gave a tortured cry at the scene of destruction before them. Plants on the ground, the pots smashed. Dirt everywhere, as if someone had dug through the soil in search of something. Tables overturned. Papers scattered and torn.

"Bloody hell," Pippa breathed, her stomach roiling.

She wrapped her arms around Jane. Her cousin's shoulders shuddered as she cried.

"All my research," she sobbed. "All my little plants—" She broke off, her voice too choked for speech.

Pippa heard footsteps in the hall and craned her head around. Perhaps Lady Rowling had come to explain? But it was the patroness's servant who approached, eyeing the weeping Jane with an anguished expression.

Dev lifted a hand as if to touch Jane's back in comfort, but he hesitated and dropped his hand to his side. Jane seemed to realize they were no longer alone, and she lifted her head from Pippa's shoulder.

"Miss Jane," he said, his voice nearly a whisper. "I am so sorry. This is all my fault—" He stopped abruptly and looked down at his hands. His neck moved with a swallow.

Jane stared at him in silence.

Dev's eyes glowed like stones flashing under the ripples of a stream when he finally looked up. "If you need assistance—any assistance at all—please know I will do all in my power to help you." He bowed. "Goodbye, Miss Jane," he whispered before disappearing down the hallway.

Jane pulled back from Pippa's arms. She wiped her sleeve across her face. "I...I think I'll try to salvage some of m-my work here." She drew a shuddering breath. "Why don't you check on your room?"

Pippa gave her arm a squeeze before slipping down the hall. She paused, her hand on the doorknob of the room where she'd spent countless hours training, both with *Señor* Martín and on her own, practicing again and again until she had each move committed to muscle memory.

She inhaled. Pippa turned the handle.

The wooden chest was overturned, her training clothes strewn about the room. Training mats were shredded, the padding spilling out from violent rents. Books on fencing strategy as well as *Señor* Martín's carefully written notes for exercises and training lay on the ground, trampled under the unknown marauder's feet.

Pippa leaned against the doorframe, uncertain her legs could hold her weight.

After a minute of deep breaths, she picked her way through the mess. She righted the chest, folding her training clothes into sloppy bundles before tossing them in. Next, she collected the books, smoothing out the pages.

Why was she even doing this?

With the LCA closing, this was no longer her training room. She couldn't bring her fencing gear home. How would she hide it from her mother or the servants?

Pippa opened the window, a light breeze cooling her face but doing little to assuage the fiery anger inside her.

It wasn't fair.

It wasn't fair her father had been murdered. It wasn't fair a little girl of ten witnessed such horror. It wasn't fair she'd lived with fear ever since, at times unable to leave the safety of her home. It wasn't fair she finally felt safe because of her training here, but it was being taken away.

She had to stop this.

The LCA could not close.

Pippa's eyes scanned the backyard, and she remembered Jack scaring her during her cool down and the deal they'd made.

Jack.

Just the thought of him sent her entire nervous system into a flutter. Pippa turned away from the window. Perhaps anger over the burglary and the LCA closure was better than this strange yearning for something she didn't fully understand.

Was Lydia's disappearance connected to the burglary?

The idea rolled around in her mind. There were no facts to support the theory, but the timing certainly suggested the two events were connected.

They must find Lydia.

If the people behind her disappearance would risk sneaking into a marchioness's guarded home and tearing up the place, then it was likely they'd have no qualms with harming a young lady with no one the wiser.

And if Lydia was recovered, safe and sound, and this threat to the LCA neutralized, then Lady Rowling would have to reconsider her decision to shut down the organization.

Pippa dashed down the stairs into the breakfast room where an assortment of fruit, pastries, and cheese sat on the sideboard, as was the custom. And at the end of the table lay the day's newspapers.

Snatching up an apple and slices of cheese, Pippa sorted through the stack until she found *Democratiam Liberum's* new article. Usually, a new piece was published every few days, but she remembered her mother commenting on a new article this morning.

She scanned it, then reread slowly line by line.

The House of Commons represents the will of the people, unlike the House of Lords which is comprised solely of inherited positions. Men of property from each borough are allowed to vote for their chosen representative for the Commons. This is fair and ensures the voice of the people has a place in England's government. Recent laws passed by the Commons prove that body's honor, commitment, and valor, such as the Estate Authorization Statute Tax. Other notable laws include...

Pippa tapped her finger against her cheek. For a second day in a row, *Democratiam Liberum*'s message was a complete reversal from the usual arguments. And although she didn't know the name of every parliamentary act, she couldn't recall reading anything about the Estate Authorization statute Tax.

The path ahead of her was clear. If she wanted to save Lydia and in turn save the LCA, she'd have to take this investigation to the next level.

Chapter Sixteen

J ACK SCOWLED THROUGH his carriage window at the sign on the stone building. *This* was where Pippa wanted to meet him for "a most urgent matter"? He pulled the note he'd received from her an hour ago out of his pocket and double-checked the address.

It appeared he'd be paying a call to the newspaper that printed *Democratiam Liberum*'s articles. Although they'd stumbled upon the manufacturing warehouse where the paper did its printing, the actual offices were in a more well-heeled part of town.

At least no murderous gang of thieves would accost them here, although, honestly, that hardly seemed likely to keep Pippa out of trouble.

He thought about last night, and his blood heated. The memory of Pippa's skin, warm and smooth, the wanton enthusiasm of her kisses, the abandon on her face when she'd found her release… And him, spilling in his night clothes like a randy school boy. She'd completely unraveled him.

Warmth spread up his cheeks.

Shoving open the carriage door, Jack jumped onto the sidewalk. It was stuffy in the carriage was all. He pulled out his pocket watch.

"Going to make me wear a hair shirt for being two minutes late?" asked a familiar voice.

Jack's heart leapt. He schooled his expression before facing her.

"Well, some consider it rude to keep others waiting." He hoped she didn't notice the ridiculous happiness radiating through him at her presence.

Pippa stared, her cheeks blossoming with rosy color. Her eyes dropped to his mouth.

Jack's skin was suddenly too tight for his body. The air didn't contain enough oxygen for his thirsty lungs. His eyes devoured her beautiful blush.

He wanted to haul her up against him, kiss her for hours, and lock her away from any dueling bastards who would slice open her precious skin.

Instead of suggesting they get naked in his carriage, he said, "I suppose you've cooked up some wild scheme involving the newspaper?"

The brightness in Pippa's eyes dimmed, and he looked away. "I decided to question the editor of the newspaper," she answered, her voice stiff. "I thought I'd offer you the courtesy of joining."

Jack shifted his weight from one foot to the other, feeling wretched for hurting her but needing to create distance between them. Distance was good. Distance kept him focused on what mattered—his sister.

"Lydia isn't the author of the *Democratiam Liberum* articles. I'm certain of it."

Pippa frowned. "What makes you so sure?"

"Yesterday's article mentioned an act passed by parliament, but the act doesn't exist. Lydia's very bright. She'd never take such shortcuts in research."

Pippa titled her head in consideration. "Today's article also mentioned an act I've never heard of."

"Well, clearly there's no need to question the newsp—"

She cut him off. "Perhaps it does have meaning though. The writer was always very accurate before." She tapped her finger against her lips. Her sweet, pink lips.

Jack forced his gaze elsewhere.

"Well, we're both here. There's certainly no harm in pursuing this lead, and we're running out of time." Pippa headed to the double doors of the newspaper office.

Jack caught up to her. "What do you mean, running out of time?"

Pippa's jaw tightened. "Lady Rowling is closing the LCA."

Jack halted. "What?"

She turned around, two steps ahead of him. "There was a burglary last night. The entire place was searched. Everything's in shambles, as if they were searching for something." She drew a deep breath. "Lady Rowling says it's not safe to continue the Academy."

A dozen thoughts chased each other around Jack's mind. Was this connected to Lydia? What would she say when she returned and found her group disbanded? And Pippa—what about her fencing? He knew it mattered a great deal to her. And those orphans they'd met the other day. Who would bring them pinafores and the world's ugliest booties?

Pippa's chin wobbled in obvious distress, and something cracked inside Jack's chest. He wanted to gather her close against him and say all would be well.

Instead, Jack took her hand. "I'm so sorry." Her fingers tightened around him. "When we find Lydia, perhaps it will convince Lady Rowling to reconsider."

Pippa's neck moved as she swallowed. She nodded before climbing the rest of the stairs.

Inside the offices, men bustled about a vast, open workspace, a score of desks strewn with paper and quills.

"Excuse me," Pippa called to a man with an ink-splattered cravat rushing by. "We wish to speak to the person in charge."

The man skidded to a halt. "You mean the editor-in-chief?"

Pippa nodded.

"Best of luck to you." The man jerked his head toward a

staircase and dashed off.

Pippa and Jack exchanged a questioning glance before picking their way through the melee to the stairs. At the top, a series of doors lined a hallway open on one side to the newsroom below.

"That one." Jack pointed to the furthermost door.

"How do you know?"

"It's the only one with a secretary posted out front."

A man with a sharp widow's peak eyed them with distrust as they approached. "May I help you?" he asked in a voice that implied he likely wouldn't.

Pippa offered a charming smile. "We wish to speak to the editor-in-chief."

The man sniffed. "Mr. Rumbold isn't to be disturbed."

Jack adopted a supercilious expression. "Please inform Rumbold that the Earl of Hartwick wishes to speak with him on an urgent matter."

The secretary's eyes widened. "Yes, my lord. Right away, my lord," he stammered, hopping up.

A moment later, he returned, gesturing to the door. "Mr. Rumbold will see you."

Jack followed Pippa inside the office. Rumbold sat behind a vast desk, its scarred surface peeking out between haphazard piles of paper, accounting books, old newspaper, and several abandoned teacups.

"To what do I owe the pleasure?" the editor-in-chief asked without looking up from a letter.

Jack cleared his throat. Rumbold finally glanced up, his blond eyebrows pulled together in annoyance.

"We have some questions for you," Pippa said. "About *Democratiam Liberum*."

Rumbold's annoyance transformed into appreciation as his gaze roamed up and down Pippa. Jack gritted his teeth.

The editor came around his desk and took Pippa's hand, bowing low to bestow a kiss upon her gloved knuckles. "It always brightens the newsroom when a pretty girl visits."

Jack pondered which would hurt more—a punch to the throat or a toss down the stairs.

Pippa disentangled her hand. "You are too kind."

"My secretary mentioned Lord Hartwick, but he failed to tell me your name, Miss…" He trailed off, his white teeth gleaming in his wide smile.

"Miss Jones."

Jack stifled a grin. He knew it was irrational to be pleased Pippa kept her true identity from this oaf, and yet pleased he was.

The editor finally looked at Jack. "So, you want to know about *Democratiam Liberum*."

"I've been tasked by a special sub-committee in the House of Lords to investigate the legitimacy of *Democratiam Liberum's* claims about the Commons." Jack decided to follow Pippa's lead and lie with impunity.

Rumbold frowned. "I haven't heard anything about this."

"It's very hush-hush." Jack peered down his nose. "I hope we may trust your discretion."

The editor shot him an incredulous look. "I run one of London's largest newspapers. Only a candidate for Bedlam would believe I'd be discreet."

Pippa laughed. "Oh, Mr. Rumbold, what a cut-up you are." She twinkled at him. "I'm certain we can count on you to wait until Lord Hartwick has finished his report, and then he'll grant you an exclusive story."

Rumbold perched on the edge of his desk, causing a landslide of papers. He was either too lost in thought to notice or didn't care. "Fine, I agree to your terms—my information on *Democratiam Liberum* in exchange for an exclusive…*before* the report is filed with the Lords."

Jack pretended to mull the deal over, then reached out for a handshake.

And he didn't even feel guilty about lying.

"Well," the editor said, "you aren't the first to inquire about *Democratiam Liberum*. In fact, many a blue blood has wanted to know the identity of the mystery man. Hughes, Torrington, and that windbag Somerset have all come by. Even that coal investor, Nathaniel Hinds, who some whisper is rather fond of handing out bribes, came awhile back. Seems both the aristos and the rich merchants aren't taking too kindly to *Democratiam Liberum*'s claims."

Jack stifled his impatience. Those men likely hoped to win the wager on the betting book at White's about the author's real identity, but Jack just wanted to find his sister.

"Do you know who *Democratiam Liberum* is?" Pippa asked.

The editor shook his head ruefully. "I wish I did. I could make a pretty penny off of the story, but he's careful to hide his tracks. Sends his articles in with a street urchin. Little scamp with a shock of red hair. Wants a few pence for the delivery too." Rumbold scowled as if the payment of the smallest coin was a personal affront.

"Red hair." Pippa frowned.

Jack gave her a searching look, but she shook her head.

He turned his attention back to Rumbold. "And you never tried to follow the boy?"

Rumbold barked in laughter. "Course I tried. But the scamp was slippery as an eel and lost my tail every time."

Pippa clasped her hands together. "I'm sure you've noticed that the, ah, tenor of *Democratiam Liberum*'s articles has radically changed."

Rumbold pinched the bridge of his nose. "I didn't know what to make of it. The scamp's not making the deliveries anymore. And articles are arriving every day now, instead of twice weekly. Deucedly odd." He shook his head. "If it weren't for the handwriting being the same, I'd think it was someone else pretending."

"May we see the handwriting?" Jack asked, trying to keep his voice level.

"I've got it right here." The editor excavated through the piles on his desk until he held up a piece of parchment for Jack.

Pippa leaned against him as they scanned the page that had become today's article.

"Damn." Jack's shoulders sagged.

The handwriting was Lydia's.

Pippa's eyes searched his own, and he knew she'd come to the same realization. Lydia was most definitely involved with the *Democratiam Liberum* articles. This was proof beyond a shadow of a doubt.

She took the paper from his numb fingers and read. Jack tried to focus on the words—his sister's words—but his brain could make no sense of what was on the page.

"You said the boy is no longer making the deliveries?" Pippa handed the paper back.

"Haven't seen him all week." Rumbold tossed the article onto his desk. "A big bruiser of a man missing a few teeth brought the last article by. A weedy gent reeking of garlic delivered them the two days before that. Both came in without a by-your-leave and hurried off without a word. No pattern to the time of day. That's three days in a row now without the boy."

Three days in a row.

Lydia had vanished four days ago.

Jack's stomach churned.

He felt Pippa's worried gaze on him, and then she made their goodbyes, reiterating promises of an exclusive interview that would never happen and leading him down the stairs.

She stuffed him into his carriage before clambering in herself, pulling the door closed.

"It really is her." Jack stared out the window.

"Yes." Pippa shifted in her seat. "And she was delivering the articles out of the LCA."

Jack turned toward her. "How do you know?"

"The red-haired scamp Rumbold mentioned is the son of one of Lady Rowling's servants. He likes to deliver messages and run errands for the LCA ladies for a few coins."

Jack's entire body felt heavy, weighed down with the

knowledge that his sister was, without any lingering doubt, the radical political writer.

Pippa took his hand. He stared down at their intertwined fingers. Why did they both have gloves on? He should be able to feel the warmth of her hand, the callouses earned through her dedication to her training, a tangible symbol of the essence of Pippa—strong and faithful.

Jack tugged off his glove, then reached for hers. The air between them trembled as Jack traced the lines of her palm, caressed her callouses, and pressed a kiss on her palm before interlacing their fingers once more.

Leaning her head against his shoulder, they rode to his home in silence. Pippa somehow knew that a discussion about *Democratiam Liberum* would tip him over the edge. Instead, she offered silent comfort and perhaps took some for herself as well.

Jack closed his eyes. Her light, clean scent filled his nose. The gentle weight of Pippa against his side steadied him, surrounded him, and helped him remain tethered to the earth.

The carriage slowed to a stop and the door flew open, one of his footmen peering inside.

"My lord, two letters arrived for you. Thorpe said you'd want to see them at once." The footman thrust his hand forward.

Jack grabbed the letters. One was sealed with the insignia of the Bow Street runners. *Gormley.* The other was on thin paper with a plain script and an unadorned seal.

"Leave us," he ordered the footman without looking up. The door clicked shut.

"Who are they from?" Pippa leaned forward.

"It seems Gormley has finally deigned to write." He broke the Bow Street runner seal. Pippa read beside him.

Lord Hartwick,

After considerable investigating throughout London and its environs, I have concluded that your sister spent a night in the unsavory company of many low people who doubtlessly encour-

aged her to drink strong spirits. After carousing around the town, she tipped over a bridge into the Thames and perished. This is my conclusion based upon my many years as a runner. I have also interviewed several eyewitnesses who can testify to seeing her upon the bridge the night she disappeared. I'm most terribly sorry for your loss. Your bill for services rendered shall be sent forthwith.

Your servant, etc.,
Gormley

Jack's stomach churned, and he swallowed back nausea. "He's lying."

Jack started at Pippa's vehement words, his heart barely contained inside his chest. "What?" he managed to gasp.

"Gormley is lying." She glared at the letter. "I have no idea why, but I'm quite certain. After all, we have proof she's alive with the letters we just saw at the newspaper."

Pippa took Jack's hand in hers and squeezed. Jack concentrated on breathing in and out. His heart returned to its normal residence inside his chest. The churning in his stomach quieted.

"I...I believed him," he murmured, and she squeezed his hand again. He huffed out a loud breath of air, shaking his head. "Damn. Do you think he did any investigating at all?"

Pippa's eyes narrowed. "It's hard to know, but he completely disregarded the note we found from Aubrey Andrews when we went to Bow Street. And told us Lydia had been snatched off the streets and murdered, without a shred of evidence." She stared into space as she thought. "If I had to guess, I'd say someone paid him off."

Jack's mouth tightened into a hard line. "We can't trust the runners."

Pippa nodded in agreement. "I don't know if it was Andrews, or someone involved in the *Democratiam Liberum* articles—or perhaps a party we haven't thought of yet—but I'd bet all my pin money that someone got to Gormley before we showed up at

Bow Street."

Jack sat up straight in the carriage, his eyes flinty. "Damn. I remember when we arrived, a young man noticed when we entered and then disappeared down the hall. Gormley probably had him watching for us, so he could get to us before any of the other runners."

Pippa frowned. "This whole thing was planned. Whoever did this figured you'd go to the runners. I don't think we can trust anyone there. We don't know who else might be in on it."

Jack's eyes narrowed and he sank back against the carriage seat. They were alone in their investigation. Just him and Pippa. Finding Lydia was entirely up to them.

He met Pippa's eyes, and the determination he found there buoyed him.

"Let's hope the second letter contains better news than the first." Jack broke the plain wax seal and read.

Dear Lord Hartwick,

Pardon my presumption in sending this express, but I'm thinking you won't mind paying to frank my letter. I told you I hadn't seen hide nor hair of the gentleman you described when you visited my fine establishment. However, when I told my missus, she rang me a fine peal saying as how a gentleman of that exact description had come in two days before your visit. She was the one what served him on account of me being in the back, tending to my ale. Folks in these parts say it's the finest ale in the county. I thought you'd want to know the news, and if your offer of a reward still stands, my missus would be most obliged. She has her eye on a new hat.

Your humble servant,
John Babcock, Proprietor of The Golden Lion

Jack exhaled. Thank God.

Pippa, reading alongside him, clutched his arm. "We must go!"

Jack, halfway through a second read of the letter, spoke without glancing up. "Go?"

"Go north again, to The Golden Lion. We need to speak to the innkeeper's wife—find out what she knows. This could lead us straight to Lydia!"

Pippa shook his arm, and he looked to find her eyes sparking.

Jack's mind flashed to the end—he and Pippa finding Lydia, safe and smiling, holed away at some nearby cottage the innkeeper's wife directed them to. His sister scribbling away on parchment. Her squire, Andrew Aubrey, was staying in some other cottage, on the other side of the village. No, in another village entirely. Actually, he'd already returned home. In Lydia's cottage, there was a matronly chaperone, knitting in the corner as she kept close watch on her charge. It had all been a misunderstanding, Lydia would explain. She'd been on her way to visit a friend. No, the articles weren't hers. What a silly notion! And who is this? Oh, your new friend, Miss Philippa Chester? Pleased to make your acquaintance. Yes, you must come over for dinner sometime soon. We can have a nice family coze, and I'll tell you all about my brother and what he was like when he was little. Ha ha ha. And our parents—

Jack's imaginings scudded to a halt.

He blinked, aware of Pippa staring at him, concern in her blue eyes.

"Jack?"

Was the innkeeper's lead better than trying to follow the men who delivered the articles to the newspaper? Different men on different days and no pattern to the timing, the editor had said.

Jack's gut said to follow the trail of the innkeeper.

"Yes, I must go north," he murmured.

"If you give me an hour, I can be back here, ready to go." She bit her lip, looking to the side as if plotting what to pack, the fastest route, and how many swords and knives to bring.

Swords and knives.

He pictured her arm, the vicious slice across her tender skin. He could no more put her at risk again than he could fly to the moon.

"Horseback would be fastest," she muttered, "but the carriage would allow us to carry on through the night if needed."

"No."

"In case we *do* need to head all the way to Scotland, I should bring—"

"Pippa," he said, louder.

She finally looked up. "What?"

"I'm going alone."

She gave an incredulous laugh. "Of course not. You said you needed me, that I'm so observant and…" She trailed off, perhaps seeing the resolve in his eyes.

"It's not safe," Jack said. "It's certain to be an overnight trip. You said it yourself—your reputation matters to you. And," he added, softening his tone, "it matters to me as well."

Pippa's mouth opened. Jack stared at her plump lower lip. God, he wanted to kiss her, to gently nibble on that soft, pink lip.

He jerked his eyes away. "I'll have the carriage take you home." He began to clamber toward the door.

"No." Her voice was *épée* sharp.

He stopped, fingers on the door handle. "Yes," he replied, trying—and likely failing—to match her tone.

Pippa folded her arms across her chest. "I'm part of this now. You can't shut me out—it's too late for that. And besides, this involves me too."

"Involves you how?" He sunk back into the seat across from her.

"Lady Rowling shut the LCA down. If we find your sister, it might stop whatever else is going on. It would show her the members are all safe. It could keep the LCA open, and I need—" She blinked her eyes. "I *need* the LCA to stay open." Her voice wobbled but she stared at him, her heart, her pain, all her feelings right there in her eyes.

Jack was sinking into all she was, all she felt there in her perfect, blue eyes. He knew, with an unsettling certainty, that he couldn't deny her. Pippa was her own person, and if she was determined to go, she'd go, whether he approved or not.

"Fine," he conceded, regretting it despite its inevitability. "My carriage will take you home and return in an hour. Be ready."

Jack hopped out of the carriage, his mind a jumble. Whatever lay ahead, he'd have Pippa by his side. For the rest of the day.

And for the entire night.

Chapter Seventeen

PIPPA PACED THE length of the entryway, twisting her hands into knots. She glanced at the clock in the entryway and grimaced. Too much time had already been wasted with her dithering. She took a bracing breath and opened the door to the sitting room.

"Oh Pippa, what a treat!" her mother's friend, Eugenia exclaimed, glancing up from her needlework. "Your mother was just telling me about your recent headaches. I'll give you the name of my physician. He'll whip up a tincture and you'll be right as rain and back in the ballrooms." The woman beamed at her, looking inordinately pleased at the thought of getting Pippa back onto the dancefloor where she assumed all young women yearned to be.

"You are very kind." Pippa didn't have to force her answering smile. Eugenia was kindhearted, and her mother had expressed more than once how grateful she was for Eugenia's friendship, especially in the dark days after Pippa's father's death.

"Everything all right at the LCA, my dear? You and Jane dashed out of here so quickly earlier." Her mother set her needle point aside.

Pippa soaked in her mother's face—her kind, open, trusting face.

She swallowed.

"It turned out to be good news, actually." Pippa affected a casual air by examining the colored threads in her mother's needlepoint basket. Several lovely shades of gold and brown, like Jack's eyes... She jerked her hand away.

"Oh?"

Pippa sank to the couch beside her mother. "Ah, yes. Lady Rowling has invited the members to her estate up north, near Leicester."

Pippa had worked out her cover story during the carriage ride from Jack's home. With her fear of scandal and exposure, Lady Rowling would keep a low profile following the burglary, so no one would be the wiser that she remained in town. Hopefully.

A wide smile broke out across her mother's face. "Oh, a house party. How lovely! When is it? I'll see about getting the carriage ready for us—"

"Actually, it's just for LCA members," Pippa interrupted. "We'll be doing charity work and...*erm*...'strategize' for our future projects. It would be quite boring for anyone who's not a member. And Lady Rowling will be there to chaperone, so it's all quite proper."

Josephine Chester, the dowager viscountess of Everleigh, narrowed her blue eyes, so similar to Pippa's. "And when is this *strategizing*"—she lingered on the word as if testing it for spoilage—"to occur?"

Pippa met her mother's eyes although staring unblinking into the sun for a full minute would have been easier. "Today."

Her mother arched an elegant eyebrow.

"Oh, isn't it lovely how these young ladies are so committed to their service?" Eugenia's cheery voice broke through the stillness. She leaned forward, saying conspiratorially, "I imagine when the time comes to cast out lures for a husband, it doesn't hurt to have this reputation for kind charity, eh Pippa?

"Just think, Josephine," her mother's friend continued, "if we'd had a Lady Rowling in our corner back when we made our debuts, the men of the *ton* would've bent the knee on the daily with our virtuous deeds held up for all to see." She winked.

Pippa's mother frowned.

"Oh, let the girl go," Eugenia continued. "Heaven knows she deserves a little fun. And weren't you just telling me how you wished she'd get out of the house more?"

Pippa's stomach clenched. Merciful heavens, did the entire world have to discuss her social anxieties and ineptitude?

Her mother sighed. "I suppose a few days away is acceptable. But," she held up a finger, "make sure Lady Rowling doesn't leave you girls unattended. You have no idea what sort of trouble a young lady can get into without proper oversight."

PIPPA WAVED OFF the footman as he reached for her valise. "I can take it," she said, hoisting up her luggage with a soft grunt. "It hardly weighs a thing." She staggered out the front door and down the steps.

"No need, no need," she called over her shoulder when she realized the footman was following. He froze on the steps, shifting from foot to foot in apparent indecision.

Drat, it seemed her attempt to keep the servants away from Jack's carriage only made things more suspicious.

A footman hopped down to take her bag. He wasn't dressed in Hartwick livery, Pippa was relieved to notice. And when he reached for the carriage door, Pippa grinned at the sight of wet paint gleaming in the place where the Hartwick crest had been only an hour before.

She climbed into the carriage and settled in beside Jack. "You are shockingly talented at subterfuge."

"You're taking on enough risk as it is with this trip," Jack grumbled. "I could hardly whisk you away in broad daylight without a few modifications."

"I've become quite proficient at lying myself," Pippa replied.

"Perhaps we should become spies next?"

Jack didn't reply.

The sound of the coachman clucking to the horses filtered into the carriage, followed by a low rumble as the wheels turned across cobblestones.

He stared out the window.

"Jack?"

Pippa touched his shoulder. His muscles tensed, and he remained facing the window. She stared at him a moment more, waiting, giving him a chance to engage with her. When he remained mute, she let her hand drop.

Pippa scooted against her side of the carriage so there were a few inches between them. Her excitement at this new adventure, the hope of finding Lydia and rescuing the LCA from ruin, deflated in the face of his cold demeanor.

The carriage rolled on, the contrast between the noises of the bustling city just outside and the cool stillness within further eroding Pippa's optimism.

Soon, they were once again on the Great North Road. It was just a regular road. Pippa no longer needed to feel afraid. Trees, fields, and horses passed by through Pippa's window. The shadows on the ground grew in length as the hours of afternoon ticked by.

"I'm sorry."

Pippa started as Jack's words broke the lengthy silence.

"What?" Was he apologizing for being a grumpy recluse?

"I'm sorry for what I did to you. After the duel." He continued to face the window.

Pippa flashed to the euphoric bliss of his touch, her spiral into the pinnacle of pleasure. Pleasure from *his* hands. In *his* bed. And now she was receiving his apology. *Yet again.*

Her face burned. "Go to hell." Oh, he was lucky her knives were packed away.

He turned from the window. His brown eyes sparked with heat.

"I shouldn't have taken advantage," he said, his voice rough. "But I could no more stop myself from kissing you, from…touching you"—he breathed the last words as if he were there still, his fingers moving with skill, with desire, with reverence over her most secret place—"than I could stop myself from breathing."

His chest moved with his great, gusting breaths.

Pippa's lips parted. He wanted her. He wanted her still.

"I…"

He shook his head. "I know you'll say nothing was done *to* you, that you were willing and had a choice." His cheekbones grew ruddy. He swallowed before continuing. "But you were an innocent—*are* an innocent. I should've known better. I should've kept control."

Pippa stared, torn between the desire to crawl onto his lap and kiss him senseless and her burning curiosity to know him, to know why he needed to always keep control. She'd had an inkling of it the other morning in his breakfast room when they'd examined the newspaper articles. She'd meant to dig deeper at the ball, but then Westerly had accosted her and the plan had been forgotten.

"Jack." She kept her voice slow and deliberate. It seemed any misspoken word could throw everything off kilter. "I *did* have a choice, and I chose to be with you. I don't regret it."

His eyes flickered.

"If you regret it for your own sake, that's fine. But don't regret it for mine."

Their gazes tangled, his hot, searching and pained, and hers—well, she didn't know what he'd find there, but she hoped the truth of her words was visible.

Jack's mouth tightened, but he nodded.

"I wonder…" She trailed off, uncertain how to tread through the precarious morass ahead. "I wonder *why* you are as you are."

He jerked back.

Pippa lifted a conciliatory hand. "I'm not criticizing. I happen to *like* you as you are, but I'm also curious about the roots of certain…elements of your personality."

He stared, his hands fisted in his lap.

Pippa drew a deep breath. If she wanted him to share the secrets of his past, then it was only fair that she did as well. "For example, I witnessed a brutal crime when I was young, and that made me afraid to leave my house and be around strangers for a very long time."

Jack's eyes widened.

She continued, "I can look back and see, analytically, how my past shaped and molded me. And that knowledge helps me to move forward. That's why…" She paused, swallowing. "That's why the LCA is so important to me. Do you see?"

Jack faced forward. His jaw muscles pulsed.

Pippa held her breath, waiting. Would he say anything? As the seconds ticked by, her chest grew tighter and tighter.

"My parents…" he said at last.

Pippa thought for a moment she might topple over from both the shock and oxygen deprivation after holding her breath for so long.

"My parents were…different." He flicked his eyes to the side, and she nodded to show she was listening. "As the earl and countess, they had a great many responsibilities. But…" He paused, seeming to need a moment. "But they didn't…"

Pippa laid her hand across his, fisted on his thigh. His tight hand eased open, and she laced their fingers together.

Jack exhaled, long and slow. "When I was quite young, I took over responsibility for the estate. I took over responsibility for my sister. I was the only one who would do it, who *could* do it. And so…yes, my past shaped me. I need to be in charge. I need to have control, or else…or else I—"

Jack broke off as the carriage jerked. The horses slowed, and he glanced out the window. "We're here."

He sounded relieved, the scoundrel! Well, he wasn't off the hook yet. It was clear the conversation was difficult for him, but

Pippa needed to know. It mattered that she understood him as they worked together, and searched for his sister, and…and worked together.

Well, it mattered. Perhaps she didn't understand the details of why, but she knew it did.

A servant opened the door, and Jack unthreaded his fingers from Pippa's before exiting the carriage. Pippa scowled at The Golden Lion sign before she clambered out after him.

JACK GULPED BRACING lungfuls of air as he headed toward the inn.

He was truly the greatest idiot in all of England.

Pippa alternated between making his cock hard, his blood boil, and his discretion vanish. And he'd hopped into a carriage with her for an overnight jaunt up the Great North Road.

Perfect.

He knew jumping out of the carriage and entering the inn without Pippa was ungentlemanly, but if he'd stayed in there one more minute…

He exhaled with a great gust.

She was no bit of muslin to be tumbled, and she was certainly no vicar to hear his confession. What in the name of all that was holy was he doing, burning for her with the intensity of the sun one minute and then spilling his guts to her about his past the next?

And what had she said about her own past? That she'd witnessed a crime when she'd been a child and it had made her afraid? His chest constricted at the thought of Pippa living in fear. It was so contrary to who she was. He'd ask her more about it later.

He threw open the door to the inn with such force that it banged off the wall and bounced back toward him. The innkeeper glanced up from clearing a table with a scowl, but once he clapped eyes on Jack his thunderous look vanished.

"My lord," he greeted loudly, drawing all eyes in the dining room. "I see you received my letter about that particular friend of yours."

Jack ground his teeth together. A performance for the score of diners at The Golden Lion would not prove beneficial to his sister's reputation. As Pippa arrived at his side, he tensed.

"Hello, Mr. Babcock." She smiled warmly.

"Pleased to see you again, my lady." He bobbed his head.

"Just Miss but thank you." Pippa twinkled at the innkeeper.

That was the only way to describe it, Jack realized. Pippa *twinkled*. She could woo a smile from a rabid dog. She'd certainly wooed one from him.

"Is there perhaps a private place we could speak with you?" She kept her voice low.

"Ah, yes. Privacy." Mr. Babcock nodded, copying her quiet tone. "I've a private dining room in the back, for when the upper crust come to visit. They all come a'clamoring for a pint of my ale, don't you know."

"A private dining room sounds perfect," Pippa said. "And we wouldn't say no to another delicious pint."

The innkeeper beamed and even offered her his arm. Jack rolled his eyes and followed. The room was cozy and clean. The innkeeper took a moment to light the wood in the fireplace and call through the door for three pints.

"Well now." He eased into a chair once the ale had arrived. "Come to hear about your friend, have you?"

Jack nodded. "We're most grateful for your letter. Please give our regards to your wife for her keen memory." Jack reached into his purse and pulled out a large handful of coins.

The innkeeper nodded his appreciation, tucking the money away before drawing a long drink of ale.

"Ah, that hits the spot after a long day," he sighed, plunking down the tankard. He laced his fingers over his round stomach and leaned back. "Well, let's see now. My missus scolded me something fierce when I told her about you asking on your friend with the streak of white hair. Ah, sure, she says to me, and you don't bother asking your own wife who keeps the inn for you while you're out playing with your kegs. Playing with my kegs! As if that's all I do out in the back." Babcock frowned into his tankard.

"But what about—"

Pippa cut Jack off with the press of her hand to his thigh under the table.

"I wonder, perhaps, if we could meet your wife?" Pippa asked gently.

The innkeeper frowned. "Meet the missus? But I can tell you what she told me. Said the gentleman came through, two days before you came along asking questions. That's what she said."

"Mr. Babcock," Pippa said, leaning forward. "You've been such a tremendous help to us, and we're so grateful for your assistance. You know how women can be though, taking note of clothing and remembering little details. I'm just curious if she could recall any of those for us."

The innkeeper's eyebrows raised in surprise. "Well, I don't suppose there's any harm in her joining us." He lumbered to the door. "Molly!" he shouted. "Molly, set that aside and come here."

A petite woman, as tiny as her husband was broad, popped in, a tray of dirty dishes in her hand.

"Need me to tidy up?" she asked, surveying the table.

"Molly, this here is Lord Hartwick and his…erm…companion. They're the ones I told you about who were searching for their friend with the streak of white hair."

"Oh!" Molly's eyes lit up. "They got your letter, John. Good on you." She smiled at her husband, and he rested his meaty hand on the curve of her hip.

Jack felt like a voyeur witnessing this tender moment between them. And he felt…jealous. It was doubtful he'd ever experience that kind of easy affection. He shot a glance at Pippa and found she was watching them as well, a soft expression on her face.

"They thought perhaps you could tell 'em the details from that day—what they wore, that sort of thing," Mr. Babcock said.

Molly set the tray of dishes on a side table before slipping into a chair. "Apologies, but when you're on your feet all day, you take breaks when you can." She sighed as she settled in.

"Well, t'is the dark-haired bloke with the striped hair you're interested in, is it?" she asked, her eyes bright with curiosity. "A friend of yours, John said?"

"Yes, he's my friend." Jack nearly choked on the word, "and I must locate him on an urgent manner. He, ah, left town in a rush, and I've had a deuced time tracking him down."

The woman nodded. "I remember him all right. Quite a distinct look with that shock of white hair, just like a skunk. That's what sparked my memory when my John mentioned it a couple of days later. I said, why John, that skunk man *did* come through here. Why didn't you ask me about it, I says. You know I'm the one who's in charge when you're out back, playing with those silly kegs and barrels."

"Now, Molly," John began, a thundercloud forming on his face.

Molly winked at Jack and Pippa before turning to her husband. "Oh, I just like to rile you up a bit, I do. Best part of my day sometimes. You know I love that ale of yours, John my love."

The innkeeper cast his eyes heavenward, shaking his head, but a hint of a smile played across his mouth. "Woman, what am I to do with you?"

"Oh, I think you know, Mr. Babcock." Molly giggled.

Pippa's eyes widened and she peeked at Jack. He contemplated giving her a wink of his own, but decided it wasn't the prudent course.

What must it be like to know someone so well, to have such a comfortable, easy rapport?

Pippa cleared her throat. "Well, Mrs. Babcock, we are quite thankful you took notice of him and had your husband send word. I was wondering, are there any details you remember? Did he stay the night?" She paused, then added, "Was he traveling with a companion, perhaps?"

Jack kept his face still. He wouldn't betray his anxiety by so much as a blink.

" 'Course I remember," Mrs. Babcock replied. "Wouldn't be much of an innkeeper if I couldn't remember who came through our doors each day, now would I?"

Jack ground his teeth together.

"Let's see." The woman cocked her head to the side. "He was dressed rather middlish. Not a swell, but not a laboring man either, if you know what I mean. He did pull up in quite a carriage though. That was the first thing I noticed—that grand, gleaming carriage pulled by a team of four matching grays."

"Was there a crest on the carriage?" Jack tried to sound like a normal human and not someone being slowly tortured word by word.

Mrs. Babcock frowned. "No, no crest on it. And when he helped the lady down—"

"The lady?" Jack bit out, earning a frown from everyone at the table.

"Aye, a sweet-looking lady with blond hair and a pretty blue dress. When he helped her down, I wondered at first if a lord and lady had arrived at our inn, but once he was seated, it was clear he wasn't a lord."

Jack frowned.

"What do you mean by that, Mrs. Babcock?" Pippa asked gently.

"Well, he inquired about the cost of the meal before he ordered. A nob wouldn't do such a thing, now would he?"

"And the lady?" Jack asked, trying to turn the conversation back to Lydia. Blond lady in a pretty blue dress? It was her, it *had* to be.

"Oh, she was very polite. Quiet. Kept smiling at him, like she was trying to get him to pay her some attention. He was distracted like, kept pulling out his pocket watch. I remember thinking I felt sorry for her if he was her husband."

Jack ran his hand over his face. Dear lord, please let Andrew Aubrey or Aubrey Andrews or whatever his name was not be Lydia's husband. If she'd eloped…

He swallowed.

Well, he'd have to cross that bridge when he came to it.

"Mrs. Babcock, you've been so helpful." Pippa smiled at the woman. "Did they spend the night?"

The innkeeper's wife shook her head. "They got back into their fine carriage after their meal. Shepherd's pie, it was. Most folks around here say that I've the best shepherd's pie in the county, you know."

"Did they say where they were headed next?" Jack asked, his voice brusque.

Pippa touched his thigh under the table again. He wanted to dust her hand away. He wanted to grab it and press it tighter to him. He was slowly going mad listening to tales of ale and shepherd's pie.

Mrs. Babcock shook her head. "If they spoke of their destination, I didn't hear it. I'm sorry."

"We appreciate your time," Pippa said. "Thank you."

Jack reached into his purse again, handing these coins to Mrs. Babcock. "With gratitude."

The Babcocks hurried out, doubtlessly eager to get back to their waiting guests.

"This is good news," Pippa said once the door was shut.

Jack swiveled in his seat. "Good news?" he growled. "Tell me what's good about my sister traveling unchaperoned up the Great North Road with that bounder Andrew Aubrey?"

"Aubrey Andr—"

"I don't care!" Jack yelled.

She started, then narrowed her eyes at him. "I know you're upset," she said, each word sharp and clear. "But you haven't any right to bellow at me like a fishwife. Drink your ale and try again."

She turned away, lifted her chin and sipped her beer, studiously ignoring him.

Jack gulped back half the pint. Staring into the fire, he tried to sort out his emotions. He sighed. She was right, as usual.

"I'm sorry," he murmured. "I've been the grumpiest bastard in all of England today. It's not fair to you, and I'll try to be better."

Her cool hand rested upon his, the gentle weight both familiar and startling.

"I forgive you."

They sat in companionable silence, watching the small fire leap and crackle in the hearth.

"What shall we do next?" she asked.

Jack turned his hand over, lacing their fingers together. "What do you think?"

She smiled, her eyes glowing. "Thank you for asking me."

Jack lost himself for a moment in the simple pleasure in her eyes. All he'd done was ask her opinion, yet it clearly made her happy.

Perhaps he ought to relinquish control more often.

Starting now.

Chapter Eighteen

AT PIPPA'S SUGGESTION, they'd continued up the Great North Road to inquire about the skunk-headed man traveling in a grand carriage with a polite blond woman in a blue dress. Pippa had been hopeful their more detailed description would jog the memory of the innkeepers who they'd already questioned on their previous visit up. However, all the innkeepers just shook their heads.

"I suppose they wouldn't have stopped again so soon after their meal at The Golden Lion." Pippa dabbed at her lips with a napkin. Her stomach had audibly growled as they'd questioned the last innkeeper, so Jack had ordered them dinner.

He narrowed his eyes in thought. "So, we should continue north then?"

Pippa's stomach flipped over. Her mother thought her safely ensconced at Lady Rowling's country estate. No one would miss her for days. Was she really going to continue on this scandalous journey with Jack?

"Yes, I suppose we must." A shiver tingled down her body as she realized what this would mean. Days of just the two of them. Nights in inns, unchaperoned. No one to watch. No one to know.

He looked up from his plate, his eyes guarded. "We can turn back if you want. With the carriage, we could travel through the night even."

Pippa dropped her eyes, chasing her peas across the plate with her fork. What did she want to do? Her heartbeat sped up. She knew what she wanted.

She wanted him.

"We should keep going. I'll stay with you."

She peeked up in time to see his neck slide up and down as he swallowed. His hands flexed before he busied himself with his meal once more.

After he'd paid the bill, they hopped back into the carriage. After only a few minutes of driving, Jack pounded on the roof and the carriage pulled over on the side of the dirt road. Pippa peeked out the window, confused why there would be another inn so close to the last one. However, a wide, grassy field flanked by a rock wall was all she saw.

"Why have we stopped?"

Jack helped her out of the carriage. "I owe you a lesson."

Pippa's brow knit in confusion as he raised one of the carriage seats and pulled out a case.

"We need to hurry before it grows too dark." Jack offered his hand.

"What are we doing?" She placed her hand in his.

He smiled, a glint in his eyes. "You'll see."

They crossed the field to the rock wall. Jack set the case on it, then hunted about on the ground. He found a clod of dried dirt, a large rock, and a round cross-section from a felled tree trunk. He placed them in intervals on the wall.

Then he opened the case.

The orange glow of the setting sun gleamed on pistol barrels.

Pippa's breath caught in her throat.

"Today, Miss Philippa Chester, you learn to shoot."

She launched herself at him. "Oh, Jack!" She twined her arms around his neck and rained kisses on his face.

His arms encircled her. "Are you happy?"

Pippa pulled back and smiled. "I'm *so* happy." She lay her head on his shoulder and squeezed tightly before pulling away.

"Now teach me!"

He grinned, and something flipped over inside her chest. It was a physical ache. Her senses whirled as her feeling crystalized.

She loved him.

Pippa looked away. She must grab hold of her emotions before they ran away with her. But she feared it was too late.

"What do I do?" Was she speaking to him or to herself? A crazed giggle escaped her. Oh, she was delirious with it.

"First, we load the pistol." He instructed her on the mechanisms of the gun, powder, and bullets.

Pippa drew a bracing breath and concentrated on his words. He was teaching her to shoot.

Jack Dashwood, Earl of Hartwick was giving her, a supposedly fragile woman, a lesson on the use of firearms. What had he said when she'd asked him for a shooting lesson last time?

I have the pistol. I'm here to protect you. You don't need to know how to shoot.

But he'd changed his mind. Had he, perhaps, grown to care for her?

She peeked at him, the golden light of the sun low in the sky setting his hair aglow.

He glanced up from the pistol. "Ready?"

Pippa nodded, and they walked halfway across the field.

"You hold it like this." He demonstrated a straight arm. "Look down the barrel at your target, and then after each shot, we'll reload."

Pippa copied Jack's stance and stared down the smooth barrel of the gun at the clod of dirt on the rock wall.

"That's not quite right. Here." Jack came up behind her, one hand on her hip as he adjusted her stance.

The heat of his touch through her gown tingled along Pippa's skin. His chest pressed against her back, his arm outstretched along her own, making small adjustments to her hold.

She inhaled, filling her lungs with his clean, masculine scent.

"Are you ready?" he murmured against her ear.

She nodded. Oh yes, she was ready.

"Then pull the trigger," he whispered.

Pippa's finger tightened. The gun fired. It jerked in her hand, the air rent by the sharp bang.

"Oh my." Her hand tingled from the kickback, and she lowered it to her side. The clod of dirt remained undisturbed.

Jack stepped back. "Well done."

Her body cried out at the absence of his solid warmth behind her.

"Here, fire again." He handed her the second pistol. He suggested a few adjustments to her stance but allowed her to shoot on her own.

This time when Pippa fired, the clod of dirt exploded, showering the ground and wall in a spray of dried earth.

"I hit it!"

He dropped a fierce kiss onto her mouth. Before she could kiss him back, he pulled away, tending to the pistols.

Pippa traced her lips with her fingers.

He handed her a reloaded gun, smiling. "Try again."

Pippa practiced shooting until dusk replaced the golden light of sunset. Her technique improved with each round, and toward the end, she was hitting the target at least half the time. And she'd blown up a handful of dirt clods, an action just as satisfying as sinking her dagger into a wooden post from twenty feet away.

"That was wonderful," she sighed as he packed up the pistols. "Thank you so much."

He glanced up with a warm smile. "You're a natural." He looked back at the case and cleared his throat. "I'm sorry I didn't show you before when you asked."

"A lifetime of learned misogyny can't vanish in an instant," she replied pertly.

His head shot up. "Misog—wait...*what?*"

Pippa raised an eyebrow. "Do you deny it?"

Although she'd asked the question in a joking tone, her stomach tightened with nerves. Society *did* have a separate set of rules for women than it did for men, a more repressive, restrictive standard. Could he see it? Could he understand the unfairness?

No one spoke of it. It wasn't polite, after all, and in polite aristocratic society, what did people have except their firm belief in the status quo and the importance of manners above all else?

But his answer mattered to her. She wanted to be seen by him, to be known. And her choice to live outside society's restrictions with her fencing was a large part of who she was.

Jack closed the case and fiddled with the handle. "I want to deny it, but that would be a lie."

Their eyes met before he looked away, staring across the field. "The idea that women are the weaker sex permeates our society. I suppose it's in the air we breathe, like the city's pollution. I've been breathing it all my life. We all have." He sighed, closing his eyes.

Pippa's hands clenched at her sides. Was he saying he was…he was *poisoned* with the smog of misogyny?

Jack opened his eyes. His warm-brown gaze met hers, his stare unwavering. "However, I find I prefer this fresh clean air of the countryside."

Pippa nodded, not trusting her voice. She stepped forward, linking her hand to his. They breathed together as the sky darkened above them. Across the field, one of the horses harnessed to the waiting carriage whinnied.

Pippa whispered, "Let's find an inn for tonight."

PIPPA RAN SOAP over her leg, watching as the bubbles slid down her shin, around her calf, and then disappeared down the back of her thigh. Her foot was propped on the edge of a hip tub filled with steaming water. How could someone as tall as Jack fit in such a small bath? The image of soap bubbles dripping down *his* skin flashed through her mind. The bubbles sliding down the ridges and planes of his chest and stomach…and lower…

The soap shot out of her tight grip and plopped into the water.

Pippa exhaled. She should have headed straight to bed once "Mr. Jones and his sister" had checked into the inn. However, a proper bath sounded just the thing after a long day of travel.

Pippa rinsed, dried with a thin towel, and then donned her night rail. A knock sounded at the door. Pippa's heart skipped a beat, but it was just the maid with two companions to remove the tub.

She sat in front of the fire, brushing her wet hair when a knock sounded once more.

It was just the maid returning, but her silly heart continued to dance to a merry beat.

"Come," she called.

The door opened.

It wasn't the maid.

Jack filled the doorway, his damp hair brushed back from his forehead. She licked her lips as she realized that while wet, soapy bubbles had been trailing over her naked skin, they'd also been trailing over his. At the same time. Both of them naked. Separated only by a wall.

And now he was here.

He cleared his throat. "I wanted to be sure you had everything you needed."

Pippa rose, her hairbrush clenched in her hand. The fire crackled in the grate behind her. Jack's eyes widened as his gaze traveled from her bare feet up to the little tie at the neck of her night rail.

Her skin tingled in the wake of his stare.

"Would you…would you care for…" She cast about the room, looking for something she could offer him, something to keep him here. There was no wine. No dessert or book to read together in front of the fire.

"Yes, I would," he answered, his voice low. He shut the door and turned the key in the lock. Jack prowled across the room toward her, the flames of the fire reflected in his eyes. Or perhaps the heat in his gaze was internal.

Pippa's heart pounded with each footstep. Jack stopped a handbreadth away, the air between them crackling like the sky before a lightning storm. He lifted a hand and paused, his palm a mere inch from her chest.

"Pippa." His voice was rough as gravel. "If you want me to leave, just tell me."

She knew what he was asking.

She knew the consequences.

And she didn't care.

She whispered, "Stay."

His body twitched as if he held himself in check by sheer dint of will.

And then he lowered his hand to the bare skin above her night rail. He traced the line of her clavicle and the indent at the base of her throat. His fingertips scorched her, a trace of fire left where ever he touched. Her breath came in uneven gasps.

"Pippa," he murmured, and then his mouth was on hers. His lips moved, cajoling her to open for him.

She sighed as his tongue teased her, the slick heat of their mouths becoming one. She pressed against his firm chest, her breasts tingling at the contact.

"Jack," she murmured as he trailed kisses across her face, behind her ear, and down her neck. His lips forged new paths across her skin. They marked the territory of her body like an explorer planting a flag in unchartered land. Her skin would forever bear the echoes of his touch, the pleasure reverberating through her memory until the end of her days.

She was determined to leave her mark upon him as well.

Pippa ran her palms up his chest, the taut muscles so different from her own softness. She wanted to feel his skin, to see him. With trembling fingers, she untied his simple cravat and slid the top buttons of his shirt out of their holes.

His shirt gaped open, exposing the strong column of his neck, a dusting of hair across his chest, and the contours of his muscles. Her fingers continued their work, exposing more of him. Jack's stomach was ridged, firm, and bisected by a narrowing band of hair. At last, the shirt was open completely, and she pushed it off his shoulders. It slid to the ground. She stared.

He was magnificent.

She gasped as his large hands roamed down her back to squeeze her bottom. He pulled her tightly against him, and she felt the hard length of his arousal against her belly.

"The way you look at me," he growled, his breath hot in her ear. "It makes me want to devour you."

Pippa shivered.

He kissed her again, his mouth frantic as he made good on his promise. Pippa ran her hands across his chest and shoulders, marveling at the unfettered access to his skin, his muscle and sinew, and flesh, to the place at the center of his chest where she felt a fierce pounding.

Jack's fingers plucked at the front of her night rail, pulling the tie. The neckline loosened and sagged. One finger caught the edge atop her shoulder and pulled it down, then repeated on the other side. Her garment slid and caught at her elbows. He looked at her bare breasts, his eyes blazing with heat, and need, and desire.

"I want you." He pulled her against him, her breasts pressing against his bare chest for the first time.

Pippa moaned. She wiggled side to side, the hair on his chest gently abrading her sensitive skin. A bolt of pleasure shot from her nipples to her core.

She whimpered at the sensation.

She wanted more.

She *needed* more.

"Touch me," she commanded.

Jack's mouth curled in a satisfied smile. "Yes," he murmured. "I want nothing more than to touch you."

He walked her backward until her legs grazed the edge of the mattress. "Arms down."

Pippa lowered her arms, and her night rail slithered to the ground. She was bare before him.

"You are so beautiful," he whispered, his gaze like a physical touch.

She *felt* beautiful, here in the heat of his desire. Pippa licked her lips. "Now you."

She watched as his hands rose to his trousers. Jack's fingers moved across his falls, sliding the buttons out until the pants gaped open. He leaned down to remove a boot, then hopped on one foot as he worked on the other. Pippa stifled a giggle.

Jack peeked up, his eyes dancing. "You find this funny?"

She nodded before succumbing to a devilish temptation. Reaching out with one finger, Pippa gave him the *tiniest* push. He tumbled over sideways onto the bed.

"Oh no, you don't." He grabbed her hand, pulling her down on top of him.

A gasp of laughter escaped her, and they rolled back and forth across the bed. She tickled his stomach. His fingers played across her ribs like piano keys.

"Stop, stop," she cried, laughing. Their entwined bodies rolled to a halt. They were both gasping for breath, their faces an inch apart as they lay on their sides.

His eyes sparkled. "You are a delight."

She smiled, a flash of joy filling her with such brightness that she wouldn't have been surprised if beams of light shone from her eyes, her open mouth, and her ears.

He traced one finger down her cheek, and the need returned. No, it didn't return, for it had never left. The brief respite from desire provided by their shared humor had only increased their connection, their unity in this sharing of smiles and touches and bodies and passion.

He shook his legs, kicking off the remaining boot and his trousers.

And now, there was nothing between them. Skin to skin, top to toe.

Pippa stared, taking in his skin. His muscles. The angles and planes of his body.

And that part of him that was very different than her own body. *Oh my.*

Pippa breathed, the sight of him, the nearness of him, permeating every part of her.

With languid slowness, he closed the distance between their mouths, kissing her reverently, deeply, tenderly.

Pippa's eyes pricked at the sweetness of his kiss.

She cupped his cheek, wanting him to feel how she cherished him too. How she loved him. She couldn't say the words, but she could show him.

She stroked down his face, trailed along his muscular shoulder, glided along the smoothness of his side, and cupped his taut rear, pulling him close. She arched into him, rubbing and stretching sinuously like a cat.

Jack growled. "Pippa." He flexed forward, his erection brushing her core.

He lifted her thigh, draping it over his leg. She was open to him, and her breath stuttered as his hand drifted down her stomach and over her curls.

"Do you want this?" he asked, his fingers stilling.

Pippa nodded, tilting her hips forward in invitation.

Jack touched her.

Even though he'd touched her in this way earlier that morning—had it only been that morning? It felt like they'd been together for eons—this felt different. This was the precursor to something else. Something more.

When his fingers slid through her folds, she gasped at the sizzle of sensation. He rubbed against her most sensitive spot, sending crackles of energy pulsing through her as he circled and pressed her nub.

"Oh God," she moaned, throwing her head back.

It was too much. She couldn't contain this pleasure. It engulfed her, overwhelming her, building and building, and crashing through her.

She screamed as the peak hit. Jack covered her mouth with his own, stifling the sound. And still, he pressed and rubbed and circled as the pleasure came and came.

She slumped against him, completely boneless in the aftermath of her climax.

"Pippa," he murmured, stroking her back, kissing her temple, and hugging her close.

Her heartbeat slowed. She cracked her eyes open. He watched her carefully, his liquid brown eyes so serious, so full of desire and tenderness. She smiled, and something leaped in his eyes.

She kissed him. It started slow and easy, but the fire between them flared once more. She reached between them and took that part of him—his *cock* she'd heard it called—into her hand.

Jack gasped, thrusting into her grasp.

"You are so..." She trailed off, uncertain how to describe the silky softness encasing such rigid strength.

"You make me that way," he murmured, his fingers tracing her nipple.

She began to understand the rhythm, and her fingers circled his length, stroking up and down.

"Pippa, I want to be with you fully." He moaned as she tightened her grip. "But we can...we can just touch if you'd rather. We don't have to—"

"I want to," she interrupted, pressing against him. "I want all of you."

He kissed her in a frenzy, his tongue tangling with hers, their lips fused. He rolled her onto her back and settled into the cradle between her thighs.

"I want to make this good for you." He slid his length along her slick seam.

"Yes." She arched her hips off the bed, seeking him.

She felt the head of his cock at her entrance, the blunt tip opening her. She held her breath as he pressed. Her body stretched. She gasped. How could he fit? How could this work?

He leaned forward and kissed her, the sensuous pleasure of his mouth distracting her from the fear of pain. He nudged forward and she froze. Again, he kissed her, and once more she grew lost in the melding of their lips. He reached between them, pressing against the center of her pleasure. She arched off the mattress, and he slid inside her body.

Pippa gasped as pleasure and pain swirled together. Jack remained still, fully seated within her, giving her long, slow kisses as her body grew accustomed to the unfamiliar intrusion.

Pippa knew there was more from the idle talk of maids who thought they were alone. But she hoped it was more like what she'd felt when Jack had touched her with his fingers than what was happening now.

But slowly, the pain subsided. An achy wanting grew, bidding Pippa to move. She tilted her hips and swiveled against him.

Jack swore. "Woman, what you do to me," he growled, and then he began to move.

Pippa's skin tingled and her nub pulsed in pleasure at his touch. She was so *full*, with him inside her. His fingers pressed and rubbed above where they were joined. He kissed her, and her breasts tingled when his chest slid against her.

The pleasure rose in her once more. He slid in and out, faster and faster still, their breaths both coming in pants now.

"Jack," she moaned, closing her eyes.

"Oh, God." Faster he thrust, and his fingers rubbed her *right there. Right there. Oh, God right there right there right there.*

Her mouth opened on a silent scream as she shattered, pulses of blinding pleasure spiraling out from her core.

Jack pulled out and thrust against her belly. He groaned, his entire body rigid. Warmth seeped across her stomach.

Pippa was dead. She'd died and could never move again. She was limp and sated and boneless. She didn't even have the strength to open her eyes.

"Dear heart," Jack murmured, pressing kisses along her jaw.

"Mmm," she replied, still dead to the world from their pleasure.

"You are…" he kissed her neck, her breasts, her mouth. "You are incredible."

"Mmm."

He rose from the bed. She could hear him pattering around the room, the sound of water trickling, the bed sinking as he returned, and then a cool cloth against her tender flesh.

She cracked one eye open.

"Are you sore?" His mouth tightened in concern.

"Mmm."

"I'm so—"

"If you apologize, I'll castrate you," she managed to slur.

She felt the tremors of his silent chuckle, and she smiled.

He cleaned off her belly as well, set the cloth aside, and then pulled her against him, her back tucked against his front with his arm around her. She was safe. She was warm.

She fell asleep in the arms of her lover.

Chapter Nineteen

JACK AWOKE IN the middle of the night, his arms full of soft, warm woman. Soft, warm Pippa.

His Pippa.

His arms contracted, pulling her closer. They'd turned in their sleep, her head nestled against his chest. He ran his hand down her back, along her side to her bottom, and back up.

She stirred, her fingers caressing his chest.

He pressed a kiss to the top of her head. The clean, fresh scent of her hair filled his nose.

He wanted to stay like this, tucked away in this soft, warm bed in the dark, cozy room with her snuggled up beside him forever.

Forever.

Jack frowned.

If there was any hope, if there was any chance of a forever between them, then he must tell her who he really was. What he'd experienced.

And he'd have to marry her, of course. After what they'd done, it was the only option. But they would sort that out when they'd found Lydia. Once he knew his sister was safe, then he could turn his attention to convincing the incredibly independent woman in his arms that she belonged at his side forever as his wife.

"Pippa," he murmured into her hair.

He paused, trying to discern if she was really awake. Her breathing had changed, and her fingers continued to move across his chest. She was listening.

"In the carriage earlier today, you asked me why I'm like this."

She nodded.

Jack drew a deep breath before plunging into the frigid water of his past.

"My parents were artists." He swallowed. He could do this. "My mother painted, and my father wrote poetry. They surrounded themselves with people like them…philosophers, scientists, and other artists. When I was a child, there were always people over, huge salons—more like parties, really—where they'd debate the existence of God, compare French Renaissance artists to Italian, or recite Shakespeare's sonnets. It was an incredible way to grow up, surrounded by so many ideas, so many thinkers."

He paused.

"It was also a terrible way to grow up."

Pippa's back muscles tightened under his hand. He stroked up and down, uncertain if the touch was to soothe her or himself.

"My father neglected the estate. They both neglected their duties." Jack unclenched his jaw. "And their children." He breathed. "When I was ten, something happened, something bad with the servants, and they came to me for help."

Jack stared into the darkness. He could recall that day so vividly despite the years…

His parents had thrown yet another of their grand parties. Jack wove through the throng of guests, but the Earl and Countess of Hartwick were difficult for a small boy of ten to spot amongst the forest of adults.

Jack switched tactics. Wedged between a painter gushing over the use of pickles to portray masculinity in his latest work and a poet reciting her newest verse which rhymed *aggrandize* with *muscular thighs*, he waited, listening.

And there it was—the distinctive, throaty laughter of his mother. Jack pushed his way through a debate on astronomy, a lecture on the evils of divine monarchs, and what sounded like an opera-singing lesson.

He finally spotted her. "Mother." She was at the center of a circle of admirers, her head tossed back as she laughed and fluttered her fan.

"Mother." He tugged on her skirts.

She peered down, blinking owlishly before recognition registered on her face. "Jack. Whatever are you up to?"

"Please come at once."

"And leave my guests?" She fanned herself. "Run along and we shall visit tomorrow."

"But the butler says the estate agent made off with all the silver."

She stared for a moment, but then her pale eyes slid away. "What nonsense! I'm sure your father will sort it all out. Tomorrow."

"But—"

"Tomorrow. Now off with you." And with a little smack of her fan on his rump, Jack's mother dismissed him.

"Now, what say you about Kant's writings on reason?" asked one of her salon guests, and Jack was rendered invisible once more.

The butler and housekeeper exchanged a knowing glance when Jack returned alone.

"Couldn't locate them, Master Jack?" Mrs. Abbott twisted her hands.

"Wouldn't come, more like," grumbled the butler, but he shut his mouth when the housekeeper's elbow connected with his ribs.

Jack shuffled his feet. "She said they'd sort it out tomorrow."

The housekeeper puffed up her chest. "The entire collection of silver has vanished, and she says *tomorrow*?" Mrs. Abbott shook her head. "I've never seen the like in all my years in service. These fancy salons day and night, no one keeping track of what's what, servants not been paid since last quarter—"

Jack blinked. Even at ten, he knew the possibility of the entire household staff abandoning ship trumped the case of the missing silver. "My father hasn't paid you?"

"The estate agent was supposed to, but now we know what sort of fellow he is," the butler groused.

"I know where the cash box is in my father's study." Jack stood a little straighter. "I could pay everyone." He swallowed. "Right now."

The housekeeper and butler exchanged a look.

"I don't suppose it would hurt," Mrs. Abbott murmured. "After all, we're owed, and if wages aren't issued soon, I suspect there won't be any servants left before the week is out."

The butler nodded.

Jack led the way to the study. He made them face away while he felt for the hidden key under the lip of his father's dusty desk. He unlocked the bottom drawer and pulled out a small metal box before calling them over.

"You tell me what everyone's owed," Jack said flipping up the lid, "and I can make a note—"

He glanced down, his words grounding to a halt.

"Empty," the butler moaned, shaking his head as if he'd suspected it all along.

"But why is there no money?" Jack ran his hands around the inside of the box, not trusting his eyes.

The housekeeper sighed. "I heard a rumor from the cook's niece whose man farms out at the country estate. Word is no one's been 'round to collect the rents yet this quarter."

Jack stared up at the two adults, hoping they'd tell him what he should do.

Or his parents! They'd be able to fix this. He'd just go downstairs and tell them—

His chest tightened.

It was no use.

He knew exactly what would happen. His parents would ignore him, all their attention on their guests. Tomorrow they'd sleep away most of the day, and if he brought up any of this business with them, they'd merely pat him on the head and say *tomorrow.*

He loved his parents, but they'd have been better as artists, not an earl and countess responsible for running an estate with countless tenants, servants, and houses. Not even their roles as mother and father to Jack or his baby sister Lydia could compete for their attention. Jack gently closed the lid on the cash box and wiped his hands on his pants.

He looked at the housekeeper. "Please arrange to have the carriage readied first thing tomorrow."

Mrs. Abbott nodded, a question in her eyes.

"And have the cook pack a lunch for two." He slid the key into his pocket.

"Two?"

Jack set his jaw. "You and I are going to the tenants to collect the rents."

Jack blinked, his mind returning to the present. The inn. A dark room. Pippa lying beside him.

"And did you?" she asked, her voice soft in the darkness.

"Did I what?"

"Collect the rents with the housekeeper in tow?"

Jack sighed. "I did. We went to every tenant, and I collected the money they owed." He chuckled, but the sound held no merriment even to his own ears. "You can imagine the farmers' and sheep herders' shock when a scrawny ten-year-old approached, asking for the rent. Thank goodness for Mrs. Abbott. She'd cast a stern eye and start to scribble down some nonsense in a ledger. As soon as they saw someone behaving with authority, they all rushed home and brought out the money."

"Ten years old," Pippa murmured, kissing his chest.

"I paid the servants, and there was enough left to maintain

the estate until the next quarter. And I…" Jack stared unblinking into the dark night. "I kept the cash box. My father finally heard what was going on and demanded it." He breathed. "And I refused."

Pippa's hand stilled on his chest.

"He threatened to spank me, to lock me in my room, and to disown me."

"What did you do?" she whispered.

He swallowed. "I staged a mutiny."

She was silent, waiting.

Jack tightened his arms around her. "I had everyone—maids, footmen, cook, butler, and my new ally, Mrs. Abbott—line up behind me in the study. I told my father the servants answered to me, that I paid their wages and not one of them would allow him to punish me."

"Oh, Jack," Pippa said, her hand tightening into a fist on his chest.

He could feel her heartbeat against his side.

"My father sputtered and threatened, but it was all for show. He went back to his poetry that same day. He was likely relieved he didn't have to worry about pesky things like rent and wages and…and children anymore."

Pippa made a little sound of distress before smoothing her hand across his chest as if she could smooth away the pain from his heart.

He drew a shuddering breath. "My sister…I took over with her as well. I hired a proper governess, made sure she had an adequate wardrobe and sent her off to finishing school when the time came. I looked after her, the estate, and my parents."

"And who looked after you?" Pippa's voice was laced with sorrow.

Jack didn't respond. He couldn't. Besides, she already knew the answer.

No one. No one had looked after him.

He'd looked after himself.

Only by keeping total control had he ensured his family, the estate, and the title didn't fall into shambles.

Control was everything.

But he couldn't control Pippa. He couldn't control the passion and connection blazing between them.

And he was learning he couldn't control Lydia either.

There was much he couldn't control, it turned out. Perhaps it had been an illusion all along.

Pippa had helped him to see that. With her blunt questions and disregard for propriety, Pippa allowed him to see how his past shaped who he'd become. And it was time for a change.

She was brilliant, his woman. Brilliant and bright and full of passion and commitment to fairness.

And he loved her.

The thought raced through him like fire across a dry field. *He loved her.*

"Pippa," he murmured, rolling toward her.

He kissed her, and her face was damp. She'd been crying. For him.

"Don't cry, my dear heart." He stroked the tears from her face.

"I can't help it." She sniffled. "It's so terrible, what happened to you and your sister."

"Help me set the pain aside." He kissed her again. "Help me create something new."

"Yes," she gasped, and they were ablaze with passion once more.

He trailed kisses down her throat to her breasts. Her nipples tightened in his mouth as he sucked the delicious tips, laving them with his tongue. Pippa cried out, arching her back and pressing her breasts against him. Her hand ran through his hair, fingers tightening as she pressed him closer to her chest. The slight tingle of pain on his scalp only intensified Jack's pleasure.

"I want to be with you again," he said, looking up at her, "but I imagine you're sore. I have something else in mind, if you'll let me."

She stilled, and he could almost see her mind spinning.

Pippa nodded. Jack smiled, something like happiness lodged in his chest, before returning his attention to her breasts. They were soft and full, and he could spend all night loving them. But he had other places to explore.

Jack trailed a path of kisses down her sternum, along her belly, and to the downy hair below.

"Jack!" She tried to clamp her legs shut, but his head blocked the way. "What are you—surely people don't—oh!"

"Trust me," he murmured, kissing her thigh.

He felt her rise on the bed and could imagine her wide eyes. "Trust me," he repeated, blowing gently against her center. She shuddered in pleasure before laying back.

He parted her folds and ran his tongue up her seam. Pippa gasped, then allowed her legs to fall open more fully. Jack grinned, pleased she didn't shy away from her pleasure.

He settled his mouth on her little bundle of nerves, licking and stroking as his fingers danced along her slick heat. Pippa's breathing became ragged as her pleasure increased. Her sweet, salty tang filled his mouth as she grew wetter.

Her hips pumped in an ancient rhythm as she chased her pleasure. Jack hummed and pinched her outer lips. Pippa cried out, her climax hitting her. Jack stayed with her through her peak. Her head tossed back and forth against the bed. Her hips continued their little jerks until she collapsed into the mattress.

"Oh, Jack," she sighed.

He climbed up the bed, pulling her into his arms. "Did you like that?"

Pippa buried her head against his chest, nodding.

Jack ran his hands along her hair. "You've created a bird's nest back here with all your thrashing." He smiled into her locks.

She tilted her head and kissed him. "You made me into a wild, wanton woman," she murmured. Pippa's fingers stroked his chest. Could she feel the pounding of his heart? "I want to make you feel good."

Jack swallowed. "Touch me," he said, his voice raspy.

He groaned when her fingers—so skilled at gripping a sword—wrapped around his erection.

"Ah, Pippa." He moaned, the pleasure of her touch, at first tentative but growing in confidence, consuming all his senses. He kissed her. He filled his hands with her soft breasts.

She pulled back and slid down the bed.

"I want to do to you like you did to me," she said, her bold words in contrast with the slight flutter of her hand against his thigh.

"You don't—you don't have to—"

Jack broke off as the wet heat of her mouth surrounded him. Her tongue darted across his tip, and Jack resisted the temptation to seize her hair and thrust into her mouth.

She peeked up at him. "Is this right?"

"You feel so good."

Pippa's mouth moved up and down his length, and Jack saw stars as his cock grew even harder.

"Oh, Pippa. Oh, God. Yes," he cried as everything clenched. "Come off," he warned her.

But she continued, and he came with a long, low growl. Pleasure rushed through him like a galloping horse, and he spurted into her tight, hot mouth. Jack collapsed onto the mattress, chest heaving.

Pippa snuggled back into his arms. "That was..." She trailed off.

"I'm sor—"

She smacked him lightly on the shoulder. "Don't you dare say it." Her voice was a cat's purr, all satisfaction and pleasure.

Jack smiled. "I was just going to say I'm sorry I didn't warn you better, about what would happen when I—"

She interrupted. "I'm not a complete ninny. I know what happened before when we..."

Jack could picture her pink cheeks. Heavens, but she was

adorable when she blushed, even when he could only imagine it.

She continued, "I was going to say, before, that it was wonderful."

"Wonderful," Jack agreed, dropping a kiss to her head.

He tightened his arms around her, and soon her breathing was slow and even as she drifted into sleep. But Jack stayed awake for a long time, staring into the darkness, as the devastating memories of his childhood shifted until they were no longer quite so central to who he was now.

It seemed something else had lodged itself at his very center.

PIPPA SCRATCHED HER nose. Something tickled her face—a blanket maybe? She rubbed at her nose again, and her hand encountered something warm. Flesh. Dusted with ticklish hair.

Pippa jolted upright in bed, her heart pounding in panic.

The morning sun glowed at the edges of the curtains, filling the inn room with hazy light.

The inn. Jack. Last night. The two of them…

Pippa's eyes flew to her bedmate.

Jack cracked one eye open and yawned. "Time to get up already?"

She stared at the handsome, naked man in her bed. The bedsheets pooled low at his waist. As she watched, the sheet began to rise as a particular part of Jack's anatomy stirred to life.

Oh my.

Pippa's cheeks burned.

Clearing her throat, she scooted back until his arm around her dropped away. "I, uh…it's morning."

She felt his eyes on her, but the thought of meeting his gaze, of looking eye-to-eye with the man who had, well, *done things* to her and with her—and all right, if she was being honest with herself, she'd done things to him too—was just too embarrassing.

Jack finally spoke. "I'd best be getting up." He stood and

began hunting for his clothes.

Draping herself in a blanket, Pippa slid from the bed.

"Ah, my stockings," Jack announced as if finding footwear was the most engrossing thing in the world.

Keeping her eyes averted, Pippa rummaged through her portmanteau. She hunched under the blanket and shimmied into a chemise before putting on her stays. She began to search for her shoes. She circled the room, her eyes downcast.

"Oof." She collided into Jack, and they both sprung back as if facing a venomous adder.

"Oh, my pardons." He offered a little bow of his head.

"My humblest apologies," Pippa murmured in reply, curtseying.

She bit her lip. Had she just curtseyed to Jack, the man whose mouth had recently been on her—

She shook her head and finished dressing. Jack stood beside the door, looking every inch the perfect, although slightly rumpled, gentleman.

"Well." He cleared his throat. "I suppose I shall return to my chambers now."

Pippa jerked her head in a nod. When the door slid shut again with a snick, she sank onto the bed, resting her head in her hands.

What had she done? Had becoming intimate with Jack doomed their friendship as well as their quest to find Lydia and save the LCA? Had her selfish desires ruined the one thing in her life that truly mattered, the Ladies Covert Academy?

Her heart protested the thought that the LCA was the only thing with meaning in her life.

"Bloody hell," Pippa groaned. The naughty flash of satisfaction from swearing dulled a fraction of her worry.

Well, she couldn't undo it, and—truth be told—she didn't wish to. The night with Jack had been a revelation. Her finger trailed across her lips, and she remembered the feel of his kiss as he'd devoured her last night. Recalling the caress of his hand, the heat of his skin, and the press of his sex against her own brought a quickening in her core.

"Oh," Pippa breathed. She lay back in the bed and pulled his pillow to her, inhaling his scent. *Fool.* He'd just been here, and she hadn't been able to look him in the eye, but the minute he walked out the door, she wished he was here again, doing lovely, sensual, naughty things to her.

She pulled the pillow over her head and screamed, wriggling back and forth on the bed as she kicked her heels.

Enough.

She had to channel this nervous energy into something productive.

Pippa finished her morning ablutions, then surveyed the room until her eyes lit upon the stack of wood next to the fire.

She slid the table flush against the wall and propped a fat log on top. Pippa dug through clothing and the stack of *Democratiam Liberum* articles she'd clipped from the newspaper until she found her sheathed dagger.

Crossing to the far corner of the room, she eyed the wood as if it had insulted her honor and let the dagger fly. It sank into the wood with a satisfying thwonk. She pried the knife out and threw it again. And again. And again, until her world had narrowed to the heft of the dagger, the flick of her wrist, and the sound of it biting into the wood.

She was so engrossed that she shrieked when a rattle sounded off to the side.

She wheeled around, the knife ready to fly.

"Well, I didn't know I'd done *that* badly," Jack drawled.

Pippa froze, taking in the sight of him—her *lover*—standing in the doorway with a breakfast tray in his hands.

He eyed the knife still held up beside her head.

The corners of his mouth twitched. Pippa bit back a grin. A muffled snort escaped his mouth, and she giggled.

Soon they were both laughing. Pippa's shoulders shook with mirth. What a pair they made. He, carrying a tray, including a little flower in a bud vase, basically performing the duties of a maid. Her, with the knife, murdering villainous logs.

He pushed the door shut with his foot and set the tray down on the table next to the wood.

"Come here, my dear heart." He opened his arms.

Pippa dropped the knife, tip down, to the floor where it safely implanted, then flew into his arms. She nuzzled her face into his neck, inhaling his clean, masculine, comforting scent.

Pippa hummed in contentment as his hands stroked down her back.

"That's more like it," he murmured.

"Earlier was so…" She trailed off, uncertain how to label their awkward tension.

"I know. I should have pulled you to me and kissed you senseless. Instead, I hunted for my boots while you hid under a blanket like you were staving off hypothermia."

Pippa giggled. "Well, it was chilly without you beside me."

His arms tightened around her. "Perhaps I should warm you up after breakfast?"

Pippa leaned back. "We have things to do today."

"Well, tonight perhaps?" His eyes glinted with delightful naughtiness.

Pippa returned to his embrace. "Tonight."

They held each other, the connection warming the parts of her that had grown chilly from second-guessing, guilt, and remorse.

This wasn't anything to feel guilt over, she decided, squeezing him tightly before turning to the breakfast tray.

"I'm famished," she said, setting out the dishes. "Thanks for finding breakfast."

Jack assisted, dishing out the eggs, sausage, and pastries onto their plates while she poured tea. They both tucked into the food with gusto.

Once she'd made an offering to the growling monsters in her stomach, Pippa asked, "Where shall we search today?"

He dabbed at his mouth with a napkin. "I vote we head north

and continue asking at every inn. With the information from Mrs. Babcock at The Golden Lion, we know they came this way, but we don't know how far they traveled." He frowned. "Although I have my suspicions."

"Gretna Green?" Pippa lay a hand across his arm.

He nodded, mouth flattened into a hard line.

"What will you do if they've eloped?"

Jack's chest rose with a deep breath. "I suppose I'll have to kill my brother-in-law."

Pippa pinched his arm in disapproval. "Perhaps he's a kind man and your sister will be happy. I doubt making Lydia a widow will endear you to her."

Jack scowled. "Well, I won't shake his hand, that much is certain."

Pippa cast her eyes heavenward and sipped her tea. It was going to be a long day.

Chapter Twenty

AFTER BREAKFAST, THEY loaded into the carriage and continued up the Great North Road. Pippa leaned her head against Jack's shoulder, glad their earlier awkwardness had evaporated.

"Are you tired?" he asked, his voice a low rumble.

"A little." In truth, she'd never before contemplated how a night of sin would tire a body so.

"You could take a nap," he suggested. "I'll wake you when we reach the next inn."

Pippa snuggled against him. "No, I'll be fine." But she didn't mention the reason she was staying awake—she didn't want to miss out on a single minute of being close to him.

What a soft-hearted romantic she was turning into.

The morning was fine, and she and Jack spent much of the next hour enjoying the views from the windows. Jack showed her a deer grazing in a meadow. She pointed out a group of children with fishing poles sitting on a little bridge over a creek.

"I wonder if they'll catch anything," she said as the children passed out of sight.

"Have you ever fished?"

"Never. My father said he'd take me someday, but he…" She trailed off, a lump forming in her throat.

Jack squeezed her hand. She returned the pressure before changing the subject to wildflowers. After a year of visiting Jane's office, Pippa had absorbed a surprising knowledge of flora.

The time passed quickly, and soon they pulled up at the next inn.

Jack helped her down from the carriage and led the way into the dim, smoky interior. Pippa picked her way carefully across the sticky floor, grateful they hadn't spent the night here.

Although the innkeeper gladly took Jack's coin in exchange for entertaining his questions, the tall beanpole of a man had no information about a blond lady traveling with a stripe-haired man in a grand coach.

Jack slouched against the seat when they returned to the carriage.

Pippa linked her arm through his. "Perhaps the next one."

But the next one had the same answer, as did the one after that. Pippa frowned as Jack's face grew stonier with each inn.

"I'll meet you at the carriage shortly," she said as they crossed the inn toward the exit. "I have to take care of something."

He opened his mouth, but Pippa darted off before he could question her.

Soon, she clambered into the carriage where Jack waited, plunking a wicker basket onto the floor with a thud.

He eyed the basket. "What's that?"

Pippa grinned. "I ordered a picnic lunch. I thought our spirits were in need of a little cheer."

Jack's eyes softened. "Thank you."

Pippa kept vigilant watch out the window, and when she saw a fallen pine tree with three other trees growing out of its side along the edge of the road, she banged on the ceiling. The carriage slowed as their driver pulled over.

Jack raised his eyebrows in question.

"I asked the innkeeper about a picnic spot, and he said there was a short trail to a pretty meadow that began at the tree with babies. I wasn't sure what he meant until I saw this." She gestured to the trees growing out of their fallen companion.

"I'm glad humans don't have to drop dead in order to reproduce." Jack reached under the carriage seat, fishing around in the storage area. He emerged with a blanket and grabbed the basket as well.

Pippa pictured herself with a round belly, carrying Jack's child. *Their* child. Maybe a little girl with his brown eyes and Pippa's terrible knitting skills. Or a boy with her dark brown locks and Jack's dry humor. Her chest pinched, and Pippa thrust the thought away.

She hopped out of the carriage. As Jack stood by the horses speaking to the footman in a hushed voice, she examined the fallen tree and its three so-called babies and recalled Jane once talking about nursery logs. Perhaps the innkeeper wasn't so far off the mark.

Jack approached, nodding toward the faint trail through the underbrush. "Shall we?"

Pippa led the way. She kept her eyes on the ground in front of her feet for much of the time as the trail was bisected by roots and other tripping hazards. After a handful of minutes, it opened up into a meadow.

"Oh, it's lovely," Pippa breathed, turning in a circle. The meadow was ringed with trees on three sides and a winding brook on the fourth. Perhaps it was the same stream where those children had fished. In the meadow, the grass was spotted with wildflowers and short bushes. The chirping of birdsong wove together with the gurgle from the brook, soothing Pippa's senses.

Jack took her hand. "Thank you for this. I was turning into a crotchety grump again and did need a bit of cheering up." He smiled, his warm eyes crinkling at the corners.

Something flipped over in Pippa's chest. "Shall we sit by the brook?"

At his nod, she spread the blanket. He unpacked the basket, revealing a meal of cold chicken, apples and cheese, pear turnovers, a loaf of fragrant bread, and a flagon of a cool beverage. Pippa pulled the cork and inhaled.

"Beer," she reported, grinning. "I hope it's Babcock's ale."

"Turning into a salt-of-the-earth type now, are you?" he asked, a teasing glint in his eyes. He served food onto their plates. "Once you begin to drink ale, it's only a short fall until you're talking back to the actors on Drury Lane and attending a suffragist protest of the elections."

"And what's wrong with protesting the elections?" She pursed her lips. "Don't you think women should have the right to vote?"

Jack opened his mouth to reply, but Pippa plowed ahead.

"From reading your sister's articles, it's clear the Commons is in need of reform—"

Jack raised a finger, but Pippa kept talking.

"—and who better to bring about reform than the ladies?"

Jack's lips twitched. "May I speak now?"

Pippa sniffed. "I suppose you may."

Jack attempted to mask his snicker with a cough, and Pippa rolled her eyes.

"Well," he answered, after swallowing a bite of chicken. "I'd likely have given you a different answer a handful of days ago. But with what I know now about Lydia's apparent talent for political treatises and an entire cadre of women engaging in unorthodox pursuits, I say society be damned. I'm inclined to let the ladies vote."

Pippa blinked. *This was unexpected.*

"Did I surprise you?"

She blinked again, then cleared her throat. "Yes, rather."

Jack laughed. "Ah, never rule out people's ability to change. I'm only beginning to understand the phenomenon myself, but it does seem rather powerful."

Pippa returned his smile and then focused on her pear turnover before he could read the emotion in her eyes. It would not do for him to know how much his support for women's suffrage meant to her. To know how much *he* meant to her.

"Pippa, I have a question for you," Jack said after laying a piece of cheese atop an apple slice. "But you don't have to answer if you'd rather not."

Pippa set down her pear turnover, deciding perhaps she'd enjoy the dessert more when she wasn't facing a potentially daunting query. She nodded.

"You've told me about the true nature of the LCA," Jack began, his voice low, "and you've hinted your involvement is connected to your father's passing. I was wondering…" He trailed off and set the apple and cheese down, seeming uncertain how to word his question.

Perhaps he feared upsetting her.

Wise man.

"You want to know why I learned to fence," she finished for him, deciding it was time to bare all. He'd told her about his neglectful parents last night, and the story had spun invisible threads around her heart, binding her tighter to Jack with each word.

Now it was time for her do to the same.

"If you feel comfortable telling me." He leaned back on one elbow. His face was open and neutral, the face of a listener, but she could see the faint worry behind his eyes.

Worry for her.

Pippa exhaled slowly. Her hands pleated the blanket as she thought about where to start.

"When I was a little girl, I had the perfect life." She stared at the ripples on the surface of the brook. "My parents were very loving, and I was so happy when my brother was born. He was so sweet and tiny." She swallowed. "Everything was perfect."

Pippa tracked the dancing flashes of sunlight reflecting off the stream. She'd spent so many years of her life feeling tossed about like a little rowboat on the open ocean, with no control or power over her direction.

But no more.

She exhaled. "My parents and I left our home in London to visit our country estate. We left my brother behind with the nanny so my mother could have a little break. He was quite a demanding baby, for all his sweetness. I sat next to my father in our carriage, like I usually did." A smile came unbidden as she recalled her father's kind face, the laugh lines spreading out from the corners of his blue eyes.

She could recall that day so clearly.

Young Pippa had leaned against her father's firm arm, the gentle sway of the carriage tempting her to close her eyes.

"How much longer?" She stifled a yawn.

"Another two hours or so, sweeting," her father answered with a smile. "I can move to the bench with your mother if you wish to lay down."

Pippa glanced across the carriage. The dim light of early evening didn't hide the view of her mother sprawled across the entire seat, her mouth open as she snored delicately.

Pippa stifled a giggle with her hand and peeked at her father. His eyes danced with laughter.

"Perhaps I'd best stay on this side with you." He pitched his voice low so as not to wake his sleeping wife.

Pippa nodded. It was understandable why her mother was so tired. Caring for a new baby was an awful lot of work, her father had told her, and that was one of the reasons the baby had been left behind in London with the wet nurse and nanny. Mama needed a little break, he'd confided, and their country estate was just the place for it.

The comfortable rumbling noises of the carriage were rent by a sharp bang. The carriage jerked and swayed. Pippa shrieked and clutched her father's arm, nearly losing her seat as the carriage shuddered to a halt.

"Wha'?" her mother mumbled, pushing herself up.

"There's trouble. Pippa, sit with your mother and stay quiet."

Once Pippa had moved to the other bench, her father lifted their now-vacant seat cushion, feeling about in the dark storage area beneath.

Pippa's mother held her close. "What's happening, Henry?"

Pippa could feel her mother's hands trembling.

"It might be highwaymen." He turned, a pistol in his hand.

Pippa had never seen her father's face like it was now. Where were his teasing smiles, his twinkling eyes, his reassuring glances?

They could hear loud voices from outside, and her father lowered the window shade and peered into the dusk.

"Henry!" Her mother reached out a hand as if to pull him back from the eye of danger and keep him safe.

He placed a finger over his mouth, never taking his eyes off the exposed strip of window.

"Papa?" Pippa's voice trembled, her fear a palpable thing, clawing and grasping at her from the inside.

He pulled away from the window. "Everything will be fine," he whispered, kissing them each. "Just stay calm and quiet."

A second later, he was gone, the carriage vast and empty without his big, warm presence to fill it.

Pippa stared at the door, willing it to open. Willing her father to return and their voyage to continue.

Please, Father. Please.

The rumble of her father's voice was followed by loud retorts. Her mother's arms were a vice around her, but Pippa needed to see. If she could just keep her eye on her father, she knew he'd be safe. She squirmed, sliding out of her mother's grasp.

"Pippa, no," her mother breathed, reaching for her.

But Pippa was at the door, pulling the window shade all the way down. Her father's broad, strong back was to her. Three men, their faces partially-hidden with scarves and lowered hats, were on horseback. One had a pistol pointed at her father and another aimed a shotgun toward the front of the carriage where the driver sat.

The man with a pistol snarled at her father, the words indistinguishable in the carriage. Her father reached into his pocket with one hand, each movement slow and deliberate. The other hand, she could now see, held a pistol trained on the highwayman. Her father produced a purse and tossed it to the man. The man caught it and hefted its weight, an ugly grin creasing his dirty face.

The man said something and nodded at the carriage. Pippa gasped.

Would the men come in here?

One of the highwaymen slid off his horse and moved toward the carriage. Her father shouted, but the man didn't stop. Her father pivoted and a loud bang tore through the air. Another bang, then another ripped through the evening's muted glow.

Pippa screamed.

The highwaymen shouted. They whirled on their horses and thundered away.

Pippa scrabbled at the door. She dashed into the cool night air.

Her father was on the ground. She threw herself onto him. "Papa!"

Her mother pulled her back.

"Henry!" Pippa's mother ran her hands over his still form. She lifted them into the last dregs of daylight. The illumination showed the red smear across her palms. "No," her mother gasped.

"Milady." The coachman staggered toward them. He gripped his upper arm with the opposite hand, blood visible between his fingers.

"Help us," her mother whispered.

Grimacing, the coachman clambered to the ground. He lay his hand upon her father's chest.

Pippa held her breath.

"Milady…" The coachman's voice was heavy with sorrow.

"No." Her mother shook her husband. "No, you're wrong. You're wrong! Henry, wake up. Wake up!"

Pippa saw the truth etched on the coachman's face. Her father was dead.

Her father was dead.

Disbelief turned her to stone. She couldn't cry or speak or move. All she could do was stare at the body of her father, bleeding into the dirt.

A fish jumped in the brook. Pippa's breath jerked in her chest, breaking her out of her reverie. She blinked. She was in the meadow. Jack's hand engulfed her own, his thumb stroking her skin in soothing circles.

She exhaled, her mind slowly returning from the painful memory.

"How old were you?"

Pippa swallowed, her eyes darting around the meadow. "Ten," she finally answered. "Same age as you when you had to grow up."

Their gazes locked, and Pippa saw her own pain reflected in his eyes.

Pippa felt wrung out. She lay back on the blanket. Jack copied her pose, their fingers tangling together. She watched a cloud drift by overhead, its shape reminiscent of a dragon.

"Thank you for telling me," Jack said after several minutes of comfortable silence. "I'm so sorry your father was killed, Pippa, and that you witnessed it. No child should see such violence."

Pippa swallowed, knowing she owed him more of the story. No, it wasn't owing. She *wanted* to tell him. She wanted him to know why she'd become who she was.

"It stayed with me." A bird chirped, its cheery warble lending her strength to continue. "A few weeks after it happened, my brother's nanny insisted we visit the park. Constant mourning was no good for youngsters, she said. My governess complied, happy for an hour or two to herself. So away we went. The nanny was distracted when my brother started crying. I wandered off, playing with another child." Pippa paused, her heart racing at the memory.

Jack squeezed her hand in comfort.

"When the other child left, I couldn't find the nanny. We'd wandered far off. I looked all around, trying to find her, trying to find safety. Some men walked by. I thought one of them held a pistol. I...I was terrified." Pippa shivered at the memory. "It was actually a riding crop, but by then I was certain the highwaymen were after me. And then a horse galloped by, and I completely panicked. I ran and hid in a thicket. I was there for hours. The nanny notified my mother who sent the entire household of servants to search the park." Pippa breathed in and out, trying to calm her pulse.

"When they found me, I was covered in scratches from the brambles. It was dark. I'd scared them all half to death. They brought me home, and my mother held me and cried. I remember I patted her on the back and told her it was all right, that it was safe at home, and I would stay there."

It's safe at home. I'll stay here.

Pippa's stomach turned. She breathed shallowly, trying to dispel the nausea.

She could feel remnants of her fear from all those years ago and the power of its grip, like a wolf's jaw mercilessly clenched around its prey. She felt it trying to wrap around her even now.

"How long did you stay home?"

Pippa opened her mouth, but the words wouldn't come. She licked her lips and tried again to answer him. "Four years."

Jack's hand flinched against hers. He swore.

Pippa stared straight up at the sky. She wouldn't cry. She wouldn't.

"You didn't leave at all for four years?"

"I refused." Pippa tried to keep her voice matter of fact. "If my mother tried to take me out, I became hysterical. Completely unhinged." She flinched at the edge to her voice. Would he think her completely unhinged now? "She finally decided to let me have my way. And so, I stayed home where I believed I was safe for four years."

Jack stroked her hand. "What changed?"

"My brother." Pippa stared up at the sky, her muscles relaxing a fraction at the memory of the chubby, smiling four-year-old. "Thomas was the sweetest little boy. He loved to play in the park and take walks with the nanny. And he loved me." The wolf's jaw loosened its grip around her. "He'd run into my room, all cute and roly-poly like little children are. And he'd ask me to play outside with him. I'd say no, of course, and then he'd cry."

Pippa could picture it so clearly, his big blue eyes spilling over with tears, his lower lip quivering.

"And one day, as he sobbed on the floor, I just...I just couldn't do it anymore. I couldn't allow my fear to sadden him. And so, I went into the backyard and played ball with my brother. And...highwaymen didn't kill us." Pippa shrugged. "I guess it was just that simple."

"Oh, I doubt it was simple," Jack muttered, his hand squeezing hers.

Pippa huffed. "Well, I was still afraid, of course." She shook her head. "I hated going to social functions. Every time I crossed the threshold to leave the house, I'd get the shivers and breathe like I'd just run up a mountain. It was still debilitating, my fear. But at least I was no longer a shut-in."

Jack rolled onto his side. "Tell me about the fencing."

Pippa turned to face him. His hair was mussed from laying on the ground, and she smoothed a lock back. Jack closed his eyes as if savoring her touch, and Pippa's heart swelled.

"One night, my mother made me go to the theater with her." Pippa made a little noise of annoyance. "So many stories. Are you finding this all quite dull?"

Jack's eyes bored into hers. "You and your stories are anything but dull. I could listen to you talk all day." He glanced away as if self-conscious. "Actually, the very first day I met you, I imagined you talking to me as I soaked in your soothing voice."

Pippa held her breath. "Really?" she asked, once her heart no longer felt like bursting from her chest.

He met her gaze and nodded. He stroked a finger along her cheek. "Tell me the story."

Pippa sighed. "This was a little over a year ago. We'd just left the theater and were waiting out front along with everyone else for our carriage. Most people were talking about the show or gossiping, but I...I couldn't. I was never relaxed when I was outside or in a crowd. So, I was looking around, keeping an eye out for danger. I saw a gentleman get attacked by footpads in an alley across the square. I was frozen, watching it all happen. I should have shouted for help, but..." She shook her head, panged with guilt.

Pippa exhaled. "It turned out the gentleman didn't need me to call for assistance." She smiled wryly. "He had a sword in his walking stick. He fought off the footpads. I watched him defend himself, and it was like some place deep inside me that had been shrouded in darkness ever since my father's death was suddenly seeing daylight." Pippa rubbed a finger across the callouses on her palm. "And I knew, I just *knew*, that if I could defend myself like that man, I wouldn't have to live in fear anymore."

"You're so brave," Jack whispered, his fingers feathering along her cheek, over her brow, and across her hair.

He left little sparks of pleasure in his wake.

"I wasn't though," she said. "I'm still not. I get frightened every day. But I fight back now. Jane is the one to thank since she was a member of the LCA. You have to be sponsored by a member to join. Lady Rowling can't exactly advertise." Pippa quirked her eyebrows. "So, my cousin vouched for me, and I had an interview with Lady Rowling. She secured my wonderful fencing instructor, *Señor* Martín."

Pippa smiled, thinking of how patient *Señor* Martín had been those first few weeks when she'd been nothing but jittery nerves and weak arms.

Jack pulled her close, so her head rested on his chest. "That's quite a tale, Miss Philippa Chester."

The sun warmed her hair, and Jack's heart beat a steady tempo under her ear. Pippa exhaled, feeling lighter than she had in a long time.

"I'm glad I told you," she whispered.

His arms tightened in a hug. "I'm glad you trusted me."

They breathed together, the warm sunshine and calming

gurgle of the brook soothing the rough and ragged places exposed by her story.

Pippa sighed. "Should we head back to the carriage?" She didn't want this idyllic time to end, but there were inns to visit.

"Not quite yet. I have a surprise for you."

Chapter Twenty-One

JACK ENJOYED WATCHING Pippa pop up from the blanket like a jack-in-the-box, her hands clasped together in delight.

"A surprise?"

"Wait here." He winked before trekking across the meadow to the trail. About twenty feet down the path lay the item he'd asked the driver to deliver.

He walked back on the shaded path, thoughts tumbling with all she'd revealed. He ached for Pippa and her painful past. A child so young witnessing her father's murder... He could barely process it. And overcoming her fear for the sake of her brother as well as herself—it was truly inspiring.

Jack wanted to tell her how he felt about her. However, he scarcely understood it himself. All he knew was being with her, and being challenged by her, made him feel truly alive.

Perhaps this surprise would show her. He approached, holding it behind his back.

"What is it?" She tried to peek around him.

"I know we still have inns to visit, but..." Jack brought the item forward. "I thought this would be a good time to continue your lessons." He handed her the box of pistols.

Pippa grinned. "I was hoping you'd let me shoot again."

She sat back on the blanket to load the guns. Her eyebrows creased in a delightful manner as she concentrated, and Jack's fingers itched to caress the little furrows.

She asked a few questions, but they were mostly to further her understanding of the pistol mechanics. Her hands were steady and confident as she poured the gunpowder and inserted the bullets.

"What shall we aim for this time?"

Jack looked around the clearing. "See that tree over there, the one with the *Y* in its trunk?"

Pippa nodded, and they relocated to the center of the clearing. She took the proper stance, arms steady and back straight. Slowly, Pippa exhaled and squeezed the trigger. A branch on the tree jumped.

She grinned at him. "Think I'll be a crack shot by the end of the day?"

Jack raised an eyebrow. "I'll show you what being a crack shot looks like."

He picked up the second pistol and scanned the tree. "See that burl on the side?"

"That tiny thing?" Pippa eyed him with open skepticism.

"Oh, just you wait." Jack raised his right arm, sighting down the barrel of the pistol to the burl. He took a moment to assess the direction of the slight breeze, then narrowed his focus to the target, his finger on the trigger, and the weight of the pistol in his hand. He breathed. He squinted. His finger tightened…

Bang.

Bark exploded off the side of the tree. Jack lowered the gun.

"Did you…?" Pippa jogged to the tree and touched where the burl had once been. "You shot it clean off. My goodness."

Jack's chest puffed up with pride. Yes, he'd just shown off to impress a lady. What a buck he'd become, basically showing off his massive antlers to get her attention.

Pippa continued her practice with renewed determination. Jack gave occasional pointers, but mostly he watched her hone her technique. He could imagine her during fencing lessons, all focus and determination as she perfected a difficult move. Those were qualities he'd associated with men in the past. Was Pippa unique, or were most women just as focused but with little opportunity to display it?

"Just think of the wagging tongues if people could see you right now," he said after she'd hit her target three times in a row.

"What?" She turned to face him, her arms stiff at her side.

"Oh, I was just thinking about the reaction from polite society if they could see you now, blasting your targets better than most men." Jack smiled.

Pippa's face froze for a moment before she smiled back. Her gaze remained on his cravat.

She cleared her throat. "I suppose we should be getting on?"

Together, they cleaned the pistols and packed up everything before heading back to the carriage.

⟫⟫⟫✳⟪⟪⟪

PIPPA STARED OUT the window, oblivious to the view of the trees rushing by. Her hands knotted together in her lap.

Just think of the wagging tongues if people could see you right now.

Pippa knew she was different. Her debilitating fear following her father's death kept her apart from everyone else. But she hadn't realized the full implication for her future until Jack's comments in the meadow.

…the reaction from polite society if they could see you now, blasting your targets better than most men…

She was a complete and utter scandal.

She could never be a proper lady. She could never, for example, be a countess. Using marriage to an earl to underscore her internal point should have been preposterous, only it wasn't. She *could* imagine marrying Jack and spending the rest of her life with him.

At least, she could until he'd made that comment.

The horses pulled them further up the Great North Road. The rhythmic sound of their hooves acted as a tranquilizer on

Jack, his head propped against the side of the carriage. But Pippa remained awake, her spinning thoughts her sole companion on the drive to the next inn.

What had she imagined happening? She and Jack would find Lydia, save the LCA, and then he'd get down on one knee?

An impossible dream.

Pippa blinked back tears.

More likely, they'd find Lydia already married to that rogue from the law office. They'd be unable to keep the news of her scandalous elopement a secret, and then the gossips would really have something to sink their teeth into once it became known that Lydia Dashwood, sister to the Earl of Hartwick, was none other than the infamous firebrand *Democratiam Liberum*.

Lydia and Jack's reputations would be in tatters, hanging onto polite society by the merest of threads.

One more scandal and they'd be given the cut direct, cast out, and shunned by all.

One more scandal…such as a liaison with a woman who practiced fencing daily.

A woman who posed as a man and fought in a duel.

A woman who battled a gang of thieves, spent the night at an inn with a man not her husband, and belonged to a secret academy that allowed ladies to—heaven forbid!—pursue the fields that interested them.

Pippa wrapped her arms around herself, trying to stave off the chill creeping along her skin with each realization.

She couldn't have Jack. It would ruin him. And she loved him too much to be the cause of his downfall.

All she could have was this trip.

Once they returned home, she'd have to let him go. Never see or speak to him again. Never press her lips to his. Never look into his laughing eyes that were such a contrast to the serious lines of his face. Would she ever have this feeling of connection, of wanting, of belonging again?

She was a novice at love, but even she knew it wasn't likely for lightning to strike twice.

The rhythm of the horses' hoof beats changed. They must be at the next inn. Pippa wiped at her eyes and adopted a serene expression before Jack stirred.

"What's it?" he slurred, rubbing his face. His hair stood up in wild disarray. He was warm and sleepy and gorgeous. Pippa's chest ached from just looking at him. It would be so satisfying to simply burst into tears. Instead, she stretched her lips in an approximation of a smile. "Wake up, sleepyhead. We're at the next inn. Perhaps we'll find news of Lydia."

LATER THAT DAY, the carriage stopped at yet another inn. Jack stretched his restless limbs once his feet touched the ground.

"Shall we see about dinner while we're here?" He helped Pippa out of the carriage.

She shook her head. "I think we can make it to at least one more inn before it's too dark to travel."

Jack searched her gaze, but she wouldn't meet his eyes. Something was bothering her, although she'd said she was simply tired when he'd inquired. But things were different between them now. The obvious reason was they'd spent the night together. However, once they'd gotten over their initial awkwardness this morning, things had been good. Better than good.

He'd been happy.

And she'd been happy as well; he'd have staked his title on it.

But now she was subdued, as if a cloud had passed over the sun. And, truly, that was Pippa—the bright warmth of the sun shining into his life.

So why did he feel like he was in a shadow?

Jack opened his mouth to question her once more, but she'd already walked away.

Another hour, another inn. How many had they visited over the course of these two days? Twenty? And no one, aside from the innkeeper's wife at The Golden Lion, had seen hide nor hair of Lydia and that scallywag.

Jack sighed and followed in Pippa's footsteps.

They had their routine down to a science. Take a table, order an ale, and ask the innkeeper their questions, all while making sure several tempting coins were in sight. And after a few sips of beer, they continued north. He was certain they'd be at the Artic Circle any day now.

Jack slid into a seat across the table from Pippa. Another innkeeper, short and bald this time, approached. His answers were the same as his predecessors. No, he'd not seen anyone fitting Lydia or Aubrey Andrew's description in the last week. Yes, he'd gladly keep an eye out and notify Jack if they came through.

Pippa's mouth turned down in a little frown of commiseration, and hungry puppy that he was, Jack lapped up the emotion of her pity. Pushing aside his tankard of ale, Jack rose to his feet. He stretched out a hand, but Pippa seemed not to notice and rose on her own.

"Hartwick!" bellowed a voice from across the crowded inn. "I say, Hartwick!"

Jack scanned the room. He groaned when he saw a man disentangle himself from a table laden with tankards, platters of food, and bored gentlemen. Pippa's eyebrows shot up in concern. She opened her mouth, but a heavy hand clamped down on his shoulder before she could speak.

"I thought that was you, old man," crowed a tall, beefy man, his neck as thick as his head. He pounded Jack on the back in a greeting that would be labeled an assault in some circles.

"Hello, Powell," Jack replied to his former Eton classmate. He stepped out of back thumping range and angled his body to remove Pippa from the conversation. With any luck, the big lug wouldn't realize she was with him.

"What brings you this way?" Powell seemed oblivious to Jack's lack of enthusiasm for this conversation.

Jack cleared his throat. "Ah, just visiting some friends up north."

"You should come over to my place, just a few miles to the west. A bunch of the old gang is over." Powell gestured to the gentlemen at the table with his giant hand. "We're to have a bit of sport tomorrow. Pheasant season, you know."

Jack scanned the table, finding several men from his school days. He'd be hard pressed to gather together a group of men with a greater aptitude for bullying, drunkenness, or leering at women. *Shit.* He had to get Pippa out of this inn.

As if Jack had telegraphed his thoughts, Powell's head swiveled to Pippa who was slowly inching away.

"Oh ho, what's hiding over here?" Powell gave her a thorough perusal, eyes gleaming with wicked glee.

The few sips of ale sat like cement in Jack's stomach.

Powell licked his thick lips. "Off for a sport of a different sort, are you?" He dug his elbow into Jack's ribs, chortling.

Jack's jaw ached from clenching so tightly.

Now he'd have to call the bastard out and he'd be a murderer and Pippa would never forgive him for not letting her do it herself.

He opened his mouth, but Pippa jumped into the fray.

"What sort of insinuations are these, sir, to make to a respectable lady?" Pippa seemed to grow several inches as her back went ramrod stiff. "I'm the companion to Lord Hartwick's sister, and I'll have your apology at once!"

And she glared down her nose with such frostiness that even Jack felt like he was in trouble with his old governess.

"I-I beg your pardon, miss," the once mighty Powell stammered, cut down to size by Pippa who wielded a weapon he was completely unfamiliar with. Apparently even the uncouth cowered before outraged respectability.

Powell apologized to Jack as well. He was inching his way back toward his table when he suddenly asked, "Where *is* your sister, by the way? Would love a chance to say hello."

Beside him, Pippa stiffened.

"She's upstairs resting. Had a bit of a megrim after a long day of travel. You know how delicate women can be." Jack wanted to punch himself in the face, but his words did the trick.

"Quite right, fairer sex and all that." Powell laughed, order restored to his world once again now that women were weak and ill instead of whipping him into submission with naught but their stare. He bid Jack farewell and returned to his friends.

"Quick thinking," Pippa whispered.

Jack's fingers itched to weave with hers and tug her close, but this was neither the time nor the place. "This means we're staying here tonight," he replied, stuffing his hands into his pockets instead.

At her questioning look, he added, "It would raise suspicion if we suddenly depart with Lydia allegedly resting upstairs. And knowing these bounders, they'll be here in their cups until the wee hours."

Pippa nodded, her face reflecting her disappointment.

"I know," he commiserated, "but I can't risk your reputation if that dunderhead Powell starts asking more questions."

"My reputation?" Pippa stared at him.

"Of course, your reputation." Jack stared back. Was she really that clueless as to how precious she'd become to him? Well, he'd have to rectify that tonight, if she agreed to admit him to her chambers once more.

"Come on, we'd best see about securing rooms."

Soon, the innkeeper had them settled in two adjacent rooms with a promise of dinner trays arriving soon.

Jack paced across the tired floorboards of his chamber, raking his fingers through his hair as he cursed.

What a disaster this had turned into. Pippa had nearly been exposed. Even now, it was possible Powell and his cronies were piecing together her identity. She was a member of the ton, after all, and despite her years homebound, she'd been seen at social events recently. If they figured out who she was, she'd be ruined.

Jack kicked the leg of the table, then grunted in pain as he hopped on one foot.

He flopped back onto the bed and stared at the water-stained ceiling.

Defeat.

He was defeated. He couldn't find Lydia. He couldn't protect Pippa. It was time to give up. Jack exhaled, feeling like he'd been pricked by a pin and all his energy was draining out of him.

He and Pippa would head home to London tomorrow, only stopping to change the horses. He'd call upon the Bow Street runners to hire more men. Although Gormley had proven less than useless, perhaps other runners were more capable, or at least honest.

Jack would sacrifice anything to have his sister home safe. However, he was discovering he wasn't so keen to sacrifice Pippa.

A knock at the door interrupted his thoughts.

"Come," he called, wondering what the innkeeper had brought for dinner.

Instead, Pippa slipped into his room and turned the key in the lock behind her.

PIPPA PRESSED HER hands into the smooth wood of the door behind her, trying to absorb some of the old timber's strength. She'd done bold, wild things, but this took the cake.

She was going to seduce Jack and soak up as much passion and affection and *him* as she could. And then she was going to say goodbye.

Madness.

And yet, it was the only way.

"I..." She trailed off, uncertain what to say, but his eyes darkened as they roamed over her. Could he see the arousal in her flushed cheeks or leaping pulse?

Jack crossed the room. And then his hands were in her hair

and his lips on her mouth and oh God, nothing had felt so good in her entire life.

She kissed him like it was everything, like she was going to die.

And a part of her *would* die when this was over.

She moaned, pressing her chest against him. His hands trailed down her hair, along the column of her neck, and down to cup her bottom. He pulled her flush against him, and Pippa gasped at the pleasure of his hard arousal pressing into her softness.

"Oh, please," she begged.

Jack stared down, his eyes smoldering. "What changed?" he rasped, his jaw hard.

Pippa shook her head in denial. "N-nothing."

He traced a finger along her cheek, his warm-brown eyes seeing straight into her. He opened his mouth but seemed to change his mind about speaking and kissed her instead, long drugging kisses that caused Pippa to forget anything but the taste of pleasure.

He scooped her up and she gasped, clinging to his neck. He nuzzled against her hair as he walked.

"What you do to me," he whispered before setting her on the bed.

Jack shrugged out of his jacket and waistcoat, then tugged off his boots. Pippa knelt on the bed, making short work of his shirt buttons. She sighed when her hand finally rested against his bare chest.

His hands hadn't remained idle, and her gown soon gaped. They each undressed the other in a frenzy of buttons and ties and fabric. Clothes were thrown to the floor without care. As soon as she was naked, Jack wrapped his arm around her waist, and they tumbled onto the bed together.

Pippa kissed him with abandon, pouring all her love into the feverish movement of lips and tongue. Did he know how she felt? Could he sense it?

Jack moaned. His hand slid over her hip and up to her breast.

Pippa gasped as he plucked at her nipple, and a jolt of lust zinged along her skin to her center.

She opened her eyes, wanting to absorb this experience with as many senses as possible. Jack's eyelashes trembled then flickered open. Their gazes locked as they kissed. Pippa shuddered at the intensity of the openness, at the vulnerability as he peered into her soul.

It had never been like this.

And it never would again.

Overwhelmed, she closed her eyes. Jack kissed along her neck and down to her breasts. He laved her tight peaks with his tongue, and Pippa cried out. Her fingers burrowed into his hair, holding him tightly to her.

"You are so beautiful," he murmured as he moved from one side to the other.

Pippa's pulse pounded through her. Her skin was aflame. It felt as if only one more touch would send her over the edge.

"Jack," she moaned.

He must have heard the desperate need in her voice, for he lifted his head and his eyes danced with wicked intentions. "Never fear, my heart. I have plans for you."

Pippa's heart stuttered. She watched, wide-eyed, as he kissed his way down her stomach. Her muscles jerked and fluttered at his touch. He dipped his head lower.

Pippa's head lolled back onto the bed as torrents of pleasure rolled through her. This thing he was doing, that he'd done once before, was completely scandalous.

And glorious.

His tongue swirled while his fingers traced her slippery folds. All her senses were focused right there, at that tiny point of enormous pleasure. The pressure from his mouth, the wet heat of his tongue…

Pippa tightened and tightened and tightened and exploded into a shuddering conduit of sensation. "Oh Jack, oh Jack, oh oh oh!" she chanted as her peak continued, his clever mouth prolonging her bliss.

Pippa's fingers gripped the sheets. Her body shuddered. She moaned and then lay supine. She had barely enough energy to pant. She threaded her hands through his hair. "Jack."

He kissed the inside of her thigh. "Pippa," he replied, his voice warm and deep.

"That was very naughty," she whispered.

"Oh, you didn't like it?" His face was all innocence. Too bad his eyes gleamed with wicked glee.

"Well, perhaps if you showed me again…"

Jack laughed, and they smiled at one another, reveling in their mutual delight. Pippa's heart pulsed. Oh, this man. How she loved him.

He dipped his head and set his tongue upon her once more. Lightly, lightly he traced her secret place.

Pippa gasped. She was on the verge with just that simple touch.

Jack's fingers smoothed up along the sides of her plump lips. His tongue flicked, and Pippa was again engulfed in a whirlwind of pleasure. Her head tilted back, her mouth open on a silent scream. Her hips jerked. That bit of friction hurled her further into her bliss.

She gasped for breath. Her entire body trembled. Coherent thought was forsaken, replaced by more primitive instincts like *mine* and *more*.

Jack ran lazy fingers along her sprawled thighs. "So?" His eyes danced in devilish mirth.

Pippa's lips twitched. "I suppose if one has to pass the time…"

Jack pinched her leg. "Minx," he scolded before soothing the spot with a kiss. Jack climbed up the bed and took her in his arms.

"I adore you," he murmured into her ear, and then he kissed her, and Pippa wanted to hold him forever and she wanted to bawl, and she wanted this night to never end.

Jack's hard length pressed against her belly as they kissed. Pippa arched her hips, and he inhaled sharply.

She kissed down his neck to his chest, following the path he'd forged on her own body. She feathered her fingers across his abdomen, trailing her tongue over the bumps and ridges of his muscles. His skin was warm and tasted of soap and salt.

"Pippa," he gasped as she moved lower.

She dropped a soft kiss on the tip of his cock, and he groaned. Glancing up, she found his face taut and eyes glittering. She hid a smile of pride. Pippa kissed him again, then ran her tongue up his length. He was strength encased in softness. It was the opposite of who he was as a man: a soft heart surrounded by a tough exterior.

Pippa took him in her mouth, feeling more confident of the rhythm this time. Jack rested his hands on the back of her head, his fingertips flexing into her hair. He moaned as she took him in deep. Pippa trailed curious fingers along the heavy sac below. Jack drew in a shuddering breath when she dusted her fingers across that curious place again.

"Oh God, that feels so good," he gasped, his fingers tightening in her hair.

Pippa increased the tempo, keeping a steady pressure with her lips as she slid her wet mouth along his heat. Her fingers continued to stroke below.

Jack stiffened and cried out. He spurted into her mouth. Pippa continued to suck until he relaxed, sinking into the mattress.

"Oh, my dear heart," he sighed, gently combing his fingers through her locks. "What you do to me."

Pippa crawled into his arms, her head resting against his chest. The steady thumping of his heartbeat echoed the rhythm of her own, their two hearts beating in time.

Chapter Twenty-Two

JACK STROKED HIS fingers along Pippa's arm. She nestled her head against his chest and sighed. His body buzzed with satisfied contentment, but something scratched at his thoughts.

"Happy?" he murmured, chest tightening as he waited for her answer.

"Hm." She pressed a kiss onto his skin.

Jack's fingers paused. "Are you upset we haven't saved the LCA yet?"

Pippa didn't answer.

"Are you mad at me for not punching that idiot Powell earlier?"

She snorted.

Jack swallowed. "Are you upset with *me*?"

Pippa was silent for what felt like ten years but was likely a handful of seconds. "I'm not upset with you. Why all these questions?"

Jack weighed several responses. "It just seems like something's troubling you."

Pippa wiggled away, pulling the sheet up over her breasts. "Well, nothing's troubling me, aside from our inability to find Lydia, the threat of scandal if the true identity of *Democratiam Liberum* is discovered, the closure of my secret academy, and fear of discovery."

Jack sat up against the headboard. "You don't say," he drawled.

She had the grace to look abashed. "I'm sorry, Jack. I know you have the same worries." She looked away. "I suppose…I suppose I feel guilty, for taking time for pleasure when we're in the middle of all of this." Her cheeks turned a delightful shade of pink.

A knock at the door prevented Jack's response. "Who is it?"

"I've got yer supper here, milord," called a voice.

"Leave it outside the door."

"And the miss next door didn't answer either, milord," the servant added.

"She's likely resting," Jack called, offering Pippa a half smile. "Leave hers outside her door as well."

Once the servant's footsteps retreated, Jack slipped into his trousers and shirt. He padded barefoot to the door. No one was in the hallway, so he collected both their dinner trays.

"Your meal is served, madam." He offered a bow.

Pippa slipped into her chemise before joining him at the table.

Jack eyed the rosy hue of her nipples through the thin fabric while she rearranged the items on the tray—a bowl of stew, a glass of wine, a hearty roll on the side, and a folded newspaper.

"This is quite good," she said after a bite of stew. "And you can stop trying to peek down my chemise. T'would be a shame for your food to grow cold just because of a nice bosom."

"Well, I shall do my best"—Jack pointed at her with his spoon—"but I'd say it's more like a *magnificent* bosom."

Pippa tried to hide her smile in her wine cup.

"I'll send word to the innkeeper to have a breakfast packed for our early departure tomorrow." Jack spread butter onto his roll.

"Do you think we'll reach Scotland tomorrow?"

Jack tried to calculate how many miles they'd make if they left at dawn. "We're not going to Scotland," he answered, distracted.

Pippa's spoon froze midair. "What?"

"We're returning to London. The chances of you being discovered are just too high."

Her eyes widened. "But—"

"We'll get you back safe and sound, and then I'll contact the Bow Street runners. I'll do some background checking to make sure they're not corrupt like Gormley." He shook his head.

She frowned. "But Jack—"

"When that muttonhead Powell saw us, I realized how selfish I've been. Your entire future would've been ruined if he'd figure out who you are."

Pippa leaned forward. "But I don't care—"

"I've decided." Jack held up his hand to block her protestations. "We're heading back on the morrow, and that's that."

Pippa's eyes narrowed and she crossed her arms. "Oh, *you've* decided, have you? Just when I think you've changed, you go and act like a controlling arse all over again."

Jack clenched his jaw. Oh, he was an arse now, was he? Her response only confirmed his conclusion. *He* needed to make the decisions. Only *he* could see the clear path ahead of them.

She'd see he was right once he explained. "If you just calm down—"

Pippa laughed, but the sound was without mirth. "Oh no, you didn't just tell me to *calm down*. Since the dawn of time, has a man saying that to an upset woman ever once worked?"

She pushed back from the table and pulled on the rest of her clothes. "I don't know where you're heading tomorrow, but I'll be traveling in the correct direction. North." She glared before seizing her dinner tray. "Sleep well, my lord." Somehow, she made his title sound like an insult.

Pippa marched out of his room. Jack stared at the open doorway, his jaw slack. Somehow things had gone quite, quite sideways.

⟫⟩⟨⟪

"IDIOT." PIPPA BANGED the door to her room shut with her hip and set down her tray.

How dare he make decisions without her? Tell her to calm down as if she was some feeble-minded hysteric? And so calmly declare they were headed home for *her* sake?

Pippa pounded a foot against the floor to punctuate her anger.

Her stomach growled. Dropping into the chair, she took a bite of stew and chewed with great force. She'd show the stew who was boss.

The newspaper tucked behind her bowl caught her eye. Perhaps reading would soothe her anger. She smoothed it out across the table with one hand and noticed it was from London.

Pippa held her breath while she flipped the pages.

There it was—another article from *Democratiam Liberum*.

She spooned her dinner into her mouth, scarcely tasting the food as she read.

The House of Commons impressed the people of England with its common-sense legislation. Of particular note this year were the Judicial Acts Concerning Kent, the Highway Excise Levy Post, and the Landowning Yeomen Debt Indemnity Act. Despite their struggle to garner support for these pieces of legislation from the House of Lords, the members of Parliament in the Commons debated the merits of each piece of legislation before...

Pippa reread the article a second time, her nose scrunched in concentration. Something tugged at the back of her mind, but she couldn't quite bring it into focus.

At the very least, it was clear the recent tone remained a complete turnaround from *Democratiam Liberum*'s original writing. Before Lydia had vanished, *Democratiam Liberum*'s articles condemned the corruption within not only the House of Commons, but also in how the country was partitioned into irregularly sized boroughs that allowed for voting manipulation.

And after Lydia's disappearance, the articles sang the Commons' praises, always listing obscure and unfamiliar pieces of legislation. It was almost as if the writer had made them up.

Pippa froze, her spoon halfway to her mouth. Her thoughts, tumbling about like a tornado, suddenly stilled in the eye of the storm.

It was almost as if the writer had made them up.

She grabbed the newspaper, holding it close to her face to scan the article once more.

Judicial Acts Concerning Kent.

Highway Excise Levy Post.

Landowning Yeomen Debt Indemnity Act.

Pippa's mouth fell open. Her eyes scanned the first letter of each word.

JACK.

HELP.

LYDIA.

She dropped her spoon. "Oh my God."

Fear chilled Pippa's blood. Lydia had sent a hidden message. She must be in terrible trouble. She hadn't run away to elope with that weaselly attorney, her political heart softened by incandescent love. She'd been kidnapped.

Pippa scurried to her valise, digging beneath her clothes for her collection of articles. She breathed in hurried gasps as she skimmed through each one. Where were the names of supposed legislation?

Here was one from an earlier article. Pippa's hand shook so much, she had to lay it flat on her lap. The Statute of Militia edicts Regulating Services, etc. & Taxation. TSMRST didn't make any sense though. Maybe this wasn't a clue? She looked at it again. Perhaps the smaller words were used some of the time, but not all. After a minute, Pippa decided it was supposed to say SOMERSET.

"Somerset." She tested the word out loud. What did it mean? Her mind spun, and then she recalled hearing about a Lord

Somerset when Eugenia was visiting and relaying the latest gossip.

Pippa continued her search and found reference to the Estate Authorization statute Tax. "East," Pippa muttered, frowning. East of what?

She scoured through every article several times, then gathered up the ones containing clues and ran down the hall, wrenching Jack's door open without bothering to knock.

"Pippa!" He turned from the washstand. Jack's lower face was covered in suds, and he held a shaving blade in one hand.

She stared, gaping. Seeing him grooming himself felt…*intimate*. Domestic.

"What's wrong?" He dropped the blade and wiped off the suds before striding to her side.

"I found clues," she said in a rush. "Lydia left them. I mean, *Democratiam Liberum* left them. In the articles. She spelled things out—it was hard to see at first. But I found them. I—I don't know what it means though."

Jack gripped her upper arms, his eyes searching. "What are you saying?"

Pippa opened her mouth, but her thoughts were too jumbled to explain. "Here." She shoved the articles at him. "The laws. Look at the first letters. You'll see."

Jack frowned, scanning the articles. "We've already been through these."

"Look—this one is new." She pulled the full page, bigger than the articles she'd clipped at home, from the bottom of the stack. "Here, read this paragraph."

Jack read. She watched his eyes scan left to right, left to right. He blinked and his entire body stilled. Pippa held her breath, waiting.

He looked up, his face drained of color. "Jack help Lydia," he whispered, each word clearly an agony.

She nodded.

"My sister…" He opened and closed his mouth.

"We can find her." Pippa touched his hand where it clenched the articles.

He inhaled. "What else?"

Pippa showed him Somerset and East. They both stared at the clues.

"I didn't find any others, but that doesn't mean they aren't there," she said.

Jack lay the articles out on the table, and they both pored over each one, the room silent except for the faint rumble of voices from below in the common area.

"I don't see anything else," Jack finally announced, leaning back in his chair. His hair stood up in wild disarray.

Pippa's heart flipped over. Some of his dishevelment was from their lovemaking. The rest of the blame lay solely at the feet of whoever held Lydia captive.

Jack save Lydia.

If any harm befell Jack's sister... Pippa shivered. She couldn't even complete the thought.

"So, who's Somerset?" Pippa asked.

Jack stared pensively at the scattered articles. "We need a copy of Debrett's."

Pippa frowned. "I doubt there's one here."

He looked up, his mouth tight. "Powell."

"That man who accosted you downstairs? How likely is he to have a copy in his pocket?"

He shook his head. "He lives just a few miles from here, remember? Every peer has a copy stuck on some dusty library shelf."

Pippa stood. "Let's go."

Jack's jaw tightened. "You'll stay here."

Raising her chin, she gave him her steeliest glare. "If you think for one minute that I'm the sort who will be left behind, you don't know me at all."

Jack rose to his feet and crossed his arms over his chest. "And if you think I'm the sort to allow my woman to waltz into danger, then you don't know *me* at all."

Gazes locked, they stood in a silent battle of wills. Pippa tried to ignore his *my woman* comment, although it was difficult to maintain her *épée*-sharp glare of defiance when her heart had softened to the consistency of porridge.

But she was only his woman when he could control her, and she couldn't be his woman in truth, since she was a scandal waiting to happen. If—no, *when*—word got out about her fencing, the LCA, and her duel, a relationship would ruin both Jack and his sister, and Pippa couldn't allow that to happen.

Jack sighed in defeat, running his fingers through his hair. "Fine. How should we do this?"

Pippa tilted her head to the side, considering first one crazy plan followed by another. Her skin broke out in goosebumps, and she smiled. "I have an idea…"

JACK SWEPT INTO the common room of the inn. His hands were clammy with nerves, but he kept a grin plastered onto his face. In order for this to work, he'd need to quickly establish some bonhomie with Powell and his friends.

"Har'wick?" Powell slurred when Jack clapped him on the back.

"Thought I'd join you chaps for a pint. After days of traveling with my sister, I'm in need of some masculine company. One can only listen to talk of lace for so long, am I right, gentlemen?"

The men—most with glazed eyes and flushed cheeks—roared their agreement, tankards sloshing as they toasted. Jack was ushered to an empty seat, and a fresh tankard of ale arrived.

"So, I's just telling the chaps," Powell said, spitting as he talked, "tha' we're going to get the biggest…fattest…juiciest pheasants tha' anyone has ever seen. Isn' tha' right, Freddie?"

Freddie, seated beside Powell with eyelids at half mast, nodded. "Hunting," he slurred.

"Hunting!" Powell bellowed, raising his tankard once more. His friends obliged with another toast.

"You know, I can afford to delay my travels by a day." Jack kept his voice casual. "I could join you, if your offer still stands."

"Join us?" Powell slurred. "Yesh, join us, Hartwicksdonington."

Jack rolled his eyes at the creative license Powell took with his name. "Shall we be off?"

"Off?" Powell peered at him. "Now?"

"Well, you never know when you might come across a yellow-breasted pheasant. Most delicious bird in all of England. Nocturnal, you know." Jack made a show of glancing at the inn's black windows. "Now's the perfect time to search for the rare yellow-breasted pheasant." He shrugged. "But perhaps the thrill of the hunt doesn't interest you fellows. I'd hate to get your hopes up…although I've heard of several nesting areas between here and your estate."

"Wait." Powell held up a hand. "Jush wait. Noc'teral pheasants? With…breasts?" The man's eyes went in and out of focus. "An' we might catch one…on the way home?"

Jack nodded.

Powell propped his head up on his fist. "Then I says we go righ' now and look for one of the boobie birdies…pheasants…what have you. And we catch one tonight. Yesh, let's catch one tonight!" He thumped his fist on the thick, scarred table, and his companions jumped.

"Now?" Freddie peered at his companion as if the man had lost his mind.

"Yesh, now!" Powell yelled, rising to unsteady feet. "Innkeeper? Have our horses saddled."

Jack bit back a smile as the band of drunken imbeciles made their way to the yard, their swaying interspersed with slurred boasts about catching the pheasant. He hoped Pippa was enjoying this display of the imbecility of men from her safe location in the inn's yard. Thankfully, none of the men realized they had no hunting equipment.

He'd not look that gift horse in the mouth. Jack would abandon the scheme rather than risk Pippa's safety to an inebriated hunter aiming a rifle at a fictitious bird in the dead of the night.

Soon the yard was full of saddled mounts as well as Jack's gleaming carriage.

"Nice horsies, Hartwickson," Powell slurred, patting a bay on the head like a puppy.

Listing dangerously to one side, Powell then made his way along the horse's length to the carriage. "Will we be able to shee out the window as we travel?" His hand fumbled at the door.

Jack sprung forward, grabbing Powell's arm. "What's this?" he attempted to drawl around the sudden knot in his throat. "Surely you'll have a better view from your mount."

Powell frowned. "Mine mount…" He squinted and surveyed the yard where his friends were slouched in their saddles or still trying to clamber onto their horses. "Ah," he proclaimed, his face lighting up with the insight of a deeply drunk man who has just recalled the obvious. "My mount is unmountable!"

Jack's eyebrows shot up.

"My mount got a…an injury on his…her…its leg," he continued. "I'll jus' hop in with you, shall I?" And with the speed of a striking snake, Powell lunged, yanking open the carriage door.

"No!" Jack shouted, but it was too late.

Powell stared, wide-eyed at the interior of the carriage. *Hell and damnation.* Defeat tightened around Jack's chest. After all his work to protect her, it had come to this. If there was any justice in the world, the lout would be too soused to piece together who Pippa was and—

"Good evening, my lord," a cheerful voice came from behind him. "Shall I help the gentlemen into the carriage before we head to Lord Powell's estate?"

Jack closed his eyes briefly before turning.

A very familiar-looking groomsman smiled cheekily at him.

Jack cleared his throat. "Ah, we shan't be needing assistance at the moment. But thank you regardless."

Pippa winked, then climbed up beside the coachman.

Jack exhaled with relief before assisting Powell into the carriage. The man's breath—blasted onto Jack's face as he muscled him into his seat—could slay any number of wild beasts, but Jack didn't mind. Pippa had strayed from the plan, and for once he was glad. Whatever instinct had led her to don her male garb and sit up front rather than inside the carriage had preserved her reputation. Well, at least for one more day, but at this point, they'd take whatever they could get.

After five minutes of nearly incoherent questions regarding the behavior of the mythical pheasant, Powell passed out. His snores filled the carriage as they traveled toward his estate.

Jack lay his hand against the carriage wall behind him. Pippa sat there, just a small barrier between them. Pippa, his stubborn, clever, brave, resourceful love.

Mixed in with his relief that her identity remained undetected lurked his escalating worry for Lydia.

Jack help Lydia.

Without Pippa's keen sense of observation, they'd have missed his sister's clues.

Jack closed his eyes. Dear lord, please let her be unharmed.

He thought of all the restrictions he'd placed on his sister in his attempts to keep her safe, to keep their world ordered and controlled. How misplaced his energies had been. Instead of opening up to him about her political ideals and writing, she'd gone behind his back.

He'd given her no other choice.

He was too controlling, too rigid, and too certain of his own point of view. Pippa had shown him that. And how had he repaid her?

He replayed their interaction from earlier in the evening, how he'd issued his edict that they'd return home. He hadn't asked for her opinion or considered a compromise. Jack had shown zero faith in her ability to protect herself or choose her path. He'd deserved her glare and the slammed door. He'd deserved much more, truth be told.

"Damn," Jack whispered, his words swallowed by the noise of horses and snoring.

The carriage lumbered to a halt. Glancing out the window, he saw a grand house limned in moonlight. Several windows blazed with light, and the front door opened for a few servants who must be accustomed to their master's erratic hours.

The carriage door swung open to reveal a footman standing at attention. The lord of the manor snorted before jerking upright in his seat. "Wha'?" Powell wiped the drool from his chin.

Jack cast his eyes heavenward. He hopped out of the carriage, leaving Powell to the footman's devices. Hopefully, the servant was well-compensated.

Jack found Pippa on the other side of the horses, holding the reins as the coachman spoke to one of the footmen about the stables.

With drunk lords teetering atop their mounts and servants dashing to and fro, trying to prevent the idiots from breaking their necks, Jack could hardly pull his alleged footman into an embrace and inquire about his welfare.

He ached with the need to hold Pippa, to weave his fingers through her hair, to feel her soft curves pressed against him. Instead, he settled for a questioning tilt of his head. She nodded.

All was well. Jack felt his shoulder muscles relax.

He followed the stream of staggering lords into the front door. Now all he had to do was sneak into the library, find a copy of Debrett's amongst the many leather-bound books, and hope to hell that there was an entry for Somerset with an obvious estate in the east. If not, Jack couldn't even fathom how he and Pippa would find Lydia.

"To th' billiards room," Powell decreed, finger thrust up in the air like a knight of old leading the charge into battle. The men tottered after their ringleader down the lavish hallway.

"My coachman and footman," Jack said to the wizened servant in the foyer with a long-suffering expression. Jack could only surmise he was the butler.

"Our servants will see they're set to rights below stairs, my lord."

Jack nodded, tugging at his cravat. The idea of Pippa eating day-old bread and tepid water in the kitchen where the ashes lay cold in the fireplace… He shook his head.

This was a grand estate, not Newgate prison. Surely visiting servants were given a nourishing meal, hot tea, and a comfortable place to rest.

Jack followed the raucous noises of Powell, Freddie, and the rest to the billiards room.

"No boobie-breasted birdies," the gray-faced Freddie said mournfully while hugging his pool cue.

"Not tonight." Jack clapped him on the back. The fellow listed dangerously to the side.

"Perhaps some water?" Jack suggested, finding himself genuinely concerned for the young gent. Freddie hadn't been with them at Eton, so perhaps his worry stemmed from simply a lack of association with bullying and loutish behavior.

"Water," Freddie sneered. He turned his back on Jack as if he'd suggested inviting a Frenchman to sit on England's throne.

So much for concern. Jack rolled his eyes and girded himself for a long night of inanity.

After an hour of sophomoric conversation circling between the charms of light skirts, liquor, and hunting, Jack made his escape. Most of the men were passed out on the leather couches and chairs against the walls. A few, including Powell, still attempted to play billiards.

Jack closed the door behind him with care, then slunk down the hallway toward the library.

He peeked inside the room, finding cheerful flames dancing in the fireplace and casting the room in a warm glow. Keeping watch on the hallway, he backed into the room. He eased the door shut and made to turn around, but he bumped into something behind him.

Or someone.

Jack inhaled sharply and pivoted. His fists came up, ready to make battle.

"Jack."

Air whooshed out of him in relief. "You scared a year off my life," he murmured, pulling Pippa into his arms.

She lay her head against him. "I can feel your heart trying to leap out of your chest."

He breathed, the adrenaline burning off and the comfort of her presence soothing all the sore and tender places inside him. She, too, seemed content to merely hold him before they resumed their mission.

"Were you worried back at the inn, when Powell opened the carriage?"

Jack groaned. "I thought the knucklehead was going to ruin everything."

Pippa chuckled. "After you went downstairs, I rethought the plan and decided it would be safer if I wasn't sitting in the carriage. And since I had my fencing outfit packed..."

"You were right about that," he said, his throat thick with emotion. "You've been right about so many things. Pippa—"

"We'd best find the book." She pulled back.

Jack swallowed his disappointment. She was right. They had to find information on Somerset and rescue Lydia. Declarations could come later.

Pippa lit candles from the fire for them, and they each took one wall of the library.

Jack scanned the shelves, holding his candle up as he peered at the spines. If Powell's library held the most recent copy of Debrett's, then it would be red leather with the title embossed in gold. However, older copies might be green or brown.

"This is a shocking number of books," Pippa murmured from across the room, "for a man who gives the impression of illiteracy."

Jack stifled a laugh. His shoulders felt lighter than they had a few minutes ago. Damn, but spending time with those men had put him in a bad mood. He hadn't even realized it until he'd breathed the same air as Pippa once more and his world had righted.

"Found it." She crossed the room, Debrett's in hand.

They sat by the fire, and Jack flipped through the book until he came to the correct entry.

"Viscount Somerset is the courtesy title for the Duke of Lambert's heir." He continued to skim the passage. "He currently sits in the House of Commons until he inherits from his father."

Jack placed his finger on the page to mark his spot and looked at Pippa. "Could that be the connection? That he's in the Commons?"

Pippa tilted her head. "But the heir to a duchy? It seems odd he'd care two figs about the Commons when he'll sit in the House of Lords someday."

Jack frowned. "The Commons wields more power than most realize, though. No act makes it out of Parliament without the Commons' approval. Perhaps Somerset believed his current position of power was threatened by Lydia's writing."

Pippa gripped his arm. "We have to find her, Jack. Once he believes he's neutralized her earlier writing, she's at risk."

Jack's breath seized in his lungs. What if they were already too late?

"Which estate is east?" Pippa seized up the book.

"Look under Lambert," Jack mumbled. "Any land is likely owned by his father."

He sat, frozen, while she thumbed through Debrett's.

"The Duke of Lambert owns handfuls of estates. There's land in Cornwall, Stafford, Derby, and Cumberland," she read, her brows pinched together.

Jack's stomach contracted. *Merciful heavens.* His Lydia. *She could be anywhere.*

Pippa stilled. "There is an estate in Lincoln. It's the only county listed that's in the east."

"Are you…" Jack paused to clear his throat. "Are you sure?"

Pippa took a moment to scan the entry again. "Yes, it's just outside of Horncastle. Look."

Jack gripped the book tightly to prevent his hands from trembling. He read the passage on the duke's holdings, comparing the list to the mental map of England's counties he'd memorized back in his schoolroom days. Thank goodness for strict tutors.

"Horncastle," he said.

She nodded, her eyes watchful.

"If we leave now—"

"*We?*" She arched a brow.

Jack set the book down and took her hand. He caressed the callouses on her palm, the sign of both her fear and her bravery. The sick churning in his stomach eased. He breathed deeply.

"You and I together." He held her gaze. "Until the end."

She blinked. He squeezed her hand.

Pippa's perfect pink lips tipped up at the corners, and she leaned forward, pressing her mouth to his.

Jack's eyes slid closed. The kiss was gentle. Sweet. A sharing.

The loud bang sounded, and Jack pulled away.

Freddie swayed in the open doorway, his eyes traveling sluggishly between the two of them on the couch. His mouth fell open as he took in Pippa in her male garb.

"You," he pointed at Jack, "are kissing *him?*"

"This is who I'm kissing, yes," Jack answered.

Freddie swayed. "Two men?" he asked, apparently requiring double confirmation.

"It does look that way, doesn't it?" Jack's lips twitched.

Pippa elbowed him in the ribs. He quirked a brow to ask, *well, what should I have said?* She rolled her eyes, a smile ghosting across her face.

Freddie spoke, his words slurred. "Is that…"

Jack waited, curious to see what word the young man would

say.

"...nice?"

Jack bit back a grin. "It is, rather." He rose, holding out a hand for Pippa. "Hate to miss the hunting tomorrow, but we must be off. Give my regards to Powell. Take care, Freddie." He patted the man on the shoulder as they slipped by. "And drink some water before you pass out."

"Take care," Freddie murmured behind them, his voice dazed. "Drink water."

"I think you've given that boy a shock," Pippa whispered as they let themselves out the front door.

"He won't remember a lick of it tomorrow," Jack predicted. "And if he does, it'll be good for him. Broaden his horizons and all that. Which way to the stables?"

Pippa pointed, and a few minutes later, they were zooming along in the comfort of his carriage, Pippa's hand in his as they headed toward Horncastle.

Chapter Twenty-Three

PIPPA STRETCHED, ARCHING up off the carriage seat. They'd traveled through the remainder of the night after leaving Powell's estate. She ached from the cramped quarters and awkward sleeping positions.

She turned to Jack, blinking against the bright daylight filtering through the carriage window shades.

Pippa shrieked.

The strange man beside her jolted upright. He rubbed a worn hand over his weathered face as he blinked awake.

"Miss," he finally croaked. "'Tis me. No need for alarm. Lord Hartwick spelled me for a bit wi' the driving is all."

Pippa slumped back against the seat in relief. Now that *she* was fully awake, she recognized their coachman. She'd spent miles perched on the seat beside him last night. But merciful heavens—what a start he'd given her!

"Lord Hartwick was most insistent," he continued. "Said twasn't safe for me to drive through the whole night an' into the day, so we swapped places a' the last stop. He's a kind man, Lord Hartwick." The coachman smiled, the deep lines on his face crinkling. "Said you wouldn't mind, miss, but I do 'pologize for giving you a start."

Pippa lay her hand on the man's arm. "We must apologize to *you*, having you drive through the entire night. If it weren't an emergency—"

"Milord tol' me about his sister."

Pippa stared. *Jack had told him?*

"An' he promised me twenty pounds as a bonus for my work, so don't you fret none, miss." The coachman patted her hand. "I'm a tough old bird. And," he added, his mouth flattening into a grim line, "I know Lady Lydia is tougher than she seems. Aye." He nodded. "And clever. She'll be right as rain in the end, you'll see."

Pippa thanked him before retreating to the corner of the seat. She leaned her head against the side, ostensibly to sleep, but her thoughts were too jumbled to rest.

Jack was driving his own carriage.

An earl was driving so his tired coachman could rest.

Was this a man afraid of scandal? Her heart yearned to freely embrace her feelings for Jack, for surely such a man wouldn't be afraid to tie himself to an outrageous woman who fenced and dueled.

And yet…

And yet, her mind knew otherwise. Her practical, clear-headed mind squashed her hopeful heart, reminding that silly organ that even if he forgot himself during this adventure, eventually he'd regret such a connection. Jack was too controlled to slip the reins for long.

And his regret would squash her soul as surely as a bug was squashed by the trampling hoof of a passing horse.

"We're slowing," the coachman murmured.

Pippa pulled up the shade to peer out the window. They were on a country lane with nothing but trees in sight. The coach eased into a small clearing alongside the road. A moment later, Jack opened the door.

His hair was windblown, his clothes covered in a layer of dust, and his eyes underscored by shadows of exhaustion.

He was the most handsome man she'd ever seen.

Jack's expression gentled as he seemed to drink her in. "Good morning." His husky voice rasped over her in the best way.

Pippa's heart flipped over. How was she to say goodbye to this man?

Jack spoke to the coachman. "I didn't manage it as smoothly as you, but we're here at last."

The coachman cackled before clambering out of the carriage. "I'd best check that you haven't tangled the lines." He headed to the horses.

Jack shook his head. "Tangled the lines," he scoffed, but his eyes twinkled.

"Enjoyed your time playing coachman, did you?" She wanted to absorb his nearness. Every inch of her craved every inch of him.

He removed his gloves and trailed a finger across her cheek. "I'd rather have been in here with you." His voice was full of promises.

Pippa's heart skipped a beat. "Are we really at Somerset's estate?"

"It's about a half mile back. We can't just charge in, so I thought we'd best approach on foot and surveille the area first."

Pippa nodded. They risked Lydia's safety if they simply knocked on the door and announced themselves. Plus, Lord Somerset would likely deny he held her, and then what?

He held out a hand. "Ready?"

Soon, Pippa and Jack were walking along a footpath toward the estate. They each munched on apples and cheese.

Cresting a hill, the woods opened up onto a wide, manicured lawn. Sprawling at its center lay a gray stone manor, its two squat wings stretching out from the taller center of the house.

Pippa and Jack hid behind the line of trees, watching. She sensed Jack's tension, his body stiff beside her.

Long minutes stretched by, interrupted only by the sounds of the leaves rustling in the breeze and the occasional bird chirping. Below, there was no movement from the manor.

Pippa tried to ignore her discomfort. Surely her desire for a bath, soft bed, and hot meal was nothing compared to what Lydia suffered.

"There." Jack pointed. "Do you see that window?"

Pippa followed the line of his finger. One of the second-floor windows toward the end of the left wing was boarded over.

Was that where Lydia was being held? There were always other explanations, of course, like the window needing repair, but it was the likeliest place to begin their search.

"We have company," Pippa whispered.

Two men rounded the corner of the manor. Pippa and Jack both stepped further back into the trees. The men circled the building, their heads swiveling about. One kept his hand in his pocket the entire time.

"Armed guards," Pippa murmured.

Jack nodded.

"That means she's still here." Pippa turned to him. "And she's—" She broke off, horrified at what she'd been about to say.

"That she's alive," Jack finished for her, his voice grim.

Laying her hand on the center of his back, Pippa hoped to offer some small measure of reassurance or comfort.

She felt the shudder of his indrawn breath.

"Well," he finally said, "we can't storm the place during the day with those guards on patrol. I think we'd best return once it's dark. We'll find a way into that boarded-up room."

Pippa nodded. "I can pick locks, you know."

He stared at her.

"It gets very boring, being confined at home for years on end." She shrugged.

Jack's mouth twitched. "And so, you filled your days training to be a burglar?"

"It was either that or the feminine arts, and you've seen my knitting."

A low laugh escaped him, and Pippa smiled in reply. Perhaps it was unseemly to jest but cutting their worry with a small bit of humor couldn't hurt.

They circled the house part-way, staying hidden in the trees as they noted the servants' entrance and other points of entry. Then they picked their way along the path with care until they were far enough from the estate to not worry about noise. Most likely, the increasing winds would cover any sounds they might make. Pippa peered through the waving branches overhead to the dull gray sky. It seemed a storm was on its way.

The coachman raised bushy eyebrows at their approach.

"To the inn in town," Jack told him. "We'll return tonight."

The man nodded, and within an hour Pippa was relaxing into a steaming bath with a meal on the way.

A knock sounded at the door, and Pippa directed the maid without opening her eyes. "You can set the tray on the table."

"I thought you might want some help scrubbing your back."

Pippa's breath caught.

A devilish idea took hold and wouldn't let go.

Continuing to face away from the door, she leaned back further in the tub. She raised a leg out of the water and ran the washcloth along her skin. A trail of bubbles followed, slowly dripping across her warm flesh.

Behind her, a low noise escaped her visitor. Pippa smiled and gave her other leg the same treatment. Her skin felt newly aware of the lap of the water, the slide of the cloth, and the slickness of the soap now that he was here. Watching her. Waiting to touch her.

To scrub her back.

She finally peered over her shoulder. Jack's hand gripped the knob of the closed door. His hair curled damply, evidence of his own bath, and his eyes gleamed with hunger.

Hunger for her.

"I thought you were here to help me wash," she purred. "It seems I've been a very dirty girl lately."

His breath caught. A little huff of laughter followed, as if he were both astounded and affected by her audacious comment.

Well, *she* found it affecting. She'd never uttered such vixen-like words in her life.

A smile curved her lips. She held up the washcloth and bar of soap, raising her eyebrows in challenge.

Jack crossed the room in a few long strides and wrenched off his jacket before tossing it onto a chair. He rolled up his shirtsleeves, staring down at her all the while. Pippa peeked down. The few bubbles floating on the water's surface did little to hide the view.

He dropped to his knees and plucked the soap and washcloth out of her hand. "Milady." The contrast between his servant-like words and pose and his gravelly voice sparked something inside Pippa.

She swallowed as her nipples tightened and a sweet ache grew between her legs.

Leaning forward, she exposed her back. Jack made a show of casting aside the washcloth. He dipped his hands in the water and slowly circled his wet hands around the soap to create a lather. His eyes remained fixed on her, heat and promise in their gray depths.

He leaned forward, running his hands across her back. The slippery slide of his fingers left sparks in their wake.

Pippa sighed as he massaged muscles sore from many hours in the carriage. What a feat for his touch to bring both comfort and sensual pleasure at the same time.

"Are you dirty here?" His hands roamed over her shoulders and down her arms.

Pippa nodded.

"Here?" His fingers traveled from her arm to her chest.

"Oh, yes," she moaned.

She arched her back, pressing her breasts into his naughty, slippery hands. His fingers circled her nipples, lightly pinching and plucking. Pippa cried out, the ache in her core intensifying.

"And here?" he whispered, hot in her ear. "Are you dirty here?"

Pippa whimpered as his hand dipped below the surface of the

water.

"Oh, you're so dirty," he moaned, his fingers sliding along her seam. "I need to clean you. Very thoroughly."

Pippa shuddered as pleasure from both his naughty, naughty words and his nimble fingers sparked through her.

"Jack," she gasped, throwing her head back against the edge of the tub.

"What do you want?" His fingers circled and pressed.

"You," she cried. "I want you."

Jack reached for the nearby towel. He pulled her to her feet, and Pippa leaned in for a kiss.

"You'll never get dry if you distract me," he muttered in between kisses.

"I don't care." Pippa darted her tongue into his slick mouth.

Jack growled, pulling her close. He swiped at her with the towel before carrying her to the bed.

"You're so beautiful." His eyes traced her damp skin while he stripped off his clothes.

Pippa licked her lips as his shirt and trousers dropped to the floor. Each time she saw him naked, she was amazed anew at the beauty of the male form. Of Jack's form.

He eased down onto the bed.

"What you do to me." He stroked over her cheekbones and across her lips.

"Jack." Pippa pressed against him, her legs twining with his.

His heart beat in time to her own. Their lips met, a tangle of tongue and breath and heat.

The drag and abrasion of his hard, hair-roughened body against her legs and breasts made her skin prickle with delicious awareness. She slid against him, stroking her softness against his masculine roughness.

Jack's lips trailed down her neck to her breasts, each aching peak receiving lavish attention from his tongue.

"Oh, yes," Pippa moaned.

Her legs moved restlessly as her ache grew with each lick and nibble. She reached down, taking his stiff erection in her hand. Jack groaned, thrusting into her grasp.

"I want you so much I ache with it," he whispered.

Pippa's heart flipped over in her chest.

She loved him so much—his touch and his smile and the ferocity of his determination. She loved all parts of him, even the parts that drove her half mad at times. And he could be hers…but only for today.

Tomorrow, she'd have to release her claim.

And claim him she had. She'd claimed his laughter, the comforting circle of his arms, and his kisses. Today, at this moment, in this bed, he belonged to her and her alone.

Pippa's claim rose in her, hot, fierce, and powerful.

She pushed and rolled until she straddled him. Jack's cock was trapped beneath her, hard and insistent.

His hands moved to her hips, urging her up. Pippa rose, arching her hips until they were aligned. She sank down. Pippa moaned as he filled and stretched her.

"Pippa," he breathed, his fingers flexing against her hips.

She moved, experimenting with tempo and swivels until she found her rhythm. His eyes were slitted, watching her breasts bounce and her hair sway. Pippa ran her fingers across his chest and abdomen, his muscles jumping beneath her touch.

Jack reached between them. He circled in just the right spot. Pippa moaned, riding him harder. Jack's chest rose and fell like a bellows beneath her hand.

"Oh," Pippa cried as her pleasure peaked, drowning her with undulating waves of sensation. She shuddered and pulsed, aware only of him inside her, him touching her, him beneath her.

Jack rolled so he was on top. He withdrew, thrusting against her stomach with a long moan. "Pippa, Pippa, Pippa," he chanted, his eyes locked on hers as he jerked against her. He spilled, hot and wet, low on her abdomen, then collapsed on top of her.

Pippa wrapped her arms around him, relishing his weight.

"I love you," he breathed into her neck.

Her breath froze in her chest.

He stroked her hair back from her face. "I love you, Pippa," he said again, pressing kisses against her neck and jaw.

She held her breath, knowing that if she exhaled, a sob would escape along with it.

He must have felt the tension in her body that had been languid with pleasure only moments before because he rolled to the side. He studied her, his expression both hopeful and wary.

Pippa closed her eyes. She struggled to find the words she knew she had to say.

⫸⫷

FEAR SLICED THROUGH Jack's chest when Pippa's eyelids fell, shuttering the desolation in their blue depths.

Desolation?

He said he loved her, and she looked as if he'd announced that the world was ending.

He reached out to touch her cheek. "Pippa—"

She shook her head. "I can't," she whispered.

His hand froze midair. He pulled back, resting his fist on the bed. "Why?" His voice was choked. He should have felt embarrassed, but his fear trumped all else.

She was slipping away from him at this very moment. Even as his seed cooled on her belly, she fled. He could sense her heart's retreat despite their skin pressed together.

"I hold you in high regard," she said stiffly, finally opening her eyes. "B-but love…" Her gaze skittered away from him, landing somewhere over his shoulder. "I fear you have assumed too much, my lord."

Jack flinched. The formal language sliced him as sharply as any sword.

He pulled away, sitting on the edge of the bed with his back to her. Without her nearness, his skin felt icy. His *heart* felt icy.

He laughed, the sound tight and bitter.

"So that's all then?" He stared at the floor. "You hold me in high regard, and I've assumed too much?"

There was only silence.

Jack leaned forward, resting his forehead on hands that trembled.

Breathe in, breathe out. Don't fall apart. Don't perish right here on the side of the bed. It's just a broken heart. It doesn't really matter. Take control.

Take control.

The familiar message steadied him and gave him something to cling to.

He'd spent years having all the control. No one else was to be trusted to take care of things. Not his irresponsible parents. Not the handful of stewards he'd hired over the years to help with the estates and finances, all of whom failed to meet his exacting standards.

And not Pippa.

He couldn't share the load with her. He must carry it, all alone. As he had before.

Something inside him protested, declaring it was too lonely, the load was too heavy for one person to bear.

He silenced the protest with ruthless efficiency.

Jack stood, the path before him clear.

Crossing the room, he knelt in front of Pippa's valise. He rummaged through until he found her stays.

"Jack?"

He ignored her, focusing on his task. His heart flickered when his hand touched the delicate cloth of her undergarment, this fabric that cupped such a lovely, intimate part of her. This too he ruthlessly silenced. His fingers no longer shook, and he pulled out what he needed.

Jack rose, filling his lungs with a steadying breath. This next part wouldn't be easy, but it was necessary. To have control, he needed to know she wasn't in harm's way, that it was he alone who traveled this last portion of the journey.

He rushed to the bed, pinning Pippa beneath him.

"Jack?" Disbelief crossed her face before it was replaced by something else, something much harder to witness—fear.

"Jack, what are you doing?" She bucked against him even as he applied his full weight, trapping her. "Jack, stop!"

He ignored her pleas. He ignored her thrashing. He ignored his aching heart.

Jack grabbed a hand and tied the string from her stays around her wrist. The knot was tight, but he left just enough slack so her hand wouldn't go numb.

"Jack, no! Why are you doing this? Please—please stop. Oh God, Jack!"

For a moment, his hands stilled as her words pierced his determination. His eyes flicked down, taking in her white face and wide, wild eyes.

Perhaps he'd gone too far?

But no. This was the right path.

He'd been wrong to think they could be partners, that there was more to life than constant vigilance, control, and self-reliance.

He ran the string through the headboard and tied her other hand.

"Jack, don't go," she pleaded as he rose from the bed. "Please, Jack. It's too dangerous. You need me with you."

He dressed in silence.

Before he left, he wiped her belly clean and flicked the covers over her naked body. He wouldn't want her to catch a chill.

"I'll untie you when I return." The words were sand in his mouth. He walked to the door, his feet feeling detached from the rest of him as they carried him away. Away from her light and warmth and smiles. Away from her determination and bravery. Away from the love he thought he'd seen in her eyes and felt in her kisses.

But that had been a delusion.

"Why?" she asked, her voice thick, as he began to turn the

doorknob.

"You'll be safe here." He hardly recognized his own voice.

"But *why*, Jack?"

He hunched his shoulders, the move an instinctual protection against this raw pain.

"I…" He gripped the doorknob until his knuckles showed white through his skin. "I have to do this alone."

With a steady stream of imaginative invectives hurled at his back, Jack left the room.

Chapter Twenty-Four

"YELLOW-BELLIED, GANGRENE-FACED GUTTERSNIPE," Pippa muttered, yanking against the rope.

"Arse-breathed, mangy…." She wracked her brain for a suitable ending, but she'd run out of quality insults after the first twenty minutes. The next twenty had been more creative than truly insulting, and this last bit was scraping the bottom of the barrel in terms of both word choice and venom.

The sad truth was her heart wasn't in it.

And that was because her heart was entirely, completely, irrevocably in love with Jack.

Jack, whose love she'd tossed back in his face with harrowing ease. Jack, who proceeded to tie her up in a bizarre echo of her actions the night of the duel. Jack, who was, at this very moment, entering a house of known peril. Alone.

Alone.

Her chest ached.

He'd looked so very alone as he'd absorbed the body blows of her false words. His wide, capable shoulders had slumped as if carrying a load too heavy to bear.

And she'd done that to him.

Pippa gritted her teeth and pulled. However, the string was quite sturdy, perhaps unsurprising given it was designed to aid in the herculean task of supporting a woman's bosom against the determined force of gravity.

"Festering, boil lancing, plague-ridden gravity." Now she was cursing a basic law of science. Truly, the night had reached a new low. Her arms dropped to the mattress when she realized her only progress was removing the top layers of skin from her wrists.

She stared at the ceiling, wondering if it had ever seen such a sight in its decades of housing weary travelers. Surely these old walls had witnessed heartache, arguments, and spurned affection, but a nude lady fencer tied to the bed by her lover who was setting off on a probable suicide mission? Not likely.

What about a man who rejected all ties at the first sign of difficulties? Had the ceiling witnessed that? Because although Pippa knew her words hurt him, he'd hurt her right back. She was to remain here where she'd be safe as if she were some ninny with wool for brains. He had no faith in her as a partner. He'd just about spit on her fencing skills, her courage, and her dependability in a time of crisis.

And that was painful to realize.

"Larvae-infested pile of pig slops," she whispered, tears gathering in her eyes. She jerked against her bonds, even though it was futile.

"Rancid, flatulent donkey brain." Tears trickled down her cheeks.

"Damn, shit, arsehole," she choked out between sobs.

At last, she gave up.

She couldn't get out of her bonds. She couldn't get out of this mess. And she couldn't be with Jack.

Fencing made her a scandal-in-waiting. Giving up her blade was impossible. Without her sword and knives, she'd be a frightened girl again, hiding away from the world. She'd be a shell of a person. And that was even worse than being a scandal. She'd never go back to that.

Never.

Better to be a scandal than live in fear.

Pippa's arms stilled. *Better to be a scandal than live in fear.*

She stared at the closed door, which Jack must have locked when he'd left. But the innkeeper and maids would have access...

Closing her eyes, Pippa offered up a silent apology to her good name before putting her plan into action.

JACK CREPT ALONG the perimeter of the manor, placing each foot with care as the wind buffeted his body. It wouldn't do to trip or snap a twig, alerting the armed thugs patrolling the grounds to his presence. Although who knew if they'd hear anything over the howling gusts.

The wan moonlight filtering through the angry clouds provided just enough illumination to show the way. Jack sidestepped a bush. He paused with his back against the wall, ears straining. At the low rumble of distant voices, he crept behind the bush.

Damn, why didn't this blasted plant have more leaves? If the men spotted him through the sparse foliage, he'd be in heaps of trouble.

Heart pounding, he forced his breath to slow. The men rounded the corner.

"... 'eard 'imself say we've got to take care of 'er tomorrow," the taller of the two said, scanning the grounds.

"Take care of 'er?" The smaller man scrunched up his face. "Wot? Like return 'er to 'er family?"

The tall fellow made a sound of disgust. "Are ye daft in the 'ead? We got to take 'er out to the woods and..." He ran a finger across his throat.

Jack's stomach roiled.

"Such a pity," Shorty said. "She looks jus' like an angel." He sighed, and the two men paused right in front of Jack's bush.

He felt the weight of his pistol in his pocket. Should he take the men out now while their backs were turned? But no, others would hear the shots, and then he'd never get to Lydia.

"'Oo would 'ave thunk such a pretty lass could throw the nobs into a frenzy," Shorty mused, rocking back on his heels.

"Best be sure you know how to tie yourself a knot on the morrow," his companion groused. "I've a feelin' she'll be a slippery one."

The men continued walking, their chatter fading into the night.

Jack forced his jaw to unclench. Bloody hell—those two bastards were planning to tie Lydia up, march her into the woods, and slit her throat. He wanted to beat them into a bloody pulp. Jack breathed deeply, letting the chilly wind douse the hot anger inside him. A cool head would win the day.

Sticking to the shadows, he circled the house in the opposite direction of the guards. Based on their earlier reconnaissance, the servants' entrance would be just around the corner.

After navigating around what appeared to be the cook's garden, he found the back door. Approaching on silent feet, he pressed an ear against the smooth wood. All was quiet. Holding his breath, he twisted the knob.

Damn. It was locked.

He recalled Pippa's teasing smile when she'd announced her lockpicking skills. Pippa, who wore her confidence like a second skin. He pictured her lying beneath him, cheeks flushed with passion and eyes languid as they made love. Right before he'd told her his feelings, and then she'd told him—so very, very politely—that he was in error.

Jack rubbed his chest, trying to alleviate the painful ache lodged there.

His hand squeezed the doorknob. If she was here now, she'd have this open in a thrice.

No.

She was safe at the inn, and he was here. Alone. He had to concentrate on getting inside, getting to Lydia.

He crouched down and examined the shadowed lock. Footsteps echoed inside. Damn, someone was coming to the door. Where to hide? He dove behind a row of tomato plants in the adjacent garden just as the door creaked open. The wild wind caught the door, banging it into the wall.

A rectangle of light shone on the flagstones.

"A storm's brewing." A maid peered out. "Are you sure we won't get caught?"

A footman followed, dipping his head to kiss her. "Just an hour in the washhouse," he murmured. "The weather will hold, and no one will notice we're gone."

The maid bit her lip.

"Ah, you know I'm dying for a wee taste of you." His hands reached for her bottom.

She giggled, swatting at his hands, and closed the door before they trotted off, hand in hand.

Jack counted to twenty, then rose from the garden. This time, the doorknob turned in his hand, and he slipped inside.

A banked fire limned the kitchen in a soft glow. Jack's breath caught when he spied a boy sleeping by the hearth. He crept across the room. Reaching the far hallway, he exhaled in relief.

Footsteps clattered down nearby stairs. Jack slipped into a closet until the footsteps faded. He cracked the door and found an empty hallway. Now, which way were the servants' stairs?

After only one false turn, he found the narrow staircase. Jack crept to the second floor. Pausing at the top, he reviewed his path to get his bearings. The west wing should be to the left. His heart pounding in his ears, he crept down the dim hallway. Here was the end of the wing. Counting off doors, Jack paused before the third one. If his mental map was correct, this was the door to the room with the boarded-up window.

Lydia's room.

He swallowed, pressing his hand against the cool wood.

If his little sister was unharmed, if he could get her out of this place, then he'd spend the rest of his life keeping her safe.

He tried the knob. Locked.

He tapped at the door. Inside, he heard a faint rustling.

"Lydia," he whispered.

Footsteps sounded through the wood. "I did what you demanded," a familiar voice replied. "Now let me out of here."

Jack's legs wobbled.

"Lydia, it's me," he managed to whisper through a throat gone tight. "It's Jack."

Silence, and then a thump, as if she'd fallen against the door. "Jack?" Her voice was choked.

"I've come for you."

"Oh God."

He pressed his forehead against the door. "How can I get you out quietly?"

There were sniffling sounds, and then she said, "Whenever the servants bring me food, there's a clanking sound in the hall before they unlock the door."

Jack spun to find a narrow table with a candelabra and two vases against the opposite wall. He overturned first one vase, then the other. A cool weight fell into his hands.

The key.

Jack rushed to the door and unlocked it with trembling hands.

Before he could fully enter the room, he was mobbed by a flash of arms and a tangle of dark-blond hair.

"Oh, Jack," Lydia cried, her voice tremulous.

He held her tight, not bothering to fight the heat pressing at his eyelids. "I was so scared."

"I knew you'd see the clues," she whispered. "I knew you'd find me."

It wasn't me. It was Pippa.

Pippa.

Before his thoughts could gallop away, Jack pulled back to give his sister a quick scan. Her hair was mussed, and her gown rumpled, but there were no obvious signs of injury or ill-treatment.

"Did they hurt you?"

She shook her head. "Just threats of death and dismemberment if I didn't write what they demanded."

"Those bastards will pay," he vowed. "Now let's get you out of here."

Lydia's eyes darted past his shoulders and her mouth opened. Jack's muscles flexed to pivot, but he froze at the distinctive click of a pistol being cocked.

"The bastards won't pay today," drawled a voice.

Then Jack's head exploded in pain.

PIPPA DASHED THROUGH the woods, branches lashing her as the wind howled. The trees opened up on the narrow path she and Jack had followed before. A bolt of lightning lit the sky, revealing the squat estate below. Squinting against the bright flash, Pippa marked the boarded-up window that was her target.

Despite the clamoring inside her to hurry, she hung back, waiting. It wouldn't do to be caught twice in one day in a place she shouldn't be.

Her cheeks heated at the memory of the maid opening the door after Pippa yelled for assistance, and the complete and utter shock on the poor girl's face as she'd taken in the scene. Pippa, tied to the bed, nude except for a blanket.

She'd given the maid five pounds in exchange for her promise of discretion. It was a princely sum for a servant. However, Pippa's faith that the salacious tale would remain untold was as firm as a bowl of pudding.

But she'd made her choice.

Her reputation—such as it was—was of far less value to her than the safety of the man she loved…even if she couldn't permit herself to love him.

And so here she stood, hidden in the shadows on the edge of a nobleman's estate, dressed in male clothes, with a sword at her side and a dagger in her boot, waiting to see if men with pistols were close at hand to capture or even kill her.

Truly, her boring days as a shut-in were behind her.

The storm clouds parted, allowing the anemic moonlight to illuminate the house. No guards were in sight. Pippa sprinted down the hill and across the lawn. She was halfway to the house when the heavens opened up, soaking her to the skin within moments.

She made it to the building and ducked behind a bush. Gasping for breath, she took stock of the situation. Somewhere overhead in the darkness was the boarded-up window. She needed to get up the wall. Pippa waited for the next flash of lightning. The weather complied, cracking an arc across the stormy sky. The storm was directly overhead now, booming as if it yearned to rattle the manor from its very foundation.

Pippa scanned the side of the building. The gray stones were held together with thick lines of mortar. She ran her hand across the surface. In many places, age and weather had worn away at the mortar, leaving deep indents between the stones. Was it enough for her to climb?

Pippa tugged off her leather gloves, tucking them into her waistband. She took a handful of deep breaths and waited for one more blast of lightning to show her the target.

Pippa began to climb.

She placed one foot onto a gap between stones, and after feeling about for a solid toe hold, the other foot went up. Pippa had never been so grateful for strong, calloused hands in her life. Her fingers gripped the cracks in the building, and despite the rain sluicing against her, she managed to cling to the side of the manor.

Rain trickled down her face. She blinked, scanning through the shroud of darkness for her next fingerhold. There. She reached, but just as her fingers made contact, a boom of thunder rent the air. Pippa jerked. Her fingers slipped, and she gave a muffled scream. Her other arm pulled taut but held her up.

Her breath came in rapid gasps as she found a new handhold and was stable once more. Up and up, she climbed. Pippa risked a glance down. She'd traveled halfway up the wall. Above and to her right was the boarded-up window. That wasn't her destination, however. Prying the boards loose would prove too difficult. Pippa aimed for the window of the room next door.

Tightening her jaw, she continued climbing. By the time she reached the window sill, her fingers were numb with cold and her shoulders ached. She hoisted herself up to the deep window sill, perching on its edge. Although it was tempting to rest and count her blessings over not dying yet, worry urged her on. Jack might be in trouble. He might need her.

She shoved her gloves back on before pulling the knife out of her boot. She watched for a flash of lightning, and when the thunder boomed, she struck the window with the hilt. The tinkling noise of broken glass was swallowed by the bellowing sky. She brushed away the jagged pieces, her thick leather gloves protecting her from the sharp edges. Once the hole was safe, she clambered through.

The chamber was dark as a tomb.

Walking forward slowly, Pippa kept her arms outstretched. After a few steps, she hit a large piece of furniture. A bed. Blindly following the edge, she came across a nightstand. She pulled off her gloves once more. Her bare fingers trailed along the table's surface. She sighed in relief when her hand encountered the familiar waxy taper of a candle and a box of matches. The sharp scent of burning sulfur filled the air when she struck the match and lit the candle.

A low moan sounded behind her.

The hairs on the back of Pippa's neck pricked, and she pivoted, one hand holding the candle while the other moved to her sword.

A man was tied to a chair in the middle of the room, his head lolling to the side.

Her breath froze. "Jack?"

She dashed to his side. Pippa ran her hands over him, searching for injuries. He moaned again as she skimmed the back of his head.

Pippa winced, her fingers gently tracing a goose egg.

He tried to look at her, but his eyelids kept falling shut and his head wobbled like a newborn's.

"Damn it all to hell, Jack," she whispered as she worked at the knot holding a gag in his mouth. "See what happens when you try going it alone?"

She pulled the cloth out. Jack worked his mouth and ran his tongue over lips likely gone dry.

"You…" he croaked.

"Yes, it's me, you knucklehead," she snapped back, sawing at one of the ropes binding his ankles to the chair legs with her knife.

"You've got…to get out…of here," he rasped.

"Certainly." Pippa finished one foot and moved to the other. "As soon as we find Lydia."

"Pippa—" He shook his head, still looking woozy.

The ropes binding his second ankle parted under her sharp blade. Pippa rose to get at his hands tied behind the chair.

With a bang, the door burst open.

Pippa's heart leaped as two figures rushed into the room. Each held a pistol.

"See, I told you I heard sumpin'," the smaller of the men said, wiping at his nose.

The larger man took a step forward, his stance menacing. "Drop the knife," he growled.

Pippa stared, unblinking.

The flickering candlelight showed a raised collar and a large hat pulled low on the man's head, obscuring his face. He held the pistol pointed straight at her chest.

She'd seen this before.

Pippa's blood froze in her veins. She couldn't move. She couldn't breathe.

The highwaymen, closing in on her father. Their faces covered, pistols in their hands. The very air around them crackling with menace.

"Pippa," Jack hissed. Even in the dim light, the panic in his eyes was obvious. He jerked against the ropes binding his hands. His gaze flicked to the knife in her hand.

She knew she should help him. She should slip him the knife so he could cut himself free while the men dealt with her. Or she should spring into action and cut him loose herself, then attack the men with her sword. She should do *something*.

But she couldn't.

She couldn't.

She was paralyzed with primal terror as the men descended upon her. They pried the knife from her nerveless fingers and took her sword. They retied Jack's feet. Grabbing her under her arms, they jerked her to the door. The men ignored Jack's wild shouts demanding they release him.

Him.

With the tiny part of her brain still functioning, she realized Jack had used a masculine pronoun. These men didn't realize she was a woman. At least she might avoid the abuse that could occur if they knew.

The words of the men floated by her ears like hazy wisps of fog.

"Not much fight in this one," the smaller man said, leading her down the hall. "Like a wee babe playing wif 'is mum's kitchen knife." He snorted with laughter.

"Shut yer gob," the other snapped. "We've got to tell 'isself a second man came sniffing 'round the place, trying to rescue the girl. 'E's not going to be 'appy wif the news."

Her feet plodded along as the men marched her into the next room down the hall. She barely registered their rough hands pushing her down onto a wooden chair.

Pippa slumped back, her limbs not her own as her arms were lashed behind her back and her feet tied to the legs of the chair. She was trussed up just like Jack.

"Now don't go getting any ideas 'bout trying t' escape." The small man thrust his sneering face close to hers. His breath reeked of onions and garlic. Pippa closed her eyes.

"Wot's this?" the man cried, and she felt him pull back. "Think's 'e's too good for the likes of us. Well, you'll see soon enough. Once 'isself knows about you, you'll be wishing you never stepped 'ide nor 'air in this place."

"Let's go," the other man growled.

The door clicked shut.

Pippa was alone with her insidious, clawing terror. Behind closed eyes, she saw once again the cloaked highwaymen, their pistols aimed at her father. She heard the sharp bang of their guns. She watched her father jerk back and topple onto the road. A dark puddle spread out beneath him, seeping into the dirt.

She sucked in air with rapid, shallow breaths. Her ears buzzed. Her stomach churned.

Oh God, she was being consumed by her fear, eaten alive by it. The men. The pistols. Her father. The blood. Jack. Her useless knife.

Her stomach heaved, and Pippa gagged.

Covering myself in vomit would not improve my situation.

A bubble of deranged laughter escaped her. Shockingly, the notion of vomit puddling in her lap pulled her back into the here and now, away from the very edge of hysteria.

She must calm down.

Breathe, she told herself. *Inhale. Exhale.*

Her lungs filled and steadied. The rhythm of raindrops battering the window snuck through her muffled senses. She grew aware of the sharp bite of the rope against her wrists. Pippa opened her eyes.

She was herself once more. A self who'd permitted those men to take her meekly away like a lamb to the slaughter.

Shame, hot and wretched, flooded her. "I failed," she croaked into the surrounding darkness.

She'd been determined to cast off the yoke of fear, to boldly rejoin the world around her secure in the knowledge she could defend herself against any danger.

But she'd been wrong.

She could successfully battle her enemies. Winning a duel against a disgusting pig of a man, fighting off a band of pickpockets in a dangerous alley.

But she couldn't win the battle against herself. She couldn't win the battle against her own fear. And now Jack and Lydia would die.

Oh God. *Jack.*

She tried to choke back her sobs, but she was destined to lose this battle as well. Her body jerked against the chair as she cried. Tears rolled down her face, merging with the rainwater already soaking her clothes.

As the storm and darkness continued to rage outside, the bright light inside of Pippa burned lower and lower until only the merest flicker remained.

Chapter Twenty-Five

J ACK STRAINED AGAINST his bonds, twisting and yanking at the rope until blood from his abraded wrists trickled down his fingertips. The rope didn't loosen.

Abject terror and fury swelled inside him until it overflowed his lungs, up through his throat, and out his mouth. He bellowed as the boom of thunder filled the black room.

Pippa.

Oh God.

The one thing—the only thing—preventing him from completely losing his mind was that the men hadn't realized Pippa's gender. If they found out she was a woman—

He heaved against his bonds once more, straining until he collapsed back against the chair.

How had it come to this?

Some secret political writings, shadowy forces in the House of Commons, a run-in with a lady fencer, following a trail of clues…

He exhaled, long and slow, forcing himself to acknowledge the ugly truth. There was one more reason for this horror. Perhaps the most important of them all.

His need for control.

Born from the chaos of his childhood, cultivated by running the estate instead of playing like other children, and perfected by a life of duty and schedules, his control pushed others away.

His need for control had brought them all to this point. It had forced Lydia to hide her important political work from him, allowing insidious men to deceive and kidnap her. It had forced Pippa to reject him. Now that he faced the end, there was no use hiding from the truth. Pippa had been *right* to reject him.

Who wanted to tie themselves forever to a lover who would never view them as equal?

At the first sign of trouble, he'd pushed her away. He hadn't given her time to search her heart when its contents didn't immediately match his own. And then he'd stolen her autonomy by tying her to the bed.

What a bastard he'd been. A wretched, selfish, insufferable bastard who thought he was the only one who could do anything right. And look at where it had landed them all.

His control, so necessary at first when he'd fought to save the estate and keep him and Lydia from sinking into their parent's bog of selfishness, had become his greatest fault.

If they escaped—and he prayed they did—he'd be better. He'd share both the burden and the power of making all the decisions with those he loved.

His sister.

Pippa.

He'd let them in. He'd honor their contributions.

The stuttering flashes of lightning displayed the shattered glass from the broken window on the floor—proof of Pippa's resilience and shrewd plotting. Jack stared at the open window.

How the hell had she gotten up there?

He'd been below Lydia's window earlier, hiding from the guards. There was no tree or drain sprout to climb. Just sheer wall.

He groaned, realizing she must have scaled it. Without a guide rope. Without assistance. In the rain.

He shook his head and exhaled. *He wasn't in charge.* Pippa had decided to scale the wall, and she'd done it successfully. Her life, her choice.

Jack nodded. Perhaps this whole *cede control* thing wouldn't be so terrible after all. Now he just had to fight to live another day so he could prove he was worthy of her love if she ever deigned to bestow her heart upon such a flawed man.

Filled with renewed determination, Jack formulated a plan.

Pulling deep from his meager reserve of energy, he jerked his body. The chair scooted a few inches to the side.

Toward the shards of glass.

BY THE TIME the men returned, Pippa had cried herself dry.

The pounding of their heavy footfalls across the floor rumbled in counterpoint to the bellowing thunder outside.

"Oi, 'isself wants to talk wif you." Garlic Breath sneered as he approached, a candle held high. "Best loosen yer tongue iffen you know wots good for you."

"Cut him loose from the chair," the large man ordered, gesturing at Pippa's feet.

"Whyn't you do it? I'm busy holding me pistol and the candle, ain't I?" Garlic whined.

Pippa's eyes remained unfocused. Although the old fear was gone, her fighting spirit had disappeared as well.

"Give it 'ere." The large one seized the candle from Garlic.

With a long sigh, Garlic stuffed his pistol into his pocket and pulled out a knife. Kneeling at Pippa's feet, he made quick work of the ropes. The guard grabbed her by the arm and hoisted her off the chair, her hands still tied behind her.

"Skinny little thing, ain't you," Garlic muttered, jerking her forward.

"'old up," the leader barked, raising the candle high. He stepped forward, peering into Pippa's face. "Why, he's a she," he exclaimed, his bushy eyebrows halfway up his forehead. "Don't know 'ow we missed it afore."

"A she?" Garlic leaned in for a closer look. Pippa held her breath against his fumes.

"Well, well, wot a pleasant surprise." Garlic leered, his hand reaching for her breast.

"None of that," the big one barked.

Garlic's hand dropped before making contact.

" 'isself will want 'er in one piece." The leader turned to the door. " 'as to question the prisoner and such. No time to play."

"Fine," Garlic conceded, jerking Pippa's arm as he followed his companion. "But later," he whispered into Pippa's ear, "when 'isself ain't 'round no more…"

He licked his lips and cackled.

Pippa's internal fire, dimmed to the meagerest spark, flared back to life under the dry tinder of this man's leering threat.

Pippa narrowed her eyes as she returned his stare. *Oh, this nasty piece of work was going down.* All she needed was to get her hands on the knife in his pocket.

The two lumbering guards led her down a flight of stairs. The lower level of the house was well-lit. Pippa registered the opulence of the furnishings and décor. The thick Aubusson rugs and gilded picture frames stood in stark contrast to the coarse men dressed like dock workers who escorted her. She shouldn't be surprised, however—this wasn't only the scene of evil plotting and violence but also a duke's estate.

"Speak wif respect to 'isself once you're inside," the larger man commanded.

When he spoke in the well-lit hallway, Pippa noticed holes in the man's mouth. Hadn't the newspaper editor described the new *Democratiam Liberum* article deliverer as missing several teeth? Here was one mystery solved, at least.

They neared a door, and Toothless gave a knock.

"Come," called a voice.

Garlic held the door open wide, and Toothless dragged her inside.

Pippa's eyes scanned the room, well-lit by a roaring fire and several candelabra. The place was reminiscent of a hunting lodge with a few deer heads mounted on the wall near ceremonial swords crossed above a family crest. Two men sat on a divan. A woman—Lydia!—was tied to a chair in the corner. It seemed these ruffians were creatures of habit when it came to methods of restraint.

As lightning flashed, one of the men rose to his feet. His golden hair was swept back from his forehead in the current mussed fashion. The man's bottle green waistcoat was perfectly tailored to his lean frame, and a sheathed sword dangled from his belt. He carelessly swirled his glass of amber liquor before raising it to a mouth stretched in a haughty smirk.

It was as if a sign floated above his head proclaiming, *Here stands a future duke!*

Pippa glared. "Somerset."

The man pursed his lips. "It appears my reputation precedes me," he drawled. "And who might you be, sir?"

"'Tis no sir," growled Toothless, his hand tightening around Pippa's arm. "Just discovered ourselves that 'im's a she, milord."

Somerset approached, his eyes assessing. "A girl, dressed up like a man and staging a rescue? How peculiar."

"Climbed the exterior wall, she did," Garlic chimed in as if bragging of his own accomplishment. "Didn't put up a fight when we caught 'er though. 'anded 'er knife right over, meek as a mouse."

Somerset unwound Pippa's scarf, uncovering her chin and neck and freeing the long braid she'd stuffed down her back.

Pippa jerked back from his touch and narrowed her eyes.

"And what brings you to my family's estate?" he drawled before taking a swallow from his crystal glass. Outside, thunder boomed. "Out for a pleasure stroll?" He laughed.

"Enough." The second man, still lounging on the divan, finally joined the conversation. He held a tankard of ale, the usual beverage of a working man, not an aristocrat. A round, rosy face gave the impression of a jolly fellow.

Somerset turned to his companion. "Shan't we question her?"

The other man waved his tankard. "She's not important. Let's wait for our other guest to be brought downstairs. Lads," he directed toward the two guards, "set her beside Miss Dashwood and then bring down our mystery gentleman."

The guards hustled Pippa across the room. Recognition flared in Lydia's eyes. Her hair was loose, and her clothing wrinkled, but there was no sign of bruises or blood.

"Sit 'ere." Toothless pushed her down onto the only other chair nearby, a plush, upholstered seat with armrests. Her tied-up hands rested on the seat behind her. The guard seized a length of rope from the floor and eyed the piece of furniture with consternation. After peering over his shoulder and finding the two men in quiet conversation, he shrugged. Looping the rope around Pippa's waist, he then tied it at the back of the chair. Because of the curved, padded backrest, the rope gaped at the sides. Pippa didn't move an inch, not wanting to call attention to the lout's rather shoddy tying-up-the-captive job.

"Best stay put iffen you know what's good fer you," he muttered.

The guards left. Somerset and the jolly-looking fellow with the tankard of ale were seated once more on the divan, conversing quietly and ignoring the women completely.

Pippa turned to Lydia.

The woman stared, her blue eyes wide and alert. "Miss Chester?"

Pippa nodded before whispering, "I've been searching for you with your brother."

Lydia leaned forward, pulling the ropes tight. "You came with Jack? But I thought he was alone."

Pippa's chest tightened.

He was alone.

She cleared her throat. "We'd teamed up the day after your disappearance, but he…he left me behind to come for you."

Lydia's piercing gaze scanned her face, undoubtedly trying to piece together all the things left unsaid. Pippa startled when Lydia's assessing expression changed as she huffed and rolled her eyes. "He left you behind and came to do it all himself. Typical Jack."

Pippa's mouth fell open.

"Come now." Lydia pushed back her blond hair with hands bound together in front of her. "If you've been working in tandem, surely you know what a terse, stiff-upper lip, schedule-following, master-of-the-universe sort of fellow he is."

Another handful of highly-flammable material landed with a whoosh on Pippa's internal fire. "I'll have you know," she whispered indignantly, "that your brother has left no stone unturned searching for you. He combed the dark alleys near the docks in the middle of the night and fought off a band of cutthroats. He challenged a man to a duel." Pippa's voice softened. "He distributed your pinafores at the orphanage and sang Hickory Dickory Dock to all the children…" She trailed off, her mind whirring.

How had she failed to notice? Jack had *changed* since their first meeting in front of the LCA. And he didn't care overly much about perceptions of propriety or twisting himself into knots to avoid gossip.

She'd been so blind.

Lydia's shoulders sagged. "I fear all your adventures with him have led you to a rather bad end."

At Pippa's questioning look, Lydia's lips thinned.

"They plan to kill us, you know. I'm so grateful you worked so hard to find me. I was uncertain if the clues in the articles would even be noticed." Lydia paused, blinking her eyes rapidly. "But there's no hope. It was all for naught."

Pippa's head jerked back as though the woman had slapped her.

All for naught?

Pippa's insides felt full of heat and light and sparks. Words tumbled out of her mouth. "It wasn't for *naught*." She felt aflame as the truth spilled forth. "It was for *love*."

Lydia froze.

Pippa leaned toward her, ignoring the rope digging into her midsection as she continued to burn. "It was for love, don't you see? Your brother loves you fiercely, even though he's rubbish at showing it."

Flames licked at her skin.

"And…and I love him." Pippa's words blazed through her in a cleansing fire. "I love him with all that I am. And that makes everything worthwhile." She welcomed the scorching heat of her realization. "The world can be a scary place. Highwaymen or evil politicians could strike you down at any moment, but it's worth the risk. *Love* is worth the risk. Without it, a person isn't even living. They're just…hiding."

Despite the ropes binding her, the armed guards, and the threat of imminent death, Pippa's heart blazed.

All those years she'd spent locked away in fear hadn't protected her from life because she hadn't been living. Not even close. And now, even though she might only have minutes left, she'd live fully, reveling in the flaming love in her heart instead of hiding it away. Like she'd hidden herself away for so long.

Pippa smiled, the heat of her revelation burning away the icy shards of paralyzing fear. She realized with a start that Lydia was smiling as well.

"What are you so happy about?"

"You," Lydia replied. "It's clear you're a woman who knows what she wants and gets things done. Since I'm an optimist by nature, I'm rather hoping we can find some crazy, clever way out of this mess." Her eyes sparkled. "And I'm so very, very happy someone besides me loves my big lug of a brother."

Pippa tamped down an entirely inappropriate laugh, given they were all slated for execution.

"A crazy, clever way out of this, hm?" she whispered instead, leaning closer to Lydia. "I have an idea…"

⟫⟫⟩⟨⟪⟪

"This one 'ere's calmed down." The shorter guard nodded sagely at his own observation once they'd descended the stairs. "I was thinking we'd 'ave a fight on our 'ands when we found 'is chair on t'other side of the room."

"Trying to throw 'imself out t'window, 'e was," the tall one replied from Jack's other side. "Giving in to 'is despair an' such."

The short one snickered.

Jack kept his face impassive. The guards had a tight grip on his upper arms. His wrists remained tied behind him, his hands in loose fists.

They turned down a wide hall and paused before an ornate door. The man knocked. His beefy fist was a bizarre counterpoint to the delicate wood carvings along the doorframe.

When they were bid to enter, the two guards jerked Jack inside. He scanned the room. His shoulders relaxed an inch when he saw Pippa and Lydia sitting in the corner, neither woman bearing obvious signs of injury.

Pippa's face was pale and drawn. And yet she had a sort of bright sparkle despite her sodden clothes and restraints. She looked him straight in the eye, and if the men hadn't been holding him tight, Jack would've rushed to her side.

Two men rose from a divan near a roaring fire, blocking his view. Both held drinks as if they were in a London drawing-room after dinner.

"Ah, our latest guest to join the party," drawled the one with the aristocratic air—likely Somerset. "Tie him up," he directed the guards.

The beefier man held on to his bound arm while the other pulled over a chair and rope.

"And who might you be?" continued Somerset.

"I'll tell you after you let the women go," Jack replied as he was shoved down onto the straight-backed, wooden chair. The shorter guard wrapped a length of rope around his waist and tied it behind the chair. He left Jack's legs unbound.

The second man spoke. "Ah, yes, the women." He jerked his head toward Pippa and Lydia. The smaller guard let go of Jack and crossed the room to his new position, standing in front of the ladies.

Jack studied the newest character in this increasingly bizarre misadventure. He was of average build with a receding hairline that marked him as middle-aged. His rosy cheeks stretched wide with a smile quite at odds with the mercenary glint in his eyes. The man shot Pippa and Lydia a patronizing look. "We wouldn't want the ladies to feel left out, even if they're hardly a threat."

"You only need to keep me. Let them go." Jack graced the smiling man—clearly the one in charge—with the unblinking stare he often used to bring recalcitrant land stewards in line.

While the man sized him up, Jack loosened his fist behind his back. A shard of glass slid down to his fingers. Moving gingerly, he grasped his makeshift tool and began to blindly saw at his restraints. Thankfully any hand movements were hidden between his body and the back of the chair.

"While I appreciate your noble gesture of offering yourself as a sacrifice for the fairer sex, there is some business to take care of." The man raised a tankard to his mouth and gulped loudly before plunking it onto a side table. He wiped at his mouth with his sleeve.

He caught Jack staring and smirked. "When you wish to rule the body that represents the common people, you must drink as the plebeians do."

"What's your role in all this?"

"Ah ah ah." The man shook his forefinger at Jack as if chastising a naughty child. "First you must tell me something. Who else knows you're here?"

"Scores of people," Pippa called from across the room. "The magistrate will be here any minute."

The man glared across the room. "I wasn't addressing you,

girl." He turned back to Jack. "Now, who else knows you've come to Somerset's estate?"

Jack raised an eyebrow. "If I were you, I'd cut my losses and run before the magistrate and my men arrive. If you leave us unharmed, I'm sure the jury will look favorably upon you during your trial."

The man approached and searched Jack's face with piercing eyes. Jack held his breath and fought to maintain a confident expression.

"You lie." Another cheery smile. "For whatever reason, you came here alone. Pity for you."

A crack of thunder underscored his words, and Jack shivered.

"Since I'm not worried about you spilling tales"—the man shot him a knowing look—"I may as well answer your question. You see, I'm Nathaniel Hinds."

Jack started. Hinds, the coal investor the newspaper editor had mentioned?

The man nodded at his expression, looking pleased. "I see you've heard of me. I do try to keep a low profile, but it's hard to be a wealthy businessman and the one pulling the strings of the Commons without garnering a modicum of attention."

"Pulling the strings?" Jack scoffed. "Pulling open the purse strings, more like. It's hardly a secret you pay to have members of Parliament in your pocket."

Hinds stuck his hands into his jacket pockets. "Hardly room for my fingers, they're so full," he boasted, wiggling his hands and laughing. "I've even got a Bow Street runner or two in here."

Somerset rolled his eyes and poured himself another drink.

Jack gritted his teeth. The bastard *had* bribed Gormley at Bow Street to make them think Lydia had died. If they got out of this alive—no, *when* they got out of this alive—Gormley was going to pay for his sins.

Jack peeked across the room at his sister. She and Pippa were each partially visible behind the shorter guard whose back was to them. Pippa leaned over, appearing to whisper into Lydia's ear.

Lydia nodded.

"It was shockingly easy to gain control of the Commons," Hinds continued, drawing Jack's attention. He clasped his hands like a vicar at the pulpit. "Miss Dashwood wasn't wrong in her *Democratiam Liberum* articles. Rotten boroughs gave seats to members who represented only a handful of voters. The lack of secret voting allowed aristocrats to pressure their tenants to elect their sons. And I," Hinds paused to rub his hands together, "had the foresight and vision to use this to my advantage."

Jack risked a glance back at the women. Lydia was slowly leaning forward.

What was she up to?

Jack sucked in a breath as she eased her bound hands toward the short guard's side, inches from where his arm hung with a loaded pistol in his grasp.

Damn it all to hell—*Lydia was picking the guard's coat pocket.*

And there was Pippa, whispering directions or encouragement into her ear, all while the guard stood but a foot away. What fools men were, always underestimating women. Jack only wished he himself had wised up sooner to women's strength and capability.

"All it took were a few well-placed bribes to men like Somerset here." Hinds jerked his head toward his companion. "Sons who were merely biding their time to inherit and take their seats in the House of Lords, discontent with a measly allowance from father dearest." He laughed. "A few words in their father's ears, and they backed their sons for a seat in the Commons. I lined the young men's pockets with a bit of blunt, and *voila*." Hinds gestured with a flourish. "The Commons was mine."

Jack feared to so much as twitch while his sister fished about with careful movements. The guard shifted his weight, and Lydia's eyes widened. Jack flicked his attention back to Hinds, who was bragging about the corrupt deals he brokered in the Commons to assist his control of the coal industry, line his own pockets, and become one of the richest non-aristocratic land owners in England.

Somerset picked at lint on his sleeve, his bored expression suggesting he'd heard this soliloquy a time or three before.

Jack glanced back to the nail-biting scene in the corner of the room. Lydia was now swaying her arms back and forth in time with the guard's side-to-side movements. And then with shocking smoothness, she pulled a dagger out of the man's pockets and hid it in her skirt folds.

Jack's heart pounded with some crazed mixture of sheer terror and complete and utter pride. He'd known Pippa was gutsy, but he hadn't expected the same boldness from Lydia. There was certainly more to his sister than he'd realized before this adventure.

The guard glanced over his shoulder at the women, and both Lydia and Pippa dropped their eyes to their laps, looking for all the world like meek, subdued prisoners.

Jack exhaled. Damn, that was the most stressful thing he'd witnessed in his entire life, and he'd once seen a boy at Eton shoot an arrow through an apple resting atop another lad's head on a dare.

"How did Andrew Aubrey come to be involved?" Jack asked, trying to keep Hinds talking. The longer he yammered on, the greater their chances of escape.

"You mean Aubrey Andrews?" Hinds chuckled, his malignant expression clashing with the sound. "Well, I needed someone in London to find out who this *Democratiam Liberum* fellow was. When Andrews did a little investigating at the newspaper office and stumbled upon a trail leading to Miss Dashwood, I directed the young man to trick her..."

While Hinds droned on about the genius of his evil plans, Jack adjusted his grip on the shard of glass. The slippery blood from his chafed wrists didn't make the task any easier. Gritting his teeth in concentration, Jack continued sawing at the ropes. He needed to be ready to spring into action when Pippa and Lydia unleashed whatever plan they'd concocted.

Chapter Twenty-Six

PIPPA TOOK A deep breath. Now wasn't the time for flashbacks and freezing like earlier. In order to make it out alive—and they *would* make it out alive—she needed to be focused and ready.

"I don't believe any further help is headed this way," Hinds announced after his long-winded monologue came to an end. His eyes, so calculating and quick, practically whirred as he seemed to reconsider Pippa's earlier claim that help was on the way.

She had underestimated him.

"First one rescuer, then another an hour later?" he mused, pacing in front of the fire. "I'm not sure why you didn't come together. I don't really care. But if the magistrate had been summoned, that old windbag would be here by now. No." He narrowed his cold, hard eyes. "I rather think it's safe to dispatch all of you."

"No," Jack roared from across the room.

"Take them into the woods," Hinds directed the guards, waving his hand. "You know what to do."

"Now," Pippa whispered.

Time slowed.

Pippa turned in her seat. The wide space created by the curved back of the chair allowed her to pivot within the confines of the rope.

She heard rustling behind her. With any luck, Lydia was picking up the stolen knife.

The guard began to turn. Pippa kicked him in the back of his knee. He fell forward with a grunt.

Shouting sounded from across the room.

The cool metal of the blade slipped between her hands.

Her ears filled with the dry rasp of rope giving way as Lydia sawed the knife, and then Pippa's hands were free. She turned around, Lydia already slicing the rope holding Pippa to the chair.

"Here." Lydia handed Pippa the knife, *her* knife, seized earlier by the guards upstairs.

Pippa leapt to her feet. She hefted the comforting weight of her dagger in her hand. The guard had just regained his footing. His arm rose, the barrel of the pistol making its menacing way up through the air. Pippa slashed across his abdomen. Warm blood gushed onto her hand.

He screeched and fell back, his pistol flying through the air.

"Pippa!" Jack yelled.

She looked up to find Toothless barreling straight toward her, his beefy mass ready to crush his opponent. Pippa whipped her arm back and flung it forward in one smooth, practiced motion. The knife flew through the air. It sunk into the guard's shoulder up to the handle.

He howled, falling to the ground.

"You bitch," Somerset yelled. He clambered toward her around pieces of furniture, his hand scrabbling for the sword at his side.

Pippa dashed to the wall. Reaching up, she grasped the hilt of an ornamental sword serving as a decoration beneath a family crest.

Please let it be functional as well.

Pippa heaved, and the sword came off the wall. Bits of plaster rained down in its wake.

"Look out," Lydia shouted.

Pippa spun, the sword whirring through the air. It met Somerset's blade with a clang.

"Pathetic," Somerset spat, moving into a counter swing.

Pippa stepped back and blocked him. She lunged, nicking his side. Somerset's eyes widened.

"You were saying?" Pippa circled him.

He grimaced.

Pippa feinted left. He followed, exposing his right side. She lunged, but he managed to sidestep at the last second.

"Damn," he grunted, as their blades danced between them. "Ladies aren't supposed to fence."

"Gentlemen aren't supposed to kidnap people." Pippa sidestepped an ottoman and easily deflected his blade. "But I suppose you aren't really a gentleman."

Pippa parried, spun to the side, and lunged. He deflected her blade and counterattacked. She stepped to the side, but her foot caught on the leg of an end table. Pippa's breath froze as she lost her footing and went down on one knee.

Somerset's thin lips curled up as if already savoring his victory. His blade whipped through the air toward her. There was no time to regain her footing and block the attack.

In a flash, Pippa remembered *Señor* Martín's lesson on the passata sotto, a maneuver to attack one's opponent from the ground.

Time slowed. Dimly, she heard shouting. The air whistled as Somerset's sword sped toward her. Pippa planted her left hand on the floor and drove up with her sword just as her instructor had demonstrated.

Her blade sank into his side. Pippa rolled to the right and out of danger.

Somerset's mouth fell open in disbelief. He staggered back, his blade falling to the floor. Toppling over, he smashed into the same table that had tripped Pippa before he fell into a heap.

Pippa jumped up, searching for Hinds. He stood beside Jack, a pistol gripped in his outstretched hand. She froze.

"I rather underestimated you, girl." He clenched his jaw, his round, rosy cheeks flexing. "Knife, sword… Too bad you don't have a gun. Like me." His lips stretched in a macabre smile.

"Set down the sword," he instructed. "Yes, just like that. Now, come closer."

Her empty hands fisted, Pippa stepped closer to Hinds. She glanced at Jack. His gaze was fixed on her, his eyes determined. His arm flexed rhythmically. Was he trying to untie the rope at his back? Pippa looked away, hoping Hinds wouldn't notice.

When Pippa was a few feet away, Hinds bade her to stop. "Face away from me," he ordered, "and get on your knees."

Pippa blanched. Good lord. *He was going to execute her.*

She risked a glance at Jack.

"Don't you bloody dare!" Jack's eyes were wild.

Whatever he was up to behind his back clearly wasn't ready yet. She was on her own.

She kept her eyes on Jack, hoping to catch Hinds unaware. Her heart thundered.

One, two, three—

Pippa lunged forward, tackling Hinds around his middle. He fell to the carpet, Pippa on top of him.

He grunted, struggling to roll out from under her. Pippa strained to keep her position. However, he outweighed her by several stones. With a heave, he pushed her to the side. They scrambled on the floor, each fighting for dominance.

Tangled legs.

Muscles straining.

Hot breath in her ear.

A blur of hands.

Jack shouting.

A pistol raised above her head.

And then…darkness.

"YOU FUCKING BASTARD!" Jack shouted as Pippa went limp from

the strike of the pistol's butt.

He strained and twisted against his bindings, but despite the sawing he'd done with the shard of glass, they didn't break. A conflagration of rage blazed inside him. He'd kill the man a thousand times for striking Pippa.

"Damn." Hinds panted for air as he pushed himself up. He knelt beside Pippa's inert form. The bastard roughly rolled her onto her back, and her head lolled to the side. Blood oozed from a gash on her temple.

That was her blood, her precious, life-sustaining blood. Jack gnashed his teeth.

"Who knew the bitch had it in her," Hinds wheezed.

Jack stared at Pippa's limp body. *She can't be dead. No no no…*

His heart turned arctic, barren as the tundra.

Hinds glanced about the room. "What a shame."

The two guards, Somerset, and Pippa were all on the floor, severely injured or possibly dead. In the corner, Lydia struggled in vain against her bonds, tears streaming down her face.

"I don't know how I'll explain the blood-stained carpet to Somerset's father. Dukes are so picky about such things." Hinds shook his head as if he were bemoaning a party running out of champagne and not the loss of human life.

Jack stared at Pippa.

Wake up, wake up…

Her eyelids flickered, and he released his breath in a giant whoosh. If he hadn't been tied to the chair, he would've tumbled over, limp with relief.

Hinds also noticed her stirring. "Well, the little warrior awakens." His smile was so cold that icicles should have dangled from his teeth. "Just in time to watch her friends die."

He lifted his arm and adjusted his grip on the pistol. "Who shall I shoot first?" He seemed to take perverse pleasure in alternating his aim between Jack and Lydia.

Hinds no longer watched Pippa on the floor, and she turned her head toward Jack. Her eyes widened.

Jack followed her gaze. A pistol lay on the floor near his feet. Jack remembered the first guard Pippa had taken out, his pistol flying through the air. Somehow in all the chaos after, it must've been kicked across the room.

Hinds aimed the gun at Lydia. "It will be so satisfying taking you out."

Fueled with desperation, Jack sawed at his bindings in a frenzy. He was so close. If he cut just a little more, he could reach down and grab the pistol and—

"After all, you caused all this trouble with those asinine articles." Hinds's voice was heavy with malice. "It's fitting your friends see your pathetic ending, as insignificant as your writing." He steadied the pistol with his other hand.

There was no time.

Jack couldn't control this situation. He couldn't carry the burden alone. Someone else would need to save the day.

A boom of thunder from outside filled the air.

Jack looked from the gun to Pippa. She nodded.

He kicked the pistol. Pippa's arm shot out and snatched it from the floor. She aimed up at Hinds just as his finger moved on the trigger.

A sharp bang rent the room.

Jack's gaze flew to Lydia. Her mouth was open in a silent cry. Jack's heart stopped. He scanned her body but saw no blood. He glanced back at the man who still stood over Pippa, his arm outstretched. Hinds's head canted to the side in puzzlement. He touched his chest and then pulled his hand away. The tips of his fingers were red.

Pippa dropped her arm, wisps of smoke drifting from her pistol's muzzle.

Hinds staggered back before collapsing in a heap. His gun skittered across the floor.

"Pippa." Jack's lips were numb.

She pushed herself up with unsteady arms and winced, gingerly touching her temple.

"Pippa," Jack said again, his voice shaky.

She looked at him.

"Jack." She smiled. "I love you."

He blinked.

"Did you hear me?" She crawled up onto his lap and wrapped her arms around his neck. "I love you, Jack. I love you so much."

Jack's chest heaved with a shuddering breath. *She loves me.*

Somehow, they'd survived this nightmare. Pippa had saved them all. Lydia was safe. And he'd learned to cede control. There were no words.

Jack leaned forward, nuzzling the side of Pippa's neck. He inhaled. Her scent, her warmth, and her words of love all settled inside him, covering every square inch of his soul and heart with the sweet brightness that was Pippa.

"I'm so sorry about what I said before." She snuggled against him. "I thought I was a scandal and would ruin your life. I thought you valued control above all else. But you… you kicked the gun to *me*, Jack. You trusted *me* to save us."

"Pippa," he began, his voice thick with emotion. Jack blinked rapidly.

She pulled back a few inches and studied him. "Are you…are you *crying?*" Her face was wreathed in astonishment.

He swallowed before croaking out, "It seems I am."

Gently, she stroked a trail of moisture away with her thumb.

After a shuddery breath, he continued, "I suppose…when a person believes his sister and"—he paused, searching her beautiful, familiar eyes—"the woman who is the very center of his heart are about to be executed, it tends to be rather unsettling."

Pippa inhaled. "Well, when you put it that way, I suppose I'd be offended if you *weren't* crying." Her mouth wobbled, and her eyes filled with tears. "I was scared, Jack. So scared I'd never have the chance to tell you how I really felt." She sniffled before giving him a stern look. "And before, I was *so* mad at you for leaving me at the inn."

He pressed kisses against her neck and cheek and hair. "I'll never be so stupid again. I swear it. Instead of me protecting you from the dangers of the world, I think it's clear you should protect me."

Pippa's lips tipped up. "Let's protect each other. And…I don't think I'll worry so much about the world's dangers anymore. I'll fight anything that comes our way, but I won't live in fear. Never again."

"Can you cut me loose?" Jack smiled. "I have a question for you, and I rather think I should be on my knees for it."

Pippa's smile lit up her entire face. Her eyes sparkled and a pink blush spread across her cheeks. Blood was smeared across her temple, her clothes were damp and rumpled, and her hair resembled a bird's nest in places.

She'd never looked lovelier.

"Excuse me!" Lydia called from across the room. "I don't mean to interrupt what is clearly a very special and touching moment for you two, but do you think you could cut me loose? Someone has to make sure these louts are tied up before they regain consciousness." She grinned. "Good thing there's no shortage of rope."

Epilogue

"VERY NICE RIPOSTE," *Señor* Martín called from the sideline.

Pippa lowered her sword. She wiped her forehead with her sleeve and grinned at the other fencer. "I admit to some jealousy. I wasn't nearly this good when I started out."

Her cousin Jane sheathed her *épée*. "To be fair, when you started out, you were stabbing at the curtains in your bedroom with a wooden dowel."

Pippa snickered.

"Why do I always miss the embarrassing stories?" Lydia called from across the room where she practiced lunges.

Señor Martín gave a mock scowl to Pippa and his two new students. "If you do not stop your chatter and begin to cool down, your muscles will—"

"—turn into rocks," Pippa, Lydia, and Jane called in unison.

Their instructor chuckled and began to tidy up the new training room. Pippa stretched her arms while Jane and Lydia compared their newest blisters.

Things had changed so much in the last few weeks.

After Pippa, Jack, and Lydia had settled things in Horncastle—which included fetching both a physician who proclaimed it a miracle all four villains lived as well as the local magistrate who promptly arrested them all—Pippa had received requests for fencing instruction from both Lydia and Jane.

However, the LCA remained closed.

When Pippa had arrived for today's fencing practice, her cousin had murmured a cryptic comment about investigating the robbery at the LCA with the help of a friend who had turned out to be more than he seemed. Given Jane's blush as she'd spoken, Pippa had a good guess as to who the friend might be. Jane hadn't gone into details. However, Pippa remembered how Dev had declared the break-in to be his fault and how he had an air of not-quite-a-servant about him. Given her own experience dealing with Lady Rowling's closely guarded secrets, Pippa wished Jane and her "friend" luck in unraveling the mystery.

With the LCA out of commission for the time being, Jack had insisted that the fencing lessons occur at his home.

Well, *their* home.

As if she'd summoned him with her thoughts, her husband of a week appeared in the doorway, a basket dangling from one arm.

"Hello, Lady Hartwick." He eyed her thin lawn shirt with interest.

Pippa approached, kissing his cheek. "Come to check on us?"

"Come to check on *you*." He captured her lips in a blistering kiss. "I missed you."

"Why sir, it's only been a few hours since you last saw me…" Pippa fluttered her eyelashes, "…naked."

"We can *hear* you!" Jane sang from across the room.

Jack winked at the ladies before tugging Pippa into the hall. With a growl, he pressed her against the wall and ran kisses down her neck to the open vee of her shirt. "You. Are. Delicious," he said between kisses.

Pippa sighed and tilted her head back in offering. A thought tickled the back of her mind, and she straightened with a gasp. "I almost forgot! What did you learn from the officials?"

Jack had been scheduled to meet with one of the prince regent's men about the charges against Hinds, Somerset, and the two guards.

He lifted his head but kept his arms tight around Pippa's waist.

"They're being deported to the penal colonies in Australia, and Parliament will investigate the issue of voting reform during the next session."

Pippa pursed her lips. "Hopefully some change will come of it. If not, *Democratiam Liberum* will have to strike again."

Jack's face darkened.

Pippa raised an eyebrow in challenge.

Jack sighed. "You're right." He smiled ruefully. "*Democratiam Liberum* can do whatever she wants. It's not up to me."

"An attitude like that should be rewarded." Pippa leaned in for a kiss.

His arms tightened, pulling her close, and something pressed into her side. She glanced down, spying the basket over his arm. "What have you got there?"

Jack cleared his throat, and to Pippa's amazement, his cheeks grew ruddy.

"Well, I know you're quite busy with fencing and helping Lydia and Jane as well. And I've handed over more of the estate accounts to my land stewards. So, I thought..." He smiled sheepishly. "Well, I thought I'd help you with your other work."

Pippa tugged the basket off his arm and reached inside. Her hands encountered soft wool. Lifting an item up, she gasped. "Is this...?"

Jack nodded. "It's a bootie."

Pippa's chest expanded as she examined the tiny garment, which was markedly less misshapen than her own.

Jack's eyes sparkled in a face that no longer carried constant lines of stress and worry. "I rather enjoyed knitting them. Your mother and Eugenia say I show potential. Plus, those women know the best gossip."

Pippa threw back her head and laughed. Her heart felt fair to bursting with emotion for this incredible man who not only accepted her as she was, but who supported her passions.

Calloused hands, sword parasols, and knitting lessons from his mother-in-law—he accepted them all.

She smiled up at him, her heart in her eyes. "I love you so much. I feel like the luckiest person in the world."

Jack grabbed the basket and bootie out of her hands and dropped them onto the floor. He pulled her tight within the strong circle of his arms. Before he kissed her, he murmured, "That makes two of us."

ACKNOWLEDGEMENTS

A huge thanks to *you* for selecting this book. I hope you've enjoyed reading Pippa and Jack's story as much as I enjoyed writing it. If you've shared love for *How to Court a Covert Lady* on social media, in a review, or to a friend, I appreciate you so very much.

I am grateful to my family for cheering me on and picking up the slack at home when I'm on a writing deadline and morph into a laptop zombie. Steve, Fiona, and Finn, you are the center of my heart.

I am so appreciative of my sisters, Coco and Sharon, who are my BF's for life. They know all my secrets and still love me unconditionally.

To my mom, who was the OG romance novel reader in my life, and my dad, who tries to read every book in his local library—thank you both for modeling a love of reading.

To all my friends at Emerald City Romance Writers, thanks for being examples of the positive power of change as we went through the disaffiliation process. ECRW is my writing home, and I'm so glad we're thriving.

To my fellow writers who have encouraged me, especially when I was in deadline despair, thank you for keeping me going! Nicole Knightley, Priscilla Smith, Maggie Menane, and Lynne Pearson were more supportive than a double-layered sports bra this past year, and I feel so lucky to call you all friend.

I wouldn't be here without my agent, Lesley Sabga, who is

enthusiastic, tenacious, and wise. I adore you!

My editor, Cynthia Blackburn, polished this manuscript up to a high gleam *and* had to deal with my many horse and pistol errors! Thank you for your keen eye and helpful edits.

And to the whole team at Dragonblade Publishing, thanks for welcoming me into the fold. I'm so glad to be here!

ABOUT THE AUTHOR

Jenny Hartwell has a confession–she loves People magazine as much as Pride and Prejudice. Her fun, pop culture adoring side shines in her contemporary rom-com set in a gourmet chocolate factory while Jenny's Regency romances feature strong damsels and swoony lords. Her writing has won or finaled in numerous contests including the Golden Heart, The Emily, Four Seasons, Fool for Love, and The Catherine. Jenny lives with her family in the verdant Pacific Northwest. She loves movies, travel, and staying up late with a good book. And, of course, chocolate. Jenny is represented by Lesley Sabga of The Seymour Agency.